Henry Harla

Comedies and Errors

Henry Harland

Comedies and Errors

1st Edition | ISBN: 978-3-75234-918-4

Place of Publication: Frankfurt am Main, Germany

Year of Publication: 2020

Outlook Verlag GmbH, Germany.

Reproduction of the original.

COMEDIES AND ERRORS

By Henry Harland

Comedies
&
Errors

By Henry Harland

John Lane
The Bodley Head
London and New York
1898

Every one who knew Rome fifteen or twenty years ago must remember Miss Belmont. She lived in the Palazzo Sebastiani, a merry little old Englishwoman, the business, the passion, of whose existence it was to receive. All the rooms of her vast apartment on the *piano nobile* were arranged as reception-rooms, even the last of the suite, in the corner of which a low divan, covered by a Persian carpet, with a prie-dieu beside it, and a crucifix attached to the wall above, was understood to serve at night as Miss Belmont's bed. Her day, as indicated by her visiting-card, was Thursday; but to those who stood in her good books her day was every day, and—save for a brief hour in the afternoon, when, with the rest of Rome, she drove in the Villa Borghese—all day long. Then almost every evening she gave a little dinner. I have mentioned that she was old. She was proud of her age, and especially proud of not looking it. "I am seventy-three," she used to boast, confronting you with the erect figure, the bright eyes, the firm cheeks, of a well-preserved woman of sixty. Her rooms were filled with beautiful and

3

precious things, paintings, porcelains and bronzes, carvings, brocades, picked up in every province of the Continent, "the spoils of a lifetime spent in rummaging," she said. All English folk who arrived in Rome decently accredited were asked to her at-homes, and all good Black Italians attended them. As a loyal Black herself, Miss Belmont, of course, knew no one in any way affiliated with the Quirinal.

One of Miss Belmont's Thursday afternoons has always persisted in my memory with a quite peculiar vividness. It was fifteen years ago, if you will; and yet I remember it, even the details of it, as clearly as I can remember the happenings of last week—as clearly indeed, but oh, how much more pleasantly! Was the world really a sweeter, fresher place fifteen years ago? Has it really grown stale in fifteen little years? It seemed, at any rate, very sweet and fresh, to my undisciplined perceptions, on that particular Thursday afternoon.

We were in December, and there was never so light a touch of frost on the air, making it keen and exhilarating. I remember walking down a long narrow street, at the end of which the sky hung like a tapestry, splendid with the colours of the sunset: a street all clamour and business and bustle, as Roman streets are apt to be when there is a touch of the *tramontano* on the air. Cobblers worked noisily, tap-tap-tapping, in their out-of-door stalls; hawkers cried their wares, and old women stopped to haggle with them; wandering musicians thrummed their guitars and mandolines, singing "Funiculi, Funiculà," more or less in tune; and cabs rattled perilously over the cobble-stones, whilst their drivers shrieked warnings at the foot-passengers, citizens soldiers, beggars, priests, like the populace in a comic opera.

But within the Palazzo Sebastiani the scene was as different as might be. Thick curtains were drawn over the windows; innumerable wax candles burned and flickered in sconces along the walls; there were flowers everywhere, lilies and roses, and the air was heady with their fragrance; there were people everywhere too, men in frock-coats, women in furs and velvets, monsignori from the Vatican lending a purple note. And there was a continuous, confused, rising, falling, murmur of conversation.

When I had made my obeisance to Miss Belmont, she said, "Come. I want to introduce you to the Contessa Bracca."

Now, this will seem improbable, of course; but you know how one sometimes has premonitions; and, upon my word, it is the literal fact: I had never heard of the Contessa Bracca, her name could convey nothing to me; and yet, when Miss Belmont said she wished to present me to her, I felt a sudden knock in my heart, I felt that something important was about to happen to me. Why?…

She was seated in an old high-backed chair of carved ebony, inlaid with mother-of-pearl, one of Miss Belmont's curiosities. She wore a jaunty little toque of Astrakhan lamb's-wool, with an aigrette springing from it, and a smart Astrakhan jacket. It was a singularly pleasant face, a singularly pretty and witty and interesting face, that looked up in the soft candle-light, and smiled, as Miss Belmont accomplished the presentation; it was a singularly pleasant voice, gentle, yet crisp, characteristic, that greeted me.

But Miss Belmont had spoken to the Contessa in English; and the Contessa spoke to me in English, with no trace of an accent. I was surprised; and I was shy and awkward. So I could think of nothing better than toexclaim—

"Oh, you are English!"

She smiled—it was a quiet little amused but kindly smile, rather a lightening of her eyes than a movement of her features—and said, "Why not?"

"I thought you would be Italian," I confessed.

She was still smiling. "And are you inconsolable to find that I'm not?" she asked.

"Oh, no. On the contrary, I am very glad," I assured her, with sincerity.

At this, her smile rippled into laughter; and she murmured something in which I caught the words "youth" and "engaging candour."

"Oh, I'm not so furiously young," I protested.

She raised her eyebrows, gazing at me quizzically.

"Aren't you?" she inquired.

"I'm twenty-two," I announced, with satisfaction.

"Oh, dear!" She laughed again. "And twenty-two you regard as the beginning of old age?" she suggested.

"At all events, one is no longer a child at twenty-two," I argued solemnly, "especially if one has seen the world a bit."

My conversation appeared to divert her more than I could have hoped; for still again she laughed.

Then, "Ah, wait till you're my age—wait till you're a hundred and fifteen," she pronounced in a hollow voice, making her face long, and shaking her head.

It was my turn to laugh now. Afterwards, "I don't believe you're much older than I am," I confided to her, with bluff geniality.

"What's the difference between twenty-two and thirty—especially when one has seen the world a bit?" she asked.

"You're never thirty," I expostulated.

"An experienced old fellow of two-and-twenty," she observed, "must surely be aware that people do sometimes live to attain the age of thirty."

"You're not thirty," I reiterated.

"Perhaps not," she said; "but unless I'm careful, I shall be, before I know it. Have you been long in Rome?"

"Oh, I'm an old Roman," I replied airily. "We used to come here when I was a child. And I was here again when I was eighteen, and again when I was twenty."

"Mercy!" she cried. "Then you will be able to put me up to the tricks of the town."

"Why, but you live here, don't you?" I wondered simply.

"Yes, I suppose I live here," she assented. "I live in the Palazzo Stricci, you must come and see me. I'm at home on Mondays."

"Oh, thank you; I'll come the very first Monday that ever is," I vowed. For, though she had teased me and laughed at me, I thought she was very charming, all the same.

"Well, and how did you get on with the Countess Bracca?" Miss Belmont asked. When I had answered her, she proceeded, as her wont was, to volunteer certain information. "She was a Miss Wilthorpe, you know—the Cumberland Wilthorpes, a staunch old Catholic family. Her mother was a Frenchwoman, a Montargier. Monsignor Wilthorpe is her cousin. Her husband, Count Bracca, held a commission in the Guardia Nobile—between ourselves, a creature of starch and whalebone, a pompous noodle. She was married to him when she was eighteen. He died three or four years ago: a good thing too. But she has continued to live in Rome, in the winter. In the summer she goes to England, to her people. Did she ask you to go and see her? Go, on the first occasion. Cultivate her. She's clever. She'll do you good. She'll form you," Miss Belmont concluded, looking at me with a critical eye.

On Monday, at the Palazzo Stricci, I was ushered through an immense sombre drawing-room, and beyond, into a gay little blue-and-white boudoir. The Contessa was there alone. "I am glad you have come early," she was good enough to say. "We can have a talk together, before any one else arrives."

She wore a delightful white frock, of some flexile woollen fabric embroidered in white silk with leaves and flowers. And I discovered that she had very lovely hair, great quantities of it, undulating richly away from her forehead; hair of an indescribable light warm brown, a sort of fawn colour, with reflections dimly red. She was seated in the corner of a sofa, leaning

7

upon a cushion of blue satin covered with white lace. I had not noticed her hair the other day at Miss Belmont's, in the vague candle-light. Now I could not take my eyes from it. It filled me with astonishment and admiration.

"Oh," I said—I suppose I blushed and stammered, but I had to say it—"you —you must let me tell you—what—what wonderful hair you have."

The poor lady! She shook her head; she lay back in her place and laughed. "Forgive me, forgive me for laughing," she said. "But—your compliment—it was a trifle point-blank—I was slightly unprepared for it. However, you're quite right. It's not bad hair," she conceded amiably. "And it was very—very natural and—and nice—of you to mention it. Now sit down here, and we will have a good long talk," she added. "You must tell me all about yourself. We must get acquainted."

There was always, perhaps, the tiniest point of raillery in that crisp voice, in those gleaming eyes, of hers; but it did not prevent them from being friendly and interested. She went on to ask me all manner of friendly, interested questions, adopting, apparently as a matter of course, the tone of maturity addressing ingenuous youth; and I found myself somehow accepting that relation without resentment. Where had I made my studies? What was I going to do in the world? She asked me everything; and I, guilelessly, fatuously no doubt, responded. I imagine I expatiated at some length, and with some fervour, upon my literary aspirations, whilst she encouraged me with her kind-glowing eyes; and I am afraid—I am afraid I even went so far as to allow her to persuade me to repeat divers of my poems. In those days one wrote things one fondly nicknamed poems. Anyhow, I know that I was enjoying myself very much indeed—when we were interrupted by the entrance of another caller.

And then a whole stream of callers passed through her dainty room: men and women, old and young; all of them people with a great deal of manner, and not much else—certainly with precious little wit. The men were faultlessly dressed, they had their hair very sleekly brushed, they caressed their hats, grinned vacuously, and clacked out set phrases; the women gossiped turbulently in Italian; and my hostess gave them tea, and smiled (was there just a tinge of irony in her smile?), and listened with marvellous endurance. But I thought to myself, "Oh, if this is the kind of human society you are condemned to, how ineffably you must be bored!"

I met her a few days later in the Villa Borghese. I was one of many hundred people walking there, in the afternoon; her victoria was one of the long procession of carriages. She made her coachman draw up, and signed to me to come and speak with her.

"If I should get down and walk with you a bit, do you think you would be heart-broken?" she asked.

I offered her my hand, and helped her to alight. She had on the toque and jacket of Astrakhan in which I had first seen her, and she carried an Astrakhan muff. The fresh air had brought a beautiful soft colour to her cheeks; her hair glowed beautifully in the sunlight. As she walked beside me, I perceived that she was nearly as tall as I was, and I noticed the strong, fine, elastic contours of her figure. We turned away from the road, and walked on the grass, among the solemn old trees; and we talked... I can't in the least remember of what— of nothings, very likely—only, I do remember that we talked and talked, and that I found our talk exceedingly agreeable. I remember, too, that at a given moment we passed a company of students from the German College, their scarlet cassocks flashing in the sun; and I remember how each of those poor priestlings stole an admiring glance at her from the corner of his eyes. But upon my calling her attention to the circumstance, though she couldn't help smiling, she tried to frown, and reproved me. "Hush. You shouldn't observe such things. You must never allow yourself to think lightly of the clergy."

When I had conducted her back to her carriage, she said, "Can't I set you down somewhere?" So I got in and drove with her, through the animated Roman streets, to the door of my lodgings. On the way, "You must come and dine with me some evening," she said. "When will you come? Will you come on Wednesday? Quite quietly, you know." And I assured her that I should be delighted to come on Wednesday.

But afterwards, when I was alone, I repeatedly caught myself thinking of her—thinking of her with enthusiasm. "She *is* a nice woman," I thought. "She's an awfully nice woman. Except my own mother, I believe she's the nicest woman I have ever known."

It may interest you to learn that I took occasion to tell her as much on Wednesday.

The other guests at her dinner had been Miss Belmont and the Contessa's cousin, Monsignor Wilthorpe, a tall, iron-grey, frigid man, of forty-something; and they left together very early, Miss Belmont remarking, "People who are not in their first youth can't afford to lose their beauty-sleep. Come, Monsignore, you must drive me home." I feared it was my duty to leave directly after them, but upon my rising to do so the Contessa cried out,

"What! Do you begrudge losing your beauty-sleep too? It's not yet ten o'clock." I was only too glad to stay.

We went from the great melancholy drawing-room, where we had taken our coffee, into her boudoir. I can't tell you how cosy and charming and intimate it seemed, in the lamplight, with its bright colours, and with all her little personal possessions scattered about, her books, bibelots, writing-materials.

"Are you allowed to smoke?" she asked.

"I don't know. Am I?" was my retort.

She laughed. "Yes. I think you deserve to, after that."

I lighted a cigarette, with gratitude; while she sat down at her piano and began to play.

"Do you care for Bach? No, you are too young to care for Bach. But you will come to him. At your age one loves Chopin. Chopin interprets the strenuous moments of life, the moments that seem all important when they are present, but matter so little in the long run. Bach interprets life as a whole, seen from a distance, seen in perspective, in its masses and proportions, in its serene symmetry, when nothing is strenuous, when everything seems right and in its place, when even sorrow seems right. At my age one prefers Bach."

She said all this as she was playing, speaking slowly, dreamily, between the chords. "If that is Bach which you are playing now, I like it very much," I made bold to affirm.

"It's the third fugue," said she. "But it's precocious of you to like it."

"Oh, I give you my word, I'm not half so juvenile as you're always trying to make me out," said I.

She looked at me with her indulgent, quizzical smile. "No, to be sure. You're a cynical old man of the world—of twenty-two," she teased.

Presently she abandoned the piano, and took her place of the other day, in the corner of her sofa.

"Tell me," she said, "what do you do here in Rome? What are your occupations? How do you spend your time?"

"Oh, my occupations are entirely commonplace," I answered her. "In the morning' I try to write. Then in the afternoon I pay calls, or go to some one's studio, or to the museums, or what not. And in the evening I generally dine with some men I know at the Caffé di Roma."

"And so, with one thing and another, you're quite happy?" she suggested.

But this recalled me, of a sudden, to the rôle I was at that season playing to myself in the human comedy. Ingenuous young men (a. friend of mine often says), if they happen to have an active imagination, are the most inveterate, the most incorrigible of poseurs. To make the matter worse, they're the first—if not the only—ones to be taken in by their pose. They believe in it heartily; they're supremely unconscious that they're posing. And so they go on, slipping from one pose to another, till in the end, by accident as like as not, they find the pose that suits them. And when a man has found the pose that suits him (I am still quoting my friend) we say that he has "found himself."

The Contessa's suggestion recalled me to my pose of the season. I repudiated the idea of happiness with scorn.

"Happy!" I echoed bitterly. "I should think not. I shall never be happy again."

"Mercy upon me!" she exclaimed. "Si jeune, et déjà Moldave-Valaque!"

"Oh," I informed her, with Byronic gloom, "it isn't a laughing matter. I'm the most miserable of men."

"Poor boy," she said compassionately; and her eyes shone with compassion too, though perhaps there still lingered in them just the faintest afterglow of amusement. "Why are you miserable? What is it all about?"

"Oh," I said, "it's the usual story. When a man's hopelessly unhappy, when his last illusion has been destroyed, it's always—I'm sorry to say it to you, but you know whether it's true—it's always a member of your sex that's to blame."

Had she a struggle to keep from laughing? If so, she came out of it victorious. Indeed, the compassion in her eyes seemed to deepen. "Poor boy," she repeated. "What have they done to you? Tell me all about it. It will do you good to tell me. Let me be your confidante," she urged gently.

And thereupon (oh, fatuity!) I strode up and down her floor, and narrated the whole history of my desperate, my fatal passion for Elsie Milray: how beautiful Elsie was, how mysteriously, incommunicably fascinating; how I had adored her; how she had encouraged me, led me on, trifled with me, and finally thrown me over—for Captain Bullen, a fellow in the Engineers, old enough to be—well, almost old enough to be her father. I fancy I swung my arms about a good deal, and quoted Heine and Rossetti, and generally made myself very tiresome and ridiculous; but my kind confidante listened with patience, with every appearance of taking my narration seriously.

"So you see," I concluded, "I've been hard hit, hit in a vital spot. My wound is one of those that never heal."

Even that did not provoke her to laughter. She gazed at me meditatively for a moment, and then she shook her head. "Your wound will heal. When our wounds are fresh, it always seems as if they would never heal. But they do heal. Yours will heal. You must try to think of other things. You must try to interest yourself in other girls—oh, platonically, I mean, of course. There are lots of nice girls in the world, you know. You must try not to think of Elsie. It's no good thinking of her, now that she's engaged to Captain Bullen. But— but when you can't help thinking of her, then you must come to me and talk it out. That is always better, healthier, than brooding upon a grief in silence. You must come to me whenever you feel you wish to. I shall always be glad when you come."

"You're a—you're an angel of kindness," I declared, with emotion. "I—I was thinking only the other day, when you had driven me home from the Borghese, I was thinking that, except my own mother, you're the—the best and dearest woman in the world."

But at this, she could be grave no longer. She laughed gaily. "If I come next to your mother in your affections," she said, "it's almost as if I were your grandmother, isn't it? Yes, that is it. I'll be a grandmother to you." And she made me a comical little *moue*.

After that, it was my excellent fortune to see the Contessa Bracca rather frequently. I called on her a good deal; she asked me to dine and lunch with her a good deal; I spent a surprising number of afternoons and evenings in her blue-and-white retiring-room. Then she used to take me to drive with her in the Villa Borghese or on the Pincian; and sometimes we would go for walks together in the Campagna. Of course, I was a regular visitor in her box at the opera: otherwise, the land had not been Italy, nor the town Rome. I liked her and enjoyed her inexpressibly; she was so witty and lively, so sympathetic, such a frank good comrade; she was so pretty and delicate and distinguished. "I can never make you understand," I confessed to her, "how much fuller and richer and more delightful life is since I have known you." I was, in fact, quite improbably happy, though I scarcely suspected it at the time. I had not forgotten that my rôle was the disconsolate lover; I must still now and again perorate about Elsie, and grieve over my painted wounds. The Contessa always listened patiently, with an air of commiseration. And I read her every line I wrote (poor woman!) whilst she criticised, suggested, encouraged. The calf is a queer animal.

You may wonder how she managed to put up with me, why I did not bore her to extermination. I can't answer—unless, indeed, it was simply that she had a sense of humour, as well as a kind heart. I am glad to be able to remember, besides, that our talks were by no means confined to subjects that had their source in my callow egotism. We talked of many things, we talked of everything: of books, pictures, music; of life, nature, religion; of Rome, its churches and palaces, its galleries and gardens; of people, of the people we knew in common, of their traits, their qualities, defects, absurdities. We talked of everything; sometimes—but all too infrequently—we talked of her. All too infrequently. I can't think how she contrived it; she was as far as possible from giving the impression of being reserved with me; yet, somehow, it was very seldom indeed that we talked of her. Somehow, for the most part—with no sign of effort, easily, imperceptibly even—she avoided or evaded the subject, or turned it if it was introduced. Only, once in a long while, once in a long, long while, she would, just for an instant, as it were, lift a corner of the curtain; tell me some little anecdote, some little incident, out of her life; allow me never so fleeting a glimpse into the more intimate regions of her experience.

One day, for example, one afternoon in February, when a faint breath of spring was on the air, we had driven out to Acqua Acetosa, and there we had left her carriage and strolled in the open country, plucking armfuls of flowers, anemones, jonquils, competing with each other to see who could gather the greatest number in the fewest minutes, and laughing and romping mirthfully. Her hair had got into some disarray, her cheeks glowed, her eyes sparkled; and her face looked so young, so young, that I exclaimed, "Do you know, you are exactly like a girl to-day. I told you once that you were the nicest woman I had ever known; but to-day I shall have to take that back, and tell you you're the nicest girl."

She laughed, sweetly, joyously. "I *am* a girl to-day," she said. But then, all at once, her eyes became sober, thoughtful; there was even a shadow of trouble in them. "You see, I never was really a girl," she went on. "I am living my girlhood now—as a kind of accidental after-thought—because I have happened to make friends with a boy. I am sowing my wild oats—gathering my wild flowers—at the eleventh hour."

"How do you mean—you were never really a girl?" I questioned stupidly.

You will guess what I felt—her eyes suddenly filled with tears.

I was stammering out some apology, but she stopped me. "No, no. It isn't your fault. I'm not crying. It's all right. I meant I was never a girl, because I

13

was married at eighteen. That is all. And I've had to be dull and middle-aged ever since," she added, smiling again. "You dull and middle-aged!" I scoffed at the notion. But her tears, and then her word about her marriage, had touched me poignantly. She had never mentioned, she had never remotely alluded to her marriage, before, in all our intercourse. Certainly, I knew, from things Miss Belmont had said, that it had not been a happy marriage. The Con-tessa's word about it now, brief as it was, slight as it was, moved me like a cry of pain. I felt a great anguish, a great anger, to think that circumstances had been cruel to her in the past; a great yearning in some way to be of comfort to her.

"Oh," I cried out—tactlessly, if you will; but my emotion was dominant; I could not stop to reflect—"oh, why—why didn't I know you in those days? Why wasn't I here—to—to help you—to defend you—to—to make it easier for you?"

We were in the carriage by this time, rolling swiftly back towards Rome. She did not speak. I did not look at her. But I felt her hand laid gently upon mine, her little light gloved hand; and then her hand pressed mine, a long soft pressure that said vastly more than speech; and then her hand rested there, lightly, lightly, and we were both silent, till we reached the Porta del Popolo.

When I had left her, I was conscious of a curious elation, a curious exaltation. It was almost as if my confidante had made me her confidant. A new honour had been conferred upon me, a new trust and responsibility. "Oh, I will devote my life to her," I vowed fervently, in my soul. "I will devote my life to making her happy, to compensating her in some measure for what she has suffered in the past. When shall I see her again?" I was consumed with eagerness, with impatience, to see her again.

I saw her, as a matter of fact, no later than the next day. I called on her in the afternoon. I went to her, meditating heroics. I would lay my life at her feet, I would ask her to let me be her knight, her servant. I looked forward to rather a fine moment. But it takes two to make a melodrama. She met me in a mood that sealed the heroics in my bosom; a teasing, elusive mood, her eyes, her voice, all mockery, all mischief. "Tiens, c'est mon petit-fils," she cried, on my arrival. "Bonjour, Toto. How nice of you to come and see your granny." There were days when she was like this, when she would never drop her joke about being my grandmother, and perpetually called me "Toto," and talked to me as if I were approaching seven. "Now, sit down on the floor before the fire," she said, "and gwandmamma will tell you a stor-wy." A sprite danced in her eyes. Her drawling enunciation of the last word was irresistible. I laughed, despite myself; and thoughts of high rhetoric had summarily to be dismissed.

When I look back upon my life as it was in those days, I protest I am filled with a sort of envy. A boy of twenty-something, his pockets comfortably supplied with money; free from morning to night, from night to morning, to do as his fancy prompted; with numberless pleasant acquaintances; and in the most beautiful country, the most interesting city, of two hemispheres—in Italy, in Rome: yes, indeed, as I look back at him, I am filled with envy.

But then, when I think of *her*.... I think of her, and she becomes visible before me, visible in all her exquisite grace and fineness, her exquisite femininity. I see her intimate little room, its gay blue and white, its pretty furniture, its hundred pretty personal trifles, tokens of her habitation; I breathe the air of it, the faint, soft perfume that was always on its air; I see her fan, her open book, her handkerchief forgotten on a table. I see her, in the room. I see her delicate white face, witty, alert, sensitive; I see her laughing eyes, her hair, the sumptuous masses of her hair. I see her hands, I touch them, slender, fragile, but warm, but firm and responsive. I see the delicious toilet she is wearing, I hear the brisk frou-frou of it. I hear her voice. I see her at her piano, I see her as she plays, the bend of her head, the motion of her body. I see her as she glances up at me, whimsically smiling, asking me something, telling me something. I gaze long at her, hungrily. And then, remembering that there was a time when I could see her like this in very reality as often as I would—oh, I can only cry out to myself of those days, "You lucky heathen, you lucky, lucky heathen! How little you realised, how little you merited, your extraordinary fortune!"

Of course, I was in love with her. But as yet, upon my conscience, I did not know it. I knew that I was tremendously fond of her, that I was never so happy as when in her presence, that I was always more or less unsatisfied and restless when out of it. I knew that I was always more or less unsatisfied and restless, too, when other men were hovering about her, when she was laughing and talking with other men. I knew that I wished to be her knight, her servant, to dedicate my existence to her welfare. But beyond that, I had not analysed my sentiment, nor given it a name.

And so, if you please, I was still able to go on prating to her of Elsie Milray!

However, there came a day when I ceased to prate of Elsie… It was during the Carnival. Miss Belmont had taken a room in the Corso, from the balcony of which, that afternoon, she and various of her friends had watched the merrymaking. The Contessa Bracca was expected, but the hours wore away, and she did not turn up. I waited for her, hoped for her, from minute to minute, to the last. Then I went home in a fine state of depression.

After dinner—and after much irresolution, ending in an abrupt resolve—I ventured to present myself at the Palazzo Stricci.

"I was alarmed about you. I was afraid you might be ill," I explained. I felt a great rush of relief, of warmth and peace, at seeing her.

She was seated in a low easy-chair, by her writing-table, with a volume of the "Récit d'une Sour" open in her lap.

"No, I'm not ill," she said, rising, and putting her book aside. "I'm not sorry you thought so, though, since it has procured me the pleasure of a visit from you," she added, smiling, as she gave me her hand.

But her face was pale, her smile seemed like a pale light that just flickered on it for an instant, and went out.

I looked at her with anxiety. "You *are* ill," I said. "There's something the matter. What is it? Tell me."

"No, no. Really. I'm all right," she insisted, with a little movement of the head, that was meant to be reassuring. "Sit down, and light a cigarette, and give me a true and faithful account of the day's doings. Who was there?"

"I don't know. You weren't. That was the important thing. We missed you awfully. Your absence entirely spoiled the afternoon," I declared.

She raised her eyebrows. "I can imagine how they must all have pined for me. Did they commission you to speak for them?"

"Well, I pined for you, at any rate," I said. "I kept looking for you, expecting you. Every minute, up to the very end, I still hoped for you. If you're not ill, or anything, why didn't you come?"

"Vanity. I was having a plain day, I didn't like to show myself."

I looked at her with anxiety, narrowly. "I say," I blurted out, "what's the use of beating about the bush? I know there's something wrong. I should have to be blind not to see it. If you're not ill, then you're unhappy about something. I can't help it—if you don't like my speaking of it, send me away. But I can't

16

sit here and talk small-talk, when I know that you're unhappy."

"If you know that I'm unhappy, you might sit here and talk small-talk, to cheer me up," she suggested.

"You—you've been crying," I exclaimed, all at once understanding an odd brightness in her eyes.

"Well, and even so? Hasn't one a right to cry, if it amuses one?" she questioned.

"What have you been crying about?" questioned I.

"I've been crying over my faded beauty—because I've had a plain day."

"Oh, I wish you wouldn't try to turn the matter to a jest," I pleaded. "I can't bear to think of you crying. I can't bear to think of you unhappy. What is it? I wish you'd tell me."

"Do you really wish it?" she asked, with a sudden approach to gravity.

"Yes—yes," I answered eagerly. "If you're unhappy, I want to know it, I want to share it with you. You're so good, you're so dear, I wish I could take every pain in the world away from you, I wish I could protect you from every breath of pain."

Her eyes softened beautifully, they shone into mine with a beautiful gentleness. "You're a dear boy," she said. "You're a great comfort to your grandmother."

"Well, then," I urged, "the least you can do is to tell me what has happened to make my grandmother unhappy."

"Nothing has happened. I've been thinking. That's all."

"Thinking what? What have you been thinking?"

"Thinking————-" she began, as if she was about to answer; but then she made a teasing little face at me, and declaimed—

> "Oh, thinking, if you like,
>
> How utterly dissociated was I,
>
> A priest and celibate, from the sad strange wife
>
> Of Guido."

And she laughed.

I threw up my hands in despair. "You're hopeless," I said. "It's no good ever expecting you to be serious."

"I'm serious enough, in all conscience," said she, "but I conceal it. I let concealment, like a worm in the bud, feed on my damask cheek. And so—I have plain days."

"I don't believe you've ever had a plain day in your life," asserted I. "You're the most beautiful woman in the world."

"I would beg you to observe that you're sitting here and talking small-talk, after all," she laughed, "That isn't small-talk. It's the solemn truth. But look here. I'm not going to let you evade the question. What have you been unhappy about?"

"I'm not unhappy any more. So what does it matter?"

"I want to know. Tell me."

"I've been puzzling over a dilemma," she said, "an excessively perplexed one."

"Yes? Go on," said I.

"I've been wondering whether I'd better marry Ciccolesi, or retire into a convent."

"Ciccolesi!" I cried, in astonishment, in dismay. "Marry Ciccolesi! You!"

"The Cavalière Ciccolesi. You've met him here on Mondays, A brown man, with curly hair. He's done me the honour of offering me his hand. Would you advise me to accept it?"

"Accept it?" I cried. "Good Lord! You must be—have you lost your reason? Ciccolesi—that automaton—that cardboard stalking-horse—that Neapolitan jackanapes! You—think of marrying him!"

I could only walk up and down the room and wave my hands.

"Ah, well," said she, "then I see there's nothing for it but the other alternative—to retire into a convent."

I halted and stared at her.

"What—what on earth has happened to make you talk like this?" I demanded, in a sort of gasp.

"I've been reflecting upon the futility of my life," she said. "I get up in the morning, and eat my breakfast. Then I fritter away an hour or two, and eat my luncheon. Then I fritter away the afternoon, and eat my dinner. Then I fritter away the evening, and go to bed. I live, apparently, to eat and sleep, like the beasts that perish. We must reform all that. I must do something to make myself of use in the world. And since you seem disinclined to sanction a marriage with Ciccolesi, what do you say to my joining some charitable sisterhood?"

She spoke lightly, even, if you will, half-jocosely. But there was a real bitterness unmistakable behind her tone. There was a bitterness in her smile.

And I—I was overwhelmed, penetrated, by a distress, by an emotion, such as I had never known before. I looked at her through a sort of mist—of pain, of passion; with a kind of aching helplessness; longing to say something, to do something, I could not tell what. Her smile had faded out; her face was white, set; her eyes were sombre. I looked at her, I longed to say something, to do something, and I could not move or speak. My mind was all a whirl, a bewilderment—till, somehow, gradually, from some place in the background of it, her name, her Christian name, struggled forward into consciousness. I seemed to see it before me, like a written word, her name, Gabrielle. And then I heard myself calling it.

"Gabrielle! Gabrielle!"

I heard my voice, I found myself kneeling beside her, holding her hands, speaking close to her face.

"Gabrielle! I can't let you—I can't allow you to think such things. *Your* life futile! Your beautiful, beautiful life! Gabrielle—my love! Oh, my love, my love!"...

By-and-by, laughing, sobbing, her eyes melting with a heavenly tenderness, she said, "It's absurd, it's impossible. You're only a boy. I'm a woman. I'm seven years older than you—in years. I'm immeasurably older in everything else. But I can't help it—I love you. You're only a boy—and yet—you're such an honest, frank, sweet boy—and my life has been passed with such artificial people, such unreal people—you're the only *man* I have ever known."

———————————————

The next morning one of her servants brought me a letter. Here it is.

"Dearest Friend,—Please do not come to see me this afternoon. I shall not be at home. I am leaving town. I am going to the Convent of Saint Veronica; I shall pass Lent there, with the good sisters.

"Dearest, do not be angry with me. I cannot accept your love, I have no right to accept it. Our friendship, our companionship, has been infinitely precious to me; it has given me a belief in human nature which I never had before. But you are young, you are still *growing*—in mind, in spirit. You must be free. I cannot cramp your youth, your growth, by accepting your love. Look, my dear, it would be an *impasse*. We could not marry. It would be monstrous if I should let you marry me—at the end of a year, at the end of six months, you would hate me, you would feel that I had spoiled your life. Yes, it is true. You must be free—you must grow. You must not handicap yourself at twenty-two by marrying a woman seven years your senior.

"Well, what then? Nothing but this—I must not accept your love, dear, I must give you up. You will go on, on; you will grow, you will outgrow the love you bear me now. You will live your life. And some day you will meet a woman of your own age.

"I know the pain this letter will give you; I know, I know. You will be unhappy, you will be angry with me. Dearest, try to forgive me. I am doing the only thing there is for me to do. You will be glad of it in the future. You will shudder to think, 'What if that woman had taken me at my word!'—Oh, why weren't you born ten years earlier, or I ten years later?

"I am going to the Convent of Saint Veronica, to pass Lent. Perhaps I shall stay longer. Perhaps—do not cry out, it is not a sudden resolution—perhaps I shall remain there, as an oblate. I could teach music, French. I must do something. I must not lead this idle futile life. Do not think of me as undergoing hardships. The rule for an oblate is not severe.

"Good-bye, dear. I pray God to bless you in every way.

"Good-bye, good-bye.

"Gabrielle."

Don't ask me what I felt, what I did....

Lent dragged itself away, but she did not return to Rome.

Then one day I received by post a copy of the *Osservatore Romano*, with a marked paragraph. It announced that the Contessa Bracca had been received into the Pious Community of Saint Veronica as a noble oblate.

Her letter, and that paragraph, cut from the *Osservatore Romano*, lie before me now, on my writing-table. Don't ask me what I feel, as I look at them.

MERELY PLAYERS

I

My dear," said the elder man, "as I've told you a thousand times, what you need is a love-affair with a red-haired woman."

"Bother women," said the younger man, "and hang love-affairs. Women are a pack of samenesses, and love-affairs are damnable iterations."

They were seated at a round table, gay with glass and silver, fruit and wine, in a pretty, rather high-ceiled little grey-and-gold breakfast-room. The French window stood wide open to the soft June day. From the window you could step out upon a small balcony; the balcony overhung a terrace; and a broad flight of steps from the terrace led down into a garden. You could not perceive the boundaries of the garden; in all directions it offered an indefinite perspective, a landscape of green lawns and shadowy alleys, bright parterres of flowers, fountains, and tall bending trees.

I have spoken of the elder man and the younger, though really there could have been but a trifling disparity in their ages: the elder was perhaps thirty, the younger seven- or eight-and-twenty. In other respects, however, they were as unlike as unlike may be. Thirty was plump and rosy and full-blown, with a laughing good-humoured face, and merry big blue eyes; eight-and-twenty, thin, tall, and listless-looking, his face pale and aquiline, his eyes dark, morose. They had finished their coffee, and now the plump man was nibbling sweetmeats, which he selected with much careful discrimination from an assortment in a porcelain dish. The thin man was drinking something green, possibly chartreuse.

"Women are a pack of samenesses," he grumbled, "and love-affairs are damnable iterations."

"Oh," cried out his comrade, in a tone of plaintive protest, "I said red-haired. You can't pretend that red-haired women are the same."

"The same, with the addition of a little henna," the pale young man argued wearily.

"It may surprise you to learn that I was thinking of red-haired women who are born red-haired," his friend remarked, from an altitude.

"In that case," said he, "I admit there is a difference—they have white eyelashes." And he emptied his glass of green stuff. "Is all this apropos of

22

boots?" he questioned.

The other regarded him solemnly. "It's apropos of your immortal soul," he answered, nodding his head. "It's medicine for a mind diseased. The only thing that will wake you up, and put a little life and human nature in you, is a love-affair with a red-haired woman. Red in the hair means fire in the heart. It means all sorts of things. If you really wish to please me, Uncle, you'll go and fall in love with a red-haired woman."

The younger man, whom the elder addressed as Uncle, shrugged his shoulders, and gave a little sniff. Then he lighted a cigarette.

The elder man left the table, and went to the open window. "Heavens, what weather!" he exclaimed fervently. "The day is made of perfumed velvet. The air is a love-philtre. The whole world sings romance. And yet you—insensible monster!—you can sit there torpidly——" But abruptly he fell silent.

His attention had been caught by something below, in the garden. He watched it for an instant from his place by the window; then he stepped forth upon the balcony, still watching. Suddenly, facing halfway round, "By my bauble, Nunky," he called to his companion, and his voice was tense with surprised exultancy, "she's got red hair!"

The younger man looked up with vague eyes. "Who? What?" he asked languidly.

"Come here, come here," his friend urged, beckoning him. "There," he indicated, when the pale man had joined him, "below there—to the right— picking roses. She's got red hair. She's sent by Providence."

A woman in a white frock was picking roses, in one of the alleys of the garden; rather a tall woman. Her back was turned towards her observers; but she wore only a light scarf of lace over her head, and her hair—dim gold in its shadows—where the sun touched it, showed a soul of red.

The younger man frowned, and asked sharply, "Who the devil is she?"

"I don't know, I'm sure," replied the other. "One of the Queen's women, probably. But whoever she is, she's got red hair."

The younger man frowned more fiercely still. "What is she doing in the King's private garden? This is a pretty state of things." He stamped his foot angrily. "Go down and turn her out. And I wish measures to be taken, that such trespassing may not occur again."

But the elder man laughed. "Hoity-toity! Calm yourself, Uncle. What would you have? The King is at a safe distance, hiding in one of his northern hunting-boxes, sulking, and nursing his spleen, as is his wont. When the

King's away, the palace mice will play—at *lèse majesté*, the thrilling game. If you wish to stop them, persuade the King to come home and show his face. Otherwise, we'll gather our rosebuds while we may; and I'm not the man to cross a red-haired woman."

"You're the Constable of Bellefontaine," retorted his friend, "and it's your business to see that the King's orders are respected."

"The King's orders are so seldom respectable; and then, I've a grand talent for neglecting my business. I'm trying to elevate the Constableship of Bellefontaine into a sinecure," the plump man explained genially. "But I'm pained to see that your sense of humour is not escaping the general decay of your faculties. What you need is a love-affair with a red-haired woman; and yonder's a red-haired woman, dropped from the skies for your salvation. Go —engage her in talk—and fall in love with her. There's a dear," he pleaded.

"Dropped from the skies," the pale man repeated, with mild scorn. "As if I didn't know my Hilary! Of course, you've had her up your sleeve the whole time."

"Upon my soul and honour, you are utterly mistaken. Upon my soul and honour, I've never set eyes on her before," Hilary asseverated warmly.

"Ah, well, if that's the case," suggested the pale man, turning back into the room, "let us make an earnest endeavour to talk of something else."

II

The next afternoon they were walking in the park, at some distance from the palace, when they came to a bridge over a bit of artificial water; and there was the woman of yesterday, leaning on the parapet, throwing bread-crumbs to the carp. She looked up as they passed, and bowed, with a little smile, in acknowledgment of their raised hats.

When they were out of earshot, "H'm," muttered Hilary, "viewed at close quarters, she's a trifle disenchanting."

"Oh?" questioned his friend. "I thought her very good-looking."

"She has too short a nose," Hilary complained.

"What's the good of criticising particular features? The general effect of her face was highly pleasing. She looked intelligent, interesting; she looked as if she would have something to say," the younger man insisted.

"It's very possible she has a tongue in her head," admitted Hilary; "but we were judging her by the rules of beauty. For my fancy, she's too tall."

"She's tall, but she's well-proportioned. Indeed, her figure struck me as exceptionally fine. There was something sumptuous and noble about it," declared the other.

"There are scores of women with fine figures in this world," said Hilary. "But I'm sorely disappointed in her hair. Her hair is nothing like so red as I'd imagined."

"You're daft on the subject of red hair. Her hair's not carrot-colour, if you come to that. But there's plenty of red in it, burning through it. The red is managed with discretion—suggestively. And did you notice her eyes? She has remarkably nice eyes—eyes with an expression. I thought her eyes and mouth were charming when she smiled," the pale man affirmed.

"When she smiled? I didn't see her smile," reflected Hilary.

"Of course she smiled—when we bowed," his friend reminded him.

"Oh, Ferdinand Augustus," Hilary remonstrated, "will you never learn to treat words with some consideration? You call that smiling! Two men take off their hats, and a woman gives them just a look of bare acknowledgment; and Ferdinand Augustus calls it smiling!"

"Would you have wished for a broad grin?" asked Ferdinand Augustus. "Her face lighted up most graciously. I thought her eyes were charming. Oh, she's certainly a good-looking woman, a distinctly handsome woman."

"Handsome is that handsome does," said Hilary.

"I miss the relevancy of that," said Ferdinand Augustus.

"She's a trespasser.'.was you yourself flew in a passion about it yesterday. Yesterday she was plucking the King's roses; to-day she's feeding the King's carp."

"'When the King's away, the palace mice will play.' I venture to recall your own words to you," Ferdinand remarked.

"That's all very well. Besides, I spoke in jest. But there are limits. And it's I who am responsible. I'm the Constable of Bellefontaine. Her trespassing appears to be habitual, We've caught her at it ourselves, two days in succession. I shall give instructions to the keepers to warn her not to touch a flower, nor feed a bird, beast, or fish, in the whole of this demesne. Really, I admire the cool way in which she went on tossing bread-crumbs to the King's carp under my very beard!" exclaimed Hilary, working himself into a fine state of indignation.

"Very likely she didn't know who you were," his friend reasoned. "And anyhow, your zeal is mighty sudden. You appear to have been letting things go at loose ends for I don't know how long; and all at once you take fire like tinder because a poor woman amuses herself by throwing bread to the carp. It's simply spite: you're disappointed in the colour of her hair. I shall esteem it a favour if you'll leave the keeper's instructions as they are. She's a damned good-looking woman; and I'll beg you not to interfere with her diversions."

"I can deny you nothing, Uncle," said Hilary, by this time restored to his accustomed easy temper; "and therefore she may make hay of the whole blessed establishment, if she pleases. But as for her good looks—that, you'll admit, is entirely a question of taste."

"Ah, well, then the conclusion is that your taste needs cultivation," laughed Ferdinand. "By-the-bye, I shall be glad if you will find out who she is."

"Thank you very much," cried Hilary. "I have a reputation to safeguard. Do you think I'm going to compromise myself, and set all my underlings a-sniggling, by making inquiries about the identity of a woman?"

"But," persisted Ferdinand, "if I ask you to do so, as your————-"

"What?" was Hilary's brusque interruption.

"As your guest," said Ferdinand.

"*Mille regrets, impossible*, as the French have it," Hilary returned. "But as your host, I give you carte-blanche to make your own inquiries for yourself—if you think she's worth the trouble. Being a stranger here, you have, as it were, no character to lose."

"After all, it doesn't matter," said Ferdinand Augustus, with resignation.

III

But the next afternoon, at about the same hour, Ferdinand Augustus found himself alone, strolling in the direction of the little stone bridge over the artificial lakelet; and there again was the woman, leaning upon the parapet, dropping bread-crumbs to the carp. Ferdinand Augustus raised his hat; the woman bowed and smiled.

"It's a fine day," said Ferdinand Augustus.

"It's a fine day—but a weary one," the woman responded, with an odd little movement of the head.

Ferdinand Augustus was perhaps too shy to pursue the conversation; perhaps he wanted but little here below, nor wanted that little long. At any rate, he passed on. There could be no question about her smile this time, he reflected; it had been bright, spontaneous, friendly. But what did she mean, he wondered, by adding to his general panegyric of the day as fine, that special qualification of it as a weary one? It was astonishing that any man should dispute her claim to beauty. She had really a splendid figure; and her face was more than pretty, it was distinguished. Her eyes and her mouth, her clear-grey sparkling eyes, her softly curved red mouth, suggested many agreeable possibilities—possibilities of wit, and of something else. It was not till four hours later that he noticed the sound of her voice. At dinner, in the midst of a discussion with Hilary about a subject in no obvious way connected with her (about the Orient Express, indeed—its safety, speed, and comfort), it suddenly came back to him, and he checked a remark upon the advantages of the corridor carriage, to exclaim in his soul, "She's got a delicious voice. If she sang, it would be a mezzo."

The consequence was that the following day he again bent his footsteps in the direction of the bridge.

"It's a lovely afternoon," he said, lifting his hat.

"But a weary one," said she, smiling, with a little pensive movement of the head.

"Not a weary one for the carp," he hinted, glancing down at the water, which boiled and bubbled with a greedy multitude.

"Oh, they have no human feelings," said she.

"Don't you call hunger a human feeling?" he inquired.

"They have no human feelings; but I never said we hadn't plenty of carp feelings," she answered him.

He laughed. "At all events, I'm pleased to find that we're of the same way of thinking."

"Are we?" asked she, raising surprised eyebrows.

"You take a healthy pessimistic view of things," he submitted.

"I? Oh, dear, no. I have never taken a pessimistic view of anything in my life."

"Except of this poor summer's afternoon, which has the fatal gift of beauty. You said it was a weary one."

"People have sympathies," she explained; "and besides, that is a watchword." And she scattered a handful of crumbs, thereby exciting a new commotion among the carp.

Her explanation no doubt struck Ferdinand Augustus as obscure; but, perhaps he felt that he scarcely knew her well enough to press for enlightment. "Let us hope that the fine weather will last," he said, with a polite salutation, and resumed his walk.

But, on the morrow, "You make a daily practice of casting your bread upon the waters," was his greeting to her. "Do you expect to find it at the season's end?"

"I find it at once," was her response, "in entertainment."

"It entertains you to see those shameless little gluttons making an exhibition of themselves!" he cried out.

"You must not speak disrespectfully of them," she reproved him. "Some of them are very old. Carp often live to be two hundred, and they grow grey, for all the world like men."

"They're like men in twenty particulars," asserted he, "though you, yesterday, denied it. See how the big ones elbow the little ones aside; see how fierce they all are in the scramble for your bounty. You wake their most evil passions. But the spectacle is instructive. It's a miniature presentment of civilisation. Oh, carp are simply brimfull of human nature. You mentioned yesterday that they have no human feelings. You put your finger on the chief point of resemblance. It's the absence of human feeling that makes them so hideously human."

She looked at him with eyes that were interested, amused, yet not altogether without a shade of raillery in their depths. "That is what you call a healthy pessimistic view of things?" she questioned.

"It is an inevitable view if one honestly uses one's sight, or reads one's newspaper."

"Oh, then I would rather not honestly use my sight," said she; "and as for the newspaper, I only read the fashions. Your healthy pessimistic view of things can hardly add much to the joy of life."

"The joy of life!". he expostulated. "There's no joy in life. Life is one fabric of hardship, peril, and insipidity."

"Oh, how can you say that," cried she, "in the face of such beauty as we have about us here? With the pure sky and the sunshine, and the wonderful peace of the day; and then these lawns and glades and the great green trees; and the sweet air, and the singing birds! No joy in life!"

"This isn't life," he answered. "People who shut themselves up in an artificial park are fugitives from life. Life begins at the park gates, with the natural countryside, and the squalid peasantry, and the sordid farmers, and the Jew money-lenders, and the uncertain crops."

"Oh, it's all life," insisted she, "the park and the countryside, and the virgin forest and the deep sea, with all things in them. It's all life. I'm alive, and I daresay you are. You would exclude from life all that is nice in life, and then say of the remainder, that only is life. You're not logical."

"Heaven forbid," he murmured devoutly. "I'm sure you're not, either. Only stupid people are logical." She laughed lightly. "My poor carp little dream to what far paradoxes they have led," she mused, looking into the water, which was now quite tranquil. "They have sailed away to their mysterious affairs among the lily-roots. I should like to be a carp for a few minutes, to see what it is like in those cool, dark places under the water. I am sure there are all sorts of strange things and treasures. Do you believe there are really water-maidens, like Undine?"

"Not nowadays," he informed her, with the confident fluency of one who knew. "There used to be; but, like so many other charming things, they disappeared with the invention of printing, the discovery of America, and the rise of the Lutheran heresy. Their prophetic souls——"

"Oh, but they had no souls, you remember," she corrected him.

"I beg your pardon; that was the belief that prevailed among their mortal contemporaries, but it has since been ascertained that they had souls, and very good ones. Their prophetic souls warned them what a dreary, dried-up planet the earth was destined to become, with the steam-engine, the electric telegraph, compulsory education (falsely so called), constitutional government, and the supremacy of commerce. So the elder ones died, dissolved in tears; and the younger ones migrated by evaporation to Neptune."

"Dear me, dear me," she marvelled. "How extraordinary that we should just have happened to light upon a topic about which you appear to have such a quantity of special knowledge! And now," she added, bending her head by way of valediction, "I must be returning to my duties."

And she moved off, towards the palace.

IV

And then, for three or four days, he did not see her, though he paid frequent enough visits to the feeding-place of the carp.

"I wish it would rain," he confessed to Hilary. "I hate the derisive cheerfulness of this weather. The birds sing, and the flowers smile, and every prospect breathes sodden satisfaction; and only man is bored."

"Yes, I own I find you dull company," Hilary responded, "and if I thought it would brisk you up, I'd pray with all my heart for rain. But what you need, as I've told you a thousand times, is a love-affair with a red-haired woman."

"Love-affairs are tedious repetitions," said Ferdinand. "You play with your new partner precisely the same game you played with the old: the same preliminary skirmishes, the same assault, the same feints of resistance, the same surrender, the same subsequent disenchantment. They're all the same, down to the very same scenes, words, gestures, suspicions, vows, exactions, recriminations, and final break-ups. It's a delusion of inexperience to suppose that in changing your mistress you change the sport. It's the same trite old book, that you've read and read in different editions, until you're sick of the very mention of it. To the deuce with love-affairs. But there's such a thing as rational conversation, with no sentimental nonsense. Now, I'll not deny that I should rather like to have an occasional bit of rational conversation with that red-haired woman we met the other day in the park. Only, the devil of it is, she never appears."

"And then, besides, her hair isn't red," added Hilary.

"I wonder how you can talk such folly," said Ferdinand.

"*C'est mon métier*, Uncle. You should answer me! according to it. Her hair's not red. What little red there's in it, it requires strong sunlight to bring out. In shadow her hair's a sort of dull brownish-yellow," Hilary persisted.

"You're colour-blind," retorted Ferdinand. "But I won't quarrel with you. The point is, she never appears. So how can I have my bits of rational conversation with her?"

"How, indeed?" echoed Hilary, with pathos.

"And therefore you're invoking storm and whirlwind. But hang a horseshoe over your bed to-night, turn round three times as you extinguish your candle, and let your last thought before you fall asleep be the thought of a newt's liver and a blind man's dog; and it's highly possible she will appear to-morrow."

I don't know whether Ferdinand Augustus accomplished the rites that Hilary prescribed, but it is certain that she did appear on the morrow: not by the pool of the carp, but in quite another region of Bellefontaine, where Ferdinand Augustus was wandering at hazard, somewhat disconsolately. There was a wide green meadow, sprinkled with buttercups and daisies; and under a great tree, at this end of it, he suddenly espied her. She was seated on the moss, stroking with one finger-tip a cockchafer that was perched upon another, and regarding the little monster with intent meditative eyes. She wore a frock the bodice part of which was all drooping creamy lace; she had thrown her hat and gloves aside; her hair was in some slight, soft disarray; her loose sleeve had fallen back, disclosing a very perfect wrist and the beginning of a smooth white arm. Altogether she made an extremely pleasing picture, sweetly, warmly feminine. Ferdinand Augustus stood still, and watched her for an instant before he spoke. Then——

"I have come to intercede with you on behalf of your carp," he announced. "They are rending heaven with complaints of your desertion."

She looked up, with a whimsical, languid little smile. "Are they?" she asked lightly. "I'm rather tired of carp."

He shook his head sorrowfully. "You will permit me to admire your fine, frank disregard of *their* feelings."

"Oh, they have the past to remember," she said. "And perhaps some day I shall go back to them. For the moment I amuse myself very well with cockchafers. They're less tumultuous. And then, carp won't come and perch on your finger. And then, one likes a change.—Now fly away, fly away, fly away home; your house is on fire, and your children will burn," she crooned to the cockchafer, giving it never so gentle a push. But instead of flying away, it dropped upon the moss, and thence began to stumble, clumsily, blunderingly, towards the open meadow.

"You shouldn't have caused the poor beast such a panic," he reproached her. "You should have broken the dreadful news gradually. As you see, your sudden blurting of it out has deprived him of the use of his faculties. Don't believe her," he called after the cockchafer. "She's practising upon your credulity. Your house isn't on fire, and your children are all safe at school."

"Your consideration is entirely misplaced," she assured him, with the same slight whimsical smile. "The cockchafer knows perfectly well that his house isn't on fire, because he hasn't got any house. Cockchafers never have houses. His apparent concern is sheer affectation. He's an exceedingly hypocritical little cockchafer."

"I should call him an exceedingly polite little cockchafer. Hypocrisy is the compliment courtesy owes to falsehood. He pretended to believe you. He would not have the air of doubting a lady's word."

"You came as the emissary of the carp," she said, "and now you stay to defend the character of their rival."

"To be candid, I don't care a hang for the carp," he confessed brazenly. "The unadorned fact is that I'm immensely glad to see you."

She gave a little laugh, and bowed with exaggerated ceremony. "*Grand merci, Monsieur; vous me faites trop d'honneur*," she murmured.

"Oh, no, not more than you deserve. I'm a just man, and I give you your due. I was boring myself into melancholy madness. The afternoon lay before me like a bumper of dust and ashes, that I must somehow empty. And then I saw you, and you dashed the goblet from my lips. Thank goodness (I said to myself), at last there's a human soul to talk with; the very thing I was pining for, a clever and sympathetic woman."

"You take a great deal for granted," laughed she.

"Oh, I know you're clever, and it pleases me to fancy that you're sympathetic. If you're not," he pleaded, "don't tell me so. Let me cherish my illusion."

She shook her head doubtfully. "I'm a poor hand at dissembling."

"It's an art you should study," said he. "If we begin by feigning an emotion, we're as like as not to end by genuinely feeling it."

"I've observed for myself," she informed him, "that if we begin by genuinely feeling an emotion, but rigorously conceal it, we're as like as not to end by feeling it no longer. It dies of suffocation. I've had that experience quite lately. There was a certain person whom I heartily despised and hated; and then, as chance would have it, I was thrown two or three times into his company; and for motives of expediency I disguised my antagonism. In the end, do you know, I found myself rather liking him?"

"Oh, women are fearfully and wonderfully made," he said.

"And so are some men," said she. "Could you oblige me with the name and address of a competent witch or warlock?" she added irrelevantly.

"What under the sun can you want with such an unholy thing?" he exclaimed.

"I want a hate-charm—something that I can take at night to revive my hatred of the man I was speaking of."

"Look here," he warned her, "I've not come all this distance, under a scorching sun, to stand here now and talk of another man. Cultivate a contemptuous indifference towards him. Banish him from your mind and conversation."

"I'll try," she consented; "though, if you were familiar with the circumstances, you'd recognise a certain difficulty in doing that." She reached for her gloves, and began to put one on. "Will you be so good as to tell me the time of day?"

He looked at his watch. "It's nowhere near time for you to be moving yet."

"You must not trifle about affairs of state," she said. "At a definite hour I have business at the palace."

"Oh, for that matter, so have I. But it's half-past four. To call half-past four a definite hour would be to do a violence to the language."

"It is earlier than I thought," she admitted, discontinuing her operation with the glove.

He smiled approval. "Your heart is in the right place, after all. It would have been inhuman to abandon me. Oh, yes, pleasantry apart, I am in a condition of mind in which solitude spells misery. And yet I am on speaking terms with but three living people whose society I prefer to it."

"You are indeed in sad case, then," she compassionated him. "But why should solitude spell misery? A man of wit like you should have plenty of resources within himself."

"Am I a man of wit?" he asked innocently.

Her eyes gleamed mischievously. "What is your opinion?"

"I don't know," he reflected. "Perhaps I might have been, if I had met a woman like you earlier in life."

"At all events," she laughed, "if you are not a man of wit, it is not for lack of courage. But why does solitude spell misery? Have you great crimes upon your conscience?"

"No, nothing so amusing. But when one is alone, one thinks; and when one thinks—that way madness lies."

"Then do you never think when you are engaged in conversation?" She raised her eyebrows questioningly.

"You should be able to judge of that by the quality of my remarks. At any rate, I feel."

"What do you feel?"

"When I am engaged in conversation with you, I feel a general sense of agreeable stimulation; and, in addition to that, at this particular moment ———But are you sure you really wish to know?" he broke off.

"Yes, tell me," she said, with curiosity.

"Well, then, a furious desire to smoke a cigarette."

She laughed merrily. "I am so sorry I have no cigarettes to offer you."

"My pockets happen to be stuffed with them."

"Then, do, please, light one."

He produced his cigarette-case, but he seemed to hesitate about lighting a cigarette.

"Have you no matches?" she inquired.

"Yes, thank you, I have matches. I was only thinking."

"It has become a solitude, then?" she cried.

"It is a case of conscience, it is an ethical dilemma. How do I know—the modern woman is capable of anything—how do I know that you may not yourself be a smoker? But if you are, it will give you pain to see me enjoying my cigarette, while you are without one."

"It would be civil to begin by offering me one," she suggested.

"That is exactly the liberty I dared not take—oh, there are limits to my boldness. But you have saved the situation." And he offered her his cigarette-case.

She shook her head. "Thank you, I don't smoke." And her eyes were full of teasing laughter, so that he laughed too, as he finally applied a match-flame to his cigarette. "But you may allow me to examine your cigarette-case," she went on. "It looks like a pretty bit of silver." And when he had handed it to her, she exclaimed, "It is engraved with the royal arms."

"Yes. Why not?" said he.

"Does it belong to the King?"

"It was a present from the King."

"To you? You are a friend of the King?" she asked, with some eagerness.

"I will not deceive you," he replied. "No, not to me. The King gave it to Hilary Clairevoix, the Constable of Bellefontaine; and Hilary, who's a careless fellow, left it lying about in his music-room, and I came along and pocketed it. It is a pretty bit of silver, and I shall never restore it to its rightful owner if I can help it."

"But you are a friend of the King's?" she repeated, with insistence.

"I have not that honour. Indeed, I have never seen him. I am a friend of Hilary's; I am his guest. He has stayed with me in England—I am an Englishman—and now I am returning his visit."

"That is well," said she. "If you were a friend of the King, you would be an enemy of mine."

"Oh?" he wondered. "Why is that?"

"I hate the King," she answered simply.

"Dear me, what a capacity you have for hating! This is the second hatred you have avowed within the hour. What has the King done to displease you?"

"You are an Englishman. Has the King's reputation not reached England yet? He is the scandal of Europe. What has he done? But no—do not encourage me to speak of him. I should grow too heated," she said strenuously.

"On the contrary, I pray of you, go on," urged Ferdinand Augustus. "Your King is a character that interests me more than you can think. His reputation has indeed reached England, and I have conceived a great curiosity about him. One only hears vague rumours, to be sure, nothing specific; but one has learned to think of him as original and romantic. You know him. Tell me a lot about him."

"Oh, I do not know him personally. That is an affliction I have as yet been spared." Then, suddenly, "Mercy upon me, what have I said!" she cried. "I must 'knock wood,' or the evil spirits will bring me that mischance to-morrow." And she fervently tapped the bark of the tree beside her with her knuckles.

Ferdinand Augustus laughed. "But if you do not know him personally, why do you hate him?"

"I know him very well by reputation. I know how he lives, I know what he does and leaves undone. If you are curious about him, ask your friend Hilary. He is the King's foster-brother. *He* could tell you stories," she added meaningly.

"I have asked him. But Hilary's lips are sealed. He depends upon the King's protection for his fortune, and the palace-walls (I suppose he fears) have ears. But you can speak without danger. He is the scandal of Europe? There's nothing I love like scandal. Tell me all about him."

"You have not come all this distance, under a scorching sun, to stand here now and talk of another man," she reminded him.

"Oh, but kings are different," he argued. "Tell me about your King."

"I can tell you at once," said she, "that our King is the frankest egotist in two hemispheres. You have learned to think of him as original and romantic? No; he is simply intensely selfish and intensely silly. He is a King Do-Nothing, a Roi Fainéant, who shirks and evades all the duties and responsibilities of his position; who builds extravagant chateaux in remote parts of the country, and hides in them, alone with a few obscure companions; who will never visit his capital, never show his face to his subjects; who takes no sort of interest in public business or the welfare of his kingdom, and leaves the entire government to his ministers; who will not even hold a court, or give balls or banquets; who, in short, does nothing that a king ought to do, and might, for all the good we get of him, be a mere stranger in the land, a mere visitor, like yourself. So closely does he seclude himself that I doubt if there be a hundred people in the whole country who have ever seen him, to know him. If he travels from one place to another, it is always in the strictest incognito, and those who then chance to meet him never have any reason to suspect that he is not a private person. His very effigy on the coin of the realm is reputed to be false, resembling him in no wise. But I could go on for ever," she said, bringing her indictment to a termination.

"Really," said Ferdinand Augustus, "I cannot see that you have alleged anything very damaging. A Roi Fainéant? But every king of a modern constitutional state is, willy-nilly, that. He can do nothing but sign bills which he generally disapproves of, lay foundation-stones, set the fashion in hats, and bow and look pleasant as he drives through the streets. He has no power for good, and mighty little for evil. He is just a State Prisoner. It seems to me that your particular King has shown some sense in trying to escape so much as he may of the prison's irksomeness. I should call it rare bad luck to be born a king. Either you've got to shirk your kingship, and then fair ladies dub you the scandal of Europe; or else you've got to accept it, and then you're as happy as a man in a strait-waistcoat. And then, and then! Oh, I can think of a thousand unpleasantnesses attendant upon the condition of a king. Your King, as I understand it, has said to himself, 'Hang it all, I didn't ask to be born a king, but since that is my misfortune, I will seek to mitigate it as much as I am able. I am, on the whole, a human being, with a human life to live, and only, probably, threescore-and-ten years in which to live it. Very good; I will live my life. I will lay no foundation-stones, nor drive about the streets bowing and looking pleasant. I will live my life, alone with the few people I find to my liking. I will take the cash and let the credit go.' I am bound to say," concluded Ferdinand Augustus, "that your King has done exactly what I should have done in his place."

"You will never, at least," said she, "defend the shameful manner in which he has behaved towards the Queen. It is for that, I hate him. It is for that, that we, the Queen's gentlewomen, have adopted '7' is a weary day as a watchword. It will be a weary day until we see the King on his knees at the Queen's feet, craving her forgiveness."

36

"Oh? What has he done to the Queen?" asked Ferdinand.

"What has he done! Humiliated her as never woman was humiliated before. He married her by proxy at her father's court; and she was conducted with great pomp and circumstance into his kingdom—to find what? That he had fled to one of his absurd castles in the north, and refused to see her! He has remained there ever since, hiding like—but there is nothing in created space to compare him to. Is it the behaviour of a gentleman, of a gallant man, not to say a king?" she cried warmly, looking up at him with shining eyes, her cheeks faintly flushed.

Ferdinand Augustus bowed. "The Queen is fortunate in her advocate. I have not heard the King's side of the story. I can, however, imagine excuses for him. Suppose that his ministers, for reasons of policy, importuned and importuned him to marry a certain princess, until he yielded in mere fatigue. In that case, why should he be bothered further? Why should he add one to the tedious complications of existence by meeting the bride he never desired? Is it not sufficient that, by his complaisance, she should have gained the rank and title of a queen? Besides, he may be in love with another woman. Or perhaps—but who can tell? He may have twenty reasons. And anyhow, you cannot deny to the situation the merit of being highly ridiculous. A husband and wife who are not personally acquainted! It is a delicious commentary upon the whole system of marriages by proxy. You confirm my notion that your King is original."

"He may have twenty reasons," answered she, "but he had better have twenty terrors. It is perfectly certain that the Queen will be revenged."

"How so?" asked Ferdinand Augustus.

"The Queen is young, high-spirited, moderately good-looking, and unspeakably incensed. Trust a young, high-spirited, and handsome woman, outraged by her husband, to know how to avenge herself. Oh, some day he will see."

"Ah, well, he must take his chances," Ferdinand sighed. "Perhaps he is liberal-minded enough not to care."

"I am far from meaning the vulgar revenge you fancy," she put in quickly. "The Queen's revenge will be subtle and unexpected. She is no fool, and she will not rest until she has achieved it. Oh, he will see!"

"I had imagined it was the curse of royalty to be without true friends," said Ferdinand Augustus. "The Queen has a very ardent one in you."

"I am afraid I cannot altogether acquit myself of interested motives," she disclaimed modestly. "I am of her Majesty's household, and my fortunes must rise and fall with hers. But I am honestly indignant with the King."

"The poor King! Upon my soul, he has my sympathy," said Ferdinand.

"You are terribly ironical," said she.

"Irony was ten thousand leagues from my intention," he protested. "In all sincerity the object of your indignation has my sympathy. I trust you will not consider it an impertinence if I say that I already count you among the few people I have met whose good opinion is a matter to be coveted."

She had risen while he was speaking, and now she bobbed him a little curtsey. "I will show my appreciation of yours, by taking flight before anything can happen to alter it," she laughed, moving away.

V

"You are singularly animated to-night," said Hilary, contemplating him across the dinner-table; "yet, at the same time, singularly abstracted. You have the air of a man who is rolling something pleasant under his tongue, something sweet and secret: it might be a hope, it might be a recollection. Where have you passed the afternoon? You've been about some mischief, I'll warrant. By Jove, you set me thinking. I'll wager a penny you've been having a bit of rational conversation with that brown-haired woman."

"Her hair is red," Ferdinand Augustus rejoined, with firmness. "And her conversation," he added sadly, "is anything you please but rational. She spent her whole time picking flaws in the character of the King. She talked downright treason. She said he was the scandal of Europe and the frankest egotist in two hemispheres."

"Ah? She appears to have some instinct for the correct use of language," commented Hilary.

"All the same, I rather like her," Ferdinand went on, "and I'm half inclined to undertake her conversion. She has a gorgeous figure—there's something rich and voluptuous about it. And there are depths of promise in her eyes; there are worlds of humour and of passion. And she has a mouth—oh, of a fulness, of a softness, of a warmth! And a chin, and a throat, and hands! And then, her voice. There's a mellowness yet a crispness, there's a vibration, there's a something in her voice that assures you of a golden temperament beneath it. In short, I'm half inclined to follow your advice, and go in for a love-adventure with her."

"Oh, but love-adventures—I have it on high authority—are damnable iterations," objected Hilary.

"That is very true; they are," Ferdinand agreed. "But the life of man is woven of damnable iterations. Tell me of any single thing that isn't a damnable iteration, and I'll give you a quarter of my fortune. The day and the night, the seasons and the years, the fair weather and the foul, breakfast and luncheon and dinner—all are damnable iterations. If there's any reality behind the doctrine of metempsychosis, death, too, is a damnable iteration. There's no escaping damnable iterations: there's nothing new under the sun. But as long as one is alive, one must do something. It's sure to be something in its essence identical with something one has done before; but one must do something. Why not, then, a love-adventure with a woman that attracts you?"

"Women are a pack of samenesses," said Hilary despondently.

"Quite so," assented Ferdinand. "Women, and men too, are a pack of samenesses. We're all struck with the same die, of the same metal, at the same mint. Our resemblance is intrinsic, fundamental; our differences are accidental and skin deep. We have the same features, organs, dimensions, with but a hair's-breadth variation; the same needs, instincts, propensities; the same hopes, fears, ideas. One man's meat is another man's meat; one man's poison is another man's poison. We are as like to one another as the leaves on the same tree. Skin us, and (save for your fat) the most skilled anatomist could never distinguish you from me. Women are a pack of samenesses; but, hang it all, one has got to make the best of a monotonous universe. And this particular woman, with her red hair and her eyes, strikes me as attractive. She has some fire in her composition, some fire and flavour. Anyhow, she attracts me; and—I think I shall try my luck."

"Oh, Nunky, Nunky," murmured Hilary, shaking his head, "I am shocked by your lack of principle. Have you forgotten that you are a married man?"

"That will be my safeguard. I can make love to her with a clear conscience. If I were single, she might, justifiably enough, form matrimonial expectations for herself."

"Not if she knew you," said Hilary.

"Ah, but she doesn't know me—and shan't," said Ferdinand Augustus. "I will take care of that."

VI

And then, for what seemed to him an eternity, he never once encountered her. Morning and afternoon, day after day, he roamed the park of Bellefontaine from end to end, in all directions, but never once caught sight of so much as the flutter of her garments. And the result was that he began to grow seriously sentimental. *"Im wunderschônen Monat Mai!"* It was June, to be sure; but the meteorological influences were, for that, only the more potent. He remembered her shining eyes now as not merely whimsical and ardent, but as pensive, appealing, tender; he remembered her face as a face seen in starlight, ethereal and mystic; and her voice as low music far away. He recalled their last meeting as a treasure he had possessed and lost; he blamed himself for the frivolity of his talk and manner, and for the ineffectual impression of him this must have left upon her. Perpetually thinking of her, he was perpetually sighing, perpetually suffering strange, sudden, half painful, half delicious commotions in the tissues of his heart. Every morning he rose with a replenished fund of hope: this day at last would produce her. Every night he went to bed pitying himself as bankrupt of hope. And all the while, though he pined to talk of her, a curious bashfulness withheld him; so that, between him and Hilary, for quite a fortnight she was not mentioned. It was Hilary who broke the silence.

"Why so pale and wan?" Hilary asked him. "Will, when looking well won't move her, looking ill prevail?"

"Oh, I am seriously love-sick," cried Ferdinand Augustus, welcoming the subject. "I went in for a sensation, and I've got a real emotion."

"Poor youth! And she won't look at you, I suppose?" was Hilary's method of commiseration.

"I have not seen her for a mortal fortnight. She has completely vanished. And for the first time in my life I'm seriously in love."

"You're incapable of being seriously in love," said Hilary.

"I had always thought so myself," admitted Ferdinand Augustus. "The most I had ever felt for any woman was a sort of mere lukewarm desire, a sort of mere meaningless titillation. But this woman is different. She's as different to other women as wine is different to toast-and-water. She has the *feu-sacré*. She's done something to the very inmost soul of me; she's laid it bare, and set it quivering and yearning. She's made herself indispensable to me; I can't live without her. Ah, you don't know what she's like. She's like some strange, beautiful, burning spirit. Oh, for an hour with her I'd give my kingdom. To touch her hand—to look into those eyes of hers—to hear her speak to me! I tell you squarely, if she'd have me, I'd throw up the whole scheme of my existence, I'd fly with her to the uttermost ends of the earth. But she has totally disappeared, and I can do nothing to recover her without betraying my identity; and that would spoil everything. I want her to love me for myself, believing me to be a plain man, like you or anybody. If she knew who I am, how could I ever be sure?"

"You *are* in a bad way," said Hilary, looking at him with amusement. "And yet, I'm gratified to see it. Her hair is not so red as I could wish, but, after all, it's reddish; and you appear to be genuinely aflame. It will do you no end of good; it will make a man of you—a plain man, like me or anybody. But your impatience is not reasoned. A fortnight? You have not met her for a fortnight? My dear, to a plain man (like me or anybody) a fortnight's nothing. It's just an appetiser. Watch and wait, and you'll meet her before you know it. And now, if you will excuse me, I have business in another quarter of the palace."

Ferdinand Augustus, left to himself, went down into the garden. It was a wonderful summer's evening, made indeed (if I may steal a phrase from Hilary) of perfumed velvet. The sun had set an hour since, but the western sky was still splendid, like a dark banner, with sombre reds and purples; and in the east hung the full moon, so brilliant, so apposite, as to seem somehow almost like a piece of premeditated decoration. The waters of the fountains flashed silverly in its light; glossy leaves gave back dim reflections; here and there, embowered among the trees, white statues gleamed ghost-like. Away in the park somewhere, innumerable frogs were croaking, croaking; subdued by distance, the sound gained a quality that was plaintive and unearthly. The long façade of the palace lay obscure in shadow; only at the far end, in the Queen's apartments, were the windows alight. But, quite close at hand, the moon caught a corner of the terrace; and here, presently, Ferdinand Augustus became aware of a human figure. A woman was standing alone by the balustrade, gazing out into the wondrous night. Ferdinand Augustus's heart began to pound; and it was a full minute before he could command himself sufficiently to move or speak.

At last, however, he approached her. "Good evening," he said, looking up from the pathway.

She glanced down at him, leaning upon the balustrade. "Oh, how do you do?" She smiled her surprise. She was in evening dress, a white robe embroidered with pearls, and she wore a tiara of pearls in her hair. She had a light cloak thrown over her shoulders, a little cape trimmed with swan's-down. "Heavens!" thought Ferdinand Augustus. "How magnificent she is!"

"It's a hundred years since I have seen you," he said.

"Oh, is it so long as that? I should have imagined it was something like a fortnight. Time passes quickly."

"That is a question of psychology. But now at last I find you when I least expect you."

"I have slipped out for a moment," she explained, "to enjoy this beautiful prospect. One has no such view from the Queen's end of the terrace. One cannot see the moon."

"I cannot see the moon from where I am standing," said he.

"No, because you have turned your back upon it," said she.

"I have chosen between two visions. If you were to authorise me to join you, aloft there, I could see both."

"I have no power to authorise you," she laughed, "the terrace is not my property. But if you choose to take the risks——"

"Oh," he cried, "you are good, you are kind." And in an instant he had joined her on the terrace, and his heart was fluttering wildly with its sense of her nearness to him. He could not speak.

"Well, now you can see the moon. Is it all your fancy painted?" she asked, with her whimsical smile. Her face was exquisitely pale in the moonlight, her eyes glowed. Her voice was very soft.

His heart was fluttering wildly, poignantly. "Oh," he began, but broke off. His breath trembled. "I cannot speak," he said.

She arched her eyebrows; "Then we have made some mistake. This will never be you, in that case."

"Oh, yes, it is I. It is the other fellow, the gabbler, who is not myself," he contrived to tell her.

"You lead a double life, like the villain in the play?" she suggested.

"You must have your laugh at my expense; have it, and welcome. But I know what I know," he said.

"What do you know?" she asked quickly.

"I know that I am in love with you," he answered.

"Oh, only that," she said, with an air of relief.

"Only that. But that is a great deal. I know that I love you—oh, yes, unutterably. If you could see yourself! You are absolutely unique among women. I would never have believed it possible for any woman to make me feel what you have made me feel. I have never spoken like this to any woman in all my life. Oh, you may laugh. It is the truth, upon my word of honour. If you could look into your eyes—yes, even when you are laughing at me! I can see your wonderful burning spirit shining deep, deep in your eyes. You do not dream how different you are to other women. You are a wonderful burning poem. They are platitudes. Oh, I love you unutterably. There has not been an hour since I last saw you that I have not thought of you, loved you, longed for you. And now here you stand, you yourself, beside me! If you could see into my heart, if you could see what I feel!"

She looked at the moon, with a strange little smile, and was silent.

"Will you not speak to me?" he cried.

"What would you have me say?" she asked, still looking away.

"Oh, you know, you know what I would have you say."

"I am afraid you will not like the only thing I can say." She turned, and met his eyes. "I am a married woman, and—I am in love with my husband."

Ferdinand Augustus stood aghast. "Oh, my God!" he groaned.

"Yes, though he has given me little enough reason to do so, I have fallen in love with him," she went on pitilessly. "So you must get over your fancy for me. After all, I am a total stranger to you. You do not even know my name."

"Will you tell me your name?" asked Ferdinand humbly. "It will be something to remember."

"My name is Marguerite."

"Marguerite! Marguerite!" He repeated it caressingly. "It is a beautiful name. But it is also the name of the Queen."

"I am the only person named Marguerite in the Queen's court," said she.

"What!" cried Ferdinand Augustus.

"Oh, it is a wise husband who knows his own wife," laughed she.

And then.... But I think I have told enough.

THE FRIEND OF MAN

The other evening, in the Casino, the satisfaction of losing my money at petits-chevaux having begun to flag a little, I wandered into the Cercle, the reserved apartments in the west wing of the building, where they were playing baccarat.

Thanks to the heat, the windows were open wide; and through them one could see, first, a vivid company of men and women, strolling backwards and forwards, and chattering busily, in the electric glare on the terrace; and then, beyond them, the sea—smooth, motionless, sombre; silent, despite its perpetual whisper; inscrutable, sinister; merging itself with the vast blackness of space. Here and there the black was punctured by a pin-point of fire, a tiny vacillating pin-point of fire; and a landsman's heart quailed for a moment at the thought of lonely vessels braving the mysteries and terrors and the awful solitudes of the sea at night....

So that the voice of the croupier, perfunctory, machine-like, had almost a human, almost a genial effect, as it rapped out suddenly, calling upon the players to mark their play. "Marquez vos jeux, messieurs. Quarante louis par tableau." It brought one back to light and warmth and security, to the familiar earth, and the neighbourhood of men.

One's pleasure was fugitive, however.

The neighbourhood of men, indeed! The neighbourhood of some two score very commonplace, very sordid men, seated or standing about an ugly green table, intent upon a game of baccarat, in a long, rectangular, ugly, gas-lit room. The banker dealt, and the croupier shouted, and the punters punted, and the ivory counters and mother-of-pearl plaques were swept now here, now there; and that was all. Everybody was smoking, of course; but the smell of the live cigarettes couldn't subdue the odour of dead ones, the stagnant, acrid odour of stale tobacco, with which the walls and hangings of the place were saturated.

The thing and the people were as banale, as unremunerative, as things and people for the most part are; and dispiriting, dispiriting. There was a hardness in the banality, a sort of cold ferocity, ill-repressed. One turned away, bored, revolted. It was better, after all, to look at the sea; to think of the lonely vessel, far out there, where a pin-point of fire still faintly blinked and glimmered in the illimitable darkness....

But the voice of the croupier was insistent.

"Faites vos jeux, messieurs. Cinquante louis par tableau. Vos jeux sont faits? Rien ne va plus." It was suggestive, persuasive, besides, to one who has a bit of a gambler's soul. I saw myself playing, I felt the poignant tremor of the instant of suspense, while the result is uncertain, the glow that comes if you have won, the twinge if you have lost. "La banque est aux enchères," the voice announced presently; and I moved towards the table.

The sums bid were not extravagant. Ten, fifteen, twenty louis; thirty, fifty, eighty, a hundred.

"Cent louis? Cent? Cent?—Cent louis à la banque," cried the inevitable voice.

I glanced at the man who had taken the bank for a hundred louis. I glanced at him, and, all at once, by no means without emotion, I recognised him.

He was a tall, thin man, and very old. He had the hands of a very old man, dried-up, shrunken hands, with mottled-yellow skin, dark veins that stood out like wires, and parched finger-nails. His face, too, was mottled-yellow, deepening to brown about the eyes, with grey wrinkles, and purplish lips. He was clearly very old; eighty, or more than eighty.

He was dressed entirely in black: a black frock-coat, black trousers, a black waistcoat, cut low, and exposing an unusual quantity of shirt-front, three black studs, and a black tie, a stiff, narrow bow. These latter details, however, save when some chance motion on his part revealed them, were hidden by his beard, a broad, abundant beard, that fell a good ten inches down his breast. His hair, also, was abundant, and he wore it long; trained straight back from his forehead, hanging in a fringe about the collar of his coat. Hair and beard, despite his manifest great age, were without a spear of white. They were of a dry, inanimate brown, a hue to which they had faded (one surmised) from black.

If it was surprising to see so old a man at a baccarat table, it was still more surprising to see just this sort of man. He looked like anything in the world, rather than a gambler. With his tall wasted figure, with his patriarchal beard, his long hair trained in that rigid fashion straight back from his forehead; with his stern aquiline profile, his dark eyes, deep-set and wide-apart, melancholy, thoughtful: he looked—what shall I say? He looked like anything in the world, rather than a gambler. He looked like a *savant*, he looked like a philosopher; he looked intellectual, refined, ascetic even; he looked as if he had ideas, convictions; he looked grave and wise and sad. Holding the bank at baccarat, in this vulgar company at the Grand Cercle of the Casino, dealing the cards with his withered hands, studying them with his deep meditative eyes, he looked improbable, inadmissible, he looked supremely out of place.

I glanced at him, and wondered. And then, suddenly, my heart gave a jump, my throat began to tingle.

I had recognised him. It was rather more than ten years since I had seen him last; and in ten years he had changed, he had decayed, terribly. But I was quite sure, quite sure.

"By Jove," I thought, "it's Ambrose—it's Augustus Ambrose! It's the Friend of Man!"

Augustus Ambrose? I daresay the name conveys nothing to you? And yet, forty, thirty, twenty years ago, Augustus Ambrose was not without his measure of celebrity in the world. If hardly any one had read his published writings, if few had any but the dimmest notion of what his theories and aims were, almost everybody had at least heard of him, almost everybody knew at least that there was such a man, and that the man had theories and aims—of some queer radical sort. One knew, in vague fashion, that he had disciples, that there were people here and there who called themselves "Ambrosites."

I say twenty years ago. But twenty years ago he was already pretty well forgotten. I imagine the moment of his utmost notoriety would have fallen somewhere in the fifties or the sixties, somewhere between '55 and '68.

And if my sudden recognition of him in the Casino made my heart give a jump, there was sufficient cause. During the greater part of my childhood, Augustus Ambrose lived with us, was virtually a member of our family. Then I saw a good deal of him again, when I was eighteen, nineteen; and still again, when I was four- or five-and-twenty.

He lived with us, indeed, from the time when I was scarcely more than a baby till I was ten or eleven; so that in my very farthest memories he is a personage—looking backwards, I see him in the earliest, palest dawn: a tall man, dressed in black, with long hair and a long beard, who was always in our house, and who used to be frightfully severe; who would turn upon me with a most terrifying frown if I misconducted myself in his presence, who would loom up unexpectedly from behind closed doors, and utter a soul-piercing *hist-hist*, if I was making a noise: a sort of domesticated Croquemitaine, whom we had always with us.

Always? Not quite always, though; for, when I stop to think, I remember there would be breathing spells: periods during which he would disappear— during which you could move about the room, and ask questions, and even (at a pinch) upset things, without being frowned at; during which you could shout lustily at your play, unoppressed by the fear of a black figure suddenly opening the door and freezing you with a *hist-hist*; during which, in fine, you could forget the humiliating circumstance that children are called into existence to be seen and not heard, with its irksome moral that they should never speak unless they are spoken to. Then, one morning, I would wake up, and find that he was in the house again. He had returned during the night.

That was his habit, to return at night. But on one occasion, at least, he returned in the daytime. I remember driving with my father and mother, in our big open carriage, to the railway station, and then driving back home with Mr. Ambrose added to our party. Why I—a child of six or seven, between whom and our guest surely no love was lost—why I was taken upon this excursion, I can't at all conjecture; I suppose my people had their reasons. Anyhow, I recollect the drive home with particular distinctness. Two things impressed me. First, Mr. Ambrose, who always dressed in black, wore a *brown* overcoat; I remember gazing at it with bemused eyes, and reflecting that it was exactly the colour of gravy. And secondly, I gathered from his conversation that he had been in prison! Yes. I gathered that he had been in Rome (we were living in Florence), and that one day he had been taken up by the policemen, and put in prison!

Of course, I could say nothing; but what I felt, what I thought! Mercy upon us, that we should know a man, that a man should live with us, who had been taken up and put in prison! I fancied him dragged through the streets by two gendarmes, struggling with them, and followed by a crowd of dirty people. I felt that our family was disgraced, we who had been the pink of respectability; my cheeks burned, and I hung my head. I could say nothing; but oh, the grief, the shame, I nursed in secret! Mr. Ambrose, who lived with us, whose standards of conduct (for children, at any rate) were so painfully exalted, Mr. Ambrose had done something terrible, and had been found out, and put in prison for it! Mr. Ambrose, who always dressed in black, had suddenly tossed his bonnet over the mills, and displayed himself cynically in an overcoat of rakish, dare-devil brown—the colour of gravy! Somehow, the notion pursued me, there must be a connection between his overcoat and his crime.

The enormity of the affair preyed upon my spirit, day after day, night after night, until, in the end, I could endure it silently no longer; and I spoke to my mother.

"Is Mr. Ambrose a burglar?" I enquired.

I remember my mother's perplexity, and then, when I had alleged the reasons for my question, her exceeding mirth. I remember her calling my father; and my father, also, laughed prodigiously, and he went to the door, and cried, "Ambrose! Ambrose!" And when Mr. Ambrose came, and the incident was related to him, even he laughed a little, even his stern face relaxed.

When, by-and-by, they had all stopped laughing, and Mr. Ambrose had gone back to his own room, my father and mother, between them, explained the matter to me. "Mr. Ambrose, I must understand, (they said), was one of the greatest, and wisest, and best men in the world. He spent his whole life "doing good." When he was at home, with us, he was working hard, all day long and late into the night, writing books H to "do good"—that was why he so often had a headache and couldn't bear any noise in the house. And when he went away, when he was absent, it was to "do good" somewhere else. I had seen the poor people in the streets? I knew that there were thousands and thousands of people in the world, grown-up people, and children like myself, who had to wear ragged clothing, and live in dreadful houses, and eat bad food, or go hungry perhaps, all because they were so poor? Well, Mr. Ambrose spent his whole life doing good to those poor people, working hard for them, so that some day they might be rich, and clean, and happy, like us. But in Rome there was a very wicked, very cruel man, a cardinal: Cardinal Antonelli was his name. And Cardinal Antonelli hated people who did good, and was always trying to kidnap them and put them in prison. And that was what had happened to Mr. Ambrose. He had been doing good to the poor people in Rome, and Cardinal Antonelli had got wind of it, and had sent his awful *sbirri* to seize him and put him in prison. But the Pope was a very good man, too; very just, and kind, and merciful; as good as it was possible for any man to be. Only, generally, he was so busy with the great spiritual cares of his office, that he couldn't pay much attention to the practical government of his City. He left that to Cardinal Antonelli, never suspecting how wicked he was, for the Cardinal constantly deceived him. But when the Pope heard that the great and good Mr. Ambrose had been put in prison, his Holiness was shocked and horrified, and very angry; and he sent for the Cardinal, and gave him a sound piece of his mind, and ordered him to let Mr. Ambrose out directly. And so Mr. Ambrose had been let out, and had come back to us."

It was a relief, no doubt, to learn that our guest was not a burglar, but I am afraid the knowledge of his excessive goodness left me somewhat cold. Or, rather, if it influenced my feeling for him in any way, I fancy it only magnified my awe. He was one of the greatest, and wisest, and best men in the world, and he spent his entire time doing good to the poor. *Bene*; that was very nice for the poor. But for me? It did not make him a bit less severe, or cross, or testy; it did not make him a bit less an uncomfortable person to have in the house.

Indeed, the character, in a story such as I had heard, most likely to affect a child's imagination, would pretty certainly have been, not the hero, but the villain. Mr. Ambrose and his virtues moved one to scant enthusiasm; but Cardinal Antonelli! In describing him as wicked, and cruel, and deceitful, my people were simply using the language, expressing the sentiment, of the country and the epoch: of Italy before 1870. In those days, if you were a Liberal, if you sympathised with the Italian party, as opposed to the Papal, and especially if you were a Catholic withal, and so could think no evil of the Pope himself—then Heaven help the reputation of Cardinal Antonelli! For my part, I saw a big man in a cassock, with a dark, wolfish face, and a bunch of great iron keys at his girdle, who prowled continually about the streets of Rome, attended by a gang of ruffian sbirri, seeking whom he could kidnap and put in prison. So that when, not very long after this, we went to Rome for a visit, my heart misgave me; it seemed as if we were marching headlong into the ogre's den, wantonly courting peril. And during the month or two of our sojourn there, I believe I was never quite easy in my mind. At any moment we might all be captured, loaded with chains, and cast into prison: horrible stone dungeons, dark and wet, infested by rats and spiders, where we should have to sleep on straw, where they would give us nothing but bread and water to eat and drink.

Charlatan. Impostor.

I didn't know what the words meant, but they stuck in my memory, and I felt that they were somehow appropriate. It was during that same visit to Rome that I had heard them. My Aunt Elizabeth, with whom we were staying, had applied them, in her vigorous way, to Mr. Ambrose (whom we had left behind us, in Florence). "Poh! An empty windbag, a canting egotist, a twopenny-halfpenny charlatan, a cheap impostor," she had exclaimed, in the course of a discussion with my father.

Charlatan, impostor: yes, that was it. A man who never did anything but make himself disagreeable—who never petted you, or played with you, or told you stories, or gave you things—who never, in fact, took any notice of you at all, except to frown, and say *hist-hist*, when you were enjoying yourself—well, he might be one of the greatest, and best, and wisest men in the world, but, anyhow, he was a charlatan and an impostor. I had Aunt Elizabeth's authority for that.

One day, after our return to Florence, my second-cousin Isabel (she was thirteen, and I was in love with her)—my second-cousin Isabel was playing the piano, alone with me, in the schoolroom, when Mr. Ambrose opened the door, and said, in his testiest manner: "Stop that noise—stop that noise!"

"He's a horrid pig," cried Isabel, as soon as his back was turned.

"Oh, no; he isn't a pig," I protested. "He's one of the greatest, and wisest, and best men in the world, so of course he can't be a horrid pig. But I'll tell you what he *is*. He's a charlatan and an impostor."

49

"Really? How do you know?" Isabel wondered. "I heard Aunt Elizabeth tell my father so."

"Oh, well, then it must be true," Isabel assented.

He lived with us till I was ten or eleven, at first in Florence, and afterwards in Paris. All day long he would sit in his room and write, (on the most beautiful, smooth, creamy paper—what wouldn't I have given to have acquired some of it for my own literary purposes!) and in the evening he would receive visitors: oh, such funny people, so unlike the people who came to see my mother and father. The men, for example, almost all of them, as Mr. Ambrose himself did, wore their hair long, so that it fell about their collars; whilst almost all the women had their hair cut short. And then, they dressed so funnily: the women in the plainest garments—skirts and jackets, without a touch of ornament; the men in sombreros and Spanish cloaks, instead of ordinary hats and coats. They would come night after night, and pass rapidly through the outer regions of our establishment, and disappear in Mr. Ambrose's private room. And thence I could hear their voices, murmuring, murmuring, after I had gone to bed. At the same time, very likely, in another part of the house, my mother would be entertaining another company, such a different company—beautiful ladies, in bright-hued silks, with shining jewels, and diamond-dust in their hair (yes, in that ancient period, ladies of fashion, on the Continent at least, used to powder their hair with a glittering substance known as "diamond-dust") and officers in gold-embroidered uniforms, and men in dress-suits. And there would be music, and dancing, or theatricals, or a masquerade, and always a lovely supper—to some of whose unconsumed delicacies I would fall heir next day.

Only four of Mr. Ambrose's visitors at all detach themselves, as individuals, from the cloud.

One was Mr. Oddo Yodo. Mr. Oddo Yodo was a small, grey-bearded, dark-skinned Hungarian gentleman, with another name, something like Polak or Bolak. But I called him Mr. Oddo Yodo, because whenever we met, on his way to or from the chamber of Mr. Ambrose, he would bow to me, and smile pleasantly, and say: "Oddo Yodo, Oddo Yodo." I discovered, in the end, that he was paying me the compliment of saluting me in my native tongue.

Another was an Irishman, named Slevin. I remember him, a burly creature, with a huge red beard, because one day he arrived at our house in a state of appalling drunkenness. I remember the incredulous dismay with which I saw a man in that condition enter our very house. I remember our old servant, Alexandre, supporting him to Mr. Ambrose's door, nodding his head and making a face the while, to signify his opinion.

Still another was a pale young Italian priest, with a tonsure, round and big as a five-shilling piece, shorn in the midst of a dense growth of blue-black hair, upon which I always vaguely longed to put my finger, to see how it would feel. I forget his name, but I shall never forget the man, for he had an extraordinary talent; he could write *upside-down*. He would take a sheet of paper, and, beginning with the last letter, write my name for me upside-down, terminating it at the first initial with a splendid flourish. You will not wonder that I remember him.

The visitor that I remember best, though, was a woman named Arseneff. She had short sandy hair, and she dressed in the ugliest black frocks, and she wore steel-rimmed spectacles; but she was a dear soul, notwithstanding. One afternoon she was shown into the room where I chanced to be studying my arithmetic lesson, to wait for Mr. Ambrose. And first, she sat down beside me, in the kindest fashion, and helped me out with my sums; and then (it is conceivable that I may have encouraged her by some cross-questioning) she told me the saddest, saddest story about herself. She told me that her husband had been the editor of a newspaper in Russia, and that he had published an article in his paper, saying that there ought to be schools where the poor people, who had to work all day, could go in the evening, and learn to read and write. And just for that, for nothing more than that, her husband and her two sons, who were his assistant-editors, had been arrested, and chained up with murderers and thieves and all the worst sorts of criminals, and forced to march, *on foot*, across thousands of miles of snow-covered country, to Siberia, where they had to work as convicts in the mines. And her husband, she said, had died of it; but her two sons were still there, working as convicts in the mines. She showed me their photographs, and she showed me a button, rather a pretty button of coloured glass, with gilt specks in it, that she had cut from the coat of one of them, when he had been arrested and taken from her. Poor Arséneff; my heart went out to her, and we became fast friends. She was never tired of talking, nor I of hearing, of her sons; and she gave me a good deal of practical assistance in my arithmetical researches, so that, at the Lycée where I was then an *externe*, I passed for an authority on Long Division.

Mr. Ambrose's visitors came night after night, and shut themselves up with him in his room, and stayed there, talking, talking, till long past bed-time; but I never knew what it was all about. Indeed, I can't remember that I ever felt any curiosity to know. It was simply a fact, a quite uninteresting fact, which one witnessed, and accepted, and thought no more of. Mr. Ambrose was an Olympian. Kenneth Grahame has reminded us with what superior unconcern, at the Golden Age, one regards the habits and doings and affairs of the Olympians.

And then, quite suddenly, Mr. Ambrose left us. He packed up his things and his books, and went away; and I understood, somehow, that he would not be coming back. I did not ask where he was going, nor why he was going. His departure, like his presence, was a fact which I accepted without curiosity. Not without satisfaction, though; it was distinctly nice to feel that the house was rid of him.

And then seven or eight years passed, the longest seven or eight years, I suppose, that one is likely ever to encounter, the seven or eight years in the course of which one grows from a child of ten or eleven to a youth approaching twenty. And during those years I had plenty of other things to think of than Mr. Ambrose. It was time more than enough for him to become a mere dim outline on the remote horizon.

My childish conception of the man, as you perceive, was sufficiently rudimental. He represented to me the incarnation of a single principle: severity; as I, no doubt, represented to him the incarnation of vexatious noise. For the rest, we overlooked each other. I had been told that he was one of the greatest and wisest and best men in the world: you have seen how little that mattered to me. It would probably have mattered quite as little if the information had been more specific, if I had been told everything there was to tell about him, all that I have learned since. How could it have mattered to a child to know that the testy old man who sat in his room all day and wrote, and every evening received a stream of shabby visitors, was the prophet of a new social faith, the founder of a new sect, the author of a new system for the regeneration of mankind, of a new system of human government, a new system of ethics, a new system of economics? What could such a word as "anthropocracy" have conveyed to me? Or such a word as "philarchy"? Or such a phrase as "Unification *versus* Civilisation"?

My childish conception of the man was extremely rudimental. But I saw a good deal of him again when I was eighteen, nineteen; and at eighteen, nineteen, one begins, more or less, to observe and appreciate, to receive impressions and to form conclusions. Anyhow, the impressions I received of Mr. Ambrose, the conclusions I formed respecting him, when I was eighteen or nineteen, are still very fresh in my mind; and I can't help believing that on the whole they were tolerably just. I think they were just, because they seem to explain him; they seem to explain him in big and in little. They explain his career, his failure, his table manners, his testiness, his disregard of other people's rights and feelings, his apparent selfishness; they explain the queerest of the many queer things he did. They explain his taking the bank the other night at baccarat, for instance; and they explain what happened afterwards, before the night was done.

One evening, when I was eighteen or nineteen, coming home from the Latin Quarter, where I was a student, to dine with my people, in the Rue Oudinot, I found Mr. Ambrose in the drawing-room. Or, if you will, I found a stranger in the drawing-room, but a stranger whom it took me only a minute or two to recognise. My father, at my entrance, had smiled, with a little air of mystery, and said to me, "Here is an old friend of yours. Can you tell who it is?" And the stranger, also—somewhat faintly—smiling, had risen, and offered me his hand. I looked at him—looked at him—and, in a minute,% I exclaimed, "It's Mr. Ambrose!"

I can see him now almost as clearly as I saw him then, when he stood before me, faintly smiling: tall and thin, stooping a little, dressed in black, with a long broad beard, long hair, and a pale, worn, aquiline face. It is the face especially that comes back to me, pale and worn and finely aquiline, the face, the high white brow, the deep eyes set wide apart, the faint, faded smile: a striking face—an intellectual face—a handsome face, despite many wrinkles—an indescribably sad face, even a tragic face—and yet, for some reason, a face that was not altogether sympathetic. Something, something in it, had the effect rather of chilling you, of leaving you where you were, than of warming and attracting you; something hard to fix, perhaps impossible to name. A certain suggestion of remoteness, of aloofness? A suggestion of abstraction from his surroundings and his company, of inattention, of indifference to them? Of absorption in matters alien to them, outside their sphere? I did not know. But there was surely something in his face not perfectly sympathetic.

I had exclaimed, "It's Mr. Ambrose!" To that he had responded, "Ah, you have a good memory." And then we shook hands, and he sat down again. His hand was thin and delicate, and slightly cold. His voice was a trifle dry, ungenial. Then he asked me the inevitable half-dozen questions about myself —how old I was, what I was studying, and so forth—but though he asked them with an evident intention of being friendly, one felt that he was all the while half thinking of something else, and that he never really took in one's answers.

And gradually he seemed to become unconscious of my presence, resuming the conversation with my father, which, I suppose, had been interrupted by my arrival.

"The world has forgotten me. My followers have dropped away. You yourself —where is your ancient ardour? The cause I have lived for stands still. My propaganda is arrested. I am poor, I am obscure, I am friendless, and I am sixty-five years old. But the great ideals, the great truths, I have taught, remain. They are like gold which I have mined. There the gold lies, between the covers of my books, as in so many caskets. Some day, in its necessities, the world will find it. What is excellent cannot perish. It may lie hid, but it cannot perish."

That is one of the things I remember his saying to my father, on that first evening of our renewed acquaintance. And, at table, I noticed, he ate and drank in a joyless, absent-minded manner, and made unusual uses of his knife and fork, and very unusual noises. And, by-and-by, in the midst of a silence, my mother spoke to a servant, whereupon, suddenly, he glanced up, with vague eyes, and the frown of one troubled in the depths of a brown study, and I could have sworn it was on the tip of his tongue to say *hist-hist!*

He stayed with us for several months—from the beginning of November till February or March, I think—and during that period I saw him very nearly every day, and heard him accomplish a tremendous deal of talk.

I tried, besides, to read some of his books, an effort, however, from which I retired, baffled and bewildered: they were a thousand miles above the apprehension of a nineteen-year-old *potache*; and I did actually read to its end a book about him: *Augustus Ambrose, the Friend of Man: an Account of his Life, and an Analysis of his Teachings. By one of his Followers. Turin: privately printed*, 1858. Of the identity of that "Follower," by-the-bye, I got an inkling, from a rather conscious, half sheepish smile, which I detected in the face of my own father, when he saw the volume in my hands. I read his *Life* to its end; and I tried to read *The Foundations of Mono-pantology, and Anthropocracy: a Remedy for the Diseases of the Body Politic, and Philarchy: a Vision* ; and I listened while he accomplished a tremendous deal of talk. His talk was always (for my taste) too impersonal; it was always of ideas, of theories, never of concrete things, never of individual men and women. Indeed, the mention of an individual would often only serve him as an excuse for a new flight into the abstract. For example, I had learned, from the *Life*, that he had been an associate of Mazzini's and Garibaldi's in '48, and that it was no less a person than Victor Emmanuel himself, who had named him—in an official proclamation, too—"the Friend of Man." So, one day, I asked him to tell me something about Victor Emmanuel, and Mazzini, and Garibaldi. "You knew them. I should be so glad to hear about them from one who knew them."

"Victor Emmanuel, Garibaldi, Mazzini, Cavour—I knew them all; I knew them well. I worked with them, fought under them, wrote for them, spoke for them, throughout the long struggle for the unification of Italy. I did so because unification is my supreme ideal, the grandest ideal the human mind has ever formed. I worked for the unification of Italy, because I was and am working for the unification of mankind, and the unification of Italy was a step towards, and an illustration of, that sublime object. Let others prate of civilisation; civilisation means nothing more than the invention and multiplication of material conveniences—nothing more than that. But unification—the unification of mankind—that is the crusade which I have preached, the cause for which I have lived. To unify the scattered nations of this earth into one single nation, one single solidarity, under one government, speaking one language, professing and obeying one religion, pursuing one aim. The religion —Christianity, with a purified Papacy. The government—anthropocratic philarchy, the reign of men by the law of Love. The language—Albigo. Albigo, which means, at the same time, both human and universal—from Albi, pertaining to man, and God, pertaining to the whole, the all. Albigo: a language which I have discovered, as the result of years of research, to exist already, and everywhere, as the base, the common principle, of all known languages, and which I have extracted, in its original simplicity, from the overgrowths which time and separateness have allowed to accumulate upon it. Albigo: the tongue which all men speak unconsciously: the universal human tongue. And, finally, the aim—the common, single aim—the highest possible spiritual development of man, the highest possible culture of the human soul."

That is what I received in response to my request for a few personal reminiscences of Victor Emmanuel, Garibaldi, and Mazzini.

You will infer that Mr. Ambrose lacked humour. But his most conspicuous trait, his preponderant trait—the trait which, I think, does more than any other to explain him, him and his fortunes and his actions—was the trait I had vaguely noticed in our first five minutes' intercourse, after my re-introduction to him; the trait which, I have conjectured, perhaps gave its unsympathetic quality to his face: abstraction from his surroundings and his company, inattention, indifference, to them.

On that first evening, you may remember, he had asked me certain questions; but I had felt that he was thinking of something else. I had answered them, but I had felt that he never heard my answers.

That little negative incident, I believe, gives the key to his character, to his fortunes, to his actions.

The Friend of Man was totally deaf and blind and insensible to *men*. Man, as a metaphysical concept, was the major premiss of his philosophy; men, as individuals, he was totally unable to realise. He could not see you, he could not hear you, he could get no "realising sense" of you. You spoke, but your voice was an unintelligible murmur in his ears; it was like the sound of the wind—it might annoy him, disturb him (in which case he would seek to silence it with a *hist-hist*), it could not signify to him. You stood up, in front of him; but you were invisible to him; he saw beyond you. And even when he spoke, he did not speak to you, he spoke to the walls and ceiling—he thought aloud. He took no account of his auditor's capacities, of the subject that would interest him, of the language he would understand. You asked him to tell you about Mazzini, and he discoursed of Albigo and the Unification of Mankind. And then, when he ceased to speak, directly he fell silent and somebody else took the word, the gates of his mind were shut; he withdrew behind them, returned to his private meditations, and so remained, detached, solitary, preoccupied, till the time came when he was moved to speak again. He was the Friend of Man, but men did not exist for him. He was like a mathematician busied with a calculation, eager for the sum-total, but heedless of the separate integers. My father—my mother—I—whosoever approached him—was a phantasm: a convenient phantasm, possibly, with a house where he might be lodged and fed, with a purse whence might be supplied the funds requisite for the publication of his works; or possibly a troublesome phantasm, that worried him by shouting at its play: but a phantasm, none the less.

Years ago, my downright Aunt Elizabeth had disposed of him with two words: a charlatan, an impostor. My Aunt Elizabeth was utterly mistaken. Mr. Ambrose's sincerity was absolute. The one thing he professed belief in, he believed in with an intensity that rendered him unconscious of all things else; his one conviction was so predominant as to exclude all other convictions. What was the one thing he believed in, the one thing he was convinced of? It would be easy to reply, himself; to declare that, at least, when she had called him an egotist, my Aunt Elizabeth had been right. It would be easy, but I am sure it would be untrue. The thing he believed in, the thing he was convinced of, the only thing in this whole universe which he saw, was his vision. That, I am persuaded, is the explanation of the man. It explains him in big and in little. It explains his career, his fortunes, his failure, his table-manners, his testiness, and the queerest of his actions.

He saw nothing in this universe but his vision; he did not see the earth beneath him, nor the people round him. Is that not enough to explain everything, almost to justify anything? Doesn't it explain his failure, for example? The fact that the world ignored him, that his followers dropped away from him, that nobody read his books? For, since he was never convinced of the world, how could he convince the world? Since he had no "realising sense" of men, how could he hold men? Since, in writing his books, he took no account of human nature, no account of human taste, endurance— since he wrote his books, as he spoke his speeches, not to you or me, not to flesh and blood, but to the walls and ceiling, to space, to the unpeopled air— how was it possible that he should have human readers? It explains his failure, the failure of a long life of unremitting labour. He was learned, he was in earnest, he was indefatigable; and the net product of his learning, his earnestness, his industry, was nil, because there can be no reciprocity established between something and nothing.

It explains his failure; and it explains—it almost excuses—in a sense it even almost justifies—the queerest of his actions. Other people did not exist for him; therefore other people had no feelings to be considered, no rights, no possessions, to be respected. They did not exist, therefore they were in no way to be reckoned with. Their observation was not to be avoided, their power was not to be feared. They could not *do* anything; they could not see what *he* did.

The queerest of his actions? You will suppose that I must have some very queer action still to record. Well, there was his action the other night at the Casino, for one thing; I haven't yet done with that. But the queerest of all his actions, I think, was his treatment of Israela, his step-daughter Israela....

During the visit Mr. Ambrose paid us in Paris, when I was nineteen, he, whose early disciples had dropped away, made a new disciple: a Madame Fontanas, a Mexican woman—of Jewish extraction, I imagine—a widow, with a good deal of money. Israela, her daughter, was a fragile, pale-faced, dark-haired, great-eyed little girl, of twelve or thirteen. Madame Fontanas sat at Mr. Ambrose's feet, and listened, and believed. Perhaps she conceived an affection for him; perhaps she only thought that here was a great philosopher, a great philanthropist, and that he ought to have some one to take permanent care of him, and reduce the material friction of his path to a minimum. Anyhow, when the spring came, she married him. I have no definite information on the subject, but I am sure in my own mind that it was she who took the initiative—that she offered, and he vaguely accepted, her hand. Anyhow, in the spring she married him, and carried him off to her Mexican estates.

Five or six years later (by the sheerest hazard) I found him living in London with Israela; in the dreariest of dreary lodgings, in a dreary street, in Pimlico. I met him one afternoon, by the sheerest hazard, in Piccadilly, and accompanied him home. (It was characteristic of him, by-the-bye, that, though we met face to face, and I stopped and exclaimed and held out my hand, he gazed at me with blank eyes, and I was obliged to repeat my name twice before he could recall me.) He was living in London, for the present, he told me, in order to see a work through the press. "A great work, the crown, the summary of all my work. *The Final Extensions of Monopantology.*

"It is in twelve volumes, with plates, coloured plates."

"And Mrs. Ambrose is well?" I asked.

"Oh, my wife—my wife is dead. She died two or three years ago," he answered, with the air of one dismissing an irrelevance.

"And Israela?" I pursued, by-and-by.

"Israela?" His brows knitted themselves perplexedly, then, in an instant, cleared. "Oh, Israela. Ah, yes. Israela is living with me."

And upon my suggesting that I should like to call upon her, he replied that he was on his way home now, and, if I cared to do so, I might come with him.

They were living in the dreariest of dreary lodgings, in the dreariest of streets. But Israela welcomed me with a warmth I had not anticipated. "Oh, I am so glad to see you, so glad, so glad," she cried, and her big, dark eyes filled with tears, and she clung to my hand. I was surprised by her emotion, because, after all, I was scarcely other than a stranger to her; a man she hadn't seen since she was a little girl, and even then had seen only once or twice. I understood it afterwards, however: when one day she confided to me that—excepting Mr. Ambrose himself, and servants and tradesmen—I was the first human being she had exchanged a word with since they had come to London! "We don't know anybody—not a soul, not a soul. He doesn't want to know people—he is so absorbed in his work. I could not make acquaintances alone. And we had been here four months, before he met you and brought you home."

Israela was tall, and very slight; very delicate-looking, with a face intensely pale, all the paler for the soft dark hair that curled above it, and the great dark eyes that looked out of it. Considering that she must have inherited a decent fortune from her mother, I wondered, rather, to see her so plainly dressed: she wore the plainest straight black frocks. And, of course, I wondered also to find them living in such dismal lodgings. However, it was not for me to ask questions; and if presently the mystery cleared itself up, it was by a sort of accident.

I called at the house in Pimlico as often as I could; and I took Israela out a good deal, to lunch or dine at restaurants; and when the weather smiled, we would make little jaunts into the country, to Hampton Court, or Virginia Water, or where not. And one day she came to tea with me, at my chambers.

"Oh, you've got a piano," was her first observation, and she flew to the instrument, and seated herself, and began to play. She played without pause for nearly an hour, I think: Chopin, Chopin, Chopin. And when she rose, I said, "Would you mind telling me why you—a brilliant pianist like you—why you haven't a piano in your own rooms?"

"We can't afford one," she answered simply.

"What do you mean—you can't afford one?"

"He says we can't afford one. Don't you know—we are very poor?"

"You can't be very poor," I exclaimed. "Your mother was rich."

"Yes, my mother was rich. I don't know what has become of her money."

"Didn't she leave a will?"

"Oh, yes, she left a will. She left a will making my step father my guardian, my trustee."

"Well, what has he done with your money?"

"I don't know. I only know that we are very poor—that we can't afford any luxuries—that we can just barely contrive to live, in the quietest manner. He hardly ever gives me any money for myself. A few shillings, very rarely, when I ask him."

"My dear child," I cried, "I see it all, I see it perfectly. You've got plenty of money, you've got your mother's fortune. But he's spending it for his own purposes. He's paying for the printing of his gigantic book with it. Twelve volumes, and plates, coloured plates! It's exactly like him. The only thing he's conscious of is the importance of publishing his book. He needs money. He takes it where he finds it. He's spending your money for the printing of his book; and that's why you have to live in dreary lodgings in the dreariest part of London, and do without a piano. *He* doesn't care how he lives—he doesn't know—he's unconscious of everything but his book. My dear child, you must stop him, you mustn't let him go on."

Israela was incredulous at first, but I argued and insisted, till, in the end, she said, "Perhaps you are right. But even so, what can I do? How can I stop him?"

"Ah, that's a question for a solicitor. We must see a solicitor. A solicitor will know how to stop him."

But at this proposal, Israela shook her head. "Oh, no, I will have no solicitor. Even supposing your idea is true, I can't set a lawyer upon my mother's husband. After all, what does it matter? Perhaps he is right. Perhaps the publication of his book *is* very important. I'm sure my mother would have thought so. It was her money. Perhaps he is right to spend it for the publication of his book."

Israela positively declined to consult a solicitor; and so they continued to live narrowly in Pimlico, and he proceeded with the issue of *The Final Extensions of Monopantology*, in twelve volumes, with coloured plates.

Meanwhile, the brown London autumn had turned into a black London winter; and Israela, delicate-looking at its outset, grew more and more delicate-looking every day.

"After all, what does it matter? The money will be his, and he can do as he wishes with it honestly as soon as I am dead," she said to me, one evening, with a smile I did not like.

"What on earth do you mean?" I asked.

"I am going to die," she said.

"You're mad, you're morbid," I cried. "You mustn't say such things. You're not *ill?* What on earth do you mean?"

"I am going to die. I know it. I feel it. I am not ill? I don't know. I think I am ill. I feel as if I were going to be ill. I am going to die—I know I am going to die."

I did what I could to dissipate such black presentiments. I refused to talk of them. I did what I could to lend a little gaiety to her life. But Israela grew whiter and more delicate-looking day by day. I was her only visitor. I had asked if I might not bring a friend or two to see her, but she had answered, "I'm afraid he would not like it. People coming and going would disturb him. He can't bear any noise," So I was her only visitor—till, by-and-by, another became necessary.

I wonder whether Mr. Ambrose ever really knew that Israela was lying in her bed at the point of death, and that the man who called twice every day to see her was a doctor? True, in an absent-minded fashion, he used to inquire how she was, he used even occasionally to enter the sick-room, and look at her, and lay his hand on her brow, as if to take her temperature; but I wonder whether he ever actually *realised* her condition? He was terribly preoccupied just then with Volume VIII, At all events, on a certain melancholy morning in April, he allowed me to conduct him to a carriage and to help him in; and together we drove to Kensal Green. He was silent during the drive—thinking hard, I fancied, about some matter very foreign to our errand.... And as soon as the parson there had rattled through his office and concluded it, Israela's step-father pulled out his watch, and said to me, "Ah, I must hurry off, I must hurry off. I've got a long day's work before me still."

That was something like ten years ago—the last time I had seen him.... Until now, to-night, on this sultry night of August, ten years afterwards, here he had suddenly reappeared to me, holding the bank at baccarat, at the Grand Cercle of the Casino: Augustus Ambrose, the Friend of Man, the dreamer, the visionary, holding the bank at baccarat, at the Grand Cercle of the Casino!

I looked at him, in simple astonishment at first, and then gradually I shaped a theory. "He has probably come pretty nearly to the end of Israela's fortune; it would be like him to spend interest and principal as well. And now he finds himself in need of money. And he is just unpractical enough to fancy that he can supply his needs by play. Or—or is it possible he has a system? Perhaps he imagines he has a system." And then I thought how old he had grown, how terribly, terribly he had decayed.

I looked at him. He was dealing. He dealt to the right, to the left, and to himself. But when he glanced at his own two cards, he made a little face. The next instant he had dropped them under the table, and helped himself to two fresh ones....

The thing was done without the faintest effort at concealment, in a room where at least forty pairs of eyes were fixed upon him.

There was, of course, an immediate uproar. In an instant every one was on his feet; Mr. Ambrose was surrounded. Men were shaking their fists in his face, screaming at him excitedly, calling him ugly names. He gazed at them placidly, vaguely. It was clear he did not grasp the situation.

Somebody must needs intervene.

"I saw what Monsieur did. I am sure it was with no ill intention. He made no effort at concealment. It was done in a fit of absence of mind. Look at him. He is a very old man. You can see he is bewildered. He does not even yet understand what has happened. He should never have come here, at his age. He should never have been allowed to take the bank. Let the croupier pay both sides. Then I will take Monsieur away."

Somehow I got him out of the Casino, and led him to his hotel, a small hotel in the least favoured quarter of the town, the name of which I had a good deal of difficulty in extracting from him. On the way thither scarcely a word passed between us. I forbore to tell him who I was; of course, he did not recognise me. But all the while a pertinacious little voice within me insisted: "He did it deliberately. He deliberately tried to cheat. With his gaze concentrated on his vision, he could see nothing else; he could see no harm in trying to cheat at cards. He needed money—it didn't matter how he obtained it. The other players were phantasms—where's the harm in cheating phantasms? Only he forgot—or, rather, he never realised—that the phantasms had eyes, that they could see. That's why he made no effort at concealment."—Was the voice right or wrong?

I parted with him at the door of his hotel; but the next day a feeling grew within me that I ought to call upon him, that I ought at least to call and take his news. They told me that he had left by an early train for Paris.

As I have been writing these last pages, a line of Browning's has kept thrumming through my head. "This high man, with a great thing to pursue... This high man, with a great thing to pursue..." How does it apply to Mr. Ambrose? I don't know—unless, indeed, a high man, with a great thing to pursue, is to be excused, is to be pitied, rather than blamed, if he loses his sense, his conscience, of other things, of small things. After all, wasn't it because he lost his conscience of small things, that he missed his great thing?

TIRALA-TIRALA...

I wonder what the secret of it is—why that little fragment of a musical phrase has always had this instant, irresistible power to move me. The tune of which it formed a part I have never heard; whether it was a merry tune or a sad tune, a pretty tune or a stupid one, I have no means of guessing. A sequence of six notes, like six words taken from the middle of a sentence, it stands quite by itself, detached, fortuitous. If I were to pick it out for you on the piano, you would scoff at it; you would tell me that it is altogether pointless and unsuggestive, that any six notes, struck at haphazard, would signify as much. And I certainly could not, with the least show of reason, maintain the contrary. I could only wonder the more why it has always had, for me, this very singular charm. As when I was a child, so now, after all these years, it is a sort of talisman in my hands, a thing to conjure with. I have but to breathe it never so softly to myself, and (if I choose) the actual world melts away, and I am journeying on wings in dreamland. Whether I choose or not, it always thrills my heart with responsive echoes, it always wakes a sad, sweet emotion.

I remember quite clearly the day when I first heard it; quite clearly, though it was more—oh, more than five-and-twenty years ago, and the days that went before and came after it have entirely lost their outlines, and merged into a vague golden blur. That day, too, as I look backwards, glows in the distance with a golden light; and if I were to speak upon my impulse, I should vow it was a smiling day of June, clothed in sunshine and crowned with roses. But then, if I were to speak upon my impulse, I should vow that it was June at Saint-Graal the whole year round. When I stop to think, I remember that it was a rainy day, and that the ground was sprinkled with dead leaves. I remember standing at a window in my grandmother's room, and gazing out with rueful eyes. It rained doggedly, relentlessly—even, it seemed to me, defiantly, spitefully, as if it took a malicious pleasure in penning me up within doors. The mountains, the Pyrenees, a few miles to the south, were completely hidden by the veil of waters. The sodden leaves, brown patches on the lawn and in the pathways, struggled convulsively, like wounded birds, to fly from the gusts of wind, but fell back fluttering heavily. One could almost have touched the clouds, they hung so low, big ragged tufts of sad-coloured cotton-wool, blown rapidly through the air, just above the writhing tree-tops. Everywhere in the house there was a faint fragrance of burning wood: fires had been lighted to keep the dampness out.

Indeed, if it had been a fair day, my adventure could scarcely have befallen. I should have been abroad, in the garden or the forest, playing with André, our farmer's son; angling, with a bit of red worsted as bait, for frogs in the pond; trying to catch lizards on the terrace; lying under a tree with *Don Quixote* or *Le Capitaine Fracasse*; visiting Manuela in her cottage; or perhaps, best of all, spending the afternoon with Hélène, at Granjolaye. It was because the rain interdicted these methods of amusement that I betook myself for solace to *Constantinople.*

I don't know why—I don't think any one knew why—that part of our house was called Constantinople; but it had been called so from time immemorial, and we all accepted it as a matter of course. It was the topmost story of the East Wing—three rooms: one little room, by way of ante-chamber, into which you entered from a corkscrew staircase; then another little room at your left; and then a big room, a long dim room, with only two windows, one at either end. And these rooms served as a sort of Hades for departed household gods. They were crowded, crowded to overflowing, with such wonderful old things! Old furniture—old straight-backed chairs, old card-tables, with green cloth tops, and brass claws for feet, old desks and cabinets, the dismembered relics of old four-post bedsteads; old clothes—old hats, boots, cloaks—green silk calashes, like bonnets meant for the ladies of Brobdingnag—and old hoop-petticoats, the skeletons of dead toilets; old books, newspapers, pictures; old lamps and candlesticks, clocks, fire-irons, vases; an old sedan-chair; old spurs, old swords, old guns and pistols; generations upon generations of superannuated utilities and vanities, slumbering in one another's shadows, under a common sheet of dust, and giving off a thin, penetrating, ancient smell.

When it rained, Constantinople was my ever-present refuge. It was a land of penumbra and mystery, a realm of perpetual wonderment, a mine of inexhaustible surprises. I never visited it without finding something new, without getting a sensation. One day, when André was there with me, we both saw a ghost—yes, as plainly as at this moment I see the paper I'm writing on;

but I won't turn aside now to speak of that. And as for my finds, on two or three occasions, at least, they had more than a subjective metaphysical importance. The first was a chest filled with jewellery and trinkets, an iron chest, studded with nails, in size and shape like a small trunk, with a rounded lid. I dragged it out of a dark corner, from amidst a quantity of rubbish, and (it wasn't even locked!) fancy the eyes I made when I beheld its contents: half-a-dozen elaborately carved, high-back tortoise-shell combs, ranged in a morocco case; a beautiful old-fashioned watch, in the form of a miniature guitar; an enamelled snuff-box; and then no end of rings, brooches, buckles, seals, and watch-keys, set with precious stones—not very precious stones, perhaps—only garnets, amethysts, carnelians; but mercy, how they glittered! I ran off in great excitement to call my grandmother; and she called my uncle Edmond; and he, alas, applied the laws of seigniory to the transaction, and I saw my trover appropriated. My other important finds were appropriated also, but about them I did not care so much—they were only papers. One was a certificate, dated in the Year III, and attesting that my grandfather's father had taken the oath of allegiance to the Republic. As I was a fierce Legitimist, this document afforded me but moderate satisfaction. The other was a Map of the World, covering a sheet of cardboard nearly a yard square, executed in pen-and-ink, but with such a complexity of hair-lines, delicate shading, and ornate lettering, that, until you had examined it closely, you would have thought it a carefully finished steel-engraving. It was signed "Herminie de Pontacq, 1818"; that is to say, by my grandmother herself, who in 1818 had been twelve years old; dear me, only twelve years old! It was delightful and marvellous to think that my own grandmother, in 1818, had been so industrious, and painstaking, and accomplished a little girl. I assure you, I felt almost as proud as if I had done it myself.

The small room at the left of the ante-chamber was consecrated to the *roba* of an uncle of my grandfather's, who had been a sugar-planter in the province of New Orleans, in the reign of Louis XVI. He had also been a colonel, and so the room was called the Colonel's room. Here were numberless mementos of the South: great palm-leaf fans, conch-shells, and branches of coral, broad-brimmed hats of straw, monstrous white umbrellas, and, in a corner, a collection of long slender wands, ending in thick plumes of red and yellow feathers. These, I was informed, the sugar-planter's slaves, standing behind his chair, would flourish about his head, to warn off the importunate winged insects that abound *là-bas*. He had died at Paris in 1793, and of nothing more romantic than a malignant fever, foolish person, when he might so easily have been guillotined! (It was a matter of permanent regret with me that *none* of our family had been guillotined.) But his widow had survived him for more than forty years, and her my grandmother remembered perfectly. A fat old Spanish Créole lady, fat and very lazy—oh, but very lazy indeed. At any rate, she used to demand the queerest services of the negress who was in constant attendance upon her. "Nanette, Nanette, tourne tête à moi. Veux"—summon your fortitude—"veux cracher!" Ah, well, we are told, they made less case of such details in those robust old times. How would she have fared, poor soul, had she fallen amongst us squeamish decadents?

―――――――――

It was into the Colonel's room that I turned to-day. There was a cupboard in its wall that I had never thoroughly examined. The lower shelves, indeed, I knew by heart; they held, for the most part, empty medicine bottles. But the upper ones?

―――――――――

I shut my eyes for a moment, and the flavour of that far-away afternoon comes back fresher in my memory than yesterday's. I am perched on a chair, in the dim light of Constantinople, at Saint-Graal; my nostrils are full of a musty, ancient smell; I can hear the rain pat-pattering on the roof, the wind whistling at the window, and, faintly, in a distant quarter of the house, my cousin Elodie playing her exercises monotonously on the piano. I am balancing myself on tip-toe, craning my neck, with only one care, one preoccupation, in the world —to get a survey of the top shelf of the closet in the Colonel's room. The next to the top, and the next below that, I already command; they are vacant of everything save dust. But the top one is still above my head, and how to reach it seems a terribly vexed problem, of which, for a little while, motionless, with bent brows, I am rapt in meditation. And then, suddenly, I have an inspiration—I see my way.

It was not for nothing that my great-aunt Radigonde (think of having had a great-aunt named Radigonde, and yet never having seen her! She died before I was born—isn't Fate unkind?)—it was not for nothing that my great-aunt Radigonde, from 1820 till its extinction in 1838, had subscribed to the *Revue Rose—La Revue Rose; Echo du Bon Ton; Miroir de la Mode; paraissant tous les mois; dirigée par une Dame de la Cour*; nor was it in vain, either, that my great-aunt Radigonde had had the annual volumes of this fashionable intelligencer bound. Three or four of them now, piled one above the other on my chair, lent me the altitude I needed; and the top shelf yielded up its secret.

It was an abominably dusty secret, and it was quite a business to wipe it off. Then I perceived that it was a box, a square box, about eighteen inches long and half as deep, made of polished mahogany, inlaid with scrolls and flourishes of satin-wood. Opened, it proved to be a dressing-case. It was lined with pink velvet and white brocaded silk. There was a looking-glass, in a pink velvet frame, with an edge of gold lace, that swung up on a hinged support of tarnished ormolu; a sere and yellow looking-glass, that gave back a reluctant, filmy image of my face. There were half-a-dozen pear-shaped bottles, of wine-coloured glass, with tarnished gilt tops. There was a thing that looked like the paw of a small animal, the fur of which, at one end, was reddened, as if it had been rubbed in some red powder. The velvet straps that had once presumably held combs and brushes, had been despoiled by an earlier hand than mine; but of two pockets in the lid the treasures were intact: a tortoise-shell housewife, containing a pair of scissors, a thimble, and a bodkin, and a tortoise-shell purse, each prettily incrusted with silver and lined with thin pink silk.

In front, between two of the gilt-topped bottles, an oval of pink velvet, with a tiny bird in ormolu perched upon it, was evidently movable—a cover to something. When I had lifted it, I saw, first, a little pane of glass, and then, through that, the brass cylinder and long steel comb of a musical box. Wasn't it an amiable conceit, whereby my lady should be entertained with tinkling harmonies the while her eyes and fingers were busied in the composition of her face? Was it a frequent one in old dressing-cases?

Oh, yes, the key was there—a gilt key, coquettishly decorated with a bow of pink ribbon; and when I had wound the mechanism up, the cylinder, to my great relief, began to turn—to my relief, for I had feared that the spring might be broken, or something; springs are so apt to be broken in this disappointing world. The cylinder began to turn—but, alas, in silence, or almost in silence, emitting only a faintly audible, rusty gr-r-r-r, a sort of guttural grumble; until, all at once, when I was least expecting it—tirala-tirala—it trilled out clearly, crisply, six silvery notes, and then relapsed into its rusty gr-r-r-r.

So it would go on and on till it ran down. A minute or two of creaking and croaking, as it were, whilst it cleared its old asthmatic throat, then a sudden silvery tirala-tirala, then a catch, a cough, and mutter-mutter-mutter. Or was it more like an old woman maundering in her sleep, who should suddenly quaver out a snatch from a ditty of her girlhood, and afterwards mumble incoherently again?

I suppose the pin-points on the cylinder, all save just those six, were worn away; or, possibly, those teeth of the steel comb were the only ones that retained elasticity enough to vibrate.

A sequence of six notes, as inconclusive as six words plucked at random from the middle of a sentence; as void of musical value as six such words would be of literary value. I wonder why it has always had this instant, irresistible power to move me. It has always been a talisman in my hands, a thing to conjure with. As when I was a child, so now, after twenty years, I have but to breathe it to myself, and, if I will, the actual world melts away, and I am journeying in dreamland. Whether I will or not, it always stirs a sad, sweet emotion in my heart. I wonder why. Tirala-tirala—I dare say, for another, any six notes, struck at haphazard, would signify as much. But for me—ah, if I could seize the sentiment it has for me, and translate it into English words, I should have achieved a sort of miracle. For me, it is the voice of a spirit, sighing something unutterable. It is an elixir, distilled of unearthly things, six lucent drops; I drink them, and I am transported into another atmosphere, and I see visions. It is Aladdin's lamp; I touch it, and cloud-capped towers and gorgeous palaces are mine in the twinkling of an eye. It is my wishing-cap, my magic-carpet, my key to the Castle of Enchantment.

The Castle of Enchantment....

When I was a child the Castle of Enchantment meant—the Future; the great mysterious Future, away, away there, beneath the uttermost horizon, where the sky is luminious with tints of rose and pearl; the ineffable Future, when I should be grownup, when I should be a Man, and when the world would be my garden, the world and life, and all their riches, mine to explore, to adventure in, to do as I pleased with! The Future and the World, the real World, the World that lay beyond our village, beyond the Forest of Granjolaye, farther than Bayonne, farther even than Pau; the World one read of and heard strange legends of: Paris, and Bagdad, and England, and Peru. Oh, how I longed to see it; how hard it was to wait; how desperately hard to think of the immense number of long years that must be worn through somehow, before it could come true.

But—tirala-tirala!—my little broken bar of music was a touchstone. At the sound of it, at the thought of it, the Present was spirited away; Saint-Graal and all our countryside were left a thousand miles behind; and the Future and the World opened their portals to me, and I wandered in them where I would. In a sort of trance, with wide eyes and bated breath, I wandered in them, through enraptured hours. Believe me, it was a Future, it was a World, of quite unstinted magnificence. My many-pinnacled Castle of Enchantment was built of gold and silver, ivory, alabaster, and mother-of-pearl; the fountains in its courts ran with perfumed waters; and its pleasaunce was an orchard of pomegranates—one had no need to spare one's colours. I dare say, too, that it was rather vague, wrapped in a good deal of roseate haze, and of an architecture that could scarcely have been reduced to ground-plans and elevations; but what of that? And oh, the people, the people by whom the World and the Future were inhabited, the cavalcading knights, the beautiful princesses! And their virtues, and their graces, and their talents Î There were no ugly people, of course, no stupid people, no disagreeable people; everybody was young and handsome, gallant, generous, and splendidly dressed. And everybody was astonishingly nice to me, and it never seemed to occur to anybody that I wasn't to have my own way in everything. And I had it. Love and wealth, glory, and all manner of romance—I had them for the wishing. The stars left their courses to fight for me. And the winds of heaven vied with each other to prosper my galleons.

To be sure, it was nothing more nor other than the day-dream of every child. But it happened that that little accidental fragment of a phrase of music had a quite peculiar power to send me off dreaming it.

I suppose it must be that we pass the Castle of Enchantment while we are asleep. For surely, at first, it is before us—we are moving towards it; we can see it shining in the distance; we shall reach it to-morrow, next week, next year. And then—and then, one morning, we wake up, and lo! it is behind us. We have passed it—we are sailing away from it—we can't turn back. We have passed the Castle of Enchantment! And yet, it was only to reach it that we made our weary voyage, toiling through hardships and perils and discouragements, forcing our impatient hearts to wait; it was only the hope, the certain hope, of reaching it at last, that made our toiling and our waiting possible. And now—we have passed it. We are sailing away from it. We can't turn back. We can only *look* back—with the bitterness that every heart knows. If we look forward, what is there to see, save grey waters, and then a darkness that we fear to enter?

———————

When I was a child, it was the great world and the future into which my talisman carried me, dreaming desirous dreams; the great world, all gold and marble, peopled by beautiful princesses and cavalcading knights; the future, when I should be grown-up, when I should be a Man.

Well, I am grown-up now, and I have seen something of the great world— something of its gold and marble, its cavalcading knights and beautiful princesses. But if I care to dream desirous dreams, I touch my talisman, and wish myself back in the little world of my childhood. Tirala-tirala—I breathe it softly, softly; and the sentiment of my childhood comes and fills my room like a fragrance. I am at Saint-Graal again; and my grandmother is seated at her window, knitting; and André is bringing up the milk from the farm; and my cousin Elodie is playing her exercises on the piano; and Hélène and I are walking in the garden—Hélène in her short white frock, with a red sash, and her black hair loose down her back. All round us grow innumerable flowers, and innumerable birds are singing in the air, and the frogs are croaking, croaking in our pond. And farther off, the sun shines tranquilly on the chestnut-trees of the Forest of Granjolaye; and farther still, the Pyrenees gloom purple.... It is not much, perhaps it is not very wonderful; but oh, how my heart yearns to recover it, how it aches to realise that it never can.

———————

In the Morning (says Paraschkine) the Eastern Rim of the Earth was piled high with Emeralds and Rubies, as if the Gods had massed their Riches there; but he—ingenuous Pilgrim—who set forth to reach this Treasure-hoard, and to make the Gods' Riches his, seemed presently to have lost his Way; he could no longer discern the faintest Glint of the Gems that had tempted him: until, in the Afternoon, chancing to turn his Head, he saw a bewildering Sight —the Emeralds and Rubies were behind him, immeasurably far behind, piled up in the West.

Where is the Castle of Enchantment? *When* do we pass it? Ah, well, thank goodness, we all have talismans (like my little broken bit of a forgotten tune) whereby we are enabled sometimes to visit it in spirit, and to lose ourselves during enraptured moments among its glistening, labyrinthine halls.

THE INVISIBLE PRINCE

At a masked ball given by the Countess Wohenhoffen, in Vienna, during carnival week, a year ago, a man draped in the embroidered silks of a Chinese mandarin, his features entirely concealed by an enormous Chinese head in cardboard, was standing in the Wintergarten, the big, dimly lighted conservatory, near the door of one of the gilt-and-white reception-rooms, rather a stolid-seeming witness of the multi-coloured romp within, when a voice behind him said, "How do you do, Mr. Field?"—a woman's voice, an English voice.

The mandarin turned round.

From a black mask, a pair of blue-grey eyes looked into his broad, bland Chinese face; and a black domino dropped him an extravagant little curtsey.

"How do you do?" he responded. "I'm afraid I'm not Mr. Field; but I'll gladly pretend I am, if you'll stop and talk with me. I was dying for a little human conversation."

"Oh, you're afraid you're not Mr. Field, are you?" the mask replied derisively. "Then why did you turn when I called his name?"

"You mustn't hope to disconcert me with questions like that," said he. "I turned because I liked your voice."

He might quite reasonably have liked her voice, a delicate, clear, soft voice, somewhat high in register, with an accent, crisp, chiselled, concise, that suggested wit as well as distinction. She was rather tall, for a woman; one could divine her slender and graceful, under the voluminous folds of her domino.

She moved a little away from the door, deeper into the conservatory. The mandarin kept beside her. There, amongst the palms, a *fontaine lumineuse* was playing, rhythmically changing colour. Now it was a shower of rubies; now of emeralds or amethysts, of sapphires, topazes, or opals.

"How pretty," she said, "and how frightfully ingenious. I am wondering whether this wouldn't be a good place to sit down. What do you think?" And she pointed with a fan to a rustic bench.

"I think it would be no more than fair to give it a trial," he assented.

So they sat down on the rustic bench, by the *fontaine lumineuse*.

"In view of your fear that you're not Mr. Field, it's rather a coincidence that at a masked ball in Vienna you should just happen to be English, isn't it?" she asked.

"Oh, everybody's more or less English, in these days, you know," said he.

"There's some truth in that," she admitted, with a laugh. "What a diverting piece of artifice this Wintergarten is, to be sure. Fancy arranging the electric lights to shine through a dome of purple glass, and look like stars. They do look like stars, don't they? Slightly over-dressed, showy stars, indeed; stars in the German taste; but stars, all the same. Then, by day, you know, the purple glass is removed, and you get the sun—the real sun. Do you notice the delicious fragrance of lilac? If one hadn't too exacting an imagination, one might almost persuade oneself that one was in a proper open-air garden, on a night in May.... Yes, everybody is more or less English, in these days. That's precisely the sort of thing I should have expected Victor Field to say."

"By-the-bye," questioned the mandarin, "if you don't mind increasing my stores of knowledge, who *is* this fellow Field?"

"This fellow Field? Ah, who indeed?" said she. "That's just what I wish you'd tell me."

"I'll tell you with pleasure, after you've supplied me with the necessary data," he promised cheerfully.

"Well, by some accounts, he's a little literary man in London," she remarked.

"Oh, come! You never imagined that I was a little literary man in London," protested he.

"You might be worse," she retorted. "However, if the phrase offends you, I'll say a rising young literary man, instead. He writes things, you know."

"Poor chap, does he? But then, that's a way they have, rising young literary persons?" His tone was interrogative.

"Doubtless," she agreed. "Poems and stories and things. And book reviews, I suspect. And even, perhaps, leading articles in the newspapers."

"*Toute la lyre enfin?* What they call a penny-a-liner?"

"I'm sure I don't know what he's paid. I should think he'd get rather more than a penny. He's fairly successful. The things he does aren't bad," she said.

"I must look 'em up," said he. "But meantime, will you tell me how you came to mistake me for him? Has he the Chinese type? Besides, what on earth should a little London literary man be doing at the Countess Wohenhoffen's?"

"He was standing near the door, over there," she told him, sweetly, "dying

73

for a little human conversation, till I took pity on him. No, he hasn't exactly the Chinese type, but he's wearing a Chinese costume, and I should suppose he'd feel uncommonly hot in that exasperatingly placid Chinese head. *I'm* nearly suffocated, and I'm only wearing a *loup*. For the rest, why *shouldn't* he be here?"

"If your *loup* bothers you, pray take it off. Don't mind me," he urged gallantly.

"You're extremely good," she responded. "But if I should take off my *loup*, you'd be sorry. Of course, manlike, you're hoping that I'm young and pretty."

"Well, and aren't you?"

"I'm a perfect fright. I'm an old maid."

"Thank you. Manlike, I confess I *was* hoping you'd be young and pretty. Now my hope has received the strongest confirmation. I'm sure you are," he declared triumphantly.

"Your argument, with a meretricious air of subtlety, is facile and superficial. Don't pin your faith to it. Why *shouldn't* Victor Field be here?" she persisted.

"The Countess only receives tremendous swells. It's the most exclusive house in Europe."

"Are you a tremendous swell?" she wondered.

"Rather!" he asseverated. "Aren't you?"

She laughed a little, and stroked her fan, a big fan of fluffy black feathers.

"That's very jolly," said he.

"What?" said she.

"That thing in your lap."

"My fan?"

"I expect you'd call it a fan."

"For goodness' sake, what would *you* call it?" cried she.

"I should call it a fan."

She gave another little laugh. "You have a nice instinct for the *mot juste*," she informed him.

"Oh, no," he disclaimed, modestly. "But I can call a fan a fan, when I think it won't shock the sensibilities of my hearer."

"If the Countess only receives tremendous swells," said she, "you must remember that Victor Field belongs to the Aristocracy of Talent."

"Oh, *quant à ça*, so, from the Wohenhoffens' point of view, do the barber and the horse-leech. In this house, the Aristocracy of Talent dines with the butler."

"Is the Countess such a snob?" she asked.

"No; she's an Austrian. They draw the line so absurdly tight in Austria."

"Well, then, you leave me no alternative," she argued, "but to conclude that Victor Field is a tremendous swell. Didn't you notice, I bobbed him a curtsey?"

"I took the curtsey as a tribute to my Oriental magnificence," he confessed. "Field doesn't sound like an especially patrician name. I'd give anything to discover who you are. Can't you be induced to tell me? I'll bribe, entreat, threaten—I'll do anything you think might persuade you."

"I'll tell you at once, if you'll own up that you're Victor Field," said she.

"Oh, I'll own up that I'm Queen Elizabeth if you'll tell me who you are. The end justifies the means."

"Then you *are* Victor Field?" she pursued him eagerly.

"If you don't mind suborning perjury, why should I mind committing it?" he reflected. "Yes. And now, who are you?"

"No; I must have an unequivocal avowal," she stipulated. "Are you or are you not Victor Field?"

"Let us put it at this," he proposed, "that I'm a good serviceable imitation; an excellent substitute when the genuine article is not procurable."

"Of course, your real name isn't anything like Victor Field," she declared, pensively.

"I never said it was. But I admire the way in which you give with one hand and take back with the other."

"Your real name——" she began. "Wait a moment... Yes, now I have it. Your real name... It's rather long. You don't think it will bore you?"

"Oh, if it's really my real name, I daresay I'm hardened to it," said he.

"Your real name is Louis Charles Ferdinand Stanislas John Joseph Emmanuel Maria Anna."

"Mercy upon me," he cried, "what a name! You ought to have broken it to

75

me in instalments. And it's all Christian name at that. Can't you spare me just a little rag of a surname, for decency's sake?" he pleaded.

"The surnames of royalties don't matter, Monseigneur," she said, with a flourish.

"Royalties? What? Dear me, here's rapid promotion! I am royal now! And a moment ago I was a little penny-a-liner in London."

"*L'un n'empêche pas l'autre.* Have you never heard the story of the Invisible Prince?" she asked.

"I adore irrelevancy," said he. "I seem to have read something about an invisible prince, when I was young. A fairy tale, wasn't it?"

"The irrelevancy is only apparent. The story I mean is a story of real life. Have you ever heard of the Duke of Zeln?"

"Zeln? Zeln?" he repeated, reflectively. "No, I don't think so."

She clapped her hands. "Really, you do it admirably. If I weren't perfectly sure of my facts, I believe I should be taken in. Zeln, as any history would tell you, as any old atlas would show you, was a little independent duchy in the centre of Germany."

"Poor dear thing! Like Jonah in the centre of the whale," he murmured, sympathetically.

"Hush. Don't interrupt. Zeln was a little independent German duchy, and the Duke of Zeln was its sovereign. After the war with France it was absorbed by Prussia. But the ducal family still rank as royal highnesses. Of course, you've heard of the Leczinskis?"

"Lecz———what?" said he.

"Leczinski," she repeated.

"How do you spell it?" "L—

e—c—z—i—n—s—k—i."

"Good. Capital. You have a real gift for spelling," he exclaimed.

"Will you be quiet," she said, severely, "and answer my question? Are you familiar with the name?"

"I should never venture to be familiar with a name I didn't know," he asserted.

"Ah, you don't know it? You have never heard of Stanislas Leczinski, who was king of Poland? Of Marie Leczinska, who married Louis XV.?"

"Oh, to be sure. I remember. The lady whose portrait one sees at Versailles."

"Quite so. Very well," she continued, "the last representative of the Leczinskis, in the elder line, was the Princess Anna Leczinska, who, in 1858, married the Duke of Zeln. She was the daughter of John Leczinski, Duke of Grodnia and Governor of Galicia, and of the Archduchess Henrietta d'.ste, a cousin of the Emperor of Austria. She was also a great heiress, and an extremely handsome woman. But the Duke of Zeln was a bad lot, a viveur, a gambler, a spendthrift. His wife, like a fool, made her entire fortune over to him, and he proceeded to play ducks and drakes with it. By the time their son was born he'd got rid of the last farthing. Their son wasn't born till '63, five years after their marriage. Well, and then, what do you suppose the Duke did?"

"Reformed, of course. The wicked husband always reforms when a child is born, and there's no more money," he generalised.

"You know perfectly well what he did," said she. "He petitioned the German Diet to annul the marriage. You see, having exhausted the dowry of the Princess Anna, it occurred to him that if she could only be got out of the way, he might marry another heiress, and have the spending of another fortune."

"Clever dodge," he observed. "Did it come off?"

"It came off, all too well. He based his petition on the ground that the marriage had never been.... I forget what the technical term is. Anyhow, he pretended that the princess had never been his wife except in name, and that the child couldn't possibly be his. The Emperor of Austria stood by his connection, like the loyal gentleman he is; used every scrap of influence he possessed to help her. But the duke, who was a Protestant (the princess was of course a Catholic), the duke persuaded all the Protestant States in the Diet to vote in his favour. The Emperor of Austria was powerless, the Pope was powerless. And the Diet annulled the marriage."

"Ah," said the mandarin.

"Yes," she went on. "The marriage was annulled, and the child declared illegitimate. Ernest Augustus, as the duke was somewhat inconsequently named, married again, and had other children, the eldest of whom is the present bearer of the title—the same Duke of Zeln one hears of, quarrelling with the croupiers at Monte Carlo. The Princess Anna, with her baby, came to Austria. The Emperor gave her a pension, and lent her one of his country houses to live in—Schloss Sanct-Andreas. Our hostess, by-the-bye, the Countess Wohenhoffen, was her intimate friend and her *première dame d'honneur.*"

"Ah," said the mandarin.

"But the poor princess had suffered more than she could bear. She died when her child was four years old. The Countess Wohenhoffen took the infant, by the Emperor's desire, and brought him up with her own son Peter. He was called Prince Louis Leczinski. Of course, in all moral right, he was the Hereditary Prince of Zeln. His legitimacy, for the rest, and his mother's innocence, are perfectly well established, in every sense but a legal sense, by the fact that he has all the physical characteristics of the Zeln stock. He has the Zeln nose and the Zeln chin, which are as distinctive as the Habsburg lip."

"I hope, for the poor young man's sake, though, that they're not so unbecoming?" questioned the mandarin.

"They're not exactly pretty," answered the mask. "The nose is a thought too long, the chin is a trifle too short. However, I daresay the poor young man is satisfied. As I was about to tell you, the Countess Wohenhoflen brought him up, and the Emperor destined him for the Church. He even went to Rome and entered the Austrian College. He'd have been on the high road to a cardinalate by this time if he'd stuck to the priesthood, for he had strong interest. But, lo and behold, when he was about twenty, he chucked the whole thing up."

"Ah? *Histoire de femme?*"

"Very likely," she assented, "though I've never heard any one say so. At all events, he left Rome, and started upon his travels. He had no money of his own, but the Emperor made him an allowance. He started upon his travels, and he went to India, and he went to America, and he went to South Africa, and then, finally, in '87 or '88, he went—no one knows where. He totally disappeared, vanished into space. He's not been heard of since. Some people think he's dead. But the greater number suppose that he tired of his false position in the world, and one fine day determined to escape from it, by sinking his identity, changing his name, and going in for a new life under new conditions. They call him the Invisible Prince. His position *was* rather an ambiguous one, wasn't it? You see, he was neither one thing nor the other. He had no *état-civil*. In the eyes of the law he was a bastard, yet he knew himself to be the legitimate son of the Duke of Zeln. He was a citizen of no country, yet he was the rightful heir to a throne. He was the last descendant of Stanislas Leczinski, yet it was without authority that he bore his name. And then, of course, the rights and wrongs of the matter were only known to a few. The majority of people simply remembered that there had been a scandal. And (as a wag once said of him) wherever he went, he left his mother's reputation behind him. No wonder he found the situation irksome. Well, there is the story of the Invisible Prince."

"And a very exciting, melodramatic little story, too. For my part, I suspect your Prince met a boojum. I love to listen to stories. Won't you tell me another? Do, please," he pressed her.

"No, he didn't meet a boojum," she returned. "He went to England, and set up for an author. The Invisible Prince and Victor Field are one and the same person."

"Oh, I say! Not really!" he exclaimed.

"Yes, really."

"What makes you think so?" he wondered.

"I'm sure of it," said she. "To begin with, I must confide to you that Victor Field is a man I've never met."

"Never met...?" he gasped. "But, by the blithe way in which you were laying his sins at my door, a little while ago, I supposed you were sworn confederates."

"What's the good of masked balls, if you can't talk to people you've never met?" she submitted. "I've never met him, but I'm one of his admirers. I like his little poems. And I'm the happy possessor of a portrait of him. It's a print after a photograph. I cut it from an illustrated paper."

"I really almost wish I *was* Victor Field," he sighed. "I should feel such a glow of gratified vanity."

"And the Countess Wohenhoffen," she added, "has at least twenty portraits of the Invisible Prince—photographs, miniatures, life-size paintings, taken from the time he was born, almost, to the time of his disappearance. Victor Field and Louis Leczinski have countenances as like each other as two halfpence."

"An accidental resemblance, doubtless."

"No, it isn't an accidental resemblance," she affirmed.

"Oh, then you think it's intentional?" he quizzed.

"Don't be absurd. I might have thought it accidental, except for one or two odd little circumstances. *Primo*, Victor Field is a guest at the Wohenhoffens' ball."

"Oh, he *is* a guest here?"

"Yes, he is," she said. "You are wondering how I know. Nothing simpler.

79

The same costumier who made my domino, supplied his Chinese dress. I noticed it at his shop. It struck me as rather nice, and I asked whom it was for. The costumier said, for an Englishman at the Hôtel de Bade. Then he looked in his book, and told me the Englishman's name. It was Victor Field. So, when I saw the same Chinese dress here to-night, I knew it covered the person of one of my favourite authors. But I own, like you, I was a good deal surprised. What on earth should a little London literary man be doing at the Countess Wohenhoffen's? And then I remembered the astonishing resemblance between Victor Field and Louis Leczinski; and I remembered that to Louis Leczinski the Countess Wohenhoffen had been a second mother; and I reflected that though he chose to be as one dead and buried for the rest of the world, Louis Leczinski might very probably keep up private relations with the Countess. He might very probably come to her ball, incognito, and safely masked. I observed also that the Countess's rooms were decorated throughout with *white lilac*. But the white lilac is the emblematic flower of the Leczinskis; green and white are their family colours. Wasn't the choice of white lilac on this occasion perhaps designed as a secret compliment to the Prince? I was taught in the schoolroom that two and two make four."

"Oh, one can see that you've enjoyed a liberal education," he apprised her. "But where were you taught to jump to conclusions? You do it with a grace, an assurance. I too have heard that two and two make four; but first you must catch your two and two. Really, as if there couldn't be more than one Chinese costume knocking about Vienna, during carnival week! Dear, good, sweet lady, it's of all disguises the disguise they're driving hardest, this particular season. And then to build up an elaborate theory of identities upon the mere chance resemblance of a pair of photographs! Photographs indeed! Photographs don't give the complexion. Say that your Invisible Prince is dark, what's to prevent your literary man from being fair or sandy? Or *vice versa?* And then, how is a little German Polish princeling to write poems and things in English? No, no, no; your reasoning hasn't a leg to stand on."

"Oh, I don't mind its not having legs," she laughed, "so long as it convinces me. As for writing poems and things in English, you yourself said that everybody is more or less English, in these days. German princes are especially so. They all learn English, as a second mother-tongue. You see, like Circassian beauties, they are mostly bred up for the marriage market; and nothing is a greater help towards a good sound remunerative English marriage, than a knowledge of the language. However, don't be frightened. I must take it for granted that Victor Field would prefer not to let the world know who he is. I happen to have discovered his secret. He may trust to my discretion."

"You still persist in imagining that I'm Victor Field?" he murmured sadly.

"I should have to be extremely simple-minded," she announced, "to imagine anything else. You wouldn't be a male human being if you had sat here for half an hour patiently talking about another man."

"Your argument," said he, "with a meretricious air of subtlety, is facile and superficial. I thank you for teaching me that word. I'd sit here till doomsday talking about my worst enemy, for the pleasure of talking with you."

"Perhaps we have been talking of your worst enemy. Whom do the moralists pretend a man's worst enemy is wont to be?" she asked.

"I wish you would tell me the name of the person the moralists would consider your worst enemy," he replied.

"I'll tell you directly, as I said before, if you'll own up," she offered.

"Your price is prohibitive. I've nothing to own up to."

"Well then—good night," she said.

Lightly, swiftly, she fled from the conservatory, and was soon irrecoverable in the crowd.

———————————

The next morning Victor Field left Vienna for London; but before he left he wrote a letter to Peter Wohenhoffen. In the course of it he said: "There was an Englishwoman at your ball last night with the reasoning powers of a detective in a novel. By divers processes of elimination and induction, she had formed all sorts of theories about no end of things. Among others, for instance, he was willing to bet her hali-dome that a certain Prince Louis Leczinski, who seems to have gone on the spree some years ago, and never to have come home again—she was willing to bet anything you like that Leczinski and I— moi qui vous parle—were to all intents and purposes the same. Who was she, please? Rather a tall woman, in a black domino, with grey eyes, or greyish-blue, and a nice voice."

In the answer which he received from Peter Wohenhoffen towards the end of the week, Peter said: "There were nineteen Englishwomen at my mother's party, all of them rather tall, with nice voices, and grey or blue-grey eyes. I don't know what colours their dominoes were. Here is a list of them."

The names that followed were names of people whom Victor Field almost certainly would never meet. The people Victor knew in London were the sort of people a little literary man might be expected to know. Most of them were respectable; some of them even deemed themselves rather smart, and patronised him right Britishly. But the nineteen names in Peter Wohenhoffen's list ("Oh, me! Oh, my!" cried Victor) were names to make you gasp.

All the same, he went a good deal to Hyde Park during the season, and watched the driving.

"Which of all those haughty high-born beauties is she?" he wondered futilely.

And then the season passed, and then the year; and little by little, of course, he ceased to think about her.

One afternoon last May, a man, habited in accordance with the fashion of the period, stopped before a hairdresser's shop in Knightsbridge somewhere, and, raising his hat, bowed to the three waxen ladies who simpered from the window.

"Oh! It's Mr. Field!" a voice behind him cried. "What are those cryptic rites that you're performing? What on earth are you bowing into a hairdresser's window for?"—a smooth, melodious voice, tinged by an inflection that was half ironical, half bewildered.

"I was saluting the type of English beauty," he answered, turning. "Fortunately, there are divergencies from it," he added, as he met the puzzled smile of his interlocutrice; a puzzled smile indeed, but, like the voice, by no means without its touch of irony.

She gave a little laugh; and then, examining the models critically, "Oh?" she questioned. "Would you call that the type? You place the type high. Their features are quite faultless, and who ever saw such complexions?"

"It's the type, all the same," said he. "Just as the imitation marionette is the type of English breeding."

"The imitation marionette? I'm afraid I don't follow," she confessed.

"The imitation marionettes. You've seen them at little theatres in Italy. They're actors who imitate puppets. Men and women who try to behave as if they weren't human, as if they were made of starch and whalebone, instead of flesh and blood."

"Ah, yes," she assented, with another little laugh. "That would be rather typical of our insular methods. But do you know what an engaging, what a reviving spectacle you presented, as you stood there flourishing your hat? What do you imagine people thought? And what would have happened to you if I had just chanced to be a policeman instead of a friend?"

"Would you have clapped your handcuffs on me?" he enquired. "I suppose my conduct did seem rather suspicious. I was in the deepest depth of dejection. One must give some expression to one's sorrow."

"Are you going towards Kensington?" she asked, preparing to move on.

"Before I commit myself, I should like to be sure whether you are," he replied.

"You can easily discover with a little perseverance."

He placed himself beside her, and together they walked towards Kensington.

She was rather taller than the usual woman, and slender. She was exceedingly well-dressed; smartly, becomingly; a jaunty little hat of strangely twisted straw, with an aigrette springing defiantly from it; a jacket covered with mazes and labyrinths of embroidery; at her throat a big knot of white lace, the ends of which fell winding in a creamy cascade to her waist (do they call the thing a *jabot?*); and then....

But what can a man trust himself to write of these esoteric matters? She carried herself extremely well, too: with grace, with distinction, her head held high, even thrown back a little, superciliously. She had an immense quantity of very lovely hair. Red hair? Yellow hair? Red hair with yellow lights burning in it? Yellow hair with red fires shimmering through it? In a single loose, full billow it swept away from her forehead, and then flowed into half-a-thousand rippling, crinkling, capricious undulations. And her skin had the sensitive colouring, the fineness of texture, that are apt to accompany red hair when it's yellow, yellow hair when it's red. Her face, with its pensive, quizzical eyes, it's tip-tilted nose, it's rather large mouth, and the little mocking quirks and curves the lips took, was an alert, arch, witty face; a delicate high-bred face; and withal a somewhat sensuous, emotional face; the face of a woman with a vast deal of humour in her soul, a vast deal of mischief; of a woman who would love to tease you, and mystify you, and lead you on, and put you off; and yet who, in her own way, at her own time, would know supremely well how to be kind.

But it was mischief rather than kindness that glimmered in her eyes at present, as she asked, "You were in the deepest depths of dejection. Poor man! Why?"

"I can't precisely determine," said he, "whether the sympathy that seems to vibrate in your voice is genuine or counterfeit."

"Perhaps it's half and half," she suggested. "But my curiosity is unmixed. Tell me your troubles."

"The catalogue is long. I've sixteen hundred million. The weather, for example. The shameless beauty of this radiant spring day. It's enough to stir all manner of wild pangs and longings in the heart of an octogenarian. But, anyhow, when one's life is passed in a dungeon, one can't perpetually be singing and dancing from mere exuberance of joy, can one?"

"Is your life passed in a dungeon?" she exclaimed.

"Indeed, indeed, it is. Isn't yours?"

"It had never occurred to me that it was."

"You're lucky. Mine is passed in the dungeons of Castle Ennui," he said.

"Oh, Castle Ennui. Ah, yes. You mean you're bored?"

"At this particular moment I'm savouring the most exquisite excitement," he professed. "But in general, when I am not working or sleeping, I'm bored to extermination—incomparably bored. If only one could work and sleep alternately, twenty-four hours a day, the year round! There's no use trying to play in London. It's so hard to find a playmate. The English people take their pleasures without salt."

"The dungeons of Castle Ennui," she repeated meditatively. "Yes, we are fellow-prisoners. I'm bored to extermination too. Still," she added, "one is allowed out on parole, now and again. And sometimes one has really quite delightful little experiences."

"It would ill become me, in the present circumstances, to dispute that," he answered, bowing.

"But the castle waits to reclaim us afterwards, doesn't it?" she mused. "That's rather a happy image, Castle Ennui."

"I'm extremely glad you approve of it. Castle Ennui is the Bastille of modern life. It is built of prunes and prisms; it has its outer court of Convention, and its inner court of Propriety; it is moated round by Respectability, and the shackles its inmates wear are forged of dull little duties and arbitrary little rules. You can only escape from it at the risk of breaking your social neck, or remaining a fugitive from social justice to the end of your days. Yes, it is a fairly decent little image."

"A bit out of something you're preparing for the press?" she hinted.

"Oh, how unkind of you!" he cried. "It was absolutely extemporaneous."

"One can never tell, with *vous autres gens-de-lettres*" she laughed.

"It would be friendlier to say *nous autres gens desprit,*' he submitted.

"Aren't we proving to what degree *nous autres gens d'esprit sont bêtes,*" she remarked, "by continuing to walk along this narrow pavement, when we can get into Kensington Gardens by merely crossing the street? Would it take you out of your way?"

"I have no way. I was sauntering for pleasure, if you can believe me. I wish I could hope that you have no way either. Then we could stop here, and crack little jokes together the livelong afternoon," he said, as they entered the Gardens.

"Alas, my way leads straight back to the Castle. I've promised to call on an old woman in Campden Hill," said she.

"Disappoint her. It's good for old women to be disappointed. It whips up their circulation."

"I shouldn't much regret disappointing the old woman," she admitted, "and I should rather like an hour or two of stolen freedom. I don't mind owning that I've generally found you, as men go, a moderately interesting man to talk with. But the deuce of it is… You permit the expression?"

"I'm devoted to the expression."

"The deuce of it is, I'm supposed to be driving," she explained.

"Oh, that doesn't matter. So many suppositions in this world are baseless," he reminded her.

"But there's the prison van," she said. "It's one of the tiresome rules in the female wing of Castle Ennui that you're always supposed, more or less, to be driving. And though you may cheat the authorities by slipping out of the prison van directly it's turned the corner, and sending it on ahead, there it remains, a factor that can't be eliminated. The prison van will relentlessly await my arrival in the old woman's street."

"That only adds to the sport. Let it wait. When a factor can't be eliminated, it should be haughtily ignored. Besides, there are higher considerations. If you leave me, what shall I do with the rest of this weary day?"

"You can go to your club."

He threw up his hand. "Merciful lady! What sin have I committed? I never go to my club, except when I've been wicked, as a penance. If you will permit me to employ a metaphor—oh, but a tried and trusty metaphor—when one ship on the sea meets another in distress, it stops and comforts it, and forgets all about its previous engagements and the prison van and everything. Shall we cross to the north, and see whether the Serpentine is in its place? Or would you prefer to inspect the eastern front of the Palace? Or may I offer you a penny chair?"

"I think a penny chair would be the maddest of the three dissipations," she decided.

And they sat down in penny chairs.

"It's rather jolly here, isn't it?" said he. "The trees, with their black trunks, and their leaves, and things. Have you ever seen such sumptuous foliage? And the greensward, and the shadows, and the sunlight, and the atmosphere, and the mistiness—isn't it like pearl-dust and gold-dust floating in the air? It's all got up to imitate the background of a Watteau. We must do our best to be frivolous and ribald, and supply a proper foreground. How big and fleecy and white the clouds are. Do you think they're made of cotton-wool? And what do you suppose they paint the sky with? There never was such a brilliant, breath-taking blue. It's much too nice to be natural. And they've sprinkled the whole place with scent, haven't they? You notice how fresh and sweet it smells. If only one could get rid of the sparrows—the cynical little beasts! hear how they're chortling—and the people, and the nursemaids and children. I have never been able to understand why they admit the public to the parks."

"Go on," she encouraged him. "You're succeeding admirably in your effort to be ribald."

"But that last remark wasn't ribald in the least—it was desperately sincere. I do think it's inconsiderate of them to admit the public to the parks. They ought to exclude all the lower classes, the People, at one fell swoop, and then to discriminate tremendously amongst the others."

"Mercy, what undemocratic sentiments!" she cried. "The People, the poor dear People—what have they done?"

"Everything. What haven't they done? One could forgive their being dirty and stupid and noisy and rude; one could forgive their ugliness, the ineffable banality of their faces, their goggle-eyes, their protruding teeth, their ungainly motions; but the trait one can't forgive is their venality. They're so mercenary. They're always thinking how much they can get out of you—everlastingly

86

touching their hats and expecting you to put your hand in your pocket. Oh, no, believe me, there's no health in the People. Ground down under the iron heel of despotism, reduced to a condition of hopeless serfdom, I don't say that they might not develop redeeming virtues. But free, but sovereign, as they are in these days, they're everything that is squalid and sordid and offensive. Besides, they read such abominably bad literature."

"In that particular they're curiously like the aristocracy, aren't they?" said she. "By-the-bye, when are you going to publish another book of poems?"

"Apropos of bad literature?"

"Not altogether bad. I rather like your poems."

"So do I," said he. "It's useless to pretend that we haven't tastes in common."

They were both silent for a bit. She looked at him oddly, an inscrutable little light flickering in her eyes. All at once she broke out with a merry trill of laughter.

"What are you laughing at?" he demanded.

"I'm hugely amused," she answered.

"I wasn't aware that I'd said anything especially good."

"You're building better than you know. But if I am amused, *you* look ripe for tears. What is the matter?"

"Every heart knows its own bitterness," he answered. "Don't pay the least attention to me. You mustn't let moodiness of mine cast a blight upon your high spirits."

"No fear," she assured him. "There are pleasures that nothing can rob of their sweetness. Life is not all dust and ashes. There are bright spots."

"Yes, I've no doubt there are," he said.

"And thrilling little adventures—no?" she questioned.

"For the bold, I dare say."

"None but the bold deserve them. Sometimes it's one thing, and sometimes it's another."

"That's very certain," he agreed.

"Sometimes, for instance," she went on, "one meets a man one knows, and speaks to him. And he answers with a glibness! And then, almost directly, what do you suppose one discovers?"

"What?" he asked.

"One discovers that the wretch hasn't the ghost of a notion who one is—that he's totally and absolutely forgotten one!"

"Oh, I say! Really?" he exclaimed.

"Yes, really. You can't deny that *that's* an exhilarating little adventure."

"I should think it might be. One could enjoy the man's embarrassment," he reflected.

"Or his lack of embarrassment. Some men are of an assurance, of a *sang froid!* They'll place themselves beside you, and walk with you, and talk with you, and even propose that you should pass the livelong afternoon cracking jokes with them in a garden, and never breathe a hint of their perplexity. They'll brazen it out."

"That's distinctly heroic, Spartan, of them, don't you think?" he said. "Internally, poor dears, they're very likely suffering agonies of discomfiture."

"We'll hope they are. Could they decently do less?" said she.

"And fancy the mental struggles that must be going on in their brains," he urged. "If I were a man in such a situation I'd throw myself upon the woman's mercy. I'd say, 'Beautiful, sweet lady! I know I know you. Your name, your entirely charming and appropriate name, is trembling on the tip of my tongue. But, for some unaccountable reason, my brute of a memory chooses to play the fool. If you've a spark of Christian kindness in your soul, you'll come to my rescue with a little clue.'.rdquo;

"If the woman had a Christian sense of the ridiculous in her soul, I fear you'd throw yourself on her mercy in vain," she warned him.

"What *is* the good of tantalising people?"

"Besides," she continued, "the woman might reasonably feel slightly humiliated to find herself forgotten in that bare-faced manner."

"The humiliation surely would be all the man's. Have you heard from the Wohenhoffens lately?"

"The—what? The—who?" She raised her eyebrows.

"The Wohenhoffens," he repeated.

"What are the Wohenhoffens? Are they persons? Are they things?"

"Oh, nothing. My enquiry was merely dictated by a thirst for knowledge. It occurred to me vaguely that you might have worn a black domino at a masked ball they gave, the Wohenhoffens. Are you sure you didn't?"

"I've a great mind to punish your forgetfulness by pretending that I did," she teased.

"She was rather tall, like you, and she had grey eyes, and a nice voice, and a laugh that was sweeter than the singing of nightingales. She was monstrously clever, too, with a flow of language that would have made her a leader in any sphere. She was also a perfect fiend. I have always been anxious to meet her again, in order that I might ask her to marry me. I'm strongly disposed to believe that she was you. Was she?" he pleaded.

"If I say yes, will you at once proceed to ask me to marry you?" she asked.

"Try it and see."

"*Ce n'est pas la peine.* It occasionally happens that a woman's already got a husband."

"She said she was an old maid."

"Do you dare to insinuate that I look like an old maid?" she cried.

"Yes."

"Upon my word!"

"Would you wish me to insinuate that you look like anything so insipid as a young girl? *Were* you the woman of the black domino?" he persisted.

"I should need further information, before being able to make up my mind. Are the—what's their name?—Wohenheimer?—are the Wohenheimers people one can safely confess to knowing? Oh, you're a man, and don't count. But a woman? It sounds a trifle Jewish, Wohenheimer. But of course there are Jews and Jews."

"You're playing with me like the cat in the adage," he sighed. "It's too cruel. No one is responsible for his memory."

"And to think that this man took me down to dinner not two months ago!" she murmured in her veil.

"You're as hard as nails. In whose house? Or—stay. Prompt me a little. Tell me the first syllable of your name. Then the rest will come with a rush."

"My name is Matilda Muggins."

"I've a great mind to punish your untruthfulness by pretending to believe you," said he. "Have you really got a husband?"

"Why do you doubt it?" said she.

"I don't doubt it. Have you?"

"I don't know what to answer."

"Don't you know whether you've got a husband?" he protested.

"I don't know what I'd better let you believe. Yes, on the whole, I think you may as well assume that I've got a husband," she concluded.

"And a lover, too?" he asked.

"Really! I like your impertinence!" She bridled. "I only asked to show a polite interest. I knew the answer would be an indignant negative. You're an Englishwoman, and you're *nice*. Oh, one can see with half an eye that you're *nice*. But that a nice Englishwoman should have a lover is as inconceivable as that she should have side-whiskers. It's only the reg'lar bad-uns in England who have lovers. There's nothing between the family pew and the divorce court. One nice Englishwoman is a match for the whole Eleven Thousand Virgins of Cologne."

"To hear you talk, one might fancy you were not English yourself. For a man of the name of Field, you're uncommonly foreign. You *look* rather foreign too, you know, by-the-bye. You haven't at all an English cast of countenance," she considered.

"I've enjoyed the advantages of a foreign education. I was brought up abroad," he explained.

"Where your features unconsciously assimilated themselves to a foreign type? Where you learned a hundred thousand strange little foreign things, no doubt? And imbibed a hundred thousand unprincipled little foreign notions? And all the ingenuous little foreign prejudices and misconceptions concerning England?" she questioned.

"Most of them," he assented.

"*Perfide Albion?* English hypocrisy?" she pursued.

"Oh, yes, the English are consummate hypocrites. But there's only one objection to their hypocrisy—it so rarely covers any wickedness. It's such a disappointment to see a creature stalking towards you, laboriously draped in sheep's clothing, and then to discover that it's only a sheep. You, for instance, as I took the liberty of intimating a moment ago, in spite of your perfectly respectable appearance, are a perfectly respectable woman. If you weren't, wouldn't I be making furious love to you, though!"

"As I am, I can see no reason why you shouldn't make furious love to me, if it would amuse you. There's no harm in firing your pistol at a person who's bullet-proof," she laughed.

"No; it's merely a wanton waste of powder and shot," said he. "However, I shouldn't stick at that. The deuce of it is…. You permit the expression?"

"I'm devoted to the expression."

"The deuce of it is, you profess to be married."

"Do you mean to say that you, with your unprincipled foreign notions, would be restrained by any such consideration as that?" she wondered.

"I shouldn't be for an instant—if I weren't in love with you."

"*Comment donc? Déjà?*" she cried with a laugh.

"Oh, *déjà!* Why not? Consider the weather—consider the scene. Is the air soft, is it fragrant? Look at the sky—good heavens!—and the clouds, and the shadows on the grass, and the sunshine between the trees. The world is made of light today, of light and colour, and perfume and music. *Tutt' intorno canta amort amor, amore!* What would you have? One recognises one's affinity. One doesn't need a lifetime. You began the business at the Wohenhoffens' ball. To-day you've merely put on the finishing touches."

"Oh, then I *am* the woman you met at the masked ball?" she cried.

"Look me in the eye, and tell me you're not," he defied her.

"I haven't the faintest interest in telling you I'm not. On the contrary, it rather pleases me to let you imagine that I am."

"She owed me a grudge, you know. I hoodwinked her like everything," he confided.

"Oh, did you? Then, as a sister woman, I should be glad to serve as her instrument of vengeance. Do you happen to have such a thing as a watch about you?" she inquired.

"Yes," he said.

"Will you be good enough to tell me what o'clock it is?"

"What are your motives for asking?"

"I'm expected at home at five."

"Where do you live?"

"What are the motives for asking?"

"I want to call upon you."

"You might wait till you're invited."

"Well, invite me—quick!"

"Never."

"Never?"

"Never, never, never," she asseverated. "A man who's forgotten me as you have!"

"But if I've only met you once at a masked ball ...."

"Can't you be brought to realise that every time you mistake me for that woman of the masked ball you turn the dagger in the wound?" she demanded.

"But if you won't invite me to call upon you, how and when am I to see you again?"

"I haven't an idea," she answered, cheerfully. "I must go now. Good bye." She rose.

"One moment," he interposed. "Before you go will you allow me to look at the palm of your left hand?"

"What for?"

"I can tell fortunes. I'm extremely good at it," he boasted. "I'll tell you yours."

"Oh, very well," she assented, sitting down again: and guilelessly she pulled off her glove.

He took her hand, a beautifully slender, nervous hand, warm and soft, with rosy, tapering fingers.

"Oho! you *are* an old maid after all," he cried. "There's no wedding ring."

"You villain!" she gasped, snatching the hand away.

"I promised to tell your fortune. Haven't I told it correctly?"

"You needn't rub it in, though. Eccentric old maids don't like to be reminded of their condition."

"Will you marry *me?*"

"Why do you ask?"

"Partly from curiosity. Partly because it's the only way I can think of, to make sure of seeing you again. And then, I like your hair. Will you?"

"I can't," she said.

"Why not?"

"The stars forbid. And I'm ambitious. In my horoscope it is written that I shall either never marry at all, or—marry royalty."

"Oh, bother ambition! Cheat your horoscope. Marry me. Will you?"

"If you care to follow me," she said, rising again, "you can come and help me to commit a little theft."

He followed her to an obscure and sheltered corner of a flowery path, where she stopped before a bush of white lilac.

"There are no keepers in sight, are there?" she questioned.

"I don't see any," he said.

"Then allow me to make you a receiver of stolen goods," said she, breaking off a spray, and handing it to him.

"Thank you. But I'd rather have an answer to my question."

"Isn't that an answer?"

"Is it?"

"White lilac—to the Invisible Prince?"

"The Invisible Prince.... Then you *are* the black domino!" he exclaimed.

"Oh, I suppose so," she consented.

"And you *will* marry me?"

"I'll tell the aunt I live with to ask you to dinner."

"But will you marry me?"

"I thought you wished me to cheat my horoscope?"

"How could you find a better means of doing so?"

"What! if I should marry Louis Leczinski...?"

"Oh, to be sure. You would have it that I was Louis Leczinski. But, on that subject, I must warn you seriously——"

"One instant," she interrupted. "People must look other people straight in the face when they're giving serious warnings. Look straight into my eyes, and continue your serious warning."

"I must really warn you seriously," said he, biting his lip, "that if you persist in that preposterous delusion about my being Louis Leczinski, you'll be most awfully sold. I have nothing on earth to do with Louis Leczinski. Your ingenious little theories, as I tried to convince you at the time, were absolute romance."

Her eyebrows raised a little, she kept her eyes fixed steadily on his—oh, in the drollest fashion, with a gaze that seemed to say "How admirably you do it! I wonder whether you imagine I believe you. Oh, you fibber! Aren't you ashamed to tell me such abominable fibs?"...

They stood still, eyeing each other thus, for something like twenty seconds, and then they both laughed and walked on.

P'TIT-BLEU

P'tit-Bleu, poor P'tit-Bleu! I can't name her without a sigh; I can't think of her without a kind of heartache. Yet, all things considered, I wonder whether hers was really a destiny to sorrow over. True, she has disappeared; and it is not pleasant to conjecture what she may have come to, what may have befallen her, in the flesh, since her disappearance. But when I remember those beautiful preceding years of self-abnegation, of great love, and pain, and devotion, I find myself instinctively believing that something good she must have permanently gained; some treasure that nothing, not the worst imaginable subsequent disaster, can quite have taken from her. It is not pleasant to conjecture what she may have done or suffered in the flesh; but in the spirit, one may hope, she cannot have gone altogether to the bad, nor fared altogether ill.

In the spirit! Dear me, there was a time when it would have seemed derisory to speak of the spirit in the same breath with P'tit-Bleu. In the early days of my acquaintance with her, for example, I should have stared if anybody had spoken of her spirit. If anybody had asked me to describe her, I should have said, "She is a captivating little animal, pretty and sprightly, but as soulless—as soulless as a squirrel." Oh, a warm-blooded little animal, good-natured, quick-witted, full of life and the joy of life; a delightful little animal to play with, to fondle; but just a little animal, none the less: a little mass of soft, rosy, jocund, sensual, soulless matter. And in her full red lips, her roguish black eyes, her plump little hands, her trim, tight little figure—in her smile, her laugh—in the toss of her head—in her saucy, slightly swaggering carriage—I fancy you would have read my appreciation justified. No doubt there must have been the spark 01 a soul smouldering somewhere in her (how, otherwise, account for what happened later on?), but it was far too tiny a spark to be perceptible to the casual observer. Soul, however, I need hardly add, was the last thing we of the University were accustomed to look for in our feminine companions; I must not for an instant seem to imply that the lack of a soul in P'tit-Bleu was a subject of mourning with any of us. That a Latin Quarter girl should be soulless was as much a part of the natural order of creation, as that she should be beardless. They were all of them little animals, and P'tit-Bleu diverged from the type principally in this, that where the others, in most instances, were stupid, objectionable little animals, she was a diverting one. She was made of sugar and spice and a hundred nice ingredients, whilst they were made of the dullest, vulgarest clay.

In my own case, P'tit-Bleu was the object, not indeed of love, but of a violent infatuation, at first sight.

At Bullier, one evening, a chain of students, some twenty linked hand in hand, were chasing her round and round the hall, shouting after her, in rough staccato, something that sounded like, "Ti-*bah!* Ti-*bah!* Ti-*bah!*"—while she, a sprite-like little form, in a black skirt and a scarlet bodice, fled before them with leaps and bounds, and laughed defiantly.

I hadn't the vaguest notion what "Ti-*bah!* Ti-*bah!* Ti-*bah!*" meant, but that laughing face, with the red lips and the roguish eyes, seemed to me immensely fascinating. Among the faces of the other young ladies present— faces of dough, faces of tallow, faces all weariness, staleness, and banality, common, coarse, pointless, insipid faces—it shone like an epigram amongst platitudes, a thing of fire amongst things of dust. I turned to some one near me, and asked who she was.

"It's P'tit-Bleu, the dancing girl. She's going to do a quadrille."

P'tit-Bleu.... It's the fashion, you know, in Paris, for the girls who "do quadrilles" to adopt unlikely nicknames: aren't the reigning favourites at this moment Chapeau-Mou and Fifi-la-Galette? P'tit-Bleu had derived hers from that vehement little "wine of the barrier," which, the song declares, "vous met la tête en feu." It was the tune of the same song, that, in another minute, I heard the band strike up, in the balcony over our heads. P'tit-Bleu came to a standstill in the middle of the floor, where she was joined by three minor dancing-girls, to make two couples. The chain of students closed in a circle round her. And the rest of us thronged behind them, pressing forward, and craning our necks. Then, as the band played, everybody sang, in noisy chorus:

"P'tit-Bleu, P'tit-Bleu, P'tit-Bleu-eu,

Ça vous met la tête en feu!

Ça vous ra-ra-ra-ra-ra,

Ça vous ra-ra-ravigotte!"

P'tit-Bleu stood with her hands on her hips, her arms a-kimbo, her head thrown impudently back, her eyes sparkling mischievously, her lips curling in a perpetual play of smiles, while her three subalterns accomplished their tame preliminary measures; and then P'tit-Bleu pirouetted forward, and began her own indescribable pas-seul—oh, indescribable for a hundred reasons. She wore scarlet satin slippers, embroidered with black beads, and black silk stockings with scarlet clocks, and simply cataracts and cataracts of white diaphanous frills under her demure black skirt. And she danced with constantly increasing fervour, kicked higher and higher, ever more boldly and more bravely. Presently her hat fell off, and she tossed it from her, calling to the member of the crowd who had the luck to catch it, "Tiens mon chapeau!" And then her waving black hair flowed down her back, and flew loose about her face and shoulders. And the whole time, she laughed—laughed—laughed. With her swift whirlings, her astonishing undulations, and the flashing of the red and black and white, one's eyes were dazzled. "Ça vous met la tête en feu!" My head burned and reeled, as I watched her, and I thought, "What a delicious, bewitching little creature! What wouldn't I give to know her!" My head burned, and my heart yearned covetously; but I was a new-comer in the Quarter, and ignorant of its easy etiquette, and terribly young and timid, and I should never have dared to speak to her without a proper introduction. She danced with constantly increasing fervour, faster, faster, furiously fast: till, suddenly—*zip!*—down she slid upon the floor, in the *grand écart,* and sat there (if one may call that posture sitting), smiling calmly up at us, whilst everybody thundered, "Bravo! Bravo! Bravo!"

In an instant, though, she was on her feet again, and had darted out of the circle to the side of the youth who had caught her hat. He offered it to her with a bow, but his pulses were thumping tempestuously, and no doubt she could read his envy in his eyes. Anyhow, all at once, she put her arm through his, and said—oh, thrills and wonders!—"Allons, mon petit, I authorise you to treat me to a bock."

It seemed as if impossible heavens had opened to me; yet there she was, clinging to my arm, and drawing me towards the platform under the musicians' gallery, where there are tables for the thirsty. Her little plump white hand lay on my coat-sleeve; the air was heady with the perfume of her garments; her roguish black eyes were smiling encouragement into mine; and her red lips were so near, so near, I had to fight down a wild impulse to stoop and snatch a kiss. She drew me towards the tables, and, on the way, she stopped before a mirror fixed in the wall, and rearranged her hair; while I stood close to her, still holding her hat, and waited, feeling the most exquisite proud swelling of the heart, as if I owned her. Her hair put right, she searched in her pocket and produced a small round ivory box, from which—having unscrewed its cover and handed it to me with a "*Tiens ça*"—she extracted a powder-puff; and therewith she proceeded gently, daintily, to dust her face and throat, examining the effect critically in the glass the while. In the end she said, "*Voilà*, that's better," and turned her face to me for corroboration. "That's better, isn't it?" "It's perfect. But—but you were perfect before, too," asseverated I. Oh, what a joy beyond measure thus to be singled out and made her confidant and adviser in these intimate affairs.... At our table, leaning back nonchalantly in her chair, as she quaffed her bock and puffed her cigarette, she looked like a bright-eyed, red-lipped bacchante.

I gazed at her in a quite unutterable ecstasy of admiration. My conscience told me that I ought to pay her a compliment upon her dancing; but I couldn't shape one: my wits were paralysed by my emotions. I could only gaze, and gaze, and revel in my unexpected fortune. At last, however, the truth burst from me in a sort of involuntary gasp.

"But you are adorable—adorable."

She gave a quick smile of intelligence, of sympathy, and, with a knowing toss of the head and a provoking glance, suggested, "Je te mets la tête en feu, quoi!" She, you perceive, was entirely at her ease, mistress of the situation. It is conceivable that she had met neophytes before—that I was by no means to her the unprecedented experience she was to me. At any rate, she understood my agitation and sought to reassure me. "Don't be afraid; I'll not eat you," she promised.

I, in the depths of my mind, had been meditating what I could not but deem an excessively audacious proposal Her last speech gave me my cue, and I risked it.

"Perhaps you would like to eat something else? If—if we should go somewhere and sup?"

"Monsieur thinks he will be safer to take precautions," she laughed. "Well —I submit."

So we removed ourselves to the cloak-room, where she put on her cloak, and exchanged her slippers for a pair of boots (you can guess, perhaps, who enjoyed the beatific privilege of buttoning them for her); and then we left the Closerie des Lilas, falsely so called, with its flaring gas, its stifling atmosphere, its boisterous merrymakers, and walked arm in arm—only this time it was *my* arm that was within *hers*—down the Boul' Miche, past the Luxembourg gardens, where sweet airs blew in our faces, to the Gambrinus restaurant, in the Rue de Médicis. And there you should have seen P'tit-Bleu devouring écrevisses. Whatsoever this young woman's hand found to do, she did it with her might. She attacked her écrevisses with the same jubilant abandon with which she had executed her bewildering single-step. She devoured them with an energy, an enthusiasm, a thoroughness, that it was invigorating to witness; smacking her lips, and smiling, and, from time to time, between the mouthfuls, breathing soft little interjections of content. When the last pink shell was emptied, she threw herself back, and sighed, and explained, with delectable unconsciousness, "I was hungry." But at my venturing to protest, "Not really?" she broke into mirthful laughter, and added, "At least, I had the appearance." Meanwhile, I must not fail to mention, she had done abundant honour to her share of a bottle of chablis.

Don't be horrified—haven't the Germans, who ought to know, a proverb that recommends it? "Wein auf Bier, das rath' ich Dir."

I have said that none of us mourned the absence of a soul in P'tit-Bleu. Nevertheless, as I looked at her to-night, and realised what a bright, joyous, good-humoured little thing she was, how healthy, and natural, and even, in a way, innocent she was, I suddenly felt a curious depression. She was all this, and yet... For just a moment, perhaps, I did vaguely mourn the lack of something. Oh, she was well enough for the present; she was joyous, and good-humoured, and innocent in a way; she was young and pretty, and the world smiled upon her. But—for the future? When it occurred to me to think of her future—of what it must almost certainly be like, of what she must almost inevitably become—I confess my jaw dropped, and the salt of our banquet lost its savour.

"What's the matter? Why do you look at me like that?" P'tit-Bleu demanded.

So I had to pull myself up and be jolly again. It was not altogether difficult. In the early twenties, troublesome reflections are easily banished, I believe; and I had a lively comrade.

After her crayfish were disposed of, P'tit-Bleu called for coffee and lit a cigarette. And then, between whiffs and sips, she prattled gaily of the subject which, of all subjects, she was probably best qualified to treat, and which assuredly, for the time being, possessed most interest for her listener—P'tit-Bleu. She told me, as it were, the story of her birth, parentage, life, and exploits. It was the simplest story, the commonest story. Her mother (*la recherche de la paternité est interdite*), her mother had died when she was sixteen, and Jeanne (that was her baptismal name, Jeanne Mérois) had gone to work in the shop of a dressmaker, where, sewing hard from eight in the morning till seven at night, with an hour's intermission at noon, she could earn, in good seasons, as much as two-francs-fifty a day. Two and a half francs a day—say twelve shillings a week—in good seasons; and one must eat, and lodge, and clothe one's body, and pay one's laundress, in good seasons and in bad. It scarcely satisfied her aspirations, and she took to dancing. Now she danced three nights a week at Bullier, and during the day gave lessons in her art to a score of pupils, by which means she contrived to keep the wolf at a respectful distance from her door. "Tiens, here's my card," she concluded, and handed me an oblong bit of pasteboard, on which was printed, "P'tit-Bleu, Professeur de Danse, 22, Rue Monsieur le Prince."

"And you have no lover?" questioned I.

She flashed a look upon me that was quite inexpressibly arch, and responded instantly, with the charmingest little pout, "But yes—since I'm supping with him."

During the winter that followed, P'tit-Bleu and I supped together somewhat frequently. She was a mere little animal, she had no soul; but she was the nicest little animal, and she had instincts. She was more than good-natured, she was kind-hearted; and, according to her unconventional standards, she was conscientious. It would have amused and touched you, for example, if you had been taking her about, to notice her intense solicitude lest you should conduct her entertainment upon a scale too lavish, her deprecating frowns, her expostulations, her restraining hand laid on your arm. And the ordinary run of Latin Quarter girls derive an incommunicable rapture from seeing their cavaliers wantonly, purposelessly prodigal. With her own funds, on the contrary, P'tit-Bleu was free-handed to a fault: Mimi and Zizette knew whom to go to, when they were hard-up. Neither did she confine her benefactions to gifts of money, nor limit their operation to her particular sex. More than one impecunious student owed it to her skilful needle that his clothes were whole, and his linen maintained in a habitable state. "Fie, Chalks! Your coat is torn, there are three buttons off your waistcoat, and your cuffs are frayed to a point that is disgraceful. I'll come round to-morrow afternoon, and mend them for you." And when poor Berthe Dumours was turned out of the hospital, in the dead of winter, half-cured, and without a penny in her purse, who took her in, and nursed her, and provided for her during her convalescence?

Oh, she was a good little thing. "P'tit-Bleu's all right. There's nothing the matter with P'tit-Bleu," was Chalks's method of phrasing it.

At the same time, she could be trying, she could be exasperating. And she had a temper—a temper. What she made me suffer in the way of jealousy, during that winter, it would be gruesome to recount. She enjoyed an exceeding great popularity in the Quarter; she was much run after. It were futile to pretend that she hadn't her caprices. And she held herself free as air. She would call no man master.

You might take what she would give, and welcome; but you must claim nothing as your due. You mustn't presume upon the fact that she was supping with you to-night, to complain if she should sup tomorrow with another. Her concession of a privilege did not by any means imply that it was exclusive. She would endure no exactions, no control or interference, no surveillance, above all, no reproaches. Mercy, how angry she would become if I ventured any, how hoighty-toighty and unapproachable.

"You imagine that I am your property? Did you invent me? One would say you held a Government patent. All rights reserved! Thank you. You fancy perhaps that Paris is Constantinople? Ah, mais non!"

She had a temper and a flow of language. There were points you couldn't touch without precipitating hail and lightning.

Thus my winter was far from a tranquil one, and before it was half over I had three grey hairs. Honey and wormwood, happiness and heartburn, reconciliations and frantic little tiffs, carried us blithely on to Mi-Carême, when things reached a crisis....

Mi-Carême fell midway in March that year: a velvety, sweet, sunlit day, Spring stirring in her sleep. P'tit-Bleu and I had spent the day together, in the crowded, crowded streets. We had visited the Boulevards, of course, to watch the triumph of the Queen of Washerwomen; we had pelted everybody with confetti; and we had been pelted so profusely in return, that there were confetti in our boots, in our pockets, down our necks, and numberless confetti clung in the black meshes of P'tit-Bleu's hair, like little pink, blue, and yellow stars. But all day long something in P'tit-Bleu's manner, something in her voice, her smile, her carriage, had obscurely troubled me; something not easy to take hold of, something elusive, unformulable, but disquieting. A certain indefinite aloofness, perhaps; an accentuated independence; as if she were preoccupied with secret thoughts, with intentions, feelings, that she would not let me share.

And then, at night, we went to the Opera Ball.

P'tit-Bleu was dressed as an Odalisque: a tiny round Turkish cap set jauntily sidewise on her head, a short Turkish jacket, both coat and jacket jingling and glittering with sequins; a long veil of gauze, wreathed like a scarf round her shoulders; then baggy Turkish trousers of blue silk, and scarlet Turkish slippers. Oh, she was worth seeing; I was proud to have her on my arm. Her black crinkling hair, her dancing eyes, her eager face and red smiling mouth—the Sultan himself might have envied me such a houri. And many, in effect, were the envious glances that we encountered, as we made our way into the great brilliantly lighted ball-room, and moved hither and thither among the Harlequins and Columbines, the Pierrots, the Toréadors, the Shepherdesses and Vivandières, the countless fantastic masks, by whom the place was peopled. P'tit-Bleu had a *loup* of black velvet, which sometimes she wore, and sometimes gave to me to carry for her. I don't know when she looked the more dangerous, when she had it on, and her eyes glimmered mysteriously through its peepholes, or when she had it off.

Many were the envious glances that we encountered, and presently I became aware that one individual was following us about: a horrid, glossy creature, in a dress suit, with a top-hat that was much too shiny, and a hugh waxed moustache that he kept twirling invidiously: an undersized, dark, Hebraic-featured man, screamingly "rasta'." Whithersoever we turned, he hovered annoyingly near to us, and ogled P'tit-Bleu under my very beard. This was bad enough; but—do sorrows ever come as single spies?—conceive my emotions, if you please, when, by-and-by, suspicion hardened into certitude that P'tit-Bleu was not merely getting a vainglorious gratification from his attentions, but that she was positively playing up to them, encouraging him to persevere! She chattered—to me, indeed, but at him— with a vivacity there was no misconstruing; laughed noisily, fluttered her fan, flirted her veil, donned and doffed her loup, and, I daresay, when my back was turned, exchanged actual eye-shots with the brute.... In due time quadrilles were organised, and P'tit-Bleu led a set. The glossy interloper was one of the admiring circle that surrounded her. Ugh! his complacent, insinuating smile, the conquering air with which he twirled his moustachios. And P'tit-Bleu.... When, at the finish, she sprang up, after her *grand écart*, what do you suppose she did?... The brazen little minx, instead of rejoining *me*, slipped her arm through *his*, and went tripping off with him to the supper-room.

Oh, the night I passed, the night of anguish! The visions that tortured me, as I tramped my floor! The delirious revenges that I plotted, and gloated over in anticipation! She had left me—the mockery of it!—she had left me her loup, her little black velvet loup, with its empty eye-holes, and its horribly reminiscent smell. Everything P'tit-Bleu owned was scented with peau-d'.spagne. I wreaked my fury upon that loup, I promise you. I smote it with my palm, I ground it under my heel, I tore it limb from limb, I called it all manner of abusive names. Early in the morning I was at P'tit-Bleu's house; but the concierge grunted, "Pas rentrée." Oh, the coals thereof are coals of fire. I returned to her house a dozen times that day, and at length, towards nightfall, found her in. We had a stormy session, but, of course, the last word of it was hers: still, for all slips, she was one of Eve's family. Of course she justified herself, and put me in the wrong. I went away, vowing I would never, never, never see her again. "Va! Ça m'est bien égal," she capped the climax by calling after me. Oh, youth! Oh, storm and stress! And to think that one lives to laugh at its memory.

For the rest of that season, P'tit-Bleu and I remained at daggers drawn. In June I left town for the summer; and then one thing and another happened, and kept me away till after Christmas.

When I got back, amongst the many pieces of news that I found waiting for me, there was one that affected P'tit-Bleu.

"P'tit-Bleu," I was told, "is 'collée' with an Englishman—but a grey-beard, mon cher—a gaga—an Englishman old enough to be her grandfather."

A stolid, implicit cynicism, I must warn you, was the mode of the Quarter. The student who did not wish to be contemned for a sentimentalist, dared never hesitate to believe an evil report, nor to put the worst possible construction upon all human actions. Therefore, when I was apprised by common rumour that during the dead season P'tit-Bleu (for considerations fiscal, *bien entendu*) had gone to live "collée" with an Englishman old enough to be her grandfather—though, as it turned out, the story was the sheerest fabrication—it never entered my head to doubt it.

At the same time, I confess, I could not quite share the humour of my compeers, who regarded the circumstance as a stupendous joke. On the contrary, I was shocked and sickened. I shouldn't have imagined her capable of that. She was a mere little animal; she had no soul; she was bound, in the nature of things, to go from bad to worse, as I had permitted myself, indeed, to admonish her, in the last conversation we had had. "Mark my words, you will go from bad to worse." But I had thought her such a nice little animal; in my secret heart, I had hoped that her progress would be slow—even, faintly, that Providence might let something happen to arrest it, to divert it. And now....!

As a matter of fact, Providence *had* let something happen to divert it; and that something was this very relation of hers with an old Englishman, in which the scandal-lovers of the Latin Quarter were determined to see neither more nor less than a mercenary "collage." The diversion in question, however, was an extremely gradual process. As yet, it is pretty certain, P'tit-Bleu herself had never so much as dreamed that any diversion was impending.

But she knew that her relation with the Englishman was an innocent relation; and of its innocence, I am glad to be able to record, she succeeded in convincing one, at least, of her friends, tolerably early in the game.

In the teeth of my opposition, and at the expense of her own pride, she forced an explanation, which, I am glad to say, convinced me.

I had just passed her and her Englishman in the street. They were crossing the Boulevard St. Michel, and she was hanging on his arm, looking up into his face, and laughing. She wore a broad-brimmed black hat, with a red ribbon in it, and a knot of red ribbon at her throat; there was a lovely suggestion of the same colour in her cheeks; and never had her eyes gleamed with sincerer fun.

I assure you, the sensation this spectacle afforded me amounted to a physical pain—the disgust, the anger. If she could laugh like that, how little could she feel her position! The hardened shamelessness of it!

Turning from her to her companion, I own I was surprised and puzzled. He was a tall, spare old man, not a grey-beard, but a white-beard, and he had thin snow-white hair. He was dressed neatly indeed, but the very reverse of sumptuously. His black overcoat was threadbare, his carefully polished boots were patched. Yet, everybody averred, it was his affluence that had attracted her; she had taken up with him during the dead season, because she had been "à sec." A detail that did nothing to relieve my perplexity was the character of his face. Instead of the florid concupiscent face, with coarse lips and fiery eye-balls, I had instinctively expected, I saw a thin, pale face, with mild, melancholy eyes, a gentle face, a refined face, rather a weak face, certainly the very last face the situation called for. He *was* a beast, of course, but he didn't look like a beast. He looked like a gentleman, a broken-down, forlorn old gentleman, singularly astray from his proper orbit.

They were crossing the Boulevard St. Michel as I was leaving the Café Vachette; and at the corner of the Rue des Ecoles we came front to front. P'tit-Bleu glanced up; her eyes brightened, she gave a little start, and was plainly for stopping to shake hands. I cut her dead....

I cut her dead, and held my course serenely down the Boulevard—though I'm not sure my heart wasn't pounding. But I could lay as unction to my soul the consciousness of having done the appropriate thing, of having marked my righteous indignation.

In a minute, however, I heard the pat-pat of rapid footsteps on the pavement behind me, and my name being called. I hurried on, careful not to turn my head. But, at Cluny, P'tit-Bleu arrived abreast of me.

"I want to speak to you," she gasped, out of breath from running.

I shrugged my shoulders.

"Will you tell me why you cut me like that just now?"

"If you don't know, I doubt if I could make you understand," I answered, with an air of, imperial disdain.

"You bear me a grudge, hein? For what I did last March? Well, then, you are right. There. I was abominable. But I have been sorry, and I ask your pardon. Now will you let bygones be bygones? Will you forgive me?"

"Oh," I said, "don't try to play the simpleton with me. You are perfectly well aware that isn't why I cut you."

"But why, then?" cried she, admirably counterfeiting (as I took for granted) a look and accent of bewilderment.

I walked on without speaking. She kept beside me.

"But why, then? If it isn't that, what is it?"

"Oh, bah!"

"I insist upon your telling me. Tell me."

"Very good, then. I don't care to know a girl who lives 'collée' with a gaga," I said, brutally.

P'tit-Bleu flushed suddenly, and faced me with blazing eyes.

"Comment done! You believe that?" she cried.

"Pooh!" said I.

"Oh, mais non, mais non, mais non, alors! You don't believe that?"

"You pay me a poor compliment. Why should you expect me to be ignorant of a thing the whole Quarter knows?"

"Oh, the whole Quarter! What does that matter to me, your Quarter? Those nasty little students! C'est de la crasse, quoi! They may believe—they may say—what they like. Oh, ça m'est bien égal!" with a shake of the head and a skyward gesture. "But you—but my friends! Am I that sort of girl? Answer."

"There's only one sort of girl in the precincts ot this University," declared her disenchanted interlocutor. "You're all of one pattern. The man's an ass who expects any good from any of you. Don't pose as better than the others. You're all a—un tas de saletés. I'm sick and tired of the whole sordid, squalid lot of you. I should be greatly obliged, now, if you would have the kindness to leave me. Go back to your gaga. He'll be impatient waiting."

That speech, I fancied, would rid me of her. But no.

"You are trying to make me angry, aren't you? But I refuse to leave you till you have admitted that you are wrong," she persisted. "It's an outrageous slander. Monsieur Long (that is his name, Monsieur Long), he lives in the same house with me, on the same landing; et voilà tout. Dame! Can I prevent him? Am I the landlord? And, for that, they say I'm 'collée' with him. I don't care what they say. But you! I swear to you it is an infamous lie. Will you come home with me now, and see?"

"Oh, that's mere quibbling. You go with him everywhere, you dine with him, you are never seen without him."

"Dieu de Dieu!" wailed P'tit-Bleu. "How shall I convince you? He is my neighbour. Is it forbidden to know one's neighbours? I swear to you, I give you my word of honour, it is nothing else. How to make you believe me?"

"Well, my dear," said I, "if you wish me to believe you, break with him. Chuck him up. Drop his acquaintance. Nobody in his senses will believe you so long as you go trapesing about the Quarter with him."

"Oh, but no," she cried, "I can't drop his acquaintance."

"Ah, there it is," cried I.

"There are reasons. There are reasons why I can't, why I mustn't."

"I thought so."

"Ah, voyons!" she broke out, losing patience.

"Will you not believe my word of honour? Will you force me to tell you things that don't concern you—that I have no right to tell? Well, then, listen. I cannot drop his acquaintance, because—this is a secret—he would die of shame if he thought I had betrayed it—you will never breathe it to a soul—because I have discovered that he has a—a vice, a weakness. No—but listen. He is an Englishman, a painter. Oh, a painter of great talent; a painter who has exposed at the Salon—quoi! A painter who is known in his country. On a même parlé de lui dans les journaux; voilà! But look. He has a vice. He has half ruined, half killed himself with a drug. Yes—opium. Oh, but wait, wait. I will tell you. He came to live in our house last July, in the room opposite mine. When we met, on the landing, in the staircase, he took off his hat, and we passed the bonjour. Oh, he is a gentleman; he has been well brought up. From that we arrived at speaking together a little, and then at visiting. It was the dead season, I had no affairs. I would sit in his room in the afternoon, and we would chat. Oh, he is a fine talker. But, though he had canvases, colours, all that is needed for painting, he never painted. He would only talk, talk. I said, 'But you ought to paint.' He said always, 'Yes, I must begin something to-morrow.' Always to-morrow. And then I discovered what it was. He took opium. He spent all his money for opium. And when he had taken his opium he would not work, he would only talk, talk, talk, and then sleep, sleep. You think that is well—hein? That a painter of talent should do no work, but spend all his money for a drug, for a poison, and then say, 'To-morrow'. You think I could sit still and see him commit these follies under my eyes and say nothing, do nothing? Ruin his brain, his health, his career, and waste all his money, for that drug? Oh, mais non. I made him the sermon. I said, 'You know it is very bad, that which you are doing there.' I scolded him. I said, 'But I forbid you to do that—do you understand? I forbid it.' I went with him everywhere, I gave him all my time; and when he would take his drug I would annoy him, I would make a scene, I would shame him. Well, in the end, I have acquired an influence over him. He has submitted himself to me. He is really trying to break the habit. I keep all his money. I give him his doses. I regulate them, I diminish them. The consequence is, I make him work. I give him one very small dose in the morning to begin the day. Then I will give him no more till he has done so much work. You see? Tu te figures que je suis sa maîtresse? Je suis plutôt sa nounou—va! Je suis sa caissière. And he is painting a great picture—you will see. Eh bien, how can I give up his acquaintance? Can I let him relapse, as he would do to-morrow without me, into his bad habit?"

I was walking with long strides, P'tit-Bleu tripping at my elbow; and before her story was finished we had left the Boulevard behind us, and reached the middle of the Pont St. Michel. There, I don't know why, we halted, and stood looking off towards Notre-Dame. The grim grey front of the Cathedral glowed softly amethystine in the afternoon sun, and the sky was infinitely deep and blue above it. One could be intensely conscious of the splendid penetrating beauty of this picture, without, somehow, giving the less attention to what P'tit-Bleu was saying. She talked swiftly, eagerly, with constantly changing, persuasive intonations, with little brief pauses, hesitations, with many gestures, with much play of eyes and face. When she had done, I waited a moment. Then, grudgingly, "Well," I began, "if what you tell me is true ——"

"*If* it is true!" P'tit-Bleu cried, with sudden fierceness. "Do you dare to say you doubt it?"

And she gazed intently, fiercely, into my eyes, challenging me, as it were, to give her the lie.

Before that gaze my eyes dropped, abashed.

"No—I don't doubt it," I faltered, "I believe you. And—and allow me to say that you are a—a damned decent little girl."

Poor P'tit-Bleu! How shall I tell you the rest of her story—the story of those long years of love and sacrifice and devotion, and of continual discouragement, disappointment, with his death at the end of them, and her disappearance?

In the beginning she herself was very far from realising what she had undertaken, what had befallen her. To exercise a little friendly supervision over her neighbour's addiction to opium, to husband his money for him, and spur him on to work—it seemed a mere incident in her life, an affair by the way. But it became her exclusive occupation, her whole life's chief concern. Little by little, one after the other, she put aside all her former interests, thoughts, associations, dropped all her former engagements, to give herself as completely to caring for, guarding, guiding poor old Edward Long, as if she had been a mother, and he her helpless child.

Throughout that first winter, indeed, she continued to dance at Bullier, continued to instruct her corps of pupils, and continued even occasionally, though much less frequently than of old time, to be seen at the Vachette, or to sup with a friend at the Gambrinus. But from day to day Monsieur Edouard (he had soon ceased to be Monsieur Long, and become Monsieur Edouard) absorbed more and more of her time and attention; and when the spring came she suddenly burned her ships.

You must understand that she had one pertinacious adversary in her efforts to wean him of his vice. Not an avowed adversary, for he professed the most earnest wish that she might be successful; but an adversary who was eternally putting spokes in her wheel, all the same. Yes, Monsieur Edouard himself. Never content with the short rations to which she had condemned him, he was perpetually on the watch for a chance to elude her vigilance; she was perpetually discovering that he had somehow contrived to lay in secret supplies. And every now and again, openly defying her authority, he would go off for a grand debauch. Then her task of reducing his daily portion to a minimum must needs be begun anew. Well, when the spring came, and the Salon opened, where his picture (*her* picture?) had been received and very fairly hung, they went together to the Vernissage. And there he met a whole flock of English folk—artists and critics, who had "just run over for the show, you know"—with whom he was acquainted; and they insisted on carrying him away with them to lunch at the Ambassadeurs.

I, too, had assisted at the Vernissage; and when I left it, I found P'tit-Bleu seated alone under the trees in the Champs-Elysées. She had on a brilliant spring toilette, with a hat and a sunshade.... Oh, my dear! It is not to be denied that P'tit-Bleu had the courage of her tastes. But her face was pale, and her lips were drawn down, and her eyes looked strained and anxious.

"What's the row?" I asked.

And she told me how she had been abandoned—"plantée là" was her expression—and of course I invited her to lunch with me. But she scarcely relished the repast. "Pourvu qu'il ne fasse pas de bêtises!" was her refrain.

She returned rather early to the Rue Monsieur le Prince, to see if he had come home; but he hadn't. Nor did he come home that night, nor the next day, nor the next. At the week's end, though, he came: dirty, haggard, tremulous, with red eyes, and nude—yes, nude—of everything save his shirt and trousers! He had borrowed a sovereign from one of his London friends, and when that was gone, he had pledged or sold everything but his shirt and trousers—hat, boots, coat, everything. It was an equally haggard and red-eyed P'tit-Bleu who faced him on his reappearance. And I've no doubt she gave him a specimen of her eloquence. "You figure to yourself that this sort of thing amuses me, hein? Here are six good days and nights that I haven't been able to sleep or rest."

Explaining the case to me, she said, "Ah, what I suffered! I could never have believed that I cared so much for him. But—what would you?—one attaches oneself, you know. Ah, what I suffered! The anxiety, the terrors! I expected to hear of him run over in the streets. Well, now, I must make an end of this business. I'm going to take him away. So long as he remains in Paris, where there are chemists who will sell him that filthiness (cette crasse) it is hopeless. No sooner do I get my house of cards nicely built up, than—piff!— something happens to knock it over. I am going to take him down into the country, far from any town, far from the railway, where I can guard him better. I know a place, a farmhouse, near Villiers-St.-Jacques, where we can get board. He has a little income, which reaches him every three months from England. Oh, very little, but if I am careful of it, it will pay our way. And then —I will make him work."

"Oh, no," I protested. "You're not going to leave the Quarter." And I'm ashamed to acknowledge, I laboured hard to dissuade her. "Think how we'll miss you. Think how you'll bore yourself. And anyhow, he's not worth it. And besides, you won't succeed. A man who has an appetite for opium will get it, coûte que coûte. He'd walk twenty miles in bare feet to get it." This was the argument that I repeated in a dozen different paraphrases. You see, I hadn't realised yet that it didn't matter an atom whether she succeeded, or whether he was worth it. He was a mere instrument in the hands of Providence. Let her succeed or let her fail in keeping him from opium: the important thing… how shall I put it? This little Undine had risen out of the black waters of the Latin Quarter, and attached herself to a mortal. What is it that love gains for Undines?

"Que veux-tu?" cried P'tit-Bleu. "I am fond of him. I can't bear to see him ruining himself. I must do what I can."

And the Quarter said, "Ho-ho! You chaps who didn't believe it was a 'collage'. He-he! What do you say now? She's chucked up everything, to go and live in the country with him."

In August or September I ran down to the farmhouse near Villiers-St.-Jacques, and passed a week with them. I found a mightily changed Monsieur Edouard, and a curiously changed P'tit-Bleu, as well. He was fat and rosy, he who had been so thin and white. And she—she was *grave*. Yes, P'tit-Bleu was grave: sober, staid, serious. And her impish, mocking black eyes shone with a strange, serious, calm light.

Monsieur Edouard (with whom my relations had long before this become confidential) drew me apart, and told me he was having an exceedingly bad time of it.

"She's really too absurd, you know. She's a martinet, a tyrant. Opium is to me what tobacco is to you, and does me no more harm. I need it for my work. Oh, in moderation; of course one can be excessive. Yet she refuses to let me have a tenth of my proper quantity. And besides, how utterly senseless it is, keeping me down here in the country. I'm dying of ennui. There's not a person I can have any sort of intellectual sympathy with, for miles in every direction. An artist needs the stimulus of contact with his fellows. It's indispensable. If she'd only let me run up to Paris for a day or two at a time, once a month say. Couldn't you persuade her to let me go back with you? She's the most awful screw, you know. It's the French lower-middle-class parsimony. I'm never allowed to have twopence in my pocket. Yet whose money is it? Where does it come from? I really can't think why I submit, why I don't break away from her, and follow my own wishes. But the poor little thing is fond of me; she attached herself to me. I don't know what would become of her if I cast her off. Oh, don't fancy that I don't appreciate her. Her intentions are excellent. But she lacks wisdom, and she enjoys the exercise of power. I wish you'd speak with her."

P'tit-Bleu also drew me apart.

"Please don't call me P'tit-Bleu any more. Call me Jeanne. I have put all that behind me—all that P'tit-Bleu signifies. I hate to think of it, to be reminded of it. I should like to forget it."

When I had promised not to call her P'tit-Bleu any more, she went on, replying to my questions, to tell me of their life.

"Of course, everybody thinks I am his mistress. You can't convince them I'm not. But that's got to be endured. For the rest, all is going well. You see how he is improved. I give him fifteen drops of laudanum, morning, noon, and night. Fifteen drops—it is nothing, I could take it myself, and never know it. And he used to drink off an ounce—an ounce, mon cher—at a time, and then want more at the end of an hour. Yes! Oh, he complains, he complains of everything, he frets, he is not contented. But he has not walked twenty miles in bare feet, as you said he would. And he is working. You will see his pictures."

"And you—how do you pass your time? What do you do?"

"I pose for him a good deal. And then I have much sewing to do. I take in sewing for Madame Deschamps, the Deputy's wife, to help make the ends meet. And then I read. Madame Deschamps lends me books."

"And I suppose you're bored to death?"

"Oh, no, I am not bored. I am happy. I never was really happy—dans le temps."

They were living in a very plain way indeed. You know what French farmhouses are apt to be. His whole income was under a hundred pounds a year; and out of that (and the trifle she earned by needlework) his canvases, colours, brushes, frames, had to be paid for, as well as his opium, and their food, clothing, everything. But P'tit-Bleu—Jeanne—with that"lower-middle-class parsimony" of hers, managed somehow. Jeanne! In putting off the name, she had put off also, in great measure, the attributes of P'tit-Bleu; she had become Jeanne in nature. She was grave, she was quiet. She wore the severest black frocks—she made them herself. And I never once noticed the odour of peau-d'.spagne, from the beginning to the end of my visit. But—shall I own it? Jeanne was certainly the more estimable of the two women, but shall I own that I found her far less exciting as a comrade than P'tit-Bleu had been? She was good, but she wasn't very lively or very amusing.

P'tit-Bleu, the heroine of Bullier, that lover of noisy pleasure, of daring toilettes, of risky perfumes, of écrevisses and chablis, of all the rush and dissipation of the Boul' Miche and the Luxembourg, quietly settling down into Jeanne of the home-made frocks, in a rough French farmhouse, to a diet of veal and lentils, lentils and veal, seven times a week, and no other pastime in life than the devoted, untiring nursing of an ungrateful old English opium-eater—here was variation under domestication with a vengeance.

And on Sunday… P'tit-Bleu went twice to church!

About ten days after my return to Paris, there came a rat-ta-ta-tat at my door, and P'tit-Bleu walked in—pale, with wide eyes. "I don't know how he has contrived it, but he must have got some money somewhere, and walked to the railway, and come to town. Anyhow, here are three days that he has disappeared. What to do? What to do?" She was in a deplorable state of mind, poor thing, and I scarcely knew how to help her. I proposed that we should take counsel with a Commissary of Police. But when that functionary discovered that she was neither the wife nor daughter of the missing man, he smiled, and remarked, "It is not our business to recover ladies' protectors for them." P'tit-Bleu walked the streets in quest of him, all day long and very nearly all night long too, for close upon a fortnight. In the end, she met him on the quays—dazed, half-imbecile, and again nude of everything save his shirt and trousers. So, again, having nicely built up her house of cards—piff!

—something had happened to topple it over.

"Let him go to the devil his own way," said I. "Really, he's unworthy of your pains."

"No, I can't leave him. You see, I'm fond of him," said she.

He, however, positively refused to return to the country. "The fact is," he explained, "I ought to go to London. Yes, it will be well for me to pass the winter in London. I should like to have a show there, a one-man show, you know. I dare say I could sell a good many pictures, and get orders for portraits." So they went to London. In the spring I received a letter from P'tit-Bleu—a letter full of orthographic faults, if you like—but a letter that I treasure. Here's a translation of it:

"My dear Friend,—I have hesitated much before taking my pen in hand to write to you. But I have no one else to turn to. We have had a dreadful winter. Owing to my ignorance of the language one speaks in this dirty town, I have not been able to exercise over Monsieur Edouard that supervision of which he has need. In consequence, he has given himself up to the evil habit which you know, as never before. Every penny, every last sou, which he could command, has been spent for that detestable filth. Many times we have passed whole days without eating, no, not the end of a crust. He has no desire to eat when he has had his dose. We are living in a slum of the most disgusting, in the quarter of London they call Soho. Everything we have, save the bare necessary of covering, has been put with the lender-on-pledges. Yesterday I found a piece of one shilling in the street. That, however, I have been forced to dispense for opium, because, when he has had such large quantities, he would die or go mad if suddenly deprived.

"I have addressed myself to his family, but without effect. They refuse to recognise me. Everybody here, of course, figures to himself that I am his mistress. He has two brothers, one of the army, one an advocate. I have besieged them in vain. They say, 'We have done for him all that is possible. We can do no more. He has exhausted our patience. Now that he has gone a step farther, and, in his age, disgraced himself by living with a mistress, as well as besotting himself with opium, we wash our hands of him for good.' And yet, I cannot leave him, because I know, without me, he would kill himself within the month, by his excesses. To his sisters, both of whom are married and ladies of the world, I have appealed with equal results. They refuse to regard me otherwise than as his mistress. But I cannot bear to see that great man, with that mind, that talent, doing himself to death. And when he is not under the influence of his drug, who is so great? Who has the wit, the wisdom, the heart, the charm, of Monsieur Edouard? Who can paint like him?

"My dear, as a last resource, I take up my pen to ask you for assistance. If you could see him your heart would be moved. He is so thin, so thin, and his face has become *blue*, yes, blue, like the face of a dead man. Help me to save him from himself. If you can send me a note of five hundred francs, I can pay off our indebtedness here, and bring him back to France, where, in a sane country, far from a town, again I can reduce him to a few drops of laudanum a day, and again see him in health and at work. That which it costs me to make this request of you, I have not the words to tell you. But, at the end ot my forces, having no other means, no other support, I confide myself to your well-tried amity.

"I give you a good kiss. Jeanne."

If the reading of this letter brought a lump into my throat and something like tears into my eyes—if I hastened to a banker's, and sent P'tit-Bleu the money she asked for, by telegraph—if I reproached her bitterly and sincerely for not having applied to me long before,—I hope you will believe that it wasn't for the sake of Monsieur Edouard.

They established themselves at St. Etienne, a hamlet on the coast of Normandy, to be farther from Paris. Dieppe was their nearest town. They lived at St.-Etienne for nearly three years. But, periodically, when she had got her house of cards nicely built up—piff!—he would walk into Dieppe.

He walked into Dieppe one day in the autumn of 1885, and it took her a week to find him. He was always ill, after one of his grand debauches. This time he was worse than he had ever been before. I can imagine the care with which she nursed him, her anxious watching by his bedside, her prayers, her hopes, the blankness when he died.

She came back to Paris, and called three times at my lodgings. But I was in England, and didn't receive the notes she left till nearly six months afterwards. I have never seen her since, never heard from her.

What has become of her? It is not pleasant to conjecture. Of course, after his death, she ought to have died too. But the Angel of this Life,

"Whose care is lest men see too much at once,"

couldn't permit any such satisfying termination. So she has simply disappeared, and, in the flesh, may have come to... one would rather not conjecture. All the same, I can't believe that in the spirit she will have made utter shipwreck. I can't believe that nothing permanent was won by those long years of love and pain. Her house of cards was toppled over, as often as she built it up; but perhaps she was all the while building another house, a house not made with hands, a house, a temple, indestructible.

Poor P'tit-Bleu!

THE HOUSE OF EULALIE

I t was a pretty little house, in very charming country—in an untravelled corner of Normandy, near the sea; a country of orchards and colza fields, of soft green meadows where cattle browsed, and of deep elm-shaded lanes.

One was rather surprised to see this little house just here, for all the other houses in the neighbourhood were rude farm-houses or labourers' cottages; and this was a coquettish little chalet, white-walled, with slim French windows, and balconies of twisted ironwork, and Venetian blinds: a gay little pleasure-house, standing in a bright little garden, among rosebushes, and parterres of geraniums, and smooth stretches of greensward. Beyond the garden there was an orchard—rows and couples of old gnarled apple-trees, bending towards one another like fantastic figures arrested in the middle of a dance. Then, turning round, you looked over feathery colza fields and yellow corn fields, a mile away, to the sea, and to a winding perspective of white cliffs, which the sea bathed in transparent greens and purples, luminous shadows of its own nameless hues.

A board attached to the wall confirmed, in roughly painted characters, the information I had had from an agent in Dieppe. The house was to let; and I had driven out—a drive of two long hours—to inspect it. Now I stood on the doorstep and rang the bell. It was a big bell, hung in the porch, with a pendent handle of bronze, wrought in the semblance of a rope and tassel. Its voice would carry far on that still country air.

It carried, at any rate, as far as a low thatched farm-house, a hundred yards down the road. Presently a man and a woman came out of the farm-house, gazed for an instant in my direction, and then moved towards me: an old brown man, an old grey woman, the man in corduroys, the woman wearing a neat white cotton cap and a blue apron, both moving with the burdened gait of peasants.

"You are Monsieur and Madame Leroux?" I asked, when we had accomplished our preliminary good-days; and I explained that I had come from the agent in Dieppe to look over their house. For the rest, they must have been expecting me; the agent had said that he would let them know.

But, to my perplexity, this business-like announcement seemed somehow to embarrass them; even, I might have thought, to agitate, to distress them. They lifted up their worn old faces, and eyed me anxiously. They exchanged anxious glances with each other. The woman clasped her hands, nervously working her fingers. The man hesitated and stammered a little, before he was able to repeat vaguely, "You have come to look over the house, Monsieur?"

"Surely," I said, "the agent has written to you? I understood from him that you would expect me at this hour to-day."

"Oh yes," the man admitted, "we were expecting you." But he made no motion to advance matters. He exchanged another anxious glance with his wife. She gave her head a sort of helpless nod, and looked down.

"You see, Monsieur," the man began, as if he were about to elucidate the situation, "you see—" But then he faltered, frowning at the air, as one at a loss for words.

"The house is already let, perhaps?" suggested I.

"No, the house is not let," said he.

"You had better go and fetch the key," his wife said at last, in a dreary way, still looking down.

He trudged heavily back to the farm-house. While he was gone we stood by the door in silence, the woman always nervously working the fingers of her clasped hands. I tried, indeed, to make a little conversation: I ventured something about the excellence of the site, the beauty of the view. She replied with a murmur of assent, civilly but wearily; and I did not feel encouraged to persist.

By-and-by her husband rejoined us, with the key; and they began silently to lead me through the house.

There were two pretty drawing-rooms on the ground floor, a pretty dining-room, and a delightful kitchen, with a broad hearth of polished red bricks, a tiled chimney, and shining copper pots and pans. The drawing-rooms and the dining-room were pleasantly furnished in a light French fashion, and their windows opened to the sun and to the fragrance and greenery of the garden. I expressed a good deal of admiration; whereupon, little by little, the manner of my conductors changed. From constrained, depressed, it became responsive; even, in the end, effusive. They met my exclamations with smiles, my inquiries with voluble eager answers. But it remained an agitated manner, the manner of people who were shaken by an emotion. Their old hands trembled as they opened the doors for me or drew up the blinds; their voices trembled. There was something painful in their very smiles, as if these were but momentary ripples on the surface of a trouble.

"Ah," I said to myself, "they are hard-pressed for money. They have put their whole capital into this house, very likely. They are excited by the prospect of securing a tenant."

"Now, if you please, Monsieur, we will go upstairs, and see the bedrooms," the old man said.

The bedrooms were airy, cheerful rooms, gaily papered, with chintz curtains and the usual French bedroom furniture. One of them exhibited signs of being actually lived in; there were things about it, personal things, a woman's things. It was the last room we visited, a front room, looking off to the sea. There were combs and brushes on the toilet-table; there were pens, an inkstand, and a portfolio on the writing-desk; there were books in the bookcase. Framed photographs stood on the mantelpiece. In the closet dresses were suspended, and shoes and slippers were primly ranged on the floor. The bed was covered with a counterpane of blue silk; a crucifix hung on the wall above it; beside it there was a *prie-dieu*, with a little porcelain holy-water vase.

"Oh," I exclaimed, turning to Monsieur and Madame Leroux, "this room is occupied?"

Madame Leroux did not appear to hear me. Her eyes were fixed in a dull stare before her, her lips were parted slightly. She looked tired, as if she would be glad when our tour through the house was finished. Monsieur Leroux threw his hand up towards the ceiling in an odd gesture, and said, "No, the room is not occupied at present."

We went back downstairs, and concluded an agreement. I was to take the house for the summer. Madame Leroux would cook for me. Monsieur Leroux would drive into Dieppe on Wednesday to fetch me and my luggage out.

On Wednesday we had been driving for something like half an hour without speaking, when all at once Leroux said to me, "That room, Monsieur, the room you thought was occupied——"

"Yes?" I questioned, as he paused.

"I have a proposition to make," said he. He spoke, as it seemed to me, half shyly, half doggedly, gazing the while at the ears of his horse.

"What is it?" I asked.

"If you will leave that room as it is, with the things in it, we will make a reduction in the rent. If you will let us keep it as it is?" he repeated, with a curious pleading intensity. "You are alone. The house will be big enough for you without that room, will it not, Monsieur?"

Of course, I consented at once. If they wished to keep the room as it was, they were to do so, by all means.

"Thank you, thank you very much. My wife will be grateful to you," he said.

For a little while longer we drove on without speaking. Presently, "You are our first tenant. We have never let the house before," he volunteered.

"Ah? Have you had it long?" I asked.

"I built it. I built it, five, six, years ago," said he. Then, after a pause, he added, "I built it for my daughter."

His voice sank, as he said this. But one felt that it was only the beginning of something he wished to say.

I invited him to continue by an interested, "Oh?"

"You see what we are, my wife and I," he broke out suddenly. "We are rough people, we are peasants. But my daughter, sir"—he put his hand on my knee, and looked earnestly into my face—"my daughter was as fine as satin, as fine as lace."

He turned back to his horse, and again drove for a minute or two in silence. At last, always with his eyes on the horse's ears, "There was not a lady in this country finer than my daughter," he went on, speaking rapidly, in a thick voice, almost as if to himself. "She was beautiful, she had the sweetest character, she had the best education. She was educated at the convent, in Rouen, at the Sacré Cour. Six years—from twelve to eighteen—she studied at the convent. She knew English, sir—your language. She took prizes for history. And the piano! Nobody living can touch the piano as my daughter could. Well," he demanded abruptly, with a kind of fierceness, "was a rough farm-house good enough for her?" He answered his own question. "No, Monsieur. You would not soil fine lace by putting it in a dirty box. My daughter was finer than lace. Her hands were softer than Lyons velvet. And oh," he cried, "the sweet smell they had, her hands! It was good to smell her hands. I used to kiss them and smell them, as you would smell a rose." His voice died away at the reminiscence, and there was another interval of silence. By-and-by he began again, "I had plenty of money. I was the richest farmer of this neighbourhood. I sent to Rouen for the best architect they have there. Monsieur Clermont, the best architect of Rouen, laureate of the Fine Arts School of Paris, he built that house for my daughter; he built it and furnished it, to make it fit for a countess, so that when she came home for good from the convent she should have a home worthy of her. Look at this, Monsieur. Would the grandest palace in the world be too good for her?"

He had drawn a worn red leather case from his pocket, and taken out a small photograph, which he handed to me. It was the portrait of a girl, a delicate-looking girl, of about seventeen. Her face was pretty, with the irregular prettiness not uncommon in France, and very sweet and gentle. The old man almost held his breath while I was examining the photograph. "Est-elle gentille? Est-elle belle, Monsieur?" he besought me, with a very hunger for sympathy, as I returned it. One answered, of course, what one could, as best one could. He, with shaking fingers, replaced the photograph in its case. "Here, Monsieur," he said, extracting from an opposite compartment a little white card. It was the usual French memorial of mourning: an engraving of the Cross and Dove, under which was printed: "Eulalie-Joséphine-Marie Leroux. Born the 16th May, 1874. Died the 12th August, 1892. Pray for her."

"The good God knows what He does. I built that house for my daughter, and when it was built the good God took her away. We were mad with grief, my wife and I; but that could not save her. Perhaps we are still mad with grief," the poor old man said simply. "We can think of nothing else. We never wish to speak of anything else. We could not live in the house—her house, without her. We never thought to let it. I built that house for my daughter, I furnished it for her, and when it was ready for her—she died. Was it not hard, Monsieur? How could I let the house to strangers? But lately I have had losses. I am compelled to let it, to pay my debts. I would not let it to everybody. You are an Englishman. Well, if I did not like you, I would not let it to you for a million English pounds. But I am glad I have let it to you. You will respect her memory. And you will allow us to keep that room—her room. We shall be able to keep it as it was, with her things in it. Yes, that room which you thought was occupied—that was my daughter's room."

Madame Leroux was waiting for us in the garden of the chalet. She looked anxiously up at her husband as we arrived. He nodded his head, and called out, "It is all right. Monsieur agrees."

The old woman took my hands, wringing them hysterically almost. "Ah, Monsieur, you are very good," she said. She raised her eyes to mine. But I could not look into her eyes. There was a sorrow in them, an awfulness, a sacredness of sorrow, which, I felt, it would be like sacrilege for me to look at.

We became good friends, the Leroux and I, during the three months I passed as their tenant. Madame, indeed, did for me and looked after me with a zeal that was almost maternal. Both of them, as the old man had said, loved above all things to talk of their daughter, and I hope I was never loth to listen. Their passion, their grief, their constant thought of her, appealed to one as very beautiful, as well as very touching. And something like a pale spirit of the girl seemed gently, sweetly, always to be present in the house, the house that Love had built for her, not guessing that Death would come, as soon as it was finished, and call her away. "Oh, but it is a joy, Monsieur, that you have left us her room," the old couple were never tired of repeating. One day Madame took me up into the room, and showed me Eulalie's pretty dresses, her trinkets, her books, the handsomely bound books that she had won as prizes at the convent. And on another day she showed me some of Eulalie's letters, asking me if she hadn't a beautiful hand-writing, if the letters were not beautifully expressed. She showed me photographs of the girl at all ages; a lock of her hair; her baby clothes; the priest's certificate of her first communion; the bishop's certificate of her confirmation. And she showed me letters from the good sisters of the Sacred Heart, at Rouen, telling of Eulalie's progress in her studies, praising her conduct and her character. "Oh, to think that she is gone, that she is gone!" the old woman wailed, in a kind of helpless incomprehension, incredulity, of loss. Then, in a moment, she murmured, with what submissiveness she could, "Le bon Dieu sait ce qu'il fait,"crossing herself.

On the 12th of August, the anniversary of her death, I went with them to the parish church, where a mass was said for the repose of Eulalie's soul. And the kind old curé afterwards came round, and pressed their hands, and spoke words of comfort to them.

In September I left them, returning to Dieppe. One afternoon I chanced to meet that same old curé in the high street there. We stopped and spoke together—naturally, of the Leroux, of what excellent people they were, of how they grieved for their daughter. "Their love was more than love. They adored the child, they idolised her. I have never witnessed such affection," the curé told me. "When she died, I seriously feared they would lose their reason. They were dazed, they were beside themselves; for a long while they were quite as if mad. But God is merciful. They have learned to live with their affliction."

"It is very beautiful," said I, "the way they have sanctified her memory, the way they worship it. You know, of course, they keep her room, with her things in it, exactly as she left it. That seems to me very beautiful."

"Her room?" questioned the curé, looking vague. "What room?"

"Oh, didn't you know?" I wondered. "Her bedroom in the chalet. They keep it as she left it, with all her things about, her books, her dresses."

"I don't think I follow you," the curé said. "She never had a bedroom in the chalet."

"Oh, I beg your pardon. One of the front rooms on the first floor was her room," I informed him.

But he shook his head. "There is some mistake. She never lived in the chalet. She died in the old house. The chalet was only just finished when she died. The workmen were hardly out of it."

"No," I said, "it is you who must be mistaken; you must forget. I am quite sure. The Leroux have spoken of it to me times without number."

"But, my dear sir," the curé insisted, "I am not merely sure; I know. I attended the girl in her last agony. She died in the farm-house. They had not moved into the chalet. The chalet was being furnished. The last pieces of furniture were taken in the very day before her death. The chalet was never lived in. You are the only person who has ever lived in the chalet. I assure you of the fact."

"Well," I said, "that is very strange, that is very strange indeed." And for a minute I was bewildered, I did not know what to think. But only for a minute. Suddenly I cried out, "Oh, I see—I see. I understand."

I saw, I understood. Suddenly I saw the pious, the beautiful deception that these poor stricken souls had sought to practise on themselves; the beautiful, the fond illusion they had created for themselves. They had built the house for their daughter, and she had died just when it was ready for her. But they could not bear—they could not bear—to think that not for one little week even, not even for one poor little day or hour, had she lived in the house, enjoyed the house. That was the uttermost farthing of their sorrow, which they could not pay. They could not acknowledge it to their own stricken hearts. So, piously, reverently—with closed eyes as it were, that they might not know what they were doing—they had carried the dead girl's things to the room they had meant for her, they had arranged them there, they had said, "This was her room; this *was* her room." They would not admit to themselves, they would not let themselves stop to think, that she had never, even for one poor night, slept in it, enjoyed it. They told a beautiful pious falsehood to themselves. It was a beautiful pious game of "make-believe," which, like children, they could play together. And—the curé had said it: God is merciful. In the end they had been enabled to confuse their beautiful falsehood with reality, and to find comfort in it; they had been enabled to forget that their "make-believe" was a "make-believe," and to mistake it for a beautiful comforting truth. The uttermost farthing of their sorrow, which they could not pay, was not exacted. They were suffered to keep it; and it became their treasure, precious to them as fine gold.

Falsehood—truth? Nay, I think there are illusions that are not falsehoods—that are Truth's own smiles of pity for us.

THE QUEEN'. PLEASURE

I am writing to you from a lost corner of the far south-east of Europe. The author of my guide-book, in his preface, observes that a traveller in this part of the world, "unless he has some acquaintance with the local idioms, is liable to find himself a good deal bewildered about the names of places." On Thursday of last week I booked from Charing Cross, by way of Dover, Paris, and the Orient Express, for Vescova, the capital of Monterosso; and yesterday afternoon—having changed on Sunday, at Belgrade, from land to water, and steamed for close upon forty-eight hours down the Danube—I was put ashore at the town of *Bckob*, in the Principality of Tchermnogoria.

I certainly might well have found myself a good deal bewildered; and if I did not—for I'm afraid I can't boast of much acquaintance with the local idioms—it was no doubt because this isn't my first visit to the country. I was here some years ago, and then I learned that *Bckob* is pronounced as nearly as may be Vscof, and that Tchermnogoria is Monterosso literally translated —*tchermnoe* (the dictionaries certify) meaning red, and *gora*, or *goria*, a hill, a mountain.

It is our fashion in England to speak of Monterosso, if we speak of it at all, as I have just done: we say the Principality of Monterosso. But if we were to inquire at the Foreign Office, I imagine they would tell us that our fashion of speaking is not strictly correct. In its own Constitution Monterosso describes itself as a *Krolevstvo*, and its Sovereign as the *Krol*; and in all treaties and diplomatic correspondence, *Krol* and *Krolevstvo* are recognised by those most authoritative lexicographers, the Powers, as equivalent respectively to King and Kingdom. Anyhow, call it what you will, Monterosso is geographically the smallest, though politically the eldest, of the lower Danubian States. (It is sometimes, by-the-bye, mentioned in the newspapers of Western Europe as one of the Balkan States, which can scarcely be accurate, since, as a glance at the map will show, the nearest spurs of the Balkan Mountains are a good hundred miles distant from its southern frontier.) Its area is under ten thousand square miles, but its reigning family, the Pavelovitches, have contrived to hold their throne, from generation to generation, through thick and thin, ever since Peter the Great set them on it, at the conclusion of his war with the Turks, in 1713.

Vescova is rarely visited by English folk, lying, as it does, something like a two days' journey off the beaten track, which leads through Belgrade and Sofia to Constantinople. But, should you ever chance to come here, you would be surprised to see what a fine town it is, with its population of upwards of a hundred thousand souls, its broad, well-paved streets, its substantial yellow-stone houses, its three theatres, its innumerable churches, its shops and cafés, its gardens, quays, monuments, its government offices, and its Royal Palace. I am speaking, of course, of the new town, the modern town, which has virtually sprung into existence since 1850, and which, the author of my guide-book says, "disputes with Bukharest the title of the Paris of the South-east." The old town—the Turkish town, as they call it—is another matter: a nightmare-region of filthy alleys, open sewers, crumbling clay hovels, mud, stench, dogs, and dirty humanity, into which a well-advised foreigner will penetrate as seldom as convenient. Yet it is in the centre of the old town that the Cathedral stands, the Cathedral of Sankt Iakov, an interesting specimen of Fifteenth Century Saracenic, having been erected by the Sultan Mohammed II., as a mosque.

Of the Royal Palace I obtain a capital view from the window of my room in the Hôtel de Russie.

"A vast irregular pile," in the language of my guide-book, "it is built on the summit of an eminence which dominates the town from the west." The "eminence" rises gradually from this side to a height of perhaps a hundred feet, but breaks off abruptly on the other in a sheer cliff overhanging the Danube. The older portions of the Palace spring from the very brink of the precipice, so that, leaning from their ramparts, you could drop a pebble straight into the current, an appalling depth below. And, still to speak by the book, these older portions "vie with the Cathedral in architectural interest." What I see from my bedroom is a formidable, murderous-looking Saracenic castle: huge perpendicular quadrangles of blank, windowless, iron-grey stone wall (*curtains*, are they technically called?), connecting massive square towers; and the towers are surmounted by battlements and pierced by meurtrières. It stands out very bold and black, gloomy and impressive, when the sun sets behind it, in the late afternoon. I could suppose the place quite impregnable, if not inaccessible; and it's a mystery to me how Peter the Great ever succeeded in taking it, as History will have it that he did, by assault.

The modern portions of the Palace are entirely commonplace and cheerful. The east wing, visible from where I am seated writing, might have been designed by Baron Haussmann: a long stretch of yellow façade—dazzling to the sight just now, in the morning sunshine—with a French roof, of slate, and a box of gay-tinted flowers in each of its countless windows.

Behind the Palace there is a large and very lovely garden, reserved to the uses of the Royal Household; and beyond that, the Dunayskiy Prospekt, a park that covers about sixty acres, and is open to the public.

The first floor, the *piano nobile*, of that east wing is occupied by the private apartments of the King and Queen.

I look across the quarter-mile of red-tiled housetops that separate me from their Majesties' habitation, and I fancy the life that is going on within. It is too early in the day for either of them to be abroad, so they are certainly there, somewhere behind those gleaming windows: Theodore *Krol*t and Anéli *Kroleva*.

She, I would lay a wager, is in her music-room, at her piano, practising a song with Florimond. She is dressed in white (I always think of her as dressed in white—doubtless because she wore a white frock the first time I saw her), and her brown hair is curling loose about her forehead, her maids not having yet imprisoned it. I declare, I can almost hear her voice: *tra-la-lira-la-la*: mastering a trill; while Florimond, pink, and plump, and smiling, walks up and down the room, nodding his head to mark the time, and every now and then interrupting her with a suggestion.

The King, at this hour, will be in his study, in dressing-gown and slippers— a tattered old dingy brown dressing-gown, out at elbows—at his big wildly-littered writing-table, producing "copy," to the accompaniment of endless cigarettes and endless glasses of tea. (Monterossan cigarettes are excellent, and Monterossan tea is always served in glasses.) The King has literary aspirations, and—like Frederick the Great—coaxes his muse in French. You will occasionally see a *conte* of his in the *Nouvelle Revue*, signed by the artful pseudonym, Théodore Montrouge.

At one o'clock to-day I am to present myself at the Palace, and to be received by their Majesties in informal audience; and then I am to have the honour of lunching with them. If I were on the point of lunching with any other royal family in Europe.... But, thank goodness, I'm not; and I needn't pursue the distressing speculation. Queen Anéli and King Theodore are—for a multitude of reasons—a Queen and King apart.

You see, when he began life, Theodore IV. was simply Prince Theodore Pavelovitch, the younger son of a nephew of the reigning Krol, Paul III,; and nobody dimly dreamed that he would ever ascend the throne. So he went to Paris, and "made his studies" in the Latin Quarter, like any commoner.

In those days—as, I dare say, it still is in these—the Latin Quarter was crowded with students from the far South-east. Servians, Roumanians, Monte-rossans, grew, as it were, on every bush; we even had a sprinkling of Bulgarians and Montenegrins; and those of them who were not (more or less vaguely) princes, you could have numbered on your fingers. And, anyhow, in that democratic and self-sufficient seat of learning, titles count for little, and foreign countries are a matter of consummate ignorance and jaunty unconcern. The Duke of Plaza-Toro, should he venture in the classical Boul' Miche, would have to cede the *pas* to the latest hero of the Beaux-Arts, or bully from the School of Medicine, even though the hero were the son of a village apothecary, and the bully reeked to heaven of absinthe and tobacco; while the Prime Minister of England would find his name, it is more than to be feared, unknown, and himself regarded as a person of quite extraordinary unimportance.

So we accepted Prince Theodore Pavelovitch, and tried him by his individual merits, for all the world as if he were made of the same flesh and blood as Tom, Dick, and Harry; and thee-and-thou'd him, and hailed him as *mon vieux*, as merrily as we did everybody else. Indeed, I shouldn't wonder if the majority of those who knew him were serenely unaware that his origin was royal (he would have been the last to apprise them of it), and roughly classed him with our other *princes valaques*. For convenience sake, we lumped them all—the divers natives of the lands between the Black Sea and the Adriatic—under the generic name, Valaques; we couldn't be bothered with nicer ethnological distinctions.

We tried Prince Theodore by his individual merits; but, as his individual merits happened to be signal, we liked him very much. He hadn't a trace of "side;" his pockets were full of money; he was exceedingly free-handed. No man was readier for a lark, none more inventive or untiring in the prosecution of one. He was a brilliant scholar, besides, and almost the best fencer in the Quarter. And he was pleasantly good-looking—fair-haired, blue-eyed, with a friendly humorous face, a pointed beard, and a slight, agile, graceful figure. Everybody liked him, and everybody was sorry when he had to leave us, and return to his ultra-mundane birthplace. "It can't be helped," he said. "I must go home and do three years of military service. But then I shall come back. I mean always to live in Paris."

That was in '82. But he never came back. For, before his three years of military service were completed, the half-dozen cousins and the brother who stood between him and the throne, had one by one died off, and Theodore himself had succeeded to the dignity of *Krolevitch*,—as they call their Heir-Presumptive. In 1886 he married. And, finally, in '88, his great-uncle Paul also died—at the age of ninety-seven, if you please—and Theodore was duly proclaimed Krol.

He didn't forget his ancient cronies, though; and I was only one of those whom he invited to come and stay with him in his Palace. I came, and stayed.... eleven months! That seems egregious; but what will you say of another of us, Arthur Fleet (or Florimond, as their Majesties have nicknamed him), who came at the same time, and has stayed ever since? The fact is, the King is a tenacious as well as a delightful host; if he once gets you within his portals, he won't let you go without a struggle. "We do bore ourselves so improbably out here, you know," he explains. "The society of a Christian is a thing we'd commit a crime for."

Theodore's consort, Anéli Isabella, *Kroleva Tcherrnnogory—vide* the *Almanach de Gotha* is the third daughter of the late Prince Maximilian of Wittenburg; sister, therefore, to that young Prince Waldemar who comes almost every year to England, and with whose name and exploits as a yachtsman all conscientious students of the daily press will be familiar; and cousin to the reigning Grand Duke Ernest.

Theoretically German, she is, however, to all intents and purposes, French; for her mother, the Princess Célestine (of Bourbon-Morbihan), was a Frenchwoman, and, until her marriage, I fancy that more than half of Anéli's life was passed between Nice and Paris. She openly avows, moreover, that she "detests Germany, the German language, the German people, and all things German, and adores France and the French." And her political sympathies are entirely with the Franco-Russ alliance.

She is a deliciously pretty little lady, with curling soft-brown hair, a round, very young-looking face, a delicate rose-and-ivory complexion, and big, bright, innocent brown eyes—innocent, yet with plenty of potential archness, even potential mischief, lurking in them. She has beautiful full red lips, besides, and exquisite little white teeth. Florimond wrote a triolet about her once, in which he described her as "une fleur en porcelaine." Her Majesty repudiated the phrase indignantly. "Why not say a wax-doll, and be done with it?" she demanded. All the same, "fleur en porcelaine" does, in a manner, suggest the general effect of her appearance, its daintiness, its finish, its crisp chiselling, its clear, pure colour. Whereas, nothing could be more misleading than "wax-doll," for there is character, character, in every molecule of her person.

The Queen's character, indeed, is what I wish I could give some idea of It is peculiar, it is distinctive; to me, at any rate, it is infinitely interesting and diverting; but, by the same token—if I may hazard so to qualify it—it is a trifle…. a trifle…. difficult.

"You're such an arbitrary gent!" I heard Florimond complain to her, one day. (I heard and trembled, but the Queen only laughed.) And that will give you an inkling of what I mean.

If she likes you, if you amuse her, and if you never remotely oppose or question her desire of the moment, she can be all that is most gracious, most reasonable, most captivating: an inspiring listener, an entertaining talker: mingling the naïveté, the inexperience of evil, the half comical, half appealing unsophistication, of a girl, of a child almost—of one who has always lived far aloof from the struggle and uncleanness of the workaday world—with the wit, the humour, the swift appreciation and responsiveness of an exceedingly impressionable, clear-sighted, and accomplished woman.

But... but....

Well, I suppose, the right way of putting it would be to say, in the consecrated formula, that she has the defects of her qualities. Having preserved something of a child's simplicity, she has not entirely lost a child's wilfulness, a child's instability of mood, a child's trick of wearing its heart upon its sleeve. She has never perfectly acquired a grown person's power of controlling or concealing her emotions.

If you *don't* happen to amuse her—if, by any chance, it is your misfortune to *bore* her, no matter how slightly; and, oh, she is so easily bored!—the atmosphere changes in a twinkling: the sun disappears, clouds gather, the temperature falls, and (unless you speedily "brisken up," or fly her presence) you may prepare for most uncomfortable weather. If you manifest the faintest hesitation in complying with her momentary wishes, if you raise the mildest objection to them—*gare à vous!* Her face darkens, ominous lightning flashes in her eyes, her under-lip swells dangerously; she very likely stamps her foot imperiously; and you are to be accounted lucky if you don't get a smart dab from the barbed end of her royal tongue. And if she doesn't like you, though she may think she is trying with might and main to disguise the fact and to treat you courteously, you know it directly, and you go away with the persuasion that she has been, not merely cold and abstracted, but downright uncivil.

In a word, Queen Anéli is hasty, she is impatient.

And, in addition to that, she is uncertain. You can never tell beforehand, by any theory of probabilities based on past experience, what will or will not, on any given occasion, cause her to smile or frown. The thing she expressed a desire for yesterday, may offend her to-day, The suggestion that offended her yesterday, to-day she may welcome with joyous enthusiasm. You must approach her gingerly, tentatively; you must feel your ground.

"Oh, most dread Sovereign," said Florimond, "if you won't fly out at me, I would submit, humbly, that you'd better not drive this afternoon in your victoria, in your sweet new frock, for, unless all signs fail, it's going to rain like everything."

She didn't fly out at him exactly; but she retorted succinctly, with a peremptory gesture, "No, it's *not* going to rain," as who should say, "It daren't." And she drove in her victoria, and spoiled her sweet new frock. "Not to speak of my sweet new top-hat," sighs Florimond, who attended her; "the only Lincoln and Bennett topper in the whole length and breadth of Monterosso."

She is hasty, she is uncertain; and then... she is *intense*. She talks in italics, she feels in superlatives; she admits no comparative degree, no emotional half-tones. When she is not *ecstatically* happy, she is *desperately* miserable; wonders why she was ever born into this worst of all possible worlds; wishes she were dead; and even sometimes drops dark hints of meditated suicide. When she is not in the brightest of affable humours, she is in the blackest of cross ones. She either *loves* a thing, or she *simply can't endure it*;—the thing may be a town, a musical composition, a perfume, or a person. She either loves you, or simply can't endure you; and she's very apt to love you and to cease to love you alternately—or, at least, to give you to understand as much —three or four times a day. It is winter midnight or summer noon, a climate of extremes.

"Do you like the smell of tangerine-skin?"

Every evening for a week, when, at the end of dinner, the fruit was handed round, the King asked her that question; and she, never suspecting his malice, answered invariably, as she crushed a bit between her fingers, and fervidly inhaled its odour, "Oh, do I *like* it? I *adore* it. It's perfect *rapture*."

She is hasty, she is uncertain, she is intense. Will you be surprised when I go on to insist that, down deep, she is altogether well-meaning and excessively tender-hearted, and when I own that among all the women I know I can think of none other who seems to me so attractive, so fascinating, so sweetly feminine and loveable? (Oh, no, I am not *in love* with her, not in the least—though I don't say that I mightn't be, if I were a king, or she were not a queen.) If she realises that she has been unreasonable, she is the first to confess it; she repents honestly, and makes the devoutest resolutions to amend. If she discovers that she has hurt anybody's feelings, her conscience will not give her a single second of peace, until she has sought her victim out and heaped him with benefits. If she believes that this or that distasteful task forms in very truth a part of her duty, she will go to any length of persevering self-sacrifice to accomplish it.

She has a hundred generous and kindly impulses, where she has one that is perverse or inconsiderate. Bring any case of distress or sorrow to her notice, and see how instantly her eyes soften, how eager she is to be of help. And in her affections, however mercurial she may appear on the surface, she is really constant, passionate, and, in great things, forbearing. She and her husband, for example, though they have been married perilously near ten years, are little better than a pair of sweethearts (and jealous sweethearts, at that: you should have been present on a certain evening when we had been having a long talk and laugh over old days in the Latin Quarter, and an evil spirit prompted one of us to regale her Majesty with a highly-coloured account of Theodore's youthful infatuation for Nina Childe!... Oh, their faces! Oh, the silence!); and then, witness her devotion to her brother, to her sisters; her fondness for Florimond, for Madame Donarowska, who was her governess when she was a girl, and now lives with her in the Palace.

"I am writing a fairy-tale," Florimond said to her "about Princess Gugglegoo and Princess Raggle-snag."

"Oh?" questioned the Queen. "And who were *they?*"

"Princess Gugglegoo was all sweetness and pinkness, softness and guilelessness, a rose full of honey, and without a thorn; a perfect little cherub; oh, such a duck! Princess Ragglesnag was all corners and sharp edges, fire and fret, dark moods and quick angers; oh, such an intolerant, dictatorial, explosive, tempestuous princess! You could no more touch her than you could touch a nettle, or a porcupine, or a live coal, or a Leyden jar, or any other prickly, snaggy, knaggy, incandescent, electric thing. You were obliged to mind your p's and q's with her! But no matter how carefully you minded them, she was sure to let you have it, sooner or later; you were sure to *rile* her, one way or another: she was that cantankerous and tetchy, and changeable and unexpected.—And then.... Well, what do you suppose?"

"I'm waiting to hear," the Queen replied, a little drily.

"Oh, there! If you're going to be grumpy, ma'am, I won't play," cried Florimond.

"I'm not grumpy. Only, your characters are rather conventionally drawn. However, go on, go on."

"There was a distinct suggestion of menace in your tone. But never mind. If you didn't really mean it, we'll pretend there wasn't.—Well, my dears," he went on, turning, so as to include the King in his audience, "you never *will* believe me, but it's a solemn, sober fact that these two princesses were twin sisters, and that they looked so much alike that nobody, not even their own born mother, could tell them apart. Now, wasn't *that* surprising? Only Ragglesnag looked like Gugglegoo suddenly curdled and gone sour, you know; and Gugglegoo looked like Ragglesnag suddenly wreathed out in smiles and graces. So that the courtiers used to say 'Hello! What *can* have happened? Here comes dear Princess Gugglegoo looking as black as thunder.' Or else—'Bless us and save us! What's *this* miracle? Here comes old

Ragglesnag looking as if butter wouldn't melt in her mouth,' Well, and then...."

"Oh, you needn't continue," the Queen interrupted, bridling. "You're tedious and obvious, and utterly unfair and unjust. I hope I'm not an insipid little fool, like Gugglegoo; but I don't think I'm quite a termagant, either, like your horrid exaggerated Ragglesnag."

"Oh, dear! Oh, dear!" wailed Florimond. "Why *will* people go and make a personal application or everything a fellow says? If I had been even remotely thinking of your Majesty, I should never have dreamed of calling her by either of those ridiculous outlandish names. Gugglegoo and Ragglesnag, indeed!"

"What *would* you have called her?" the King asked, who was chuckling inscrutably in his armchair.

"Well, I *might* have called her Ragglegoo, and I *might* have called her Gugglesnag. But I hope I'm much too discerning ever to have applied such a sweeping generalisation to her as Ragglesnag, or such a silly, sugary sort of barbarism as Gugglegoo."

"It's perfectly useless," the Queen broke out, bitterly, "to expect a *man*—even a comparatively intelligent and highly-developed man, like Florimond—to understand the subtleties of a woman's nature, or to sympathise with the difficulties of her life. When she isn't as crude, and as blunt, and as phlegmatic, and as insensitive, and as transparent and commonplace and all-of-one-piece as themselves, men always think a woman's unreasonable and capricious and infantile. It's a little *too* discouraging. Here I wear myself to a shadow, and bore and worry myself to extermination, with all the petty contemptible cares and bothers and pomps and ceremonies of this tiresome little Court; and that's all the thanks I get—to be laughed at by my husband, and lectured and ridiculed in stupid allegories by Florimond! It's a little *too* hard. Oh, if you'd only let me go away, and leave it all behind me! I'd go to Paris and change my name, and become a concert-singer. It's the only thing I really care for—to sing and sing and sing. Oh, if I could only go and make a career as a concert-singer in Paris! Will you let me? Will you? *Will* you?" she demanded, vehemently, of her husband.

"That's rather a radical measure to bring up for discussion at this hour of the night, isn't it?" the King suggested, laughing.

"But it's quite serious enough for you to afford to consider it. And I don't see why one hour isn't as good as another. *Will* you let me go to Paris and become a concert-singer?"

"What! And leave poor me alone and forlorn here in Vescova? Oh, my dear, you wouldn't desert your own lawful spouse in that regardless manner!"

"I don't see what 'lawful' has to do with it. You don't half appreciate me. You think I'm childish, and capricious, and bad-tempered, and everything that's absurd and idiotic. I don't see why I should waste my life and my youth, stagnating in this out-of-the-way corner of Nowhere, with a man who doesn't appreciate me, and who thinks I'm childish and idiotic, when I could go to Paris and have a life of my own, and a career, and do the only thing in the world I really care for. Will you let me go? Answer. Will you?"

But the King only laughed.

"And besides," the Queen went on, in a minute, "if you really missed me, you could come too. You could abdicate. Why shouldn't you? Instead of staying here, and boring and worrying ourselves to death as King and Queen of this ungrateful, insufferable, little unimportant ninth-rate make-believe of a country, why shouldn't we abdicate and go to Paris, and be a Man and a Woman, and have a little Life, instead of this dreary, artificial, cardboard sort of puppet-show existence? You could devote yourself to literature, and I'd go on the concert-stage, and we'd have a delightful little house in the Avenue du Bois de Boulogne, and be perfectly happy. Of course, Flori-mond would come with us. Why shouldn't we? Oh, if you only would Î Will you? Will you, Theo?" she pleaded earnestly.

The King looked at his watch. "It's nearly midnight, my dear," he said. "High time, I should think, to adjourn the debate. But if, when you wake up to-morrow morning, you wish to resume it, Flori-mond and I will be at your disposal. Meanwhile, we're losing our beauty-sleep; and I, for one, am going to bed."

"Oh, it's always like that!" the Queen complained. "You never do me the honour of taking seriously anything I say. It's intolerable. I don't think any woman was ever so badly treated."

She didn't recur to the subject next day, however, but passed the entire morning with Florimond, planning the details of a garden-party, and editing the list of guests; and she threw her whole soul into it too. So that, when the King looked in upon them a little before luncheon, Florimond smiled at him significantly (indeed, I'm not sure he didn't *wink* at him) and called out, "Oh, we *are* enjoying ourselves. Please don't interrupt. Go back to your counting-house and count out your money, and leave us in the parlour to eat our bread and honey."

It is in the nature of things, doubtless, that a temperament such as I have endeavoured to suggest should find the intensity of its own feelings reflected by those that it excites in others. One would expect to hear that the people who like Queen Anéli like her tremendously, and that the people who don't like her tremendously don't like her at all. And, in effect, that is precisely the lady's case. She is tremendously liked by those who are near to her, and who are therefore in a position to understand her and to make allowances. They love the woman in her; they laugh at and love the high-spirited, whimsical, impetuous, ingenuous child. But those who are at a distance from her, or who meet her only rarely and formally, necessarily fail to understand her, and are apt, accordingly, neither to admire her greatly, nor to bear her much good will. And, of course, while the people who are near to her can be named by twos and threes, those who view her from a distance must be reckoned with by thousands. And this brings me to a painful circumstance, which I may as well mention without more ado. At Vescova—as you could scarcely spend a day in the town and not become aware—Queen Anéli is anything you please but popular.

"The inhabitants of Monterosso," says M. Boridov, in his interesting history of that country, "fall into three rigidly separated castes: the nobility, a bare handful of tall, fair-haired, pure-blooded Slavs; the merchants and manufacturers, almost exclusively Jews and Germans; and the peasantry, the populace—a short, thick-set, swarthy race, of Slavic origin, no doubt, and speaking a Slavic tongue, but with most of the Slavic characteristics obliterated by admixture with the Turk…. Your true Slav peasant, with his mild blue eyes and his trustful spirit, is as meek and as long-suffering as a dumb beast of burden. But your black-browed Monterossan, your Tchermnogorets, is fierce, lawless, resentful, and vindictive, a Turk's grandson, the Turk's first cousin: though no one detests the Turk more cordially than he."

"Well, at Vescova, and, with diminishing force, throughout all Monterosso, Queen Anéli is entirely misunderstood and sullenly misliked. Her husband cannot be called precisely the idol of his people, either; but he is regarded with indulgence, even with hopefulness; he is a Monterossan, a Pavelovitch: he may turn out well yet. Anéli, on the contrary, is an alien, a German, a *Niemkashka*. The feeling against her begins with the nobility. Save the half-dozen who are about her person, almost every mother's son or daughter of them fancies that he or she has been rudely treated by her, and quite frankly hates her. I am afraid, indeed, they have some real cause of grievance; for they are most of them rather tedious, and provincial, and narrow-minded; and they bore her terribly when they come to Court; and when she is bored, as we have seen, she is likely to show it pretty plainly. So they say she gives herself airs. They pretend that when she isn't absent-minded and monosyllabic, she is positively snappish. They denounce her as vain, shallow-pated, and extravagant. They twist and torture every word she speaks, and everything she does, into subject-matter for unfriendly criticism; and they quote as from her lips a good many words that she has never spoken, and they blame her savagely for innumerable things that she has never thought of doing. But that's the trouble with the fierce light that beats upon a throne—it shows the gaping multitude so much more than is really there. Why, I have been assured by at least a score of Monterossan ladies that the Queen's lovely brown hair is a wig; that her exquisite little teeth are the creation of Dr. Evans, of Paris; that whenever anything happens to annoy her, she bursts out with torrents of the most awful French oaths; that she quite frequently slaps and pinches her maids-of-honour; and that, as for her poor husband, he gets his hair pulled and his face scratched as often as he and she have the slightest difference of opinion. Monterossan ladies have gravely asseverated these charges to me (these, and others more outrageous, which I won't repeat), whilst their Monterossan lords nodded confirmation. It matters little that the charges are preposterous. Give a Queen a bad name, and nine people in ten will believe she merits it.

"Anyhow, the nobility of Monterosso, quite frankly hating Queen Anéli, give her every bad name they can discover in their vocabularies; and the populace, the mob, without stopping to make original investigations, have convicted her on faith, and watch her with sullen captiousness and mislike. When she drives abroad, scarcely a hat is doffed, never a cheer is raised. On the contrary, one sometimes hears mutterings and muffled groans; and the glances the passers-by direct at her are, in the main, the very reverse of affectionate glances. Members of the shop-keeping class alone show a certain tendency to speak up for her, because she spends her money pretty freely; but the shop-keeping class are aliens too, and don't count—or, rather, they count against her, 'the dogs of Jews,' the *zhudovskwy sobakwy!*"

But do you imagine Queen Anéli minds? Do you imagine she is hurt, depressed, disappointed? Not she. She accepts her unpopularity with the most superb indifference. "What do you suppose I care for the opinion of such riff-raff?" I recollect her once crying out, with curling lip. "Any one who has the least individuality, the least character, the least fineness, the least originality— any one who is in the least degree natural, unconventional, spontaneous—is bound to be misconceived and calumniated by the vulgar rank and file. It's the meanness and stupidity of average human nature; it's the proverbial injustice of men. To be popular, you must either be utterly insignificant, a complete nonentity, or else a timeserver and a hypocrite. So long as I have a clear conscience of my own, I don't care a button what strangers think and say about me. I don't intend to allow my conduct to be influenced in the tiniest particular by the prejudices of outsiders. Meddlers, busybodies! I will live my own life, and those who don't like it may do their worst. I will be myself."

"Yes, my dear; but after all," the King reminded her, "one has, in this imperfect world, to make certain compromises with one's environment, for comfort's sake. One puts on extra clothing in winter, for example, however much, on abstract principles, one may despise such a gross, material, unintelligent thing as the weather. Just so, don't you think, one is by way of having a smoother time of it, in the long run, if one takes a few simple measures to conciliate the people amongst whom one is compelled to live? Now, for instance, if you would give an hour or two every day to learning Monterossan...."

"Oh, for Heaven's sake, don't begin *that* rengaine," cried her Majesty. "I've told you a hundred million times that I won't be bothered learning Monterossan."

It is one of her subjects' sorest points, by the bye, that she has never condescended to learn their language. When she was first married, indeed, she announced her intention of studying it. Grammars and dictionaries were bought; a Professor was nominated; and for almost a week the Crown Princess (Krolevna), as she then was, did little else than grind at Monterossan. Her Professor was delighted; he had never known such a zealous pupil. Her husband was a little anxious. "You mustn't work too hard, my dear. An hour or two a day should be quite enough." But she answered, "Let me alone. It interests me." And for almost a week she was at it early and late, with hammer and tongs; poring over the endless declensions of Monterossan nouns, the endless conjugations of Monterossan verbs; wrestling, *sotto voce*, with the tongue-tangling difficulties of Monterossan pronunciation; or, with dishevelled hair and inky fingers, copying long Monterossan sentences into her exercise book. She is not the sort of person who does things by halves.— And then, suddenly, she turned volte-face; abandoned the enterprise for ever. "It's idiotic," she exclaimed. "A language with thirty-seven letters in its alphabet, and no literature! Why should I addle my brains trying to learn it? Ah, bien, merci! I'll content myself with French and English. It's bad enough, in one short life, to have had to learn German, when I was a child."

And neither argument nor entreaty could induce her to recommence it. The King, who has never altogether resigned himself to her determination, seizes from time to time an opportunity to hark back to it; but then he is silenced, as we have seen, with a "don't begin *that* rengaine." The disadvantages that result from her ignorance, it must be noticed, are chiefly moral; it offends Monterossan amour-propre. Practically, she does perfectly well with French, that being the Court language of the realm.

No, Queen Anéli doesn't care a button. She tosses her head, and accepts "the proverbial injustice of men" with magnificent unconcern. Only, sometimes, when the public sentiment against her takes the form of aggressive disrespect, or when it interferes in any way with her immediate convenience, it puts her a little out of patience—when, for instance, the traffic in the street retards the progress of her carriage, and a passage isn't cleared for her as rapidly as it might be for a Queen whom the rabble loved; or when, crossing the pavement on foot, to enter a church, or a shop, or what not, the idlers that collect to look, glare at her sulkily, without doing her the common courtesy of lifting their hats. In such circumstances, I dare say, she is more or less angered. At all events, a sudden fire will kindle in her eyes, a sudden colour in her cheeks; she will very likely tap nervously with her foot, and murmur something about "canaille." Perhaps anger, though, is the wrong word for her emotion; perhaps it should be more correctly called a kind of angry contempt.

When I first came to Vescova, some years ago, the Prime Minister and virtual dictator of the country was still M. Tsargradev, the terrible M. Tsargradev,—or Sargradeff, as most English newspapers write his name,—and it was during my visit here that his downfall occurred, his downfall and irretrievable disgrace.

The character and career of M. Tsargradev would furnish the subject for an extremely interesting study. The illegitimate son of a Monterossan nobleman, by a peasant mother, he inherited the unprepossessing physical peculiarities of his mother's stock: the sallow skin, the broad face, the flat features, the prominent cheek-bones, the narrow, oblique-set, truculent black eyes, the squat, heavy figure. But to these he united a cleverness, an energy, an ambition, which are as foreign to simple as to gentle Monterossan blood, and which he doubtless owed to the fusion of the two; and an unscrupulousness, a perfidy, a cruelty, and yet a superficial urbanity, that are perhaps not surprising in an ambitious politician, half an Oriental, who has got to carry the double handicap of a repulsive personal appearance and a bastard birth. Now, the Government of Monterosso, as the King has sometimes been heard to stigmatise it, is deplorably constitutional. By the Constitution of 1869, practically the whole legislative power is vested in the Soviete, a parliament elected by the votes of all male subjects who have completed three years of military service. And, in the early days of the reign of Theodore IV., M. Tsargradev was leader of the Soviete, with a majority of three to one at his back.

This redoubtable personage stood foremost in the ranks of those whom our fiery little Queen Anéli "could not endure."

"His horrible soapy smile! His servile, insinuating manner! It makes you feel as if he were plotting your assassination," she declared. "His voice—ugh! It's exactly like lukewarm oil. He makes my flesh creep, like some frightful, bloated reptile."

"There was a Queen in Thule," hummed Florimond, "who had a marvellous command of invective. 'Eaving help your reputation, if you fell under her illustrious displeasure."

"I don't see why you make fun of me. I'm sure you think as I do—that he's a monster of low cunning, and cynicism, and craft, and treachery, and everything that's vile and revolting. Don't you?" the Queen demanded.

"To be sure I do, ma'am. I think he's a bold, bad, dreadful person. I lie awake half the night, counting up his iniquities in my mind. And if just now I laughed, it was only to keep from crying."

"This sort of talk is all very well," put in the King; "but the fact remains that Tsargradev is the master of Monterosso. He could do any one of us an evil turn at any moment. He could cut down our Civil List to-morrow, or even send us packing, and establish republic. We're dependent for everything upon his pleasure. I think, really, my dear, you ought to try to be decent to him—if only for prudence' sake."

"Decent to him!" echoed her Majesty. "I like that! As if I didn't treat him a hundred million times better than he deserves! I hope he can't complain that I'm not decent to him."

"You're not exactly effusive, do you think? I don't mean that you stick your tongue out at him, or throw things at his head. But trust him for understanding. It's what you leave unsaid and undone, rather than what you say or do. He's fully conscious of the sort of place he occupies in your esteem, and he resents it. He thinks you distrust him, suspect him, look down upon him…."

"Well, and so I do," interrupted the Queen. "And so do you. And so does everybody who has any right feeling."

"Yes; but those of us who are wise in our generation keep our private sentiments regarding him under lock and key. We remember his power, and treat him respectfully to his face, however much we may despise him in secret. What's the use of quarrelling with our bread and butter? We should seek to propitiate him, to rub him the right way."

"Then you would actually like me to *grovel*, to *toady*, to a disgusting little low-born, black-hearted cad like Tsargradev!" cried the Queen, with scorn.

"Oh, dear me, no," protested her husband. "But there's a vast difference between toadying, and being a little tactful, a little diplomatic. I should like you to treat him with something more than bare civility."

"Well, what can I do that I don't do?"

"You never ask him to any but your general public functions, your State receptions, and that sort of thing. Why don't you admit him to your private circle sometimes? Why don't you invite him to your private parties, your dinners?"

"Ah, merci, non! My private parties are my private parties. I ask my friends, I ask the people I like. Nothing could induce me to ask that horrid little underbred mongrel creature. He'd be—he'd be like—like something unclean—something murky and contaminating—in the room. He'd be like an animal, an ape, a satyr."

"Well, my dear," the King submitted meekly, "I only hope we'll never have cause to repent your exclusion of him. I know he bears us a grudge for it, and he's not a person whose grudges are to be made light of."

"Bah! I'm not afraid of him," Anéli retorted. "I know he hates me. I see it every time he looks at me, with his snaky little eyes, his forced little smile—that awful, complacent, ingratiating smirk of his, that shows his teeth, and isn't even skin deep; a mere film spread over his face, like pomatum! Oh, I know he hates me. But it's the nature of mean, false little beasts like him to hate their betters; so it can't be helped. For the rest, he may do his worst. I'm not afraid," she concluded airily.

Not only would she take no steps to propitiate M. Tsargradev, but she was constantly urging her husband to dismiss him.

"I'm perfectly certain he has all sorts of dreadful secret vices. I haven't the least doubt he's murdered people. I'm sure he steals. I'm sure he has a secret understanding with Berlin, and accepts bribes to manage the affairs of Monterosso as Prince Bismarck wishes. That's why we're more or less in disgrace with our natural allies, Russia and France. Because Tsargradev is paid to pursue, an anti-Russian, a German, policy. If you would take my advice, you'd dismiss him, and have him put in prison. Then you could explain to the Soviete that he is a murderer, a thief, a traitor, and a monster of secret immorality, and appoint a decent person in his place."

Her husband laughed with great amusement.

"You don't appear quite yet to have mastered the principles of constitutional government, my dear. I could no more dismiss Tsargradev than you could dismiss the Pope of Rome."

"Are you or are you not the King of Monterosso?"

"I'm Vice-King, perhaps. You're the King, you know. But that has nothing to do with it. Tsargradev is leader of the Soviete. The Soviete pays the bills, and its leader governs. The King's a mere fifth wheel. Some day they'll abolish him. Meanwhile they tolerate him, on the understanding that he's not to interfere."

"You ought to be ashamed to say so. You ought to take the law and the Constitution and everything into your own hands. If you asserted yourself, they'd never dare to resist you. But you always submit—submit—submit. Of course, everybody takes advantage of a man who always submits. Show that you have some spirit, some sense of your own dignity. Order Tsargradev's dismissal and arrest. You can do it now, at once, this evening. Then to-morrow you can go down to the Soviete, and tell them what a scoundrel he is —a thief, a murderer, a traitor, an impostor, a libertine, everything that's foul and bad. And tell them that henceforward you intend to be really King, and not merely nominally King; and that you're going to govern exactly as you think best; and that, if they don't like that, they will have to make the best of it. If they resist, you can dissolve them, and order a general election. Or you can suspend the Constitution, and govern without any Soviete at all."

The King laughed again.

"I'm afraid the Soviete might ask for a little evidence, a few proofs, in support of my sweeping charges. I could hardly satisfy them by declaring that I had my wife's word for it. But, seriously, you exaggerate. Tsargradev is anything you like from the point of view of abstract ethics, but he's not a criminal. He hasn't the faintest motive for doing anything that isn't in accordance with the law. He's simply a vulgar, self-seeking politician, with a touch of the Tartar. But he's not a thief, and I imagine his private life is no worse than most men's."

"Wait, wait, only wait!" cried the Queen. "Time will show. Some day he'll come to grief, and then you'll see that he's even worse than I have said. I *feel*, I *know*, he's everything that's bad. Trust a woman's intuitions. They're much better than what you call *evidence*."

And she had a nickname for him, which, as well as her general criticisms of his character, had pretty certainly reached the Premier's ear; for, as subsequent events demonstrated, very nearly every servant in the Palace was a spy in his pay. She called him the nain jaune.

Subsequent events have also demonstrated that her woman's intuitions were indeed trustworthy. Perhaps you will remember the revelations that were made at the time of M. Tsargradev's downfall; fairly full reports of them appeared in the London papers. Murder, peculation, and revolting secret debaucheries were all, surely enough, proved against him. It was proved that he was the paid agent of Berlin; it was proved that he had had recourse to *torture* in dealing with certain refractory witnesses in his famous prosecution of Count Osaréki. And then, there was the case of Colonel Alexandrevitch. He and Tsargradev, at sunset, were strolling arm-in-arm in the Dunayskiy Prospekt, when the Colonel was shot by some person concealed in the shrubberies, who was never captured. Tsargradev and his friends broached the theory, which gained pretty general acceptance, that the shot had been intended for the Prime Minister himself, and that the death of Colonel Alexandrevitch was an accident due to bad aiming. It is now perfectly well established that the death of the Colonel was due to very good aiming indeed; that the assassin was M. Tsargradev's own hireling; and that perhaps the best reason why the police could never lay hands on him had some connection with the circumstance that the poor wretch, that very night, was strangled and cast into the Danube.

Oh, they manage these things in a highly unlikely and theatrical manner, in the far south-east of Europe!

But the particular circumstances of M. Tsargradev's downfall were amusingly illustrative of the character of the Queen. *Ce que femme veult, Dieu le veult.* And though her husband talked of the Constitution, and pleaded the necessity of evidence, Anéli was unconvinced. To get rid of Tsargradev, by one method or another, was her fixed idea, her determined purpose; she bided her time, and in the end she accomplished it.

It befell, during the seventh month of my stay in the Palace, that a certain great royal wedding was appointed to be celebrated at Dresden: a festivity to which were bidden all the crowned heads and most of the royal and semi-royal personages of Christendom, and amongst them the Krol and Kroleva of Monte-rosso.

"It will cost us a pretty sum of money," Theodore grumbled, when the summons first reached him. "We'll have to travel in state, with a full suite; and the whole shot must be paid from our private purse. There's no expecting a penny for such a purpose from the Soviete."

"I hope," exclaimed the Queen, looking up from a letter she was writing, "I hope you don't for a moment intend to go?"

"We *must* go," answered the King. "There's no getting out of it."

"Nonsense!" said she. "We'll send a representative."

"I only wish we could," sighed the King. "But unfortunately this is an occasion when etiquette requires that we should attend in person."

"Oh, bother etiquette," said she. "Etiquette was made for slaves. We'll send your Cousin Peter. One must find some use for one's Cousin Peters."

"Yes; but this is a business, alas, in which one's Cousin Peter won't go down. I'm very sorry to say we'll have to attend in person."

"Nonsense!" she repeated. "Attend in person! How can you think of such a thing? We'd be bored and fatigued to death. It will be unspeakable. Nothing but dull, stodgy, suffocating German pomposity and bad taste. Oh, je m'y connais! Red cloth, and military bands, and interminable banquets, and noise, and confusion, and speeches (oh, the speeches!), until you're ready to drop. And besides, we'd be herded with a crowd of ninth-rate princelings and petty dukes, who smell of beer and cabbage and brilliantine. We'd be relegated to the fifth or sixth rank, behind people who are all of them really our inferiors. Do you suppose I mean to let myself be patronised by a lot of stupid Hohenzollerns and Grâtzhoffens? No, indeed! You can send your Cousin Peter."

"Ah, my dear, if I were the Tsar of Russia!" laughed her husband. "Then I could send a present and a poor relation, and all would be well. But—you speak of ninth-rate princelings. A ninth-rate princeling like the Krol of Tchermnogoria must make act of presence in his proper skin. It's de rigueur. There's no getting out of it. We must go."

"Well, you may go, if you like," her Majesty declared. "As for me, I won't. If you choose to go and be patronised and bored, and half killed by the fatigue, and half ruined by the expense, I suppose I can't prevent you. But, if you want my opinion, I think it's utter insane folly."

And she re-absorbed herself in her letter, with the air of one who had been distracted for a moment by a frivolous and tiresome interruption.

The King did not press the matter that evening, but the next morning he mustered his courage, and returned to it.

"My dear," he began, "I beg you to listen to me patiently for a moment, and not get angry. What I wish to say is really very important."

"Well, what is it? What is it?" she enquired, with anticipatory weariness.

"It's about going to Dresden. I—I want to assure you that I dislike the notion of going quite as much as you can. But it's no question of choice. There are certain things one has to do, whether one will or not. I'm exceedingly sorry to have to insist, but we positively must reconcile ourselves to the sacrifice, and attend the wedding—both of us. It's a necessity of our position. If we should stay away, it would be a breach of international good manners that people would never forgive us. We should be the scandal, the by-word, of the Courts of Europe. We'd give the direst offence in twenty different quarters. We really can't afford to make enemies of half the royal families of the civilised world. You can't imagine the unpleasantnesses, the complications, our absence would store up for us; the bad blood it would cause. We'd be put in the black list of our order, and snubbed, and embarrassed, and practically ostracised, for years to come. And you know whether we need friends. But the case is so obvious, it seems a waste of breath to argue it. You surely won't let a mere little matter of temporary personal inconvenience get us into such an ocean of hot water. Come now— be reasonable, and say you will go."

The Queen's eyes were burning; her under-lip had swollen portentously; but she did not speak.

The King waited a moment. Then, "Come, Anéli—don't be angry. Answer me. Say that you will go," he urged, taking her hand.

She snatched her hand away. I'm afraid she stamped her foot. "No!" she cried. "Let me alone. I tell you I *won't.*"

"But, my dear…." the King was re-commencing….

"No, no, no! And you needn't call me your dear. If you had the least love for me, the least common kindness, or consideration for my health or comfort or happiness, you'd never dream of proposing such a thing. To drag me half-way across the Continent of Europe, to be all but killed at the end of the journey by a pack of horrid, coarse, beer-drinking Germans! And tired out, and irritated, and patronised, and humiliated by people like —————— and —————! It's perfectly heartless of you. And I—when I suggest such a

142

simple natural pleasure as a trip to Paris, or to the Italian lakes in autumn—
you tell me we can't afford it! You're ready to spend thousands on a stupid,
utterly unnecessary and futile absurdity, like this wedding, but you can't
afford to take me to the Italian lakes! And yet you pretend to love me! Oh, its
awful, awful, awful!" And her voice failed her in a sob; and she hid her face
in her hands, and wept. So the King had to drop the subject again, and to
devote his talents to the task of drying her tears.

I don't know how many times they renewed the discussion, but I do know
that the Queen stood firm in her original refusal, and that at last it was
decided that the King should go without her, and excuse her absence as best
he might on the plea of her precarious state of health. It was only after this
resolution was made and registered, and her husband had brought himself to
accept it with some degree of resignation—it was only then that her Majesty
began to waver and vacillate, and reconsider, and change her mind. As the
date approached for his departure, her alternations became an affair of hours.
It was, "Oh, after all, I can't let you go alone, poor Theo. And besides, I
should die of heartbreak, here without you. So—there—I'll make the best of a
bad business, and go with you"—it was either that, or else, "No, after all, I
can't. I really can't. I'm awfully sorry. I shall miss you horribly. But, when I
think of what it *means*, I haven't the strength or courage. I simply can't"—it
was one thing or the other, on and off, all day.

"When you finally know your own mind, I shall be glad if you'll send for
me," said Theodore. "Because I've got to name a Regent. And if you're
coming with me, I shall name my Uncle Stephen. But if you're stopping here,
of course I shall name you."

There is a bothersome little provision in the Constitution of Monterosso to
the effect that the Sovereign may not cross the frontiers of his dominions, no
matter for how brief a sojourn, without leaving a Regent in command. Under
the good old régime, before the revolution of 1868, the kings of
Tchermnogoria were a good deal inclined to spend the bulk of their time—
and money—in foreign parts. They found Paris, Monte Carlo, St. Petersburg,
Vienna, and even, if you can believe me, sometimes London, on the whole
more agreeable as places of residence than their hereditary capital. (There was
the particularly flagrant case of Paul II., our Theodore's great-grandfather,
who lived for twenty years on end in Rome. He fancied himself a statuary,
poor gentleman, and produced—oh, such amazing Groups! Tons of them
repose in the Royal Museum at Vescova; a few brave the sky here and there in
lost corners of the Campagna—he used to present them to the Pope! Perhaps
you have seen his Fountain at Acqu'amarra?) It was to discourage this sort of
royal absenteeism that the patriotic framers of the Constitution slyly slipped

Sub-Clause 18 into Clause ii., of Title 3, of Article XXXVI.: *Concerning the Appointment of a Regent.*

"So," said Theodore, "when you have finally made up your mind, I shall be glad if you will let me know; for I've got to name a Regent."

But the Queen continued to hesitate; in the morning it was Yes, in the evening No; and the eleventh hour was drawing near and nearer. The King was to leave on Monday. On the previous Tuesday, in a melting mood, Anéli had declared, "There! Once for all, to make an end of it, I'll go." On Wednesday a Commission of Regency, appointing Prince Stephen, was drawn up. On Thursday it was brought to the Palace for the royal signature. The King had actually got so far as the *d* in his name, when the Queen, faltering at sight of the irrevocable document, laid her hand on his arm. She was very pale, and her voice was weak. "No, Theo, don't sign it. It's like my death-warrant. I—I haven't got the courage. You'll have to let me stay. You'll have to go alone." On Friday a new commission was prepared, in which Anéli's name had been substituted for Stephen's. On Saturday morning it was presented to the King. "Shall I sign?" he asked. "Yes, sign," said she. And he signed.

"Ouf!" she cried. "*That's* settled."

And she hardly once changed her mind again until Sunday night; and even then she only half changed it.

"If it weren't too late," she announced, "do you know, I believe I'd decide to go with you, in spite of everything? But of course I never could get ready to start by to-morrow morning. You couldn't wait till Tuesday?"

The King said he couldn't.

"And now, my dears" (as Florimond, who loves to tell the story, is wont to begin it), "no sooner was her poor confiding husband's back a-turned, than what do you suppose this deep, designing, unprincipled, high-handed young woman up and did?"

Almost the last words Theodore spoke to her were, "Do, for heaven's sake, try to get on pleasantly with Tsargradev. Don't treat him too much as if he were the dust under your feet. All you'll have to do is to sign your name at the end of the papers he'll bring you. Sign and ask no questions, and all will be well."

And the very first act of Anéli's Regency was to degrade M. Tsargardev from office and to place him under arrest.

We bade the King good-bye on the deck of the royal yacht *Nemisa*, which was to bear him to Belgrade, the first stage of his journey. Cannon bellowed from the citadel; the bells of all the churches in the town were clanging in jubilant discord; the river was gay with fluttering bunting, and the King resplendent in a gold-laced uniform, with the stars and crosses of I don't know how many Orders glittering on his breast. We lingered at the landing-stage, waving our pocket-handkerchiefs, till the *Nemisa* turned a promontory and disappeared; Anéli silent, with a white face, and set, wistful eyes. And then we got into a great gilt-and-scarlet state-coach, she and Madame Donarowska, Florimond and I, and were driven back to the Palace; and during the drive she never once spoke, but leaned her cheek on Madame Donarowska's shoulder, and cried as if her heart would break.

The Palace reached, however—as who should say, "We're not here to amuse ourselves"—she promptly dried her tears.

"Do you know what I'm going to do?" she asked. And, on our admitting that we didn't, she continued, blithely, "It's an ill wind that blows no good. Theo's absence will be very hard to bear, but I must turn it to some profitable account. I must improve the occasion to straighten out his affairs; I must put his house in order. I'm going to give Monsieur Tsargradev a taste of retributive justice. I'm going to do what Theo himself ought to have done long ago. It's intolerable that a miscreant like Tsargradev should remain at large in a civilised country; it's a disgrace to humanity that such a man should hold honourable office. I'm going to dismiss him and put him in prison. And I shall keep him there till a thorough investigation has been made of his official acts, and the crimes I'm perfectly certain he's committed have been proved against him. I'm not going to be Regent for nothing. I'm going to *rule.*"

We, her auditors, looked at each other in consternation. It was a good minute before either of us could collect himself sufficiently to speak.

At last, "Oh, lady, lady, august and gracious lady," groaned Florimond, "please be nice, and relieve our minds by confessing that you're only saying it to tease us. Tell us you're only joking."

"I never was more serious in my life," she answered.

"I defy you to look me in the eye and say so without laughing," he persisted. "What *is* the fun of trying to frighten us?"

"You needn't be frightened. I know what I'm about," said she.

"What you're about!" he echoed. "Oh me, oh my! You're about to bring your house crashing round your ears. You're about to precipitate a revolution. You'll lose your poor unfortunate husband's kingdom for him. You'll— goodness only can tell what you *won't* do. Your own bodily safety—your very life—will be in danger. There'll be mobs, there'll be rioting. Oh, lady, sweet lady, gentle lady, you mustn't, you really mustn't. You'd much better come and sing a song, along o' me. Don't meddle with politics. They're nothing but sea, sand, and folly. Music's the only serious thing in the world. Come—let's too-tootle."

"It's all very well to try to turn what I say to jest," the Queen replied loftily, "but I assure you I mean every word of it. I've studied the Constitution. I know my rights. The appointment and revocation of Ministers rest absolutely with the Sovereign. It's not a matter of law, it's merely a matter of custom, a matter of convenience, that the Ministers should be chosen from the party that has a majority in the Soviete. Well, when it comes to the case of a ruffian like Tsargradev, custom and convenience must go by the board, in favour of right and justice. I'm going to revoke him."

"And within an hour of your doing so the whole town of Vescova will be in revolt. We'll all have to leave the Palace, and fly for our precious skins. We'll be lucky if we get away with them intact. A pretty piece of business! Tsargradev, from being Grand Vizier, will become Grand Mogul; and farewell to the illustrious dynasty of Pavelovitch! Oh, lady, lady! I call it downright unfriendly, downright inhospitable of you. Where shall my grey hairs find shelter? I'm *so* comfortable here under your royal rooftree. You wouldn't deprive the gentlest of God's creatures of a happy home? Better that a thousand Tsargradevs should flourish like a green bay-tree, than that one upright man should be turned out of comfortable quarters. There, now, be kind. As a personal favour to me, won't you please just leave things as they are?"

The Queen laughed a little—not very heartily, though, and not at all acquiescently. "Monsieur Tsargradev must go to prison," was her inexorable word.

We pleaded, we argued, we exhausted ourselves in warnings and protestations, but to no purpose. And in the end she lost her patience, and shut us up categorically.

"No! Laissez moi tranquille!" she cried. "I've heard enough. I know my own mind. I won't be bothered."

It was with heavy spirits and the dismallest forebodings that we assisted at her subsequent proceedings. We had an anxious time of it for many days; and it has never ceased to be a source of astonishment to me that it all turned out as well as it did. But—*ce que femme veult....*

She began operations by despatching an aide-decamp to M. Tsargradev's house, with a note in which she commanded him to wait upon her forthwith at

146

the Palace, and to deliver up his seals of office.

At the same time she summoned to her presence General Michaïlov, the Military Governor of Vescova, and Prince Vasiliev, the leader of the scant Conservative opposition in the Soviete.

She awaited these gentleman in the throne-room, surrounded by the officers of the household in full uniform. Florimond and I hovered uneasily in the background.

"By Jove, she does look her part, doesn't she?" Florimond whispered to me.

She wore a robe of black silk, with the yellow ribbon of the Lion of Monterosso across her breast, and a tiara of diamonds in her hair. Her eyes glowed with a fire of determination, and her cheeks with a colour that those who knew her recognised for a danger-signal. She stood on the steps of the throne, waiting, and tapping nervously with her foot.

And then the great white-and-gold folding doors were thrown open, and M. Tsargradev entered, followed by the aide-de-camp who had gone to fetch him.

He entered, bowing and smiling, grotesque in his ministerial green and silver; and the top of his bald head shone as if it had been waxed and polished. Bowing and smirking, he advanced to the foot of the throne, where he halted.

"I have sent for you to demand the return of your seals of office," said the Queen. She held her head high, and spoke slowly, with superb haughtiness.

Tsargradev bowed low, and, always smiling, answered, in a voice of honey, "If it please your Majesty, I don't think I quite understand."

"I have sent for you to demand the return of your seals of office," the Queen repeated, her head higher, her inflection haughtier than ever.

"Does your Majesty mean that I am to consider myself dismissed from her service?" he asked, with undiminished sweetness.

"It is my desire that you should deliver up your seals of office," said she.

Tsargradev's lips puckered in an effort to suppress a little good-humoured deprecatory laugh. "But, your Majesty," he protested, in the tone of one reasoning with a wayward school-girl, "you must surely know that you have no power to dismiss a constitutional Minister."

"I must decline to hold any discussion with you. I must insist upon the immediate surrender of your seals of office."

"I must remind your Majesty that I am the representative of the majority of the Soviete."

"I forbid you to answer me. I forbid you to speak in my presence. You are not here to speak. You are here to restore the seals of your office to your Sovereign."

"That, your Majesty, I must, with all respect, decline to do."

"You refuse?" the Queen demanded, with terrific shortness.

"I cannot admit your Majesty's right to demand such a thing of me. It is unconstitutional."

"In other words, you refuse to obey my commands? Colonel Karkov!" she called.

Her eyes were burning magnificently now; her hands trembled a little.

Colonel Karkov, the Marshal of the Palace, stepped forward.

"Arrest that man," said the Queen, pointing to Tsargradev.

Colonel Karkov looked doubtful, hesitant.

"Do you also mean to disobey me?" the Queen cried, with a glance... oh, a glance!

Colonel Karkov turned pale, but he hesitated no longer. He bowed to Tsargradev. "I must ask you to constitute yourself my prisoner," he said.

Tsargradev made a motion as if to speak; but the Queen raised her hand, and he was silent.

"Take him away at once," she said. "Lock him up. He is to be absolutely prevented from holding any communication with any one outside the Palace."

And, somehow, Colonel Karkov managed to lead Tsargradev from the presence-chamber.

And that ended the first act of our comical, precarious little melodrama.

After Tsargradev's departure there was a sudden buzz of conversation among the courtiers. The Queen sank back, in evident exhaustion, upon the red velvet cushions of the throne. She closed her eyes and breathed deeply, holding one of her hands pressed hard against her heart.

By-and-by she looked up. She was very pale.

"Now let General Michaïlov and Prince Vasiliev be introduced," she said.

And when they stood before her, "General Michaïlov," she began, "I desire you to place the town of Vescova under martial law. You will station troops about the Palace, about the Chamber of the Soviete, about the Mint and Government offices, and in all open squares and other places where crowds would be likely to collect. I have just dismissed M. Tsargradev from office, and there may be some disturbance. You will rigorously suppress any signs of disorder. I shall hold you responsible for the peace of the town and the protection of my person."

General Michaïlov, a short, stout, purple-faced old soldier, blinked and coughed, and was presumably on the point of offering something in the nature of an objection.

"You have heard my wishes," said the Queen. "I shall be glad if you will see to their immediate execution."

The General still seemed to have something on his mind.

The Queen stamped her foot. "Is everybody in a conspiracy to disobey me?" she demanded. "I am the representative of your King, who is Commander-in-Chief of the Army. Are my orders to be questioned?"

The General bowed, and backed from the room.

"Prince Vasiliev," the Queen said, "I have sent for you to ask you to replace M. Tsargradev as Secretary of State for the Interior, and President of the Council. You will at once enter into the discharge of your duties, and proceed to the formation of a Ministry."

Prince Vasiliev was a tall, spare, faded old man, with a pointed face ending in a white imperial. He was a great personal favourite of the Queen's.

"It will be a little difficult, Madame," said he.

"No doubt," assented she. "But it must be done."

"I hardly see, Madame, how I can form a Ministry to any purpose, with an overwhelming majority against me in the Soviete."

"You are to dissolve the Soviete and order a general election."

"The general election can scarcely be expected to result in a change of parties, your Majesty."

"No; but we shall have gained time. When the new deputies are ready to take their seats, M. Tsargradev's case will have been disposed of. I expect you will find among his papers at the Home Office evidence sufficient to convict him of all sorts of crimes. If I can deliver Monterosso from the Tsargradev superstition, my intention will have been accomplished."

"Now let's lunch," she said to Florimond and me, at the close of this historic session. "I'm ravenously hungry."

I dare say General Michaïlov did what he could, but his troops weren't numerous enough to prevent a good deal of disturbance in the town; and I suppose he didn't want to come to bloodshed. For three days and nights, the streets leading up to the Palace were black with a howling mob, kept from crossing the Palace courtyard by a guard of only about a hundred men. Cries of "Long live Tsargradev!" and "Death to the German woman!" and worse cries still, were constantly audible from the Palace windows.

"Canaille!" exclaimed the Queen. "Let them shout themselves hoarse. Time will show."

And she would step out upon her balcony, in full sight of the enemy, and look down upon them calmly, contemptuously.

Still, the military did contrive to prevent an actual revolution, and to maintain the *status quo*.

The news reached the King at Vienna. He turned straight round and hurried home.

"Oh, my dear, my dear!" he groaned. "You *have* made a mess of things."

"You think so? Read this."

It was a copy of the morning's Gazette, containing Prince Vasiliev's report of the interesting discoveries he had made amongst the papers Tsargradev had left behind him at the Home Office.

There was an immediate revulsion of public feeling. The secret understanding with Berlin was the thing that "did it." The Monterossans are hereditarily, temperamentally, and from motives of policy, Russophils.

They couldn't forgive Tsargradev his secret treaty with Berlin; and they promptly proceeded to execrate him as much as they had loved him.

For State reasons, however, it was decided not to prosecute him. On his release from prison, he asked for his passport, that he might go abroad. He has remained an exile ever since, and (according to Florimond, at any rate) "is spending his declining years colouring a meerschaum."

"People talk of the ingratitude of princes," said the Queen, last night. "But what of the ingratitude of nations? The Monterossans hated me because I dismissed M. Tsargradev; and then, when they saw him revealed in his true colours, they still hated me, in spite of it. They are quick to resent what they imagine to be an injury; but they never recognise a benefit. Oh, the folly of universal suffrage! The folly of constitutional government! I used to say, 'Surely a good despot is better than a mob.' But now I'm convinced that a *bad* despot, even, is better. Come, Florimond, let us sing.... you know.... that song...."

"God save—the best of despots?" suggested Florimond.

COUSIN ROSALYS

I sn't it a pretty name, Rosalys? But, for me, it is so much more; it is a sort of romantic symbol. I look at it written there on the page, and the sentiment of things changes: it is as if I were listening to distant music; it is as if the white paper turned softly pink, and breathed a perfume—never so faint a perfume of hyacinths. Rosalys, Cousin Rosalys.... London and this sad-coloured February morning become shadowy, remote. I think of another world, another era. Somebody has said that old memories and fond regrets are the day-dreams of the disappointed, the illusions of the age of disillusion. Well, if they are illusions, thank goodness they are where experience can't touch them—on the safe side of time.

———————————

Cousin Rosalys—I call her cousin. But, as we often used to remind ourselves, with a kind of esoteric satisfaction, we were not "real" cousins. She was the niece of my Aunt Elizabeth, and lived with her in Rome; but my Aunt Elizabeth was not my "real" aunt—only my great-aunt by marriage, the widow of my father's uncle. It was Aunt Elizabeth herself however, who dubbed us cousins, when she introduced us to each other; and at that epoch, for both of us, Aunt Elizabeth's lightest words were in the nature of decrees, she was such a terrible old lady.

I'm sure I don't know why she was terrible, I don't know how she contrived it; she never said anything, never did anything, especially terrifying; she wasn't especially wise or especially witty—intellectually, indeed, I suspect she might have passed for a paragon of respectable commonplaceness: but I do know that everybody stood in awe of her. I suppose it must simply have been her atmosphere, her odylic force; a sort of metaphysical chill that enveloped her, and was felt by all who approached her —some people *are* like that. Everybody stood in awe of her, everybody deferred to her: relations, friends, even her Director, and the cloud of priests that pervaded her establishment and gave it its character. For, like so many other old ladies who lived in Rome in those days, my Aunt Elizabeth was nothing if not Catholic, if not Ecclesiastical. You would have guessed as much, I think, from her exterior. She *looked* Catholic, she *looked*

Ecclesiastical. There was something Gothic in her anatomy, in the architecture of her face: in her high-bridged nose, in the pointed arch her hair made as it parted above her forehead, in her prominent cheek-bones, her straight-lipped mouth and long attenuated chin, in the angularities of her figure. No doubt the simile must appear far-sought, but upon my word her face used to remind me of a chapel—a chapel built of marble, fallen somewhat into decay. I'm not sure whether she was a tall woman, or whether she only had a false air of tallness, being excessively thin and holding herself rigidly erect.

She always dressed in black, in hard black silk cut to the severest patterns. Somehow, the very jewels she wore—not merely the cross on her bosom, but the rings on her fingers, the watch-chain round her neck, her watch itself, her old-fashioned, gold-faced watch—seemed of a mode canonical.

She was nothing if not Catholic, if not Ecclesiastical; but I don't in the least mean that she was particularly devout. She observed all requisite forms, of course: went, as occasion demanded, to mass, to vespers, to confession; but religious fervour was the last thing she suggested, the last thing she affected. I never heard her talk of Faith or Salvation, of Sin or Grace, nor indeed of any matters spiritual. She was quite frankly a woman of the world, and it was the Church as a worldly institution, the Church corporal, the Papacy, Papal politics, that absorbed her interests. The loss of the Temporal Power was the wrong that filled the universe for her, its restoration the cause for which she lived. That it was a forlorn cause she would never for an instant even hypothetically admit. "Remember Avignon, remember the Seventy Years," she used to say, with a nod that seemed to attribute apodictic value to the injunction.

"Mark my words, she'll live to be Pope yet," a ribald young man murmured behind her chair. "Oh, you tell me she is a woman. I'll assume it for the sake of the argument—I'd do anything for the sake of an argument. But remember Joan, remember Pope Joan!" And he mimicked his Aunt Elizabeth's inflection and her conclusive nod.

I had not been in Rome since that universe-filling wrong was perpetrated—not since I was a child of six or seven—when, a youth approaching twenty, I went there in the autumn of 1879; and I recollected Aunt Elizabeth only vaguely, as a lady with a face like a chapel, in whose presence—I had almost written in whose precincts—it had required some courage to breathe. But my mother's last words, when I left her in Paris, had been, "Now mind you call on your Aunt Elizabeth at once. You mustn't let a day pass. I am writing to her to tell her that you are coming. She will expect you to call at once." So, on the morrow of my arrival, I made an exceedingly careful toilet (I remember to this day the pains I bestowed upon my tie, the revisions to which I submitted it!), and, with an anxious heart, presented myself at the huge brown Roman palace, a portion of which my formidable relative inhabited; a palace with grated windows, and a vaulted, crypt-like porte-cochère, and a tremendous Swiss concierge, in knee-breeches and a cocked hat: the Palazzo Zacchinelli.

The Swiss, flourishing his staff of office, marshalled me (I can't use a less imposing word for the ceremony) slowly, solemnly, across a courtyard, and up a great stone staircase, at the top of which he handed me on to a functionary in black—a functionary with an ominously austere countenance, like an usher to the Inquisition. Poor old Archimede! Later, when I had come to know him well and tip him, I found he was the mildest creature, the amiablest, the most obliging, and that tenebrious mien of his only a congenital accident, like a lisp or a club-foot. But for the present he dismayed me, and I surrendered myself with humility and meekness to his guardianship. He conducted me through a series of vast chambers—you know those enormous, ungenial Roman rooms, their sombre tapestried walls, their formal furniture, their cheerless, perpetual twilight—and out upon a terrace.

The terrace lay in full sunshine. There was a garden below it, a garden with orange-trees, and rosebushes, and camellias, with stretches of greensward, with shrubberies, with a great fountain plashing in the midst of it, and broken, moss-grown statues: a Roman garden, from which a hundred sweet airs came up, in the gentle Roman weather. The balustrade of the terrace was set at intervals with flowering plants, in big urn-shaped vases; I don't remember what the flowers were, but they were pink, and many of their petals had fallen, and lay scattered on the grey terrace pavement. At the far end, under an awning brave with red and yellow stripes, two ladies were seated—a lady in black, presumably the object of my pious pilgrimage; and a lady in white, whom, even from a distance, I discovered to be young and pretty. A little round table stood between them, with a carafe of water and some tumblers glistening crisply on it. The lady in black was fanning herself with a black lace fan. The lady in white held a book in her hand, from which I think she had been reading aloud. A tiny imp of a red Pomeranian dog had started forward, and was barking furiously.

This scene must have made a deeper impression upon my perceptions than any that I was conscious of at the moment, because it has always remained as fresh in my memory as you see it now. It has always been a picture that I could turn to when I would, and find unfaded: the garden, the blue sky, the warm September sunshine, the long terrace, and the two ladies seated at the end of it, looking towards me, an elderly lady in black, and a young lady in white, with dark hair.

My aunt quieted Sandro (that was the dog's name), and giving me her hand, said "How do you do?" rather drily. And then, for what seemed a terribly long time, though no doubt it was only a few seconds, she kept me standing before her, while she scrutinised me through a double eye-glass, which she held by a mother-of-pearl handle; and I was acutely aware of the awkward figure I must be cutting to the vision of that strange young lady.

At last, "I should never have recognised you. As a child you were the image of your father. Now you resemble your mother," Aunt Elizabeth declared; and lowering her glass, she added, "This is your cousin Rosalys."

I wondered, as I made my bow, why I had never heard before that I had such a pretty cousin, with such a pretty name. She smiled on me very kindly, and I noticed how bright her eyes were, and how white and delicate her face. The little blue veins showed through the skin, and there was no more than just the palest, palest thought of colour in her cheeks. But her lips—exquisitely curved, sensitive lips—were warm red. She smiled on me very kindly, and I daresay my heart responded with an instant palpitation. She was a girl, and she was pretty; and her name was Rosalys; and we were cousins; and I was eighteen. And above us glowed the blue sky of Italy, and round us the golden sunshine; and there, beside the terrace, lay the beautiful old Roman garden, the fragrant, romantic garden.... If at eighteen one isn't susceptible and sentimental and impetuous, and prepared to respond with an instant sweet commotion to the smiles of one's pretty cousins (especially when they're named Rosalys), I protest one is unworthy of one's youth. One might as well be thirty-five, and a literary hack in London.

After that introduction, however, my aunt immediately reclaimed my attention. She proceeded to ask me all sorts of questions, about myself, about my people, uninteresting questions, disconcerting questions, which she posed with the air of one who knew the answers beforehand, and was only asking as an examiner asks, to test you. And all the while, the expression of her face, of her deprecating straight-lipped mouth, of her half-closed sceptical old eyes, seemed to imply that she already had her opinion of me, and that it wouldn't in the least be affected by anything I could say for myself, and that it was distinctly not a flattering opinion.

"Well, and what brings you to Rome?" That was one of her questions. I felt like a suspicious character haled before the local magistrate to give an account of his presence in the parish; putting on the best face I could, I pleaded superior orders. I had taken my *baccalauréat* in the summer; and my father desired me to pass some months in Italy, for the purpose of "patching up my Italian, which had suffered from the ravages of time," before I returned to Paris, and settled down to the study of a profession.

"H'm," said she, manifesting no emotion at what (in my simplicity) I deemed rather a felicitous metaphor; and then, as it were, she let me off with a warning. "Look out that you don't fall into bad company. Rome is full of dangerous people—painters, Bohemians, republicans, atheists. You must be careful. I shall keep my eye upon you."

By-and-by, to my relief, my aunt's director arrived, Monsignor Parlaghi, a tall, fat, cheerful, bustling man, who wore a silk cassock edged with purple, and a purple netted sash. When he sat down and crossed his legs, one saw a square-toed shoe with a silver buckle, and an inch or two of purple silk stocking. He began at once to talk with his penitent, about some matter to which I (happily) was a stranger; and that gave me my chance to break the ice with Rosalys.

She had risen to greet the Monsignore, and now stood by the balustrade of the terrace, half turned towards the garden, a slender, fragile figure, all in white. Her dark hair swept away from her forehead in lovely, long undulations, and her white face, beneath it, seemed almost spirit-like in its delicacy, almost immaterial.

"I am richer than I thought. I did not know I had a Cousin Rosalys," said I.

It looks like a sufficiently easy thing to say, doesn't it? And besides, hadn't I carefully composed and corrected and conned it beforehand in the silence of my mind? But I remember the mighty effort of will it cost me to get it said. I suppose it is in the design of nature that Eighteen should find it nervous work to break the ice with pretty girls. At any rate, I remember how my heart fluttered, and what a hollow, unfamiliar sound my voice had; I remember that in the very middle of the enterprise my pluck and my presence of mind suddenly deserted me, and everything became a blank, and for one horrible moment I thought I was going to break down utterly, and stand there staring, blushing, speechless. But then I made a further mighty effort of will, a desperate effort, and somehow, though they nearly choked me, the premeditated words came out.

"Oh, we're not *real* cousins," said she, letting her eyes shine for a second on my face. And she explained to me just what the connection between us was. "But we will call ourselves cousins," she concluded.

The worst was over; the worst, though Eighteen was still, no doubt, conscious of perturbations. I don't know how long we stood chatting together there by the balustrade, but presently I said something about the garden, and she proposed that we should go down into it. So she led me to the other end of the terrace, where there was a flight of steps, and we went down into the garden.

The merest trifles, in such weather, with a pretty new-found Cousin Rosalys for a comrade, are delightful, when one is eighteen, aren't they? It was delightful to feel the yielding turf under our feet, the cool grass curling round our ankles—for in Roman gardens, in those old days, it wasn't the fashion to clip the grass close, as on an English lawn. It was delightful to walk in the shade of the orange-trees, and breathe the air sweetened by them. The stillness the dreamy stillness of the soft, sunny afternoon was delightful; the crumbling old statues were delightful, statues of fauns and dryads, of Pagan gods and goddesses, Pan and Bacchus and Diana, their noses broken for the most part, their bodies clothed in mosses and leafy vines. And the flowers were delightful; the cyclamens, with which—so abundant were they—the walls of the garden fairly dripped, as with a kind of pink foam; and the roses, and the waxen red and white camellias. It was delightful to stop before the great brown old fountain, and listen to its tinkle-tinkle of cold water, and peer into its basin, all green with weeds, and watch the antics of the goldfishes, and the little rainbows the sun struck from the spray. And my Cousin Rosalys's white frock was delightful, and her voice was delightful; and that perturbation in my heart was exquisitely delightful—something between a thrill and a tremor—a delicious mixture of fear and wonderment and beatitude. I had dragged myself hither to pay a duty-call upon my grim old dragon of a great-aunt Elizabeth; and here I was wandering amid the hundred delights of a romantic Italian garden, with a lovely, white-robed, bright-eyed sylph of a Cousin Rosalys.

Don't ask me what we talked about. I have only the most fragmentary recollection. I remember she told me that her father and mother had died in India, when she was a child, and that her father (Aunt Elizabeth's "ever so much younger brother") had been in the army, and that she had lived with Aunt Elizabeth since she was twelve. And I remember she asked me to speak French with her, because in Rome she almost always spoke Italian or English, and she didn't want to forget her French; and "You're, of course, almost a Frenchman, living in Paris." So we spoke French together, saying *ma cousine* and *mon cousin*, which was very intimate and pleasant; and she spoke it so well that I expressed some surprise. "If you don't put on at least a *slight* accent, I shall tell you you're almost a Frenchman too," I threatened. "Oh, I had French nurses when I was little," she said, "and afterwards a French governess, till I was sixteen. I'm eighteen now. How old are you?" I had heard that girls always liked a man to be older than themselves, and I answered that I was nearly twenty. Well, and isn't eighteen nearly twenty?.... Anyhow, as I walked back to my lodgings that afternoon, through the busy, twisted, sunlit Roman streets, Cousin Rosalys filled all my heart and all my thoughts with a white radiance.

<hr>

You will conceive whether or not, during the months that followed, I was an assiduous visitor at the Palazzo Zacchinelli. But I couldn't spend *all* my time there, and in my enforced absences I needed consolation. I imagine I treated Aunt Elizabeth's advice about avoiding bad company as youth is wont to treat the counsels of crabbed age. Doubtless my most frequent associates were those very painters and Bohemians against whom she had particularly cautioned me—whether they were also republicans and atheists, I don't think I ever knew; I can't remember that I inquired, and religion and politics were subjects they seldom touched upon spontaneously. I dare say I joined the artists' club, in the Via Margutta, the Circolo Internazionale degli Artisti; I am afraid the Caffe Greco was my favourite café; I am afraid I even bought a wide-awake hat, and wore it on the back of my head, and tried to look as much like a painter and Bohemian myself as nature would permit.

Bad company? I don't know. It seemed to me very good company indeed. There was Jack Everett, tall and slim and athletic, with his eager aquiline face, his dark curling hair, the most poetic-looking creature, humorous, whimsical, melancholy, imaginative, who used to quote Byron, and plan our best practical jokes, and do the loveliest little cupids and roses in water-colours. He has since married the girl he was even then in love with, and is still living in Rome, and painting cupids and roses. And there was d'.vignac, *le vicomte*, a young Frenchman, who had been in the Diplomatic Service, and —superlative distinction!—"ruined himself for a woman," and now was striving to keep body and soul together by giving fencing lessons; witty, kindly, pathetic d'.vignac—we have vanished altogether from each other's ken. There was Ulysse Tavoni, the musician, who, when somebody asked him what instrument he played, answered cheerily, "All instruments." I can testify from personal observation that he played the piano and the flute, the guitar, mandoline, fiddle, and French horn, the 'cello and the zither. And there was Kônig, the Austrian sculptor, a tiny man with a ferocious black moustache, whom my landlady (he having called upon me one day when I was out), unable to remember his transalpine name, described to perfection as "un Orlando Furioso—ma molto piccolo." There was a dear, dreamy, languid, sentimental Pole, blue-eyed and yellow-haired, also a sculptor, whose name I have totally forgotten, though we were sworn to "hearts' brotherhood," He had the most astonishing talent for imitating the sounds of animals, the neighing of a horse, the crowing of a cock; and when he brayed like a donkey, all the donkeys within earshot were deceived, and answered him. And then there was Father Flynn, a jolly old bibulous priest from Cork. An uncle of his had fought at Waterloo; it was great to hear him tell of his uncle's part in the fortunes of the day. It was great, too (for Father Flynn was a fervid Irish patriot), to hear him roar out the "Wearing of the Green." Between the stanzas he would brandish his blackthorn, stick at Everett, and call him a "murthering English tyrant," to our huge delectation.

There were others and others and others; but these six are those who come back first to my memory. They seemed to me very good company indeed; very merry, and genial, and amusing; and the life we led together seemed a very pleasant life. Oh, our pleasures were of the simplest nature, the traditional pleasures of Bohemia; smoking and drinking and talking, rambling arm-in-arm through the streets, lounging in studios, going to the play or perhaps the circus, or making excursions into the country. Only, the capital of our Bohemia was Rome. The streets through which we rambled were Roman streets, with their inexhaustible picturesqueness, their unending vicissitudes: with their pink and yellow houses, their shrines, their fountains, their gardens, their motley wayfarers—monks and soldiers; shaggy pifferari, and contadine in their gaudy costumes, and models masquerading as contadine; penitents, beggars, water-carriers, hawkers; priests in their vestments, bearing the Host, attended by acolytes, with burning tapers, who rang little bells, whilst men uncovered and women crossed themselves; and everywhere, everywhere, English tourists, with their noses in Baedeker. It was Rome with its bright sun, and its deep shadows; with its Ghetto, its Tiber, its Castel Sant' Angelo; with its churches, and palaces, and ruins; with its Villa Borghese and its Pincian Hill; with its waving green Campagna at its gates. We smoked and talked and drank—Chianti, of course, and sunny Orvieto, and fabled Est-Est-Est, all in those delightful pear-shaped, wicker-covered flasks, which of themselves, I fancy, would confer a flavour upon indifferent wine. We made excursions to Tivoli and Frascati, to Monte Cavo and Nemi, to Acqua Acetosa. We patronised Pulcinella, and the marionettes, and (better still) the *imitation* marionettes. We blew horns on the night of Epiphany, we danced at masked balls, we put on dominoes and romped in the Corso during carnival, throwing flowers and confetti, and struggling to extinguish other people's *moccoli*. And on rainy days (with an effort I can remember that there were *some* rainy days) Everett and I would sit with d'.vignac in his fencing gallery, and talk and smoke, and smoke and talk and talk. D'.vignac was six-and-twenty, Everett was twenty-two, and I was "nearly twenty." D'.vignac would tell us of his past, of his adventures in Spain and Japan and South America, and of the lady for the love of whom he had come to grief. Everett and I would sigh profoundly, and shake our heads, and exchange sympathetic glances, and assure him that we knew what love was—we were victims of unfortunate attachments ourselves. To each other we had confided everything, Everett and I. He had told me all about his unrequited passion for Maud Eaton, and I had rhapsodised to him by the hour about Cousin Rosalys. "But you, old chap, you're to be envied," he would cry. "Here you are in the same town with her, by Jove! You can *see* her, you can plead your cause. Think of that. I wish I had half your luck. Maud is far away in England, buried in a country-house down in Lancashire. She might as well be on another planet, for all the good I get of her. But you—why, you can see your Cousin Rosalys this very hour if you like! Oh, heavens, what wouldn't I give for half your luck!" The wheel of Time, the wheel of Time! Everett and Maud are married, but Cousin Rosalys and I…. Heigh-ho! I wonder whether, in our thoughts of ancient days, it is more what we remember or what we forget that makes them sweet? Anyhow, for the moment, we forget the dismal things that have happened since.

Yes, I was in the same town with her, by Jove; I could *see* her. And indeed I did see her many times every week. Like the villain in a melodrama, I led a double life. When I was not disguised as a Bohemian, in a velvet jacket and a wide-awake, smoking and talking and holding wassail with my boon companions, you might have observed a young man attired in the height of the prevailing fashion (his top-hat and varnished boots flashing fire in the eyes of the Roman populace), going to call on his Aunt Elizabeth. And his Aunt Elizabeth, pleased by such dutiful attentions, rewarded him with frequent invitations to dinner. Her other guests would be old ladies like herself, and old gentlemen, and priests, priests, priests. So that Rosalys and I, the only young ones present, were naturally paired together. After dinner Rosalys would play and sing, while I hung over her piano. Oh, how beautifully she played Chopin! How ravishingly she sang! Schubert's *Wohin, and Rôslein, Rôslein, Rôslein roth;* and Gounod's *Sérénade* and his *Barcarolle*:

160

"Dites la jeune belle,

Où voulez-vous aller?"

And how angelically beautiful she looked! Her delicate, pale face, and her dark, undulating hair, and her soft red lips; and then her eyes—her luminous, mysterious dark eyes, in whose depths, far, far within, you could discern her spirit shining starlike. And her hands, white and slender and graceful, images in miniature of herself; with what incommunicable wonder and admiration I used to watch them as they moved above the keys. "A woman who plays Chopin ought to have three hands—two to play with, and one for the man who's listening to hold." That was a pleasantry which I meditated much in secret, and a thousand times aspired to murmur in the player's ear, but invariably, when it came to the point of doing so, my courage failed me. "You can see her, you can plead your cause." Bless me, I never dared even vaguely to hint that I had any cause to plead. I imagine young love is always terribly afraid of revealing itself to its object, terribly afraid and terribly desirous. Whenever I was not in Cousin Rosalys's presence, my heart was consumed with longing to tell her that I loved her, to ask her whether perhaps she might be not wholly indifferent to me; I made the boldest resolutions, committed to memory the most persuasive declarations. But from the instant I *was* in her presence again—mercy, what panic seized me!

I could have died sooner than speak the words that I was dying to speak, ask the question I was dying to ask.

I called assiduously at the Palazzo Zacchinelli, and my aunt bade me to dinner a good deal, and then one afternoon every week she used to drive with Rosalys on the Pincian. There was one afternoon every week when all Rome drove on the Pincian; was it Saturday? At any rate, you may be very sure I did not let such opportunities escape me for getting a bow and a smile from my cousin. Sometimes she would leave the carriage and join me, while Aunt Elizabeth, with Sandro in her lap, drove on, round and round the consecrated circle; and we would stroll together in the winding alleys, or stand by the terrace and look off over the roofs of the city, and watch the sunset blaze and fade behind St. Peter's. You know that unexampled view—the roofs of Rome spread out beneath you like the surface of a troubled sea, and the dome of St. Peter's, an island rising in the distance, and the sunset sky behind it. We would stand there in silence perhaps, at most saying very little, while the sunset burned itself out; and for one of us, at least, it was a moment of ineffable, impossible enchantment. She was so near to me—so near, the slender figure in the pretty frock, with the dark hair, and the captivating hat, and the furs; with her soft glowing eyes, with her exquisite fragrance of girlhood; she was so near to me, so alone with me, despite the crowd about us, and I loved her so! Oh, why couldn't I tell her? Why couldn't she divine it? People said that women always knew by intuition when men were in love with them. Why couldn't Rosalys divine that I loved her, *how* I loved her, and make me a sign, and so enable me to speak?

Presently—and all too soon—she would return to the carriage, and drive away with Aunt Elizabeth; and I, in the lugubrious twilight, would descend the great marble Spanish staircase (a perilous path, amongst models and beggars and other things) to the Piazza, and seek out Jack Everett at the Caffé Greco. Thence he and I would go off to dine together somewhere, condoling with each other upon our ill-starred passions. After dinner, pulling our hats over our eyes, two desperately tragic forms, we would set ourselves upon the traces of d'.vignac and Kônig and Father Flynn, determined to forget our sorrows in an evening of dissipation, saying regretfully, "These are the evil courses to which the love of woman has reduced us—a couple of the best-meaning fellows in Christendom, and surely born for better ends." When we were children (hasn't Kenneth Grahame written it for us in a golden book?) we played at conspirators and pirates. When we were a little older, and Byron or Musset had superseded Fenimore Cooper, some of us found there was an unique excitement to be got from the game of Blighted Beings.

Oh, why couldn't I tell her? Why couldn't she divine it, and make me an encouraging sign?

But, of course, in the end I did tell her. It was on the night of my birthday. I had dined at the Palazzo Zacchinelli, and with the dessert a great cake was brought in and set before me. A number of little red candles were burning round it, and embossed upon it in frosting was this device:

A birthday-piece

From Rosalys,

Wishing birthdays more in plenty

To her cousin "nearly twenty."

And counting the candles, I perceived they were *nineteen.*

Probably my joy was somewhat tempered by confusion, to think that my little equivocation on the subject of my age had been discovered. As I looked up from the cake to its giver, I met a pair of eyes that were gleaming with mischievous raillery; and she shook her head at me, and murmured, "Oh, you fibber!"

"How on earth did you find out?" I wondered.

"Oh—a little bird," laughed she.

"I don't think it's at all respectful of you to call Aunt Elizabeth a little bird," said I.

After dinner we went out upon the terrace. It was a warm night, and there was a moon. A moonlit night in Italy—dark velvet shot with silver. And the air was intoxicant with the scent of hyacinths. We were in March; the garden had become a wilderness of spring flowers, narcissuses and jonquils, crocuses, anemones, tulips, and hyacinths; hyacinths, everywhere hyacinths. Rosalys had thrown a bit of white lace over her hair. Oh, I assure you, in the moonlight, with the white lace over her hair, with her pale face, and her eyes, her shining, mysterious eyes—oh, I promise you, she was lovely.

"How beautiful the garden is, in the moonlight, isn't it?" she said. "The shadows, and the statues, and the fountains. And how sweet the air is. They're the hyacinths that smell so sweet. The hyacinth is your birthday flower, you know. Hyacinths bring happiness to people born in March."

I looked into her eyes, and my heart thrilled and thrilled. And then, somehow, somehow... Oh, I don't remember what I said; only somehow, somehow... Ah, but I do remember very clearly what she answered—so softly, so softly, while her hand lay in mine. I remember it very clearly, and at the memory, even now, years afterwards, I confess my heart thrills again.

We were joined, in a minute or two, by Monsignor Parlaghi, and we tried to behave as if he were not unwelcome.

Adam and Eve were driven from Eden for their guilt; but it was Innocence that lost our Eden for Rosalys and me. In our egregious innocence, we had determined that I should call upon Aunt Elizabeth in the morning, and formally demand her sanction to our engagement! Do I need to recount the history of that interview? Of my aunt's incredulity, that gradually changed to scorn and anger? Of how I was fleered at and flouted, and taunted with my youth, and called a fool and a coxcomb, and sent about my business with the information that the portals of the Palazzo Zacchinelli would remain eternally closed against me for the future, and that my people "would be written to"? I was not even allowed to see my cousin to say good-bye. "And mind you, we'll have no letter writing," cried Aunt Elizabeth. "I shall forbid Rosalys to receive any letters from you."

Guilt (we are taught) can be annulled, and its punishment remitted, if we do heartily repent. But innocence? Goodness knows how heartily I repented; yet I never found that a pennyweight of the punishment was remitted. At the week's end I got a letter from my people recalling me to Paris. And I never saw Rosalys again. And some years afterwards she married an Italian, a nephew of Cardinal Badascalchi. And in 1887, at Viareggio, she died....

———————————

Eh bien, voilà! There is the little inachieved, the little unfulfilled romance, written for me in her name, Cousin Rosalys. What of it? Oh, nothing—except —except... Oh, nothing. *"All good things come to him who waits."* *Perhaps.* *But we know how apt they are to come too late; and—sometimes they come too early.*

———————————

FLOWER O' THE CLOVE

I

I n the first-floor sitting-room of a lodging-house in Great College Street, Westminster, a young man—he was tall and thin, with a good deal of rather longish light-coloured hair, somewhat tumbled about; and he wore a pince-nez, and was in slippers and the oldest of tattered coats—a man of thirty-something was seated at a writing-table, diligently scribbling at what an accustomed eye might have recognised as "copy," and negligently allowing the smoke from a cigarette to curl round and stain the thumb and forefinger of his idle hand, when the lodging-house maid-servant opened his door, and announced excitedly, "A lady to see you, sir."

With the air of one taken altogether by surprise, and at a cruel disadvantage, the writer dropped his pen, and jumped up. He was in slippers and a disgraceful coat, not to dwell upon the condition of his hair. "You ought to have kept her downstairs until———" he began, frowning upon the maid; and at that point his visitor entered the room.

She was a handsome, dashing-looking young woman, in a toilette that breathed the very last and crispest savour of Parisian elegance: a hat that was a tangle of geraniums, an embroidered jacket, white gloves, a skirt that frou-froued breezily as she moved; and she carried an amazing silver-hilted sunshade, a thing like a folded gonfalon, a thing of red silk gleaming through draperies of black lace.

Poising lightly near the threshold, with a little smile of interrogation, this bewildering vision said, "Have I the honour of addressing Mr. William Stretton?"

The young man bowed a vague acknowledgment of that name; but his gaze, through the lenses of his pince-nez, was all perplexity and question.

"I'm very fortunate in finding you at home. I've called to see you about a matter of business," she informed him.

"Oh?" he wondered. Then he added, with a pathetic shake of the head, "I'm the last man in the world whom any one could wisely choose to see about a matter of business; but such as I am, I'm all at your disposal."

"So much the better," she rejoined cheerily. "I infinitely prefer to transact business with people who are unbusinesslike. One has some chance of overreaching them."

"You'll have every chance of over-reaching me," sighed he.

"What a jolly quarter of the town you live in," she commented. "It's so picturesque and Gothic and dilapidated, with such an atmosphere of academic calm. It reminds me of Oxford."

"Yes," assented he, "it *is* a bit like Oxford. Was your business connected ——?"

"Oh, it *is* like Oxford?" she interrupted. "Then never tell me again that there's nothing in intuitions. I've never been in Oxford, but directly I passed the gateway of Dean's Yard, I felt reminded of it."

"There's undoubtedly a lot in intuitions," he agreed; "and for the future I shall carefully abstain from telling you there isn't."

"Those things are gardens, over the way, behind the wall, aren't they?" she asked, looking out of the window.

"Yes," he said, "those things are gardens, the gardens of the Abbey. The canons and people have their houses there."

"Very comfortable and nice," said she. "Plenty of grass. And the trees aren't bad, either, for town trees. It must be rather fun to be a canon. As I live," she cried, turning back into the room, "you've got a Pleyel. This is the first Pleyel I've seen in England. Let me congratulate you on your taste in pianos." And with her gloved hands she struck a chord and made a run or two. "You'll need the tuner soon, though. It's just the shadow of a shadow out. I was brought up on Pleyels. Do you know, I've half a mind to make you a confidence?" she questioned brightly.

"Oh, do make it, I pray you," he encouraged her.

"Well, then, I believe, if you were to offer me a chair, I believe I could bring myself to sit down," she admitted.

"I beg your pardon," he exclaimed; and she sank rustling into the chair that he pushed forward.

"Well, now for my business," said she. "Would you just put this thing somewhere?" She offered him her sunshade, which he took and handled somewhat gingerly. "Oh, you needn't be afraid. It's quite tame," she laughed, "though I admit it looks a bit ferocious. What a sweet room you've got—so manny, and smoky, and booky. Are they all real books?"

"More or less real," he answered; "as real as any books ever are that a fellow gets for review."

"Oh, you got them for review?" she repeated, with vivacity. "How terribly exciting. I've never seen a book before that's actually passed through a reviewer's hands. They don't look much the worse for it. Whatever else you said about them, I trust you didn't deny that they make nice domestic ornaments. But this isn't business. *You* wouldn't call this business?" she enquired, with grave curiosity.

"No, I should call this pleasure," he assured her, laughing.

"*Would* you?" She raised her eyebrows. "Ah, but then you're English."

"Aren't you?" asked he.

"Do I look English?"

"I'm not sure." He hesitated for a second, studying her. "You certainly don't dress English."

"Heaven forbid Î" She made a fervent gesture. "I'm a miserable sinner, but at least I'm incapable of that. However, if you were really kind, you'd affect just a little curiosity to know the errand to which you owe my presence."

"I'm devoured by curiosity," he declared.

Again she raised her eyebrows. "You are? Then why don't you show it?"

"Perhaps because I have a sense of humour—amongst other reasons," he suggested, smiling.

"Well, since you're devoured by curiosity, you must know," she began; but broke off suddenly—"Apropos, I wonder whether *you* could be induced to tell *me* something."

"I daresay I could, if it's anything within my sphere of knowledge." He paused, expectant.

"Then tell me, please, why you keep your Japanese fan in your fireplace," she requested.

"Why shouldn't I? Doesn't it strike you as a good place for it?"

"Admirable. But my interest was psychological. I was wondering by what mental processes you came to hit upon it."

"Well, then, to be frank, it wasn't I who hit upon it; it isn't my Japanese fan. It's a conceit of my landlady's. This is an age of paradox, you know. Would you prefer silver paper?"

"*Must* one have one or the other?"

"You're making it painfully clear," he cautioned her, "that you've never lived in lodgings."

"If you go on at this rate," she retorted, laughing, "I shall never get my task accomplished. Here are twenty times that I've commenced it, and twenty times you've put me off. Shall we now, at last, proceed seriously to business?"

"Not on my account, I beg. I'm not in the slightest hurry," protested he.

"You said you were devoured by curiosity."

"Did I say that?" He knitted his brow.

"Certainly you did."

"It must have been aphasia. I meant contentment," he explained.

"Devoured by contentment?"

"Why not, as well as by curiosity?"

"The phrase is novel," she mused.

"It's the occupation of my life to seek for novel phrases," he reminded her. "I'm what somebody or other has called a literary man."

"And you enjoy what somebody or other has called beating about the bush?"

"Hugely—with such a fellow-beater," he responded.

"You drive me to extremities." She shook her head. "I see there's nothing for it but to plunge in *médias res*. You must know, then, that I have been asked to call upon you by a friend—by my friend Miss Johannah Rothe—I beg your pardon; I never *can* remember that she's changed her name—my friend Miss Johannah Silver—but Silver *née* Rothe—of Silver Towers, in the County of Sussex."

"Ah?" said he. "Ah, yes. Then never tell me again that there's nothing in intuitions. I've never met Miss Silver, but directly you crossed the threshold of this room, I began to feel vaguely reminded of her."

"Oh, there's a lot in intuitions," she agreed. "But don't think to disconcert me. My friend Miss Silver——"

It was his turn to raise his eyebrows. "Your *friend?*"

"Considering the sacrifice I'm making on her behalf to-day, it's strange you should throw doubt upon my friendship for her," she argued.

"You make your sacrifices with a cheerful countenance. I should never have guessed that you weren't entirely happy. But forgive my interruption.

You were about to say that your friend Miss Silver——"

"My occasional friend," she substituted. "Sometimes, I confess, we quarrel like everything, and remain at daggers drawn for months. She's such a flighty creature, dear Johannah, she not infrequently gets me into a perfect peck of trouble. But since she's fallen heir to all this money, you'd be surprised to behold the devotion her friends have shown her. I couldn't very well refuse to follow their example. One's human, you see; and one can't dress like this for nothing, can one?"

"Upon my word, I'm not in a position to answer you. I've never tried," laughed he.

"In the absence of evidence to the contrary, I think we may safely assume one can't," said she. "However, here you are, beating about the bush again. I come to you as Johannah's emissary. She desires me to ask you several questions."

"Yes?" said he, a trifle uncomfortably.

"She would be glad to know," his visitor declared, looking straight into his eyes, and smiling a little gravely, "why you have been so excessively nasty to her?"

"Have I been nasty to her?" he asked, with an innocence that was palpably counterfeit.

"Don't you think you have?" She still looked gravely, smilingly, into his eyes.

"I don't see how." He maintained his feint of innocence.

"Don't you think you've responded somewhat ungraciously to her overtures of friendship?" she suggested. "Do you think it was nice to answer her letters with those curt little formal notes of yours? Look. Johannah sat down to write to you. And she began her letter *Dear Mr. Stretton*. And then she simply couldn't. So she tore up the sheet, and began another *My Dear Cousin Will*. And what did she receive in reply? A note beginning *Dear Miss Silver*. Do you think that was kind? Don't you think it was the least bit mortifying? And why have you refused in such a stiff-necked way to go down to see her at Silver Towers?"

"Oh," he protested, "in all fairness, in all logic, your questions ought to be put the other way round."

"Bother logic! But put them any way you like," said she.

"What right had Miss Silver to expect me to multiply the complications of my life by rushing into an ecstatic friendship with her? And why, being very well as I am in town just now, why should I disarrange myself by a journey into the country?"

"Why indeed?" she echoed. "I'm sure I can give no reason. Why should one ever do any one else a kindness? Your cousin has conceived a great desire to meet you."

"Oh, a great desire!" He tossed his head. "One knows these great desires. She'll live it down. A man named Burrell has been stuffing her up."

"Stuffing her up?" She smiled enquiringly. "The expression is new to me."

"Greening her, filling her head with all sorts of nonsensical delusions, painting my portrait for her in all the colours of the rainbow. Oh, I know my Burrell. He's tried to stuff *me* up, too, about her."

"Oh? Has he? What has he said?" she questioned eagerly.

"The usual rubbishy things one does say, when one wants to stuff a fellow up."

"For instance?"

"Oh, that she's tremendously good-looking, with hair and eyes and things, and very charming."

"What a dear good person the man named Burrell must be," she murmured.

"He's not a bad chap," he conceded, "but you must remember that he's her solicitor."

"And, remembering that, you weren't to be stuffed?" she said.

"If she was charming and good-looking, it was a reason the more for avoiding her," said he.

"Oh?" She looked perplexed.

"There's nothing on earth so tiresome as charming women. They're all exactly alike," asserted he.

"Thank you," his guest exclaimed, bowing.

"Oh, nobody could pretend that *you're* exactly alike," he assured her hastily. "I own at once that you're delightfully different. But Burrell has no knack for character drawing."

"You're extremely flattering. But aren't you taking a slightly one-sided point of view? Let us grant, for the sake of the argument, that it is Johannah's bad luck to be charming and good-looking. Nevertheless, she still has claims on you."

"Has she?"

"She's your cousin."

"Oh, by the left hand," said he.

She stared for an instant, biting her lip. Then she laughed.

"And only my second or third cousin at that," he went on serenely.

She looked at him with eyes that were half whimsical, half pleading. "Would you mind being quite serious for a moment?" she asked. "Because Johannah's situation, absurd as it seems, really is terribly serious for Johannah. I should like to submit it to your better judgment. We'll drop the question of cousinship, if you wish—though it's the simple fact that you're her only blood-relation in this country, where she feels herself the forlornest sort of alien. She's passed her entire life in Italy and France, you know, and this is the first visit she's made to England since her childhood. But we'll drop the question of cousinship. At any rate, Johannah is a human being. Well, consider her plight a little. She finds herself in the most painful, the most humiliating circumstances that can be imagined; and you're the only person living who can make them easier for her. Involuntarily—in spite of herself— she's come into possession of a fortune that naturally, morally, belongs to you. She can't help it. It's been left to her by will—by the will of a man who never saw her, never had any kind of relations with her, but chose her for his heir just because her mother, who died when Johannah was a baby, had chanced to be his cousin. And there the poor girl is. Can't you see how like a thief she must feel at the best? Can't you see how much worse you make it for her, when she holds out her hand, and you refuse to take it? Is that magnanimous of you? Isn't it cruel? You couldn't treat her with greater unkindness if she'd actually designed, and schemed, and intrigued, to do you out of your inheritance, instead of coming into it in the passive way she has. After all, she's a human being, she's a woman. Think of her pride."

"Think of mine," said he.

"I can't see that your pride is involved."

"To put it plainly, I'm the late Sir William Silver's illegitimate son."

"Well? What of that?"

"Do you fancy I should enjoy being taken up and patronised by his legitimate heir?"

"Oh!" she cried, starting to her feet. "You can't think I would be capable of anything so base as that."

And he saw that her eyes had suddenly filled with tears.

"I beg your pardon, I beg your pardon a thousand times," he said. "You would be utterly incapable of anything that was not generous and noble. But you must remember that I had never seen you. How could I know?"

"Well, now that you *have* seen me," she responded, her eyes all smiles again, "now that I have put my pride in my pocket, and bearded you in your den, I don't mind confiding in you that it's nearly lunchtime, and also that I'm ravenously hungry. Could you ring your bell, and order up something in the nature of meat and drink? And while you are about it, you might tell your landlady or some one to pack your bag. We take," she mentioned, examining a tiny watch, that seemed nothing more than a frivolous incrustation of little diamonds and rubies, "we take the three-sixteen for Silver Towers."

II.

Seated opposite her in the railway-carriage, as their train bore them through the pleasant dales and woods of Surrey, Will Stretton fell to studying his cousin's appearance. "Burrell was right," he told himself; "she really is tremendously good-looking," and that, in spite of a perfectly reckless irregularity of feature. Her nose was too small, but it was a delicate, pert, pretty nose, notwithstanding. Her mouth was too large, but it was a beautiful mouth, all the same, softly curved and red as scarlet, with sensitive, humorous little quirks in its corners. Her eyes he could admire without reservation, brown and pellucid, with the wittiest, teasingest, mockingest lights dancing in them, yet at the same time a deeper light that was pensive, tender, womanly. Her hair, too, he decided, was quite lovely, abundant, undulating, black, blue-black even, but fine, but silky, escaping in a flutter of small curls above her brow. "It's like black foam," he said. And he would have been ready to go to war for her complexion, though it was so un-English a complexion that one might have mistaken her for a native of the France or Italy she had inhabited: warm, dusky white, with an elusive shadow of rose glowing through it. Yes, she was tremendously good-looking, he concluded. She looked fresh and strong and real. She looked alert, alive, full of the spring and the joy of life. She looked as if she could feel quick and deep, as if her blood flowed swiftly, and was red. He liked her face, and he liked her figure—it was supple and vigorous. He liked the way she dressed—there was something daring and spirited in the uncompromising, unabashed luxury of it. "Who ever saw such a hat—or such a sunshade?" he reflected.

"There'll be no coach-and-four to meet us at the station," she warned him, as they neared their journey's end, "because I have no horses. But we'll probably find Madame Dornaye there, *piaffer*-ing in person. Can you resign yourself to the prospect of driving up to your ancestral mansion in a hired fly?"

"I could even, at a pinch, resign myself to walking," he declared. "But who is Madame Dornaye?"

"Madame Dornaye is my burnt-offering to that terrible sort of fetich called the County. She's what might be technically termed my chaperon."

"Oh, to be sure," he said; "I had forgotten. Of course, you'd have a chaperon."

"By no means of course," she corrected him. "Until the other day I'd never thought of such a thing. But it's all along o' the man named Burrell. He insisted that I mustn't live alone—that I was too young. He has such violent hallucinations about people's ages. He said the County would be horrified. I must have an old woman, a sound, reliable old woman, to live with me. I begged and implored *him* to come and try it, but he protested with tears in his eyes that he wasn't an old woman. So I sent for Madame Dornaye, who is, every inch of her. She's the widow of a man who used to be a professor at the Sorbonne, or something. I've known her for at least a hundred years. She's connected in some roundabout way with the family of my father's stepmother. She's like a little dry brown leaf; and she plays Chopin *comme pas un*; and she lends me a false air of respectability, I suppose. She calls me *Jeanne ma fille*, if you can believe it, as if my name weren't common Johannah. If you chance to please her, she'll very likely call you *Jean mon fils*. But see how things turn out. The man named Burrell also insisted that I must put on mourning, as a symbol of my grief for the late Sir William. That I positively refused to think of. So the County's horrified, all the same—which proves the futility of concessions."

"Oh?" questioned Will. "What does the County do?"

"It comes and calls on me, and walks round me, and stares, with a funny little deprecating smile, as if I were some outlandish and not very proper animal, cast up by the sea. To begin with, there's the vicar, with all his wives and daughters. *Their* emotions are complicated by the fact that I am a Papist. Then there's old Lord Belgard; and there's Mrs. Breckenbridge, with her marriageable sons; and there's the Bishop of Salchester, with his Bishopess, Dean, and Chapter. The dear good people make up parties in the afternoon, to come and have a look at me; and they sip my tea with an air of guilt, as if it smacked of profligacy; and they suppress demure little knowing glances among themselves. And then at last they go away, shaking their heads, and talking me over in awe-struck voices."

"I can see them, I can hear them," Will laughed.

"Haven't you in English a somewhat homely proverbial expression about the fat and the fire?" asked Johannah.

"About the fat getting into the fire? Yes," said Will.

"Well, then, to employ that somewhat homely proverbial expression," she went on, "the fat got into the fire at the Bishop's palace. Mrs. Rawley was kind enough to write and ask us to dinner, and she added that she had heard I sang, and wouldn't I bring some music? But nobody had ever told me that it's bad form in England to sing *well*. So, after dinner, when Mrs. Rawley said, 'Now, Miss Silver, do sing us something,' I made the incredible blunder of singing as well as I could. I sang the *Erlkônig*, and Madame Dornaye played the accompaniment, and we both did our very bestest, in our barefaced, Continental way. We were a little surprised, and vastly enlightened, to perceive that we'd shocked everybody. And by-and-by the Bishop's daughters consented to sing in their turn, and then we saw the correct British style of doing it. If you don't want to be considered rowdyish and noisy in a British drawing-room, you must sing under your breath, faintly, faintingly, as if you were afraid somebody might hear you."

"My poor dear young lady," her cousin commiserated her, "fancy your only just discovering that. It's one of the foundation-stones of our social constitution. If you sing with any art or with any feeling, you expose yourself to being mistaken for a paid professional."

"Another thing that's horrified the County," pursued Johannah, "is the circumstance that I keep no horses. I don't like horses—except in pictures. In pictures, I admit at once, they make a very pleasant decorative motive. But in life—they're too strong and too unintelligent; and they're perpetually bolting. By-the-bye, please choose a good feeble jaded one, when you engage our fly. I'm devoted to donkeys, though. They're every bit as decorative as the horse, and they're really wise—they only baulk. I had a perfect love of a little donkey in Italy; his name was Angelo. If I decide to stay in England, I shall have a spanking team of four donkeys, with scarlet trappings and silver bells. But the County say 'Oh, you *must* have horses,' and casts its eyes appealingly to heaven when I say I *won't*."

"The County lacks a sense of situations," he reflected. "It's really a deliciously fresh one—a big country house, and not a horse in the stables."

"Apropos of the house, that brings me to another point," said she. "The County feels very strongly that I ought to put the house in repair—that dear old wonderful, rambling, crumbling house. They take it as the final crushing evidence of my depravity, that I prefer to leave it in its present condition of picturesque decay. I'm sure you agree with me, that it would be high treason to allow a carpenter or mason to lay a hand on it. By-the-bye, I hope you have no conscientious scruples against speaking French; for Madame Dornaye only knows two words of English, and those she mispronounces. There she is—yes, that little black and grey thing, in the frock. She's come to meet me, because we had a bet. You owe me five shillings," she called out to Madame Dornaye, as Will helped her from the carriage. "You see, I've brought him."

Madame Dornaye, who had a pair of humorous old French eyes, responded, blinking them, "Oh, before I pay you, I shall have to be convinced that it is really he."

"I'm afraid it's really he," laughed Will; "but rather than let so immaterial a detail cost you five shillings, I'm prepared to maintain with my dying breath that there's no such person."

"Don't mind him," interposed Johannah. "He's trying to flatter you up, because he wants you to call him *Jean mon fils*, as if his name weren't common William." Then, to him, "Go," she said, with an imperious gesture, "go and find a vehicle with a good tired horse."

And when the vehicle with the good tired horse had brought them to their destination, and they stood before the hall-door of Silver Towers, Johannah looked up at the escutcheon carved in the pale-grey stone above it, and said pensively, "On a field argent, a heart gules, crowned with an imperial crown or; and the motto, 'Qu'il régne!' If, when you got my first letter, Cousin Will, if you'd remembered the arms of our family, and the motto—if you had 'let it reign'—I should have been spared the trouble and expense of a journey to town to-day."

"But I should have missed a precious experience," said he. "You forget what I couldn't help being supremely conscious of—that I bear those arms with a difference. I hope, though, that you won't begrudge the journey to town. I think there are certain aspects of your character that I might never have discovered if I'd met you in any other way."

That evening Johannah wrote a letter:

"Dear Mr. Burrell,—*Ce que femme veut, Dieu le veut.* The first part of my rash little prophecy has already come true. Will Stretton is staying in this house, a contented guest. At the present moment he's hovering about the piano, where Madame Dornaye is playing Chopin; and he's just remarked that he never hears Chopin without thinking of those lines of Browning's:

'I discern

Infinite passion, and the pain
Of finite hearts that yearn.'

I quite agree with you, he *is* a charming creature. So now I repeat the second part of my rash little prophecy: Before the summer's over he will have accepted at least a good half of his paternal fortune. *Ce que femme veut, le diable ne saurait pas l'empêcher.* He will, he shall, even if I have to marry him to make him.—Yours ever, Johannah Silver."

III

Will left his room somewhat early the next morning, and went down into the garden. The sun was shining briskly, the dew still sparkled on the grass, the air was heady with a hundred keen earth-odours. A mile away, beyond the wide green levels of Sumpter Meads, the sea glowed blue as the blue of larkspur, under the blue June sky. And everywhere, everywhere, innumerable birds piped and twittered, filling the world with a sense of gay activity, of whole-hearted, high-hearted life.

"What! up already?" a voice called softly, from behind him.

He turned, and met Johannah.

"Why not, since you are?" he responded.

She laughed, and gave him her hand, a warm, elastic hand, firm of grasp. In a garden-hat and a white frock, her eyes beaming, her cheeks faintly flushed, she seemed to him a sort of beautiful incarnation of the spirit of the summer morning, its freshness, and sweetness, and richness.

"Oh, we furriners," she explained; "we're all shocking early risers. In Italy we love the day when it is young, and deem it middle-aged by eight o'clock. But in England I had heard it was the fashion to lie late."

"I woke, and couldn't go to sleep again, so I tossed the fashion to the winds. Perhaps it was a sort of dim presentiment that I should surprise Aurora walking in the garden, that banished slumber," he suggested, with a flourish.

"Flowery speeches are best met by flowery deeds," said she. "Come with me to the rosery, and I will give you a red, red rose."

And in the rosery, as she stood close to him, pinning the red, red rose in his coat, her smooth cheek and fragrant hair so near, so near, he felt his heart all at once begin to throb, and he had to control a sudden absurd longing to put

176

his arms round her and kiss her. "Good heavens," he said to himself, "I must be on my guard."

"There," she cried, bestowing upon her task a gentle pat, by way of finish, "that makes us quits." And she raised her eyes to his, and held them for an instant with a smile that did anything but soothe the trouble in his heart, such a sly little teasing, cryptic smile. Could it possibly be, he wondered wildly, that she had divined his monstrous impulse, and was coquetting with it?

"Now let's be serious," she said, leading the way back to the lawn. "It's like a hanging-garden, high up here, with the meads and the sea below, isn't it? And àpropos of the sea, I would beg you to observe its colour. Is it blue? I would also ask you kindly to cast an eye on that line of cliffs, there to the eastward, as it goes winding in and out away to the vanishing point. Are the cliffs white?"

"Oh, yes, the cliffs are white," agreed the unwary Will.

"How can you tell such dreadful fibs?" she caught him up. "The cliffs are prismatic. White, indeed! when they gleam with every transparent tint from rose to violet, as if the light that falls on them had passed through rubies and amethysts, and all sorts of precious stones. That is an optical effect due doubtless to reflection or refraction or something—no?"

"I should say it was almost certainly due to something," he acquiesced.

"And now," she continued, "will you obligingly turn your attention to the birds? Tweet-weet-willow-will-weet. I don't know what it means, but they repeat it so often and so earnestly, I'm sure it must be true."

"It's relatively true," said he. "It means that it's a fine morning, and their digestion's good, and their affairs are prospering—nothing more than that. They're material-minded little beasts, you know."

"All truth is relative," said she, "and one's relatively a material-minded little beast oneself. Is the greensward beyond there (relatively) spangled with buttercups and daisies? Is the park (relatively) leafy, and shadowy, and mysterious, and delightful? Is the may in bloom? *Voyons donc!* you'll never be denying that the may's in bloom. And is the air like an elixir? I vow, it goes to one's head like some ethereal elixir. And yet you have the effrontery to tell me that you're pining for the flesh-pots of Great College Street, Westminster, S.W."

"Oh, did I tell you that? Ah, well, it must have been with intent to deceive, for nothing could be farther from the truth," he owned.

"The relative truth? Then you're not homesick?"

"Not consciously," said he.

"Neither am I," said she.

"Why should you be?" he asked.

"This is positively the first day since my arrival in England that I haven't been, more or less," she answered.

"Oh?" he wondered sympathetically.

"You can't think how *dépaysée* I've felt. After having lived all one's life in Prague, suddenly to find oneself translated to the mistress-ship of an English country house," she submitted.

"In Prague? I thought you had lived in Rome and Paris, chiefly," he exclaimed.

"Prague is a figure of rhetoric," she reminded him. "I mean the capital of Bohemia. Wasn't my father a sculptor? And wasn't I born in a studio? And haven't my playmates and companions always been of Florizel the loyal subjects? So whether you call it Rome or Paris or Florence or Naples, it was Prague, none the less."

"At that rate, I live in Prague myself, and we're compatriots," said Will.

"That's no doubt why I don't feel homesick any more," she responded, smiling. "Where two of the faithful are gathered together they can form a miniature Prague of their own. If I decide to stay in England, I shall send for a lot of my Prague friends to come and visit me, and you can send for an equal number of yours; and then we'll turn this bright particular corner of the British Empire into a province of Bohemia, and the County may be horrified with reason. But meanwhile, let's be Pragueians in practice as well as theory. Let's go to the strawberry beds, and steal some strawberries," was her conclusion.

She walked a little in front of him. Her garden-hat had come off, and she was swinging it at her side, by its ribbons. Will noticed the strong, lithe sway and rhythm of her body, as she moved. "What a *woman* she is," he thought; "how one feels her sex." And with that, he all at once became aware of a singular depression. "Surely," a malevolent little voice within him argued, "woman that she is, and having passed all her life with the subjects of Florizel, surely, surely, she must have had... experiences. She must have loved—she must have been loved." And (as if it was any of his business!) a kind of vague jealousy of her past, a kind of suspiciousness and irrelevant resentment, began to burn, a small dull spot of pain, somewhere in his breast.

She, apparently, was in the highest spirits. There was something expressive of joyousness in the mere way she tripped over the grass, swinging her garden-hat like a basket; and presently she fell to singing, merrily, in a light voice, that prettiest of old French songs, *Les Trots Princesses*, dancing forward to its measure:

"Derrièr' chez mon père,

(Vole, vole, mon cour, vole!)

Derrièr' chez mon père,

Ya un pommier doux,

Tout doux, et iou,

Ya un pommier doux."

"Don't you like that song?" she asked. "The tune of it is like the smell of faded rose-leaves, isn't it?"

And suddenly she began to sing a different one, possibly an improvisation:

" And so they set forth for the strawberry beds,

The strawberry beds, the strawberry beds,

And so they set forth for the strawberry beds,

On Christmas day in the morning."

And when they had reached the strawberry beds, she knelt, and plucked a great red berry, and then leapt up again, and held it to her cousin's lips, saying, "Bite—but spare my fingers." And so, laughing, she fed it to him, while he, laughing too, consumed it. But when her pink finger-tips all but touched his lips, his heart had a convulsion, and it was only by main-force that he restrained his kisses. And he said to himself, "I must go back to town to-morrow. This will never do. It would be the devil to pay if I should let myself fall in love with her."

"Oh, yes, I've felt terribly *dépaysée*," she told him again, herself nibbling a berry. "I've felt like the traditional cat in the strange garret. And then, besides, there was my change of name. I can't reconcile myself to being called Miss Silver. I can't realise the character. It's like an affectation, like making-believe. Directly I relax my vigilance, I forget, and sink back into Johannah

Rothe. I'm always Johannah Rothe when I'm alone. Directly I'm alone, I push a big *ouf*, and send Miss Silver to Cracklimbo. Then somebody comes, and, with a weary sigh, I don my sheep's clothing again. Of course, there's nothing in a name, and yet there's everything. There's a furious amount of mental discomfort when the name doesn't fit."

"It's a discomfort that will pass," he said consolingly. "The change of name is a mere formality—a condition attached to coming into a property. In England, you know, it's a rather frequent condition."

"I'm aware of that," she informed him. "But to me," she went on, "it seems symbolic—symbolic of my whole situation, which is false, abnormal. Silver? Silver? It's a name meant for a fair person, with light hair and a white skin. And here I am, as black as any Gipsy. And then! It's a condition attached to coming into a property. Well, I come into a property to which I have no more moral right than I have to the coat on your back; and I'm obliged to do it under an *alias*, like a thief in the night."

"Oh, my dear young lady," he cried out, "you've the very best of rights, moral as well as legal. You come into a property that is left to you by will, and you're the last representative of the family in whose hands it has been for I forget how many hundreds of years."

"That," said she, "is a question I shall not refuse to discuss with you upon some more fitting occasion. For the present I am tempted to perpetrate a simply villainous pun, but I forbear. Suffice it to say that I consider the property that I've come into as nothing more nor less than a present made me by my cousin, William Stretton. No—don't interrupt!" she forbade him. "I happen to know my facts. I happen to know that if Will Stretton hadn't, for reasons in the highest degree honourable to himself, quarrelled and broken with his father, and refused to receive a penny from him, I happen to know, I say, that Sir William Silver would have left Will Stretton everything he possessed in the world. Oh, it's not in vain that I've pumped the man named Burrell. So, you see, I'm indebted to my Quixotic cousin for something in the neighbourhood, I'm told, of eight thousand a year. Rather a handsome little present, isn't it? Furthermore, let me add in passing, I absolutely forbid my cousin to call me his dear young lady, as if he were seven hundred years my senior and only a casual acquaintance. A really nice cousin would take the liberty of calling me by my Christian name."

"I'll take the liberty of calling you by some exceedingly *un*Christian name," he menaced, "if you don't leave off talking that impossible rot about my making you a present."

"I wasn't talking impossible rot about your making me a present," she contradicted. "I was merely telling you how *dépaysée* I'd felt. The rest was parenthetic. So now, then, keep your promise, call me Johannah."

"Johannah," he called, submissively.

"Will," said she. "And when you feel, Will, that on the whole, Will, you've had strawberries enough, Will, quite to destroy your appetite, perhaps it would be as well if we should go in to breakfast, Willie."

IV.

They were seated on the turf, under a great tree, in the park, amid a multitude of bright-coloured cushions, Johannah, Will, and Madame Dornaye. It was three weeks later—whence it may be inferred that he had abandoned his resolution to "go back to town to-morrow." He was smoking a cigarette; Madame Dornaye was knitting; Johannah, hatless, in an indescribable confection of cream-coloured muslin, her head pillowed in a scarlet cushion against the body of the tree, was gazing off towards the sea with dreamy eyes.

"Will," she called languidly, by-and-by.

"Yes?" he responded.

"Do you happen by any chance to belong to that sect of philosophers who regard gold as a precious metal?"

"From the little I've seen of it, I am inclined to regard it as precious—yes," he answered.

"Well, then, I wouldn't be so lavish of it, if I were you," said she.

"If you don't take care," said he, "you'll force me to admit that I haven't an idea of what you're driving at."

"I'm driving at your silence. You're as silent as a statue. Please talk a little."

"What shall I talk about?"

"Anything. Nothing. Tell us a story," she decided.

"I don't know any stories."

"Then the least you can do is to invent one," was her plausible retort.

"What sort of a story would you like?"

"There's only one sort of story a woman ever sincerely likes—especially on a hot summer's afternoon, in the country," she affirmed.

"Oh, I couldn't possibly invent a love-story," he disclaimed.

"Then tell us a true one. You needn't be afraid of shocking Madame Dornaye. She's a realist herself."

"Jeanne ma fille!" murmured Madame Dornaye, reprovingly.

"The only true love-story I could tell has a somewhat singular defect," said he. "There's no heroine."

"That's like the story of what's-his-name—Narcissus," Johannah said.

"With the vastest difference. The hero of my story wasn't in love with his own image. He was in love with a beautiful princess," Will explained.

"Then how can you have the face to say that there's no heroine?" she demanded.

"There isn't any heroine. At the same time, there's nothing else. The story's all about her. You see, she never existed."

"You said it was a *true* love-story," she reproached him.

"So it is—literally true."

"I asked for a story, and you give me a riddle." She shook her head.

"Oh, no, it's a story all the same," he reassured her. "Its title is *Much Ado about Nobody*."

"Oh? It runs in my head that I've met with something or other with a similar title before," she considered.

"Precisely," said he. "Something or other by one of the Elizabethans. That's how it came to occur to me. I take my goods where I find them. However, do you want to hear the story?"

"Oh, if you're determined to tell it, I daresay I can steel myself to listen," she answered, with resignation.

"On second thoughts, I'm determined not to tell it," he teased.

"Bother! Don't be disagreeable. Tell it at once," she commanded.

"Well, then, there isn't any story," he admitted. "It's simply an absurd little freak of child psychology. It's the story of a boy who fell in love with a girl— a girl that never was, on sea or land. It happened in Regent Street, of all romantic places, 'one day still fierce 'mid many a day struck calm.' I had gone with my mother to her milliner's. I think I was ten or eleven. And while my mother was transacting her business with the milliner, I devoted my attention to the various hats and bonnets that were displayed about the shop.

And presently I hit on one that gave me a sensation. It was a straw hat, with brown ribbons, and cherries, great glossy red and purple cherries. I looked at it, and suddenly I got a vision—a vision of a girl. Oh, the loveliest, loveliest girl! She was about eighteen (a self-respecting boy of eleven, you know, always chooses a girl of about eighteen to fall in love with), and she had the brightest brown eyes, and the rosiest cheeks, and the curlingest hair, and a smile and a laugh that made one's heart thrill and thrill with unutterable blisses. And there hung her hat, as if she had just come in and taken it off, and passed into another room. There hung her hat, suggestive of her as only people's hats know how to be suggestive; and there sat I, my eyes devouring it, my soul transported. The very air of the shop seemed all at once to have become fragrant—with the fragrance that had been shaken from her garments as she passed. I went home, hopelessly, frantically in love. I loved that non-existent young woman with a passion past expressing, for at least half a year. I was always thinking of her; she was always with me, everywhere. How I used to talk to her, and tell her all my childish fancies, desires, questionings; how I used to sit at her feet and listen! She never laughed at me. Sometimes she would let me kiss her—I declare, my heart still jumps at the memory of it. Sometimes I would hold her hand or play with her hair. And all the *real* girls I met seemed so tame and commonplace by contrast with her. And then, little by little, I suppose, her image faded away.—Rather an odd experience, wasn't it?"

"Very, very odd; very strange and very pretty," Johannah murmured. "It seems as if it ought to have some allegorical significance, though I can't perceive one. It would be interesting to know what sort of real girl, if any, ended by becoming the owner of that hat. You weren't shocked, were you?" she inquired of Madame Dornaye.

"Not by the story. But the heat is too much for me," said that lady, gathering up her knitting. "I am going to the house to make a siesta."

Will rose, as she did, and stood looking vaguely after her, as she moved away. Johannah nestled her head deeper in her cushion, and half closed her eyes. And for a while neither she nor her cousin spoke. A faint, faint breeze whispered in the tree-tops; now a twig snapped, now a bird dropped a solitary liquid note. For the rest, all was still summer heat and woodland perfume. Here and there the greensward round them, dark in the shadow of dense foliage, was diapered with vivid yellow by sunbeams that filtered through.

"Oh, dear me," Johannah sighed at last.

"What is it?" Will demanded.

"Here you are, silent as eternity again. Come and sit down—here—near to me."

She indicated a position with a lazy movement of her hand. He obediently sank upon the grass.

"You're always silent nowadays, when we're alone," she complained.

"Am I? I hadn't noticed that."

"Then you're extremely unobservant. Directly we're alone, you appear to lose the power of speech. You mope and moon, and gaze off at things beyond the horizon, and never open your mouth. One might suppose you had something on your mind. Have you? What is it? Confide it to me, and you can't think how relieved you'll feel," she urged.

"I haven't anything on my mind," said he.

"Oh? Ah, then you're silent with me because I bore you? You find me an uninspiring talk-mate? Thank you," she bridled.

"You know perfectly well that that's preposterous nonsense," answered Will.

"Well, then, what is it? Why do you never talk to me when we're alone?" she persisted.

"But I do talk to you. I talk too much. Perhaps *I'm* afraid of boring *you*," he said.

"You know perfectly well that that's a preposterous subterfuge," said she. "You've got something on your mind. You're keeping something back." She paused for a second; then, softly, wistfully, "Tell me what it is, Will, *please*." And she looked eagerly, pleadingly, into his eyes.

He looked away from her. "Upon my word, there's nothing to tell," he said, but his tone was a little forced.

She broke into a merry peal of laughter, looking at him now with eyes that were derisive.

"What are you laughing at?" he asked.

"At you, Will," said she. "What else could you imagine?"

"I'm flattered to think you find me so amusing."

"Oh, you're supremely amusing. 'Refrain thou shalt; thou shalt refrain!' Is that your motto, Will? If I were a man, I'd choose another. 'Be bold, be bold, and everywhere be bold!' That should be my motto if I were a man."

"But as you're a woman————" he began.

"It's my motto, all the same," she interrupted. "Do you mean to say you've not discovered that yet? Oh, Will, if I were you, and you were I, how differently we should be employing this heaven-sent summer's afternoon." She gazed at the sky, and sighed.

"What should we be doing?" asked he.

"That's a secret. Pray the fairies to-night to transpose our souls, and you'll know by to-morrow morning—if the fairies grant your prayer. But in the meanwhile, you must try to entertain me. Tell me another story."

"I can't think of any more stories till I've had my tea."

"You shan't have any tea unless you earn it," she stipulated. "Now that Madame Dornaye's no longer present, you can tell me of some of your grown-up love affairs, some of your flesh-and-blood ones."

"I've never had a grown-up love affair," he said.

"Oh, come! you can't expect me to believe that," she cried.

"It's the truth, all the same."

"Well, then, it's high time you *should* have one," was her conclusion. "How old did you say you were?"

"I'm thirty-three."

She lifted up her hands in astonishment. "And you've never had a love affair! *Fi donc!* I'm barely twenty-eight, and I've had a hundred."

"Have you?" he asked, a little ruefully.

"No, I haven't. But everybody's had at least one. So tell me yours."

"Upon my word, I've not had even one," he reiterated.

"It seems incredible. How have you contrived it?"

"The circumstances of my birth contrived it for me. It would be impossible for me to have a love affair with a woman I could love," he said.

"Impossible? For goodness sake, why?" she wondered.

"What woman would accept the addresses of a man without a name?"

"Haven't you a name? Methought I'd heard your name was William Stretton."

"You know what I mean."

"Then permit me to remark," she answered him, "that what you mean is quite superlatively silly. If you loved a woman, wouldn't you tell her so?"

185

"Not if I could help it."

"But suppose the woman loved you?"

"Oh, it wouldn't come to that."

"But suppose it *had* come to that?" she persevered. "Suppose she'd set her heart upon you? Would it be fair to her not to tell her?"

"What would be the good of my telling her, since I couldn't possibly ask her to marry me?"

"The fact might interest her, apart from the question of its consequences," Johannah suggested. "But suppose *she* told you? Suppose *she* asked *you* to marry *her?*"

"She wouldn't," said he.

"All hypotheses are admissible. Suppose she should?"

"I couldn't marry her," he declared.

"You'd find it rather an awkward job refusing, wouldn't you?" she quizzed. "And what reasons could you give?"

"Ten thousand reasons. I'm a bastard. That begins and ends it. It would dishonour her, and it would dishonour me; and, worst of all, it would dishonour my mother."

"It would certainly *not* dishonour you, nor the woman you married. That's the sheerest, antiquated, exploded rubbish. And how on earth could it dishonour your mother?"

"For me to take as my wife a woman who could not respect her?" Will questioned. "My mother's memory for me is the sacredest of sacred things. You know something of her history. You know that she was in every sense but a legal sense my father's wife. You know why they couldn't be married legally. You know, too, how he treated her—and how she died. Do you suppose I could marry a woman who would always think of my mother as of one who had done something shameful?"

"Oh, but no woman with a spark of nobility in her soul would or could do that," Johannah cried.

"Every woman brought up in the usual way, with the usual prejudices, the usual traditions, thinks evil of the woman who has had an illegitimate child," asserted he.

"Not every woman. I, for instance. Do you imagine that I could think evil of your mother, Will?" She looked at him intensely, earnestly.

"Oh, you're entirely different from other women. You're——" But he stopped at that.

"Then—just for the sake of a case in point—if *I* were the woman you chanced to be in love with, and if I simultaneously chanced to be in love with you, you *could* see your way to marrying *me?*" she pursued him.

"What's the use of discussing that?"

"For its metaphysical interest. Answer me."

"There are other reasons why I couldn't marry *you.*"

"I'm not good-looking enough?" she cried.

"Don't be silly."

"Not young enough?"

"Oh, I say! Let's talk of something reasonable."

"Not old enough, perhaps?"

He was silent.

"Not wise enough? Not foolish enough?" she persisted.

"You're foolish enough, in all conscience," said he. "Well, then, why? What are the reasons why you couldn't marry *me?*"

"What *is* the good of talking about this?" he groaned.

"I want to know. A man has the hardihood to inform me to my face that he'd spurn my hand, even if I offered it to him. I insist upon knowing why." She feigned high indignation.

"You know why. And you know that 'spurn' is very far from the right word," was his rejoinder.

"I don't know why. I insist upon your telling me," she repeated, fiercely.

"You know that you're Sir William Silver's heiress, I suppose," he suggested.

"Oh, come! that's not *my* fault. How could *that* matter?"

"Look here, I'm not going to make an ass of myself by explaining the obvious," he declared.

"I daresay I'm very stupid, but it isn't obvious to me."

"Well, then, let's drop the subject," he proposed.

"I'll not drop the subject till you've elucidated it. If you were in love with me, Will, and I were in love with you, how on earth could it matter, my being Sir William Silvers heiress?"

"Wouldn't I seem a bit mercenary'if I asked you to marry me?"

"Oh, Will!" she remonstrated. "Don't tell me you're such a prig as that. What! if you loved me, if I loved you, you'd give me up, you'd break my heart, just for fear lest idiotic people, whose opinions don't matter any more than the opinions of so many deep-sea fish, might think you mercenary! When you and I both knew in our own two souls that you really weren't mercenary' in the least! You'd pay me a poor compliment, Will. Isn't it conceivable that a man might love me for myself?"

"You state the case too simply. You make no allowances for the shades and complexities of a man's feelings."

"Bother shades and complexities. Love burns them up. Your shades and complexities are nothing but priggishness and vanity," she asserted hotly. "But there! I'm actually getting angry over a purely supposititious question. For, of course, we don't really love each other the least bit, do we, Will?" she asked him softly.

He appeared to be giving his whole attention to the rolling of a cigarette; he did not answer. But his fingers trembled, and presently he tore his paper, spilling half the tobacco in his lap.

Johannah watched him from eyes full of languid, half mocking, half pensive laughter.

"Oh, dear, oh, dear," she sighed again, by-and-by.

He looked at her; and he had to catch his breath. Lying there on the turf, the skirts of her frock flowing round her in a sort of little billowy white pool, her head deep in the scarlet cushion, her black hair straying wantonly where it would about her face and brow, her eyes lambent with that lazy, pensive laughter, one of her hands, pink and white, warm and soft, fallen open on the grass between her and her cousin, her whole person seeming to breathe a subtle scent of womanhood, and the luxury and mystery of womanhood—oh, the sight of her, the sense of her, there in the wide green stillness of the summer day, set his heart burning and beating poignantly.

"Oh, dear, oh, dear," she sighed, "I wish the man I *am* in love with were only here."

"Oh! You *are* in love with some one?" he questioned, with a little start.

"Rather!" said she. "In love! I should think so. Oh, I love him, love him, love him. Ah, if he were here! *He* wouldn't waste this golden afternoon as you're doing. He'd take my hand—he'd hold it, and press it, and kiss it; and he'd pour his soul out in tumultuous celebration of my charms, in fiery avowals of his passion. If he were here! Ah, me!"

"Where is he?" Will asked, in a dry' voice.

"Ah, where indeed? I wish I knew."

"I've never heard you speak of him before," he reflected.

"There's none so deaf as he that *will* not hear. I've spoken of him to you at least a thousand times. He forms the staple of my conversation."

"I must be veryy deaf indeed. I swear this is absolutely news to me."

"Oh, Will, you *are* such a goose—or such a hypocrite," said she. "But it's tea-time. Help me up."

She held out her hand, and, he took it and helped her up. But she tottered a little before she got her balance (or made, at least, a feint of doing so), and grasped his hand tight as if to save herself, and all but fell into his arms.

He drew back a step.

She looked straight into his eyes. "You're a goose, and a hypocrite, and a prig, and—a *dear*," she said.

V.

Their tea was served in the garden, and whilst they were dallying over it, a footman brought Johannah a visiting-card.

She glanced at the card; and Will, watching her, noticed that a look of annoyance—it might even have been a look of distress—came into her face.

Then she threw the card on the tea-table, and rose. "I shan't be gone long," she said, and set out for the house.

The card lay plainly legible under the eyes of Will and Madame Dornaye. "Mr. George Aymer, 36, Boulevard Rochechouart" was the legend inscribed upon it.

"*Tiens*," said Madame Dornaye; "Jeanne told me she had ceased to see him."

Will suppressed a desire to ask, "Who is he?"

But Madame Dornaye answered him all the same.

"You have heard of him? He is a known personage in Paris, although English. He is a painter, a painter of great talent; very young, but already decorated. And of a surprising beauty—the face of an angel. With that, a thorough-paced rascal. Oh, yes, whatever is vilest, whatever is basest. Even in Montmartre, even in the corruptest world of Paris, among the lowest journalists and painters, he is notorious for his corruption. Johannah used to see a great deal of him. She would not believe the evil stories that were told about him. And with his rare talent and his beautiful face, he has the most plausible manners, the most winning address. We were afraid that she might end by marrying him. But at last she found him out for herself, and gave him up. She told me she had altogether ceased to see him. I wonder what ill wind blows him here."

Johannah entered the drawing-room.

A man in grey tweeds, the red ribbon of the Legion of Honour gleaming in his buttonhole, was standing near a window: a man, indeed, as Madame Dornaye had described him, with a face of surprising beauty—a fine, clear, open-air complexion, a clean-cut, even profile, a sensitive, soft mouth, big, frank, innocent blue eyes, and waving hair of the palest Saxon yellow. He could scarcely have been thirty; and the exceeding beauty of his face, its beauty and its sweetness, made one overlook his figure, which was a trifle below the medium height, and thick-set, with remarkably square, broad shoulders, and long arms.

Johannah greeted him with some succinctness. "What do you want?" she asked, remaining close to the door.

"I want to have a talk with you," he answered, moving towards her. He drawled slightly; his voice was low and soft, conciliatory, caressing almost. And his big blue eyes shone with a faint, sweet, appealing smile.

"Would you mind staying where you are?" said she. "You can make yourself audible from across the room."

"What are you afraid of?" he asked, his smile brightening with innocent wonder.

"Afraid? You do yourself too much honour. One does not like to find oneself in close proximity with objects that disgust one," she explained.

He laughed; but instead of moving further towards her, he dropped into a chair. "You were always brutally outspoken," he murmured.

"Yes; and with advancing years I've become even more so," said Johannah, who continued to stand.

"You're quite sure, though, that you're not afraid of me?" he questioned.

"Oh, for that, as sure as sure can be. If you've based any sort of calculations upon the theory that I would be afraid of you, you'll have to throw them over."

He flushed a little, as if with anger; but in a moment he said calmly, "You've come into a perfect pot of money since I last had the pleasure of meeting you."

"Yes, into something like eight thousand a year, if the figures interest you."

"I never had any head for figures," he answered, smiling. "But eight thousand sounds stupendous. And a lovely place, into the bargain. The park, or so much of it as one sees from the avenue, could not be better. And I permitted myself to admire the façade of the house and the view of the sea."

"They're not bad," Johannah assented.

"It's heart-rending," he remarked, "the way things are shared in this world. Here are you, rich beyond the dreams of avarice, you who have done nothing all your life but take your pleasure; and I, who've toiled like a galley-slave, I remain as poor as any church-mouse. It's monstrous."

Johannah did not answer.

"And now," he went on, "I suppose you've settled down and become respectable? No more Bohemia? No more cakes and ale? Only champagne and truffles? A County Family! Fancy your being a County Family, all by yourself, as it were! You must feel rather like the reformed rake of tradition—don't you?"

"I mentioned that I am not afraid of you," she reminded him, "but that doesn't in the least imply that I find you amusing. The plain truth is, I find you deadly tiresome. If you have anything special to say to me, may I ask you to say it quickly?"

Again he flushed a little; then again, in a moment, answered smoothly, "I'll say it in a sentence. I've come all the way to England, for the purpose of offering you my hand in marriage." And he raised his bright blue eyes to her face with a look that really was seraphic.

"I decline the offer. If you've nothing further to keep you here, I'll ring to have you shown out."

Still again he flushed, yet once more controlled himself. "You decline the offer! *Allons donc!* When I am prepared to do the right thing, and make an honest woman of you."

"I decline the offer," Johannah repeated.

"That's foolish of you," said he.

"If you could dream how remotely your opinion interests me, you wouldn't trouble to express it," said she.

His anger this time got the better of him. He scowled, and looked at her from the corners of his eyes. "You had better not exasperate me," he said in a suppressed voice.

"Oh," said she, "you must suffer me to be the mistress of my own actions in my own house. Now—if you are quite ready to go?" she suggested, putting her hand upon the bell-cord.

"I'm not ready to go yet. I want to talk with you. To cut a long business short, you're rich. I'm pitiably poor. You know how poor I am. You know how I have to live, the hardships, the privations I'm obliged to put up with."

"Have you come here to beg?" Johannah asked.

"No, I've come to appeal to your good-nature. You refuse to marry me. That's absurd of you, but—*tant pis!* Whether you marry me or not, you haven't the heart to leave me to rot in poverty, while you luxuriate in plenty. Considering our oldtime relations, the thing's impossible on the face of it."

"Ah, I understand. You *have* come here to beg," she said.

"No," said he. "One begs when one has no power to enforce."

"What is the use of these glittering aphorisms?" she asked wearily.

"If you are ready to behave well to me, I'll behave handsomely to you. But if you refuse to recognise my claims upon you, I'm in a position to take reprisals," he said very quietly.

Johannah did not answer.

"I'm miserably, tragically poor; you're rich. At this moment I've not got ten pounds in the world; and I owe hundreds. I've not sold a picture since March. You have eight thousand a year. You can't expect me to sit down under it in silence. As the French attorneys phrase it, *cet état de choses ne peut pas durer.*"

Still Johannah answered nothing.

"You must come to my relief," said he. "You must make it possible for me to go on. If you have any right feeling, you'll do it spontaneously. If not—you know I can compel you."

"Oh, then, for goodness' sake, compel me, and so make an end of this entirely tedious visit," she broke out.

"I'd immensely rather not compel you. If you will lend me a helping hand from time to time, I'll promise never to take a step to harm you. I shall be moderate. You've got eight thousand a year. You'd never miss a hundred now and then. You might simply occasionally buy a picture. That would be the best way. You might buy my pictures."

"I should be glad to know definitely," remarked Johannah, "whether I have to deal with a blackmailer or a bagman."

"Damn you," he exploded, with sudden savagery, flushing very red indeed.

Johannah was silent.

After a pause, he said, "I'm staying at the inn in the village—at the Silver Arms."

Johannah did not speak.

"I've already scraped acquaintance with the parson," he went on. Then, as she still was silent, "I wonder what would become of your social position in this County if I should have a good long talk about you with the parson."

"To a man of your intelligence, the solution of that problem can surely present no difficulty," she replied wearily.

"You admit that your social position would be smashed up?"

"All the king's horses and all the king's men couldn't put it together again," she said.

"I'm glad to find at least that you acknowledge my power," said he.

"You have it in your power to tell people that I was once inconceivably simple enough to believe that you were an honourable man, that I once had the inconceivable bad taste to be fond of you. What woman's character could survive *that* revelation?"

"And I could add—couldn't I?—that you once had the inconceivable weakness to become my mistress?"

"Oh, you could add no end of details," she admitted.

"Well, then?" he questioned.

"Well, then?" questioned she.

"It comes to this, that if you don't want your social position, your reputation, to be utterly smashed up, you must make terms with me."

"It's a little unfortunate, from that way of looking at it," she pointed out, "that I shouldn't happen to care a rush about my social position—as you call it."

"I think I'll have a good long talk with the parson," he said.

"Do by all means," said she.

"You'd better be careful. I may take you at your word," he threatened.

"I wish you would. Take me at my word—-and go," she urged.

"You mean to say you seriously don't care?"

"Not a rush, not a button," she assured him.

"Oh, come! You'll never try to brazen the thing out," he exclaimed.

"I wish you'd go and have your long talk with the parson," she said impatiently.

"It would be so easy for you to give me a little help," he pleaded.

"It would be so easy for you to 'smash up' my reputation with the parson," she rejoined.

"You never used to be close-fisted. It's incomprehensible that you should refuse me a little help. Look. I'm willing to be more than fair. Give me a hundred pounds, a bare little hundred pounds, and I'll send you a lovely picture."

"Thank you, I don't want a picture."

"You won't give me a hundred pounds—a beggarly hundred pounds?" He looked incredulous.

"I won't give you a farthing."

"Well, then, by God, you jade," he cried, springing to his feet, his face crimson, "by God, I'll make you. I swear I'll ruin you. Look out!"

"Are you really going at last?" she asked brightly.

"No, I'm not going till it suits my pleasure. You've got a sort of bastard cousin staying here with you, I'm told," he answered.

"I would advise you to moderate your tone or your language," said she. "If my sort of bastard cousin should by any chance happen to hear you referring to him in those terms, he would not be pleased."

"I want to see him," said he.

"I would advise you not to see him," she returned.

"I want to see him," he insisted.

"If you really wish to see him, I'll send for him," she consented. "But it's only right to warn you that he's not at all a patient sort of man. If I send for him, he will quite certainly make things disagreeable for you."

"I'm not afraid of him. You know well enough that I'm not a coward."

"My cousin is more than a head taller than you are," she mused. "He would be perfectly able and perfectly sure to kick you. If there's any other possible way of getting rid of you, I'd rather not trouble him."

"I think I had better have a talk with your cousin, as well as with the parson," he considered.

"I think you had better confine your attentions to the parson. I do, upon my word," she counselled him.

"I am going to make a concession," said Aymer. "I'm going to give you a night in which to think this thing over. If you care to send me a note, with a cheque in it, so that I shall receive it at the inn by to-morrow at ten o'clock, I'll take the next earliest train back to town, and I'll send you a picture in return. If no note comes by ten o'clock, I'll call on the parson, and tell him all I know about you; and I'll write a letter to your cousin. Now, goodday."

Johannah rang, and Aymer was shown out.

VI

"|I shan't be gone long," Johannah had said, when she left Madame Dornaye and Will at tea in the garden; but time passed, and she did not come back. Will, mounting through various stages and degrees of nervousness, restlessness, anxiety, at last said, "What on earth can be keeping her?" and Madame Dornaye replied, "That is precisely what I am asking myself." They waited a little longer, and then, "Shall we go back to the house?" he suggested. But when they reached the house they found the drawing-room empty, and—no trace of Johannah.

"She may be in her room. I'll go and see," said Madame Dornaye.

More time passed, and still no Johannah. Nor did Madame Dornaye return to explain her absence.

Will walked about in a state of acute misery. What could it be? What could have happened? What could this painter, this George Aymer, this thorough-paced rascal with the beautiful face, this man of whom Johannah, in days gone by, "had seen a great deal," so that her friends had feared "she might end by marrying him"—what could he have called upon her for? What could have passed between them? Why had she disappeared? Where was she now? Where was he? Where was Madame Dornaye, who had gone to look for her? Could—could it possibly be—that he—this man notorious for his corruption even in the corruptest world of Paris—could it be that he was the man Johannah meant when she had talked of the man she was in love with? And Will, fatuous imbecile, had vainly allowed himself to imagine.... Oh, why did she not come back? What *could* be keeping her away from him all this time? ... "I have had a hundred, I have had a hundred." The phrase echoed and echoed in his memory. She had said, "I have had a hundred love affairs." Oh, to be sure, in the next breath, she had contradicted herself, she had said, "No, I haven't." But she had added, "Everybody has had at least one." So she had had at least one. With this man, George Aymer? Madame Dornaye said she had broken with him, ceased to see him. But—it was certain she had seen him to-day. But—lovers' quarrels are made up; lovers break with each other, and then come together again, are reunited. Perhaps... Perhaps... Oh, where was she? Why did she remain away in this mysterious fashion? What could she be doing? What could she be doing?

The dressing-bell rang, and he went to dress for dinner.

"Anyhow, I shall see her now, I shall see her at dinner," he kept telling himself, as he dressed.

But when he came downstairs the drawing-room was still empty. He walked backwards and forwards.

"We shall have to dine without our hostess," Madame Dornaye said, entering presently. "Jeanne has a bad headache, and will stay in her room."

VII

Will left the house early the next morning, and went out into the garden. The sun was shining, the dew sparkled on the grass, the air was keen and sweet with the odours of the earth. A mile away the sea glowed blue as larkspur; and overhead innumerable birds gaily piped and twittered. But oh, the difference, the difference! His eyes could see no colour, his ears could hear no music. His brain felt as if it had been stretched and strained, like a thing of india-rubber; a lump ached in his throat; his heart was sick with the suspense of waiting, with the questionings, the fears, suspicions, that had beset it through the night.

"Will!" Johannah's voice called behind him.

He turned.

"Thank God!" The words came without conscious volition on his part. "I thought I was never going to see you again."

"I have been waiting for you," said she.

She wore her garden-hat and her white frock; but her face was pale, and her eyes looked dark and anxious.

He had taken her hand, and was clinging to it, pressing it, hard, so hard that it must have hurt her, in the violence of his emotion.

"Oh, wait, Will, wait," she said, trying to draw her hand away; and her eyes filled with sudden tears.

He let go her hand, and looked into her tearful eyes, helpless, speechless, longing to speak, unable, in the confusion of his thoughts and feelings, to find a word.

"I must tell you something, Will. Come with me somewhere—where we can be alone. I must tell you something."

She moved off, away from the house, he keeping beside her. They passed out of the garden, into the deep shade of the park.

"*Do* you remember," she began, all at once, "do you remember what I said yesterday, about my motto? That my motto was 'Be bold, be bold, and everywhere be bold'."

"Yes," he said.

"I am going to be very bold indeed now, Will. I am going to tell you something—something that will make you hate me perhaps—that will make you despise me perhaps," she faltered.

"You could not possibly tell me anything that could make me hate you or despise you. But you must not tell me anything at all, unless it is something you are perfectly sure you will be happier for having told me," he said.

"It is something I wish to tell you, something I must tell you," said she. Then after a little pause, "Oh, how shall I begin it?" But before he could have spoken, "Do you think that a woman—do you think that a girl, when she is very young, when she is very immature and impressionable, and very impulsive, and ignorant, and when she is alone in the world, without a father or mother—do you think that if she makes some terrible mistake, if she is terribly deceived, if somebody whom she believes to be good and noble and unhappy and misunderstood, somebody whom she—whom she loves—do you think that if she makes some terrible mistake—if she—if she—oh, my God!—if——" She held her breath for a second, then suddenly, "Can't you understand what I *mean?*" she broke down in a sort of wail, and hid her face in her hands, and sobbed.

Will stood beside her, holding his arms out towards her. "Johannah! Johannah!" was all he could say.

She dropped her hands, and looked at him with great painful eyes. "Tell me —do you think that a woman can never be forgiven? Do you think that she is soiled, degraded, changed utterly? Do you think that when she—that when she did what she did—it was a sin, a crime, not only a terrible mistake, and that her whole nature is changed? Most people think so. They think that a mark has been left upon her, branded upon her; that she can never, never be the same again. Do you think so, Will? Oh, it is not true; I know it is not true. A woman can leave that mistake, that terror, that horror—she can leave it behind her as completely as she can leave any other dreadful thing. She can blot it out of her life, like a nightmare. She *isn't* changed—she remains the same woman. She isn't utterly changed, and soiled, and defiled. In her own conscience, no matter what other people think, she knows, she knows she isn't. When she wakes up to find that the man she had believed in, the man she had loved, when she wakes up to find that he isn't in any way what she had thought him, that he is base and evil and ignoble, and when all her love for him dies in horror and misery—oh, do you think that she must never, never, as long as she lives, hold up her head again, never be happy again, never love any one again? Look at me, Will. I am myself. I am what God made me. Do you think that I am utterly vile because—because——" But her voice failed again, and her eyes again filled with tears.

"Oh, Johannah, don't ask me what I think of you. I could not tell you what I think of you. You are as God made you. God never made—never made any one else so splendid."

And in a moment his arms were round her, and she was weeping her heart out on his shoulder.

ROOTS

Would Madame like a little orange-flower water in her milk?" the waiter asked. Madame thought she would, and the waiter went off to fetch it.

We were seated on the terrace of a café at Rouen, a café on the quays. There was a long rank, three deep, of small marble tables, untenanted for the most part, sheltered by a bright red-and-white striped awning, and screened from the street by a hedge of oleanders in big green-painted tubs; so that one had a fine sense of cosiness and seclusion, of refreshing shade and coolness and repose. Beyond the oleanders, one was dimly conscious of hot sunshine, of the going and coming of people on the pavement, of the passing of carts and tram-cars in the grey road, and then of the river—the slate-coloured river, with its bridges and its puffing penny steamboats, its tall ships out of Glasgow or Copenhagen or Barcelona, its high green banks, farther away, where it wound into the country, and the pure sky above it. From all the interesting things the café provided, lucent-tinted syrups, fiery-hearted, aromatic cordials, Madame (with subtle feminine unexpectedness) had chosen a glass of milk. But the waiter had suggested orange-flower water, to give it savour; and now he brought the orange-flower water in a dark-blue bottle.

It was partly, I daresay, the sight of the dark-blue bottle, but it was chiefly, perhaps, the smell of the orange-flower water, that suddenly, suddenly, whisked my thoughts far away from Rouen, far away from 1897, back ten, twenty, I would rather not count how many years back in the past, to my childhood, to Saint-Graal, and to my grandmother's room in our old rambling house there. For my grandmother always kept a dark-blue bottle of orange-flower water in her closet, and the air of her room was always faintly sweet with the perfume of it.

Suddenly, suddenly, a sort of ghost of my grandmother's room rose before me; and as I peered into it and about it, a ghost of the old emotion her room used to stir in me rose too, an echo of the old wonder, the old feeling of strangeness and mystery. It was a big room—or, at least, it seemed big to a child—a corner room, on the first floor, with windows on two sides. The windows on one side looked through the branches of a great elm, a city of birds and squirrels, out upon the lawn, with the pond at the bottom of it. On the other side, the windows looked over the terrace, into the shrubberies and winding paths of the garden. The walls of the room were hung with white paper, upon which, at regular intervals, was repeated a landscape in blue, a stretch of meadow with cows in it, and a hillside topped by a ruined castle. In

200

a corner, the inmost corner, stood my grandmother's four-post bed, with its canopy and curtains of dark-green tapestry. Then, of course, there was the fireplace, surmounted by a high, slender mantelpiece, on which were ranged a pair of silver candlesticks, a silver tray containing the snuffers and the extinguisher, and, in the middle, a solemn old buhl clock. From above the mantelpiece a picture looked down at you, the only picture in the room, the life-size portrait of a gentleman in a white stock and an embroidered waistcoat—the portrait of my grandfather, indeed, who had died long years before I was born, when my mother was a schoolgirl. And then there was the rest of the furniture of the room—a chair at each window, and between the various windows my grandmother's dressing-table, her work-table, her armoire-à-glace, her great mahogany bureau, a writing-desk above, a chest-of-drawers below. In two or three places—besides the big double door that led into her room from the outer passage—the wall was broken by smaller doors, doors papered over like the wall itself, and even with it, so that you would scarcely have noticed them. One of these was the door of my grandmother's oratory, with its praying-desk and its little altar. The others were the doors of her closets: the deep black closet, where her innumerable dresses were suspended, and the closets where she kept her bandboxes and her sunshades and her regiment of bottles—chief among them the tall dark-blue bottle of orange-flower water.

I don't know, I can't think, why this room should always have awakened in me a feeling of strangeness and mystery, why it should always have set me off day-dreaming and wondering; but it always did. The mahogany bureau, the tapestried four-post bed, the portrait of my grandfather, the recurrent landscape on the wall-paper, the deep black closet where the dresses hung, the faint smell of orange-flower water—each of these was a surface, a curtain, behind which, on the impenetrable other side of which, vaguely, wonderingly, I divined strange vistas, a whole strange world. Each of these silently hinted to me of strange happenings, strange existences, strange conditions. And vaguely, longingly, I would try to formulate my feeling into some sort of distinct mental vision, try to translate into my own language their occult suggestions. They were hieroglyphs, full of meaning, if only I could understand. Was it because the things in my grandmother's room were all old things, old-fashioned things? Was the strange world they spoke of simply the world as it had been in years gone by, before I came into it, before even my mother and father came into it, when people long since dead were alive, important, the people of the day, and when these faded, old-fashioned things were fresh and new? I doubt if it could have been entirely this. There were plenty of old things in our house at Saint-Graal—in the hall, the library, the garret, everywhere; the house itself was very old indeed; yet no other part of it gave me anything like the same emotion.

My Uncle Edmond's room, for instance, gave me a directly contrary emotion, though here, too, all the furniture was old-fashioned. It gave me a sense of brisk, almost of stern, actuality; of present facts and occupations; of alert, busy manhood. As I followed Alexandre into it, in the morning, when he went to dust it and put it in order, I was filled with a kind of fearful admiration: the fear, the admiration, of the small for the big, of the weak for the strong, of the helpless for the commanding. The arrangement of the room, the lines of the room, the very colours of the room, seemed strong, and commanding, and severe. Yet, when you came to examine it, the only really severe-looking object was the bedstead; this being devoid of curtains, its four varnished pillars shone somewhat hard and bare. For the rest, there was just the natural furniture of a sleeping-room: a dressing-table, covered with a man's toilet accessories—combs and brushes, razors, scissors, shoehorns, button-hooks, shirt-studs, and bottles enclosing I know not what necessary fluids; a bigger table, with writing-materials on it, with an old epaulette-box used now to hold tobacco, and endless pipes and little pink books of cigarette-papers; a bureau like my grandmother's; a glazed bookcase; and the proper complement of chairs. The walls of the room were painted white, and ornamented by two pictures, facing each other: two steel-engravings, companion-pieces, after Rembrandt, I believe. "Le Philosophe en Contemplation" was the legend printed under one; and under the other, "Le Philosophe en Méditation." I can only remember that the philosopher had a long grey beard, and that in both pictures he was seated in a huge easy-chair. My Uncle Edmond had been in the army when he was a young man, and in his closets (besides his ordinary clothes and his countless pairs of boots) there were old uniform coats, with silver buttons, old belts, clasps, spurs, and then, best of all, three or four swords, and a rosewood case or two of pistols. Needless to say whether my awe and my admiration mounted to their climax when I peeped in upon these historic trophies. And just as the smell of orange-flower water pervaded my grandmother's room, so another, a very different smell, pervaded my Uncle Edmond's, a dry, clean smell, slightly pungent, bitter, but not at all unpleasant. I could never discover what it came from, I can't even now conjecture; but it seemed to me a manly smell, just the smell that a man's room ought to have. In my too-fruitless efforts to imitate Uncle Edmond's room in the organisation of my own, it was that smell, more than anything else, which baffled me. I could not achieve the remotest semblance of it. Of course, I was determined that when I grew up I should have a room exactly like my uncle's in every particular, and I trusted, no doubt, that it would acquire the smell, with time.

But of all the rooms at Saint-Graal, the one that gave you the thrillingest, the most exquisite emotion, was my mother's. If my grandmother's room represented the silence and the strangeness of the past, and my uncle's the actuality and activity of the present, my mother's room represented the Eternal Feminine, smiling at you, enthralling you, in its loveliest incarnation; singing to you, amid delicate luxuries, of youth and beauty and happiness, and the fine romance of mirth. In my mother's room, for example, so far from being old-fashioned, the furniture was of the very latest, daintiest design, fresh from Paris. The wallpaper was cream-coloured, with garlands of pink and blue flowers trailing over it, and here and there a shepherd's hat and a shepherd's pipes tied together by a long fluttering blue ribbon. The chairs and the sofa were covered with chintz, gayer even, if that were possible, than this paper: chintz on which pretty little bright-blue birds flew about among poppies, red as scarlet, and pale-green leaves. The window-curtains and the bed-curtains were of the same merry chintz; the bed-quilt was an eider-down of the softest blush-rose silk; the bedstead was enamelled white, and so highly polished that you could see an obscure reflection of your features in it. And then, the dressing-table, with its wide bevelled mirror, and the glistening treasures displayed upon it!—the open jewel-case, and the rings, brooches, bracelets, necklaces, that sparkled in it; the silver-backed brushes, the silver-topped bottles, the silver-framed hand-glass; the hundred shining trifles. One whole side of the room had been converted into a vast bay-window; this looked due south, over the floweriest part of our flower-garden, over the rich green country beyond, miles away, to where the Pyrenees gloomed purple. As a shield against the sun the window was fitted with Venetian blinds, besides the curtains; and every morning, when I crept in from my own adjoining room, to pay my mother a visit, it was given me to witness a marvellous transformation scene. At first all was dark, or nearly dark, so that you could only distinguish things as shadowy masses. But presently my mother's maid, Aurélie, arrived with the chocolate, and drew back the curtains, filling the room with a momentary twilight; then she opened the Venetian blinds, and suddenly there was a gush of sunlight, and the room gleamed and glittered like a room in a crystal palace. Sweet airs came in from the garden, bird-notes came in, the day came in, dancing and laughing joyously; and my mother and I joyously laughed back at it. Another transformation scene, at which I was permitted to assist, took place in this room in the evening, when my mother dressed for dinner. I would sit at a distance, not to be in the way, and watch the ceremony with eyes as round as O's doubtless, and certainly with an enravished soul; while Aurélie did my mother's hair (sprinkling it, as a culmination, with a pinch of diamond-dust, according to the mode of the period), and moved to and from the wardrobe, where my mother's bewildering confections of silks and laces were enshrined, and her satin slippers glimmered in a row on their shelf. And after the toilet was completed, and my mother, in dazzling loveliness, had kissed me good-bye and vanished, I would linger a little, to gaze about the temple in which such miracles could happen; taking up and studying one by one the combs, brushes, powder-puffs, or what not, as you would study the instruments employed by a conjurer; and removing the stoppers from the scent-bottles, to inhale their delicious fragrance....

"Don't you think," asked my companion, "that it's time you paid the waiter and we were off?"

I looked up, and suddenly there was Rouen—Rouen, the café on the quays, Madame's empty glass of milk, and Madame herself questioning me from anxious eyes.

"Yes," I said, "I think it's time we were off; and what's more, I'll tell you this: every room in the universe has not only its peculiar physiognomy and its peculiar significance, but it wakes a particular sentiment also, and has a special smell."

"Oh, I see," said Madame; "that's why you've been silent all this while."

So I paid the waiter, and we took the puffing little steamboat, down the river, between its green banks and its flowery islets, back to La Bouille.

ROSEMARY FOR REMEMBRANCE

I

I wonder why I dreamed last night of Zabetta. It is years since she made her brief little transit through my life, and passed out of it utterly. It is years since the very recollection of her—which for years, like an accusing spirit, had haunted me too often—like a spirit was laid. It is long enough, in all conscience, since I have even thought of her, casually, for an instant. And then, last night, after a perfectly usual London day and evening, I went to bed and dreamed of her vividly. What had happened to bring her to my mind? Or is it simply that the god of dreams is a capricious god?

The influence of my dream, at any rate,—the bittersweet savour of it,—has pursued me through my waking hours. All day long to-day Zabetta has been my phantom guest. She has walked with me in the streets; she has waited at my elbow while I wrote or talked or read. Now, at tea-time, she is present with me by my study fireside, in the twilight. Her voice sounds faintly, plaintively, in my ears; her eyes gaze at me sadly from a pale reproachful face.... She bids me to the theatre of memory, where my youth is rehearsed before me in mimic show. There was one—no, there were two little scenes in which Zabetta played the part of leading lady.

II

I do not care to specify the year in which it happened; it happened a terrible number of years ago; it happened when I was twenty. I had passed the winter in Naples,—oh, it had been a golden winter!—and now April had come, and my last Neapolitan day. Tomorrow I was to take ship for Marseilles, on the way to join my mother in Paris.

It was in the afternoon; and I was climbing one of those crooked staircase alleys that scale the hillsides behind the town, the salita—is there, in Naples, a Salita Santa Margherita? I had lunched (for the last time!) at the Café d'.urope, and had then set forth upon a last haphazard ramble through the streets. It was tremulous spring weather, with blue skies, soft breezes, and a tender sun; the sort of weather that kindles perilous ardours even in the blood of middle age, and turns the blood of youth to wildfire.

Women sat combing their hair, and singing, and gossiping, before the doorways of their pink and yellow houses; children sprawled, and laughed, and quarrelled in the dirt. Pifferari, in sheep-skins and sandals, followed by prowling, gaunt-limbed dogs, droned monotonous nasal melodies from their bagpipes. Priests picked their way gingerly over the muddy cobble stones, sleek, black-a-vised priests, with exaggerated hats, like Don Basilio's in the *Barbiere*. Now and then one passed a fat brown monk; or a soldier; or a white-robed penitent, whose eyes glimmered uncannily from the peep-holes of the hood that hid his face; or a comely contadina, in her smart costume, with a pomegranate-blossom flaming behind her ear, and red lips that curved defiantly as she met the covetous glances wildfire-and-twenty no doubt bestowed upon her—whereat, perhaps, wildfire-and-twenty halted and hesitated for an instant, debating whether to accept the challenge and turn and follow her. A flock of milk-purveying goats jangled their bells a few yards below me. Hawkers screamed their merchandise, fish, and vegetables, and early fruit—apricots, figs, green almonds. Brown-skinned, barelegged boys shouted at long-suffering donkeys, and whacked their flanks with sticks. And everybody, more or less, importuned you for coppers. "Mossou, mossou! Un piccolo soldo, per l'amor di Dio!" The air was vibrant with Southern human noises and dense with Southern human smells—amongst which, here and there, wandered strangely a lost waft of perfume from some neighbouring garden, a scent of jasmine or of orange flowers.

And then, suddenly, the salita took a turn, and broadened into a small piazza. At one hand there was a sheer terrace, dropping to tiled roofs twenty feet below; and hence one got a splendid view, over the town, of the blue bay, with its shipping, and of Capri, all rose and purple in the distance, and of Vesuvius with its silver wreath of smoke. At the other hand loomed a vast, discoloured, pink-stuccoed palace, with grated windows, and a porte-cochère black as the mouth of a cavern; and the upper stories of the palace were in ruins, and out of one corner of their crumbling walls a palm-tree grew. The third side of the piazza was inevitably occupied by a church, a little pearl-grey rococo edifice, with a bell, no deeper toned than a common dinner-bell, which was now frantically ringing. About the doors of the church countless written notices were pasted, advertising indulgences; beggars clung to the steps, like monster snails; and the greasy leathern portière was constantly being drawn aside, to let some one enter or come out.

III

It was here that I met Zabetta.

The heavy portière swung open, and a young girl stepped from the darkness behind it into the sunshine.

I saw a soft face, with brown eyes; a plain black frock, with a little green nosegay stuck in its belt; and a small round scarlet hat.

A hideous old beggar woman stretched a claw towards this apparition, mumbling something. The apparition smiled, and sought in its pocket, and made the beggar woman the richer by a soldo.

I was twenty, and the April wind was magical. I thought I had never seen so beautiful a smile, a smile so radiant, so tender.

I watched the young girl as she tripped down the church steps, and crossed the piazza, coming towards me. Her smile lingered, fading slowly, slowly, from her face.

As she neared me, her eyes met mine. For a second we looked straight into each other's eyes....

Oh, there was nothing bold, nothing sophisticated or immodest, in the momentary gaze she gave me. It was a natural, spontaneous gaze of perfectly frank, of perfectly innocent and impulsive interest, in exchange for mine of open admiration. But it touched the wildfire in my veins, and made it leap tumultuously.

IV

Happiness often passes close to us without our suspecting it, the proverb says.

The young girl moved on; and I stood still, feeling dimly that something precious had passed close to me. I had not turned back to follow any of the brazenly provocative contadine. But now I could not help it. Something precious had passed within arm's reach of me. I must not let it go, without at least a semblance of pursuing it. If I waited there passive till she was out of sight, my regrets would be embittered by the recollection that I had not even tried.

I followed her eagerly, but vaguely, in a tremor or unformulated hopes and fears. I had no definite intentions, no designs. Presently, doubtless, she would come to her journey's end—she would disappear in a house or shop—and I should have my labour for my pains. Nevertheless, I followed. What would you? She was young, she was pretty, she was neatly dressed. She had big bright brown eyes, and a slender waist, and a little round scarlet hat set jauntily upon a mass of waving soft brown hair. And she walked gracefully, with delicious undulations, as if to music, lifting her skirts up from the pavement, and so disclosing the daintiest of feet, in trim buttoned boots of glazed leather, with high Italian heels. And her smile was lovely—and I was twenty—and it was April. I must not let her escape me, without at least a semblance of pursuit.

She led me down the salita that I had just ascended. She could scarcely know that she was being followed, for she had not once glanced behind her.

V

At first I followed meekly, unperceived, and contented to remain so.

But little by little a desire for more aggressive measures grew within me. I said, "Why not—instead of following meekly—why not overtake and outdistance her, then turn round, and come face to face with her again? And if again her eyes should meet mine as frankly as they met them in the piazza...."

The mere imagination of their doing so made my heart stop beating.

I quickened my pace. I drew nearer and nearer to her. I came abreast of her —oh, how the wildfire trembled! I pressed on for a bit, and then, true to my resolution, turned back.

Her eyes did meet mine again quite frankly. What was more, they brightened with a little light of surprise, I might almost have fancied a little light of pleasure.

If the mere imagination of the thing had made my heart stop beating, the thing itself set it to pounding, racing, uncontrollably, so that I felt all but suffocated, and had to catch my breath.

She knew now that the young man she had passed in the piazza had followed her of set purpose; and she was surprised, but, seemingly, not displeased. They were wonderfully gentle, wonderfully winning eyes, those eyes she raised so frankly to my desirous ones; and innocent, innocent, with all the unsuspecting innocence of childhood. In years she might be seventeen, older perhaps; but there was a child's fearless unconsciousness of evil in her wide brown eyes. She had not yet been taught (or, anyhow, she clearly didn't believe) that it is dangerous and unbecoming to exchange glances with a stranger in the streets.

She was as good as smiling on me. Might I dare the utmost? Might I venture to speak to her?... My heart was throbbing too violently. I could not have found an articulate human word, nor a shred of voice, nor a pennyweight of self-assurance, in my body. .

So, thrilling with excitement, quailing in panic, I passed her again.

I passed her, and kept on up the narrow alley for half a dozen steps, when again I turned.

She was standing where I had left her, looking after me. There was the expression of unabashed disappointment in her dark eyes now, which, in a minute, melted to an expression of appeal.

"Oh, aren't you going to speak to me, after all?" they pleaded.

Wooed by those soft monitors, I plucked up a sort of desperate courage. Hot coals burned in my cheeks, something flattered terribly in my breast; I was literally quaking in every limb. My spirit was exultant, but my flesh was faint. Her eyes drew me, drew me.... I fancy myself awkwardly raising my hat; I hear myself accomplish a half-smothered salutation.

"Buon' giorno, Signorina."

Her face lit up with that celestial smile of hers; and in a voice that was like ivory and white velvet, she returned, "Buon' giorno, Signorino."

VI

And then I don't know how long we stood together in silence.

This would never do, I recognised. I must not stand before her in silence, like a guilty schoolboy. I must feign composure. I must carry off the situation lightly, like a man of the world, a man of experience. I groped anxiously in the confusion ot my wits for something that might pass for an apposite remark.

At last I had a flash or inspiration. "What—what fine weather," I gasped. "Che bel tempo!"

"Oh, molto bello," she responded. It was like a cadenza on a flute.

"You—you are going into the town?" I questioned.

"Yes," said she.

"May I—may I have the pleasure———" I faltered.

"But yes," she consented, with an inflection that wondered. "What else have you spoken to me for?"

And we set off down the salita, side by side.

VII

She had exquisite little white ears, with little coral earrings, like drops of blood; and a perfect rosebud mouth, a mouth that matched her eyes for innocence and sweetness. Her scarlet hat burned in the sun, and her brown hair shook gently under it. She had plump little soft white hands.

Presently, when I had begun to feel more at my ease, I hazarded a question. "You are a republican, Signorina?"

"No," she assured me, with a puzzled elevation of the brows.

"Ah, well, then you are a cardinal," I concluded.

She gave a silvery trill of laughter, and asked, "Why must I be either a republican or a cardinal?"

"You wear a scarlet hat—a *bonnet rouge*", I explained.

At which she laughed again, crisply, merrily.

"You are French," she said.

"Oh, am I?"

"Aren't you?"

"As you wish, Signorina; but I had never thought so."

And still again she laughed.

"You have come from church," said I.

"Già," she assented; "from confession."

"Really? And did you have a great many wickednesses to confess?"

"Oh, yes; many, many," she answered, simply.

"And now have you got a heavy penance to perform?"

"No; only twenty *aves*. And I must turn my tongue seven times in my mouth before I speak, whenever I am angry."

"Ah, then you are given to being angry? You have a bad temper?"

"Oh, dreadful, dreadful," she cried, nodding her head.

It was my turn to laugh now. "Then I must be careful not to vex you."

"Yes. But I will turn my tongue seven times before I speak, if you do," she promised.

"Are you going far?" I asked.

"I am going nowhere. I am taking a walk."

"Shall we go to the Villa Nazionale, and watch the driving?"

"Or to the Toledo, and look at the shop-windows?"

"We can do both. We will begin at the Toledo, and end in the Villa."

"Bene," she acquiesced.

After a little silence, "I am so glad I met you," I informed her, looking into her eyes.

He eyes softened adorably. "I am so glad too," she said.

"You are lovely, you are sweet," I vowed, with enthusiasm.

"Oh, no!" she protested. "I am as God made me."

"You are lovely, you are sweet. I thought—when I first saw you, above there, in the piazza—when you came out of church, and gave the soldo to the old beggar woman—I thought you had the loveliest smile I had ever seen."

A beautiful blush suffused her face, and her eyes swam in a mist of pleasure. "É vero?" she questioned.

"Oh, vero, vero. That is why I followed you. You don't mind my having followed you?"

"Oh, no; I am glad."

After another interval of silence, "You are not Neapolitan?" I said. "You don't speak like a Neapolitan."

"No; I am Florentine. We live in Naples for my father's health. He is not strong. He cannot endure the cold winters of the North."

I murmured something sympathetic; and she went on, "My father is a violinist. To-day he has gone to Capri, to play at a festival. He will not be back until to-morrow. So I was very lonesome."

"You have no mother?"

"My mother is dead," she said, crossing herself. In a moment she added, with a touch of pride, "During the season my father plays in the orchestra of the San Carlo."

"I am sure I know what your name is," said I.

"Oh? How can you know? What is it?"

"I think your name is Rosabella."

"Ah, then you are wrong. My name is Elisabetta. But in Naples everybody says Zabetta. And yours?"

"Guess."

"Oh, I cannot guess. Not—not Federico?"

"Do I look as if my name were Federico?"

She surveyed me gravely for a minute, then shook her head pensively. "No; I do not think your name is Federico."

And therewith I told her my name, and made her repeat it till she could pronounce it without a struggle.

It sounded very pretty, coming from her pretty lips, quite Southern and romantic, with its r's tremendously enriched.

"Anyhow, I know your age," said I.

"What is it?"

"You are seventeen." "No—

ever so much older." "Eighteen

then."

"I shall be nineteen in July."

VIII

Before the brilliant shop-windows of the Toledo we dallied for an hour or more, Zabetta's eyes sparkling with delight as they rested on the bright-hued silks, the tortoiseshell and coral, the gold and silver filagree-work, that were there displayed. But when she admired some one particular object above another, and I besought her to let me buy it for her, she refused austerely. "But no, no, no! It is impossible." Then we went on to the Villa, and strolled by the sea-wall, between the blue-green water and the multicoloured procession of people in carriages. And by-and-by Zabetta confessed that she was tired, and proposed that we should sit down on one of the benches. "A café would be better fun," submitted her companion. And we placed ourselves at one of the out-of-door tables of the café in the garden, where, after some urging, I prevailed upon Zabetta to drink a cup of chocolate. Meanwhile, with the ready confidence of youth, we had each been desultorily autobiographical; and if our actual acquaintance was only the affair of an afternoon, I doubt if in a year we could have felt that we knew each other better.

"I must go home," Zabetta said at last.

"Oh, not yet, not yet," cried I.

"It will be dinner-time. I must go home to dinner."

"But your father is at Capri. You will have to dine alone."

"Yes."

"Then don't. Come with me instead, and dine at a restaurant."

Her eyes glowed wistfully for an instant; but she replied, "Oh, no; I cannot."

"Yes, you can. Come."

"Oh, no; impossible."

"Why?"

"Oh, because."

"Because what?"

"There is my cat. She will have nothing to eat."

"Your cook will give her something."

"My cook!" laughed Zabetta. "My cook is here before you."

"Well, you must be a kind mistress. You must give your cook an evening out."

"But my poor cat?"

"Your cat can catch a mouse."

"There are no mice in our house. She has frightened them all away."

"Then she can wait. A little fast will be good for her soul."

Zabetta laughed, and I said, "Andiamo!"

At the restaurant we climbed to the first floor, and they gave us a table near the window, whence we could look out over the villa to the sea beyond. The sun was sinking, and the sky was gay with rainbow tints, like mother-of-pearl.

Zabetta's face shone joyfully. "This is only the second time in my life that I have dined in a restaurant," she told me. "And the other time was very long ago, when I was quite young. And it wasn't nearly so grand a restaurant as this, either."

"And now what would you like to eat?" I asked, picking up the bill of fare.

"May I look?" said she.

I handed her the document, and she studied it at length. I think, indeed, she read it through. In the end she appeared rather bewildered.

"Oh, there is so much. I don't know. Will you choose, please?"

I made a shift at choosing, and the sympathetic waiter flourished kitchenwards with my commands.

"What is that little green nosegay you wear in your belt, Zabetta?" I inquired.

"Oh, this—it is rosemary. Smell it," she said, breaking off a sprig and offering it to me.

"Rosemary—that's for remembrance," quoted I.

"What does that mean? What language is that?" she asked.

I tried to translate it to her. And then I taught her to say it in English. "Rrosemérri—tsat is forr rremembrrance."

"Will you write it down for me?" she requested. "It is pretty."

And I wrote it for her on the back of one of my cards.

IX

After dinner we crossed the garden again, and again stood by the sea-wall. Over us the soft spring night was like a dark sapphire. Points of red, green, and yellow fire burned from the ships in the bay, and seemed of the same company as the stars above them. A rosy aureole in the sky, to the eastward, marked the smouldering crater of Vesuvius. Away in the Chiaja a man was singing comic songs, to an accompaniment of mandolines and guitars; comic songs that sounded pathetic, as they reached us in the distance.

I asked Zabetta how she wished to finish the evening.

"I don't care," said she.

"Would you like to go the play?"

"If you wish."

"What do *you* wish?"

"I think I should like to stay here a little longer. It is pleasant."

We leaned on the parapet, close to each other. Her face was very pale in the starlight; her eyes were infinitely deep, and dark, and tender. One of her little hands lay on the stone wall, like a white flower. I took it. It was warm and soft. She did not attempt to withdraw it. I bent over it and kissed it. I kissed it many times. Then I kissed her lips. "Zabetta—I love you—I love you," I murmured fervently.—Don't imagine that I didn't mean it. It was April, and I was twenty.

"I love you, Zabetta. Dearest little Zabetta! I love you so."

"É vero?" she questioned, scarcely above her breath.

"Oh, si; é vero, vero, vero," I asseverated. "And you? And you?"

"Yes, I love you," she whispered.

And then I could say no more. The ecstasy that filled my heart was too poignant. We stood there speechless, hand in hand, and breathed the air of heaven.

By-and-by Zabetta drew her bunch of rosemary from her belt, and divided it into two parts. One part she gave to me, the other she kept. "Rosemary—it is for constancy," she said. I pressed the cool herb to my face for a moment, inhaling its bitter-sweet fragrance; then I fastened it in my buttonhole. On my watch-chain I wore—what everybody in Naples used to wear—a little coral hand, a little clenched coral hand, holding a little golden dagger. I detached it now, and made Zabetta take it. "Coral—that is also for constancy," I reminded her; "and besides, it protects one from the Evil Eye."

X

At last Zabetta asked me what time it was; and when she learned that it was half-past nine, she insisted that she really must go home. "They shut the outer door of the house we live in at ten o'clock, and I have no key."

"You can ring up the porter."

"Oh, there is no porter."

"But if we had gone to the theatre?"

"I should have had to leave you in the middle of the play."

"Ah, well," I consented; and we left the villa and took a cab.

"Are you happy, Zabetta?" I asked her, as the cab rattled us towards our parting.

"Oh, so happy, so happy! I have never been so happy before."

"Dearest Zabetta!"

"You will love me always?"

"Always, always."

"We will see each other every day. We will see each other to-morrow?"

215

"Oh, to-morrow!" I groaned suddenly, the actualities of life rushing all at once upon my mind.

"What is it? What of to-morrow?"

"Oh, to-morrow, to-morrow!"

"What? What?" Her voice was breathless with suspense, with alarm. "Oh, I had forgotten. You will think I am a beast."

"What is it? For heaven's sake, tell me."

"You will think I am a beast. You will think I have deceived you. To-morrow—I cannot help it—I am not my own master—I am summoned by my parents—to-morrow I am going away—I am leaving Naples."

"You are leaving Naples?"

"I am going to Paris."

"To Paris?"

"Yes."

There was a breathing-space of silence. Then, "Oh, Dio!" sobbed Zabetta; and she began to cry as if her heart would break.

I seized her hands; I drew her to me. I tried to comfort her. But she only cried and cried and cried.

"Zabetta... Zabetta.... Don't cry... Forgive me.... Oh, don't cry like that."

"Oh, Dio! Oh, caro Dio!" she sobbed.

"Zabetta—listen to me," I began. "I have something to say to you...."

"Cosa?" she asked faintly.

"Zabetta—do you really love me?"

"Oh, tanto, tanto!"

"Then, listen, Zabetta. If you really love me—come with me."

"Come with you. How?"

"Come with me to Paris."

"To Paris?"

"Yes, to-morrow."

There was another instant of silence, and then again Zabetta began to cry.

"Will you? Will you? Will you come with me to Paris?" I implored her.

216

"Oh, I would, I would. But I can't. I can't."

"Why not?"

"Oh, I can't."

"Why? Why can't you?"

"Oh, my father—I cannot leave my father."

"Your father? But—if you love me————"

"He is old. He is ill. He has no one but me. I cannot leave him."

"Zabetta!"

"No, no. I cannot leave him. Oh, Dio mio!"

"But Zabetta————"

"No. It would be a sin. Oh, the worst of sins. He is old and ill. I cannot leave him. Don't ask me. It would be dreadful."

"But then? Then what? What shall we do?"

"Oh, I don't know. I wish I were dead."

The cab came to a standstill, and Zabetta said, "Here we are." I helped her to descend. We were before a dark porte-cochère, in some dark back-street, high up the hillside.

"Addio," said Zabetta, holding out her hand.

"You won't come with me?"

"I can't. I can't. Addio."

"Oh, Zabetta! Do you————Oh, say, say that you forgive me."

"Yes. Addio."

"And, Zabetta, you—you have my address. It is on the card I gave you. If you ever need anything—if you are ever in trouble of any kind—remember you have my address—you will write to me."

"Yes. Addio."

"Addio."

She stood for a second, looking up at me from great brimming eyes, and then she turned away and vanished in the darkness of the porte-cochère. I got into the cab, and was driven to my hotel.

XI

A nd here, one might have supposed, was an end of the episode; but no.

I went to Paris, I went to New York, I returned to Paris, I came on to London; and in this journeying more than a year was lost. In the beginning I had suffered as much as you could wish me in the way of contrition, in the way of regret too. I blamed myself and pitied myself with almost equal fervour. I had trifled with a gentle human heart; I had been compelled to let a priceless human treasure slip from my possession. But—I was twenty. And there were other girls in the world. And a year is a long time, when we are twenty. Little by little the image of Zabetta faded, faded. By the year's end, I am afraid it had become very pale indeed....

It was late June, and I was in London, when the post brought me a letter. The letter bore an Italian stamp, and had originally been directed to my old address in Paris. Thence (as the numerous redirections on the big square foreign envelope attested) it had been forwarded to New York; thence back again to Paris; and thence finally to London.

The letter was written in the neatest of tiny copperplates; and this is a translation of what it said:

"Dear Friend,—My poor father died last month in the German Hospital, after an illness of twenty-one days. Pray for his soul.

"I am now alone and free, and if you still wish it, can come to you. It was impossible for me to come when you asked me; but you have not ceased to be my constant thought. I keep your coral hand.—Your ever faithful Zabetta Collaluce."

Enclosed in the letter there was a sprig of some dried, bitter-sweet-smelling herb; and, in pencil, below the signature—laboriously traced, as I could guess, from what I had written for her on my visiting-card,—the English phrase: "Rosemary—that's for remembrance."

The letter was dated early in May, which made it six weeks old.

What could I do? What answer could I send?

Of course, you know what I did do. I procrastinated and vacillated, and ended by sending no answer at all. I could not write and say "Yes, come to me." But how could I write and say "No, do not come"? Besides, would she not have given up hoping for an answer, by this time? It was six weeks since she had written. I tried to think that the worst was over.

But my remorse took a new and a longer and a stronger lease of life. A vision of Zabetta, pale, with anxious eyes, standing at her window, waiting, waiting for a word that never came,—for months I could not chase it from my conscience; it was years before it altogether ceased its accusing visits.

XII

And then, last night, after a perfectly usual London day and evening, I went to bed and dreamed of her vividly; and all day long to-day the fragrance of my dream has clung about me,—a bitter-sweet fragrance, like that of rosemary itself. Where is Zabetta now? What is her life? How have the years treated her?... In my dream she was still eighteen. In reality—it is melancholy to think how far from eighteen she has had leisure, since that April afternoon, to drift.

Youth faces forward, impatient of the present, panting to anticipate the future. But we who have crossed a certain sad meridian, we turn our gaze backwards, and tell the relentless gods what we would sacrifice to recover a little of the past, one of those shining days when to us also it was given to sojourn among the Fortunate Islands. *Ah, si jeunesse savait!*...